IN OPEN FIELDS

by
Heather Campbell

CHAPTER 1

This was our beginning in a new land. When I look back over thirty years, I marvel at our tenacity and courage. We were young and so naive, so full of hope and optimism. Yet again the venture was so immense and completely impossible that I feel I must tell of how it all came about.

We drove up to a small row of austere little rooms forming a rustic house. This plain construction, which was to be my future home, stood completely alone; about it rolled open fields as far as the eye could see.

I climbed down slowly from the carriage which had brought us from the town of Mercedes: baby Donny, his nannie Mrs. Allen, my cousin Willy and myself. My husband Donald had to remain in Mercedes because our luggage had not yet left the boat. There were also the dogs, Santa and Claus, to be landed the next day. It would have been much better had Donald come with us. The shock would have been less, I'm sure. His pride in his new property would have over-ridden any disappointment of mine.

We were all down from the carriage now. 'Well,' said Willy watching my face, 'what do you think of it?' I shrugged and turned away. How could I tell him of my true feelings? It would be too cruel if it got back to Donald; he must never know how I really felt about this house. I must pretend, although I really felt sick at heart. I walked away a little to compose myself. All of a sudden I had become a stranger even to myself, dispirited and weary, no longer a part of this great adventure of pioneering into a new land.

At the end of the old brick-floored veranda there was another room and nothing more. Open fields spread out in all directions and silent stillness prevailed equaling the dullness that gripped my heart.

I turned around and Willy said: 'Let's get the things down from the carriage and go inside, shall we?'

A climax to the long trip out from Ireland to South America.

Our journey began in September; it had been planned and talked about for so many months and now was actually be-ginning. Although the steamer was rocking about in a dreadful fashion, I still felt the thrill of excitement at what the future might hold for us.

We were quite a large party: Donald and I and our baby already seven months old; Willy coming to help work this Uruguayan farm and Mrs. Silvia Allen whom we had in charge of our child. Mrs. Allen had become widowed two years ago, a young woman of thirty with no children. She had been anxiously looking for work that would take her out of Ireland where sad memories still haunted her, into something completely new. The job of nannie to our child sounded like the very thing she was hunting for.

Now on board the steamer she was doing her best to keep on her feet, as the sea was very rough, but when she came into our cabin with Donny for his evening meal I could see she felt very seasick.

'Leave Donny with me for the present,' I told her, 'and go and lie down.' She nodded thankfully and rushed from the cabin with clenched teeth, holding back the vomit swelling up into her throat. Poor thing! I could hear her throwing up into the chamber pot in the cabin next door. For the next two days the stewardess brought me my child to be put to the breast at feeding times, Mrs. Allen being too unwell to leave her bunk.

As the sea became calmer after leaving Bordeaux, all the passengers gradually started coming out of their cabins like rabbits from their burrows, to take an active part in the life on board.

The marvelous part of our journey was now beginning, with days of sunshine, dinners and parties in the evenings. The larger luggage had been brought up from the hold to enable the passengers to get out their cooler clothes and feel comfortable.

Upon arriving at Rio de Janeiro we went ashore and visited this lovely city with a tropical vegetation unlike anything I had ever seen before, and with small green islands springing up just off the shore. We stopped for refreshments twice due to the heat before going back on board. On our return I said to Mrs. Allen: 'I insist you go ashore and see this lovely city. Someone will accompany you.'

So Silvia Allen dressed for the event and looked most elegant in her cream-coloured gown, showing off her slim waist. 'She's carrying her sunshade in gloved hands,' commented Willy as we watched her leave the steamer, 'and picks her way delicately along the rough quay.'

'She's a real lady!' laughed Donald.

That night we left Rio and started travelling south. About four days later I awoke amazed to find a thick fog covering everything. Nothing was visible, even the close-by water had a nasty grey aspect. The *Legunia* all but stopped; I could feel the engines going slow and hear the fog horn hooting its mournful warning all the time.

'Visibility nil!' Donald told me after breakfast when we went on deck as we normally did to watch the sea and enjoy the sun. 'What a change from yesterday! I can't believe it's the same world.'

We advanced cautiously under these conditions all day while people began commenting on the danger. At night it got cold and we shut down our port-holes and went to bed early.

'In sight of land!' Donald came dashing back into the cabin next morning, having arisen for an early breakfast.

'Quick, come and see our coastline!' he urged me, although I was still in the process of dressing. Without giving me time to tie back my hair correctly, he pulled me out on deck. To my intense surprise it was a fogless and fine morning and before us was a small line of coast, which truly might have been anywhere in the world, but Donald was excited about it because he knew it to be Uruguayan coast and this was special to us.

I squeezed his arm: 'It's beautiful and exciting!' His answering smile told me this was what he wanted to hear.

'It's undeveloped land, but we'll work it and we'll conquer it!'

'Yes, I know we will,' I breathed excitedly.

After Christopher Columbus discovered the new continent many
expeditions more were sent to the Americas from Spain. The Uruguayan
territory was discovered in March 1516 by the Spaniard Juan Diaz de Solis. He
and the fifty men who landed with him were attacked by the *Charrua* Indians
inhabiting the land and killed by arrows.

And now in this year of 1876, our steamer followed the same coast
on the River Plate, passing pure white sands for miles, important points
such as the Faro de La Paloma, the first light-house on this coast, and an
important peninsular called Punta del Este only a few hours before arriving
at Montevideo. We saw the mount which, as legend has it, once caused a
Portuguese sailor to call out as he saw it '*Monte Vide Eu*' (I see a mount), the
origin of the name of the capital city.

As we docked in the port, Donald came into the cabin, and we were all
packed up to leave. 'Ready?' he asked. 'Al-most, but I can't get this wretched
bag to close down! It shut perfectly when we left home, but now—' Donald
looked ruefully at the bulging bag where clothes stuck out on all sides. Rapidly
he tucked everything inside and swiftly sat on it. 'There you are!' he cried as he
snapped back the locks. 'Come on now,' he continued, 'I've hired a boy to help
with the luggage.' Heaped with bags and trunks we went ashore.

'The boy knows of a good hotel nearby,' We walked along some very
precarious sidewalks until we reached the Hotel Paris which took us in. There
we collapsed thankfully on some dubiously clean beds.

A tremendous storm was banking up all day, and it broke shortly after
we left the port on the riverboat Villa de Salto, destination Buenos Aires.
Conditions on this small boat were not adequate. The cabins were minute and
totally airless; the dirty port-hole was screwed down and impossible to open.
We tried to settle and get Donny to sleep but he was in a fit of crying — the
heat was making him uncomfortable. Mrs. Allen was unable to cope; her face
a light green, so I guessed she was about to be sick. I gave thanks that we had
employed her for firm land work.

'Here give me the baby,' I said, 'try and get some rest.' I took the child into our cabin and laid down beside him. Fortunately, he calmed down but the fury of the storm increased and the creaking and groaning of the old boat continued all night so that I could hardly rest. I thought it was like a ghost ship, where the souls of the tormented sighed and moaned and sometimes shrieked above the howling of the wind and the thrashing of the waves against the sides of the boat. I hoped the rotten woodwork would hold out until we reached the other side of this unfriendly river, the River Plate.

During the night's vigil I had ample time to recall Donald's words while we were still in Ireland: 'It's a beautiful river with the widest estuary in the world,' he had explained during one of those happy, secure evenings sitting in the drawing-room at Carrie hall. How far away the family circle seemed now. Donald went on: 'When the sun shines the water is blue-green near the Uruguayan coast because of a maritime current which brings white sands and salty water from the ocean forming lovely beaches. As one approaches the Argentine coast the water turns a light brown and is no longer transparent — this is a muddy coast.'

Tonight Donald had slept little and as daybreak came he rolled over and awoke. The baby also woke up and was hungry so I gave him a feed which satisfied him well and he began to gurgle and smile.

'Dawn!' exclaimed Donald, pulling his hand through his unruly hair. 'I'm going up to see if there's any sign of land and find out how long it will be before we dock.'

There were great grey and white clouds racing over the sky and the wind was still howling with intensity. It was cold up on deck compared to the stuffiness of the closed cabin. The coastline was well in view and great waves were thundering about making the boat pitch and sway in an alarming fashion. We had crossed the River Plate during the night but when Donald spoke to the Master of the vessel, he told him we would not dock in Buenos Aires because of the gale. To drop anchor in the port of Buenos Aires was utterly impossible because the vessel would go smashing against the waterfront rocks. Likewise, no small embarkation could leave the port to carry us ashore, so the only alternative was to sail up the River Tigre and take shelter there. The Delta del

Tigre was a sheltered river basin with lots of small islands covering the estuary. Here, where the heavy seas were reduced, we dropped anchor and were able to draw a short breath. At least it was daylight and the movement of the boat was considerably less. We had to remain there a day and a night while the great wind storm raged and the River Plate was unnavigable.

The following morning, we continued our journey up-river, soon entering the Rio Uruguay and sailing north towards the port of Fray Bentos, our final destination. All the way along this river we were in sight of land, the shores of our new country were green and wooded. There was thick vegetation in parts but also large expanses of flat open country ideal for cattle raising. Finally, we docked at Fray Bentos and I was more than relieved to get my feet on firm land once again.

'Now we'll be taken to a tavern for lunch,' Donald told us while we were standing in a shelter near the docks. We had an extremely good lunch while our spirits rose considerably. 'Pass the wine, will you Willy?' Willy pushed the bottle across the table to Donald and he and I had our second glassful.

I giggled: 'I know that Donny is going to sleep well after his midday feed. When I drink wine, it makes him sleep like a top!'

'Good! Have a drop more!' At last we were relaxed and laughing again; there had been moments on board the Villa de Salto when I thought I'd never laugh again.

The tavern was warm and friendly, the food and wine excellent, and I felt like remaining here, and not have to travel again. However, as soon as the coach arrived we drove to Mercedes, crossing another water expanse to reach the town, where we make plans to stay the night.

Picture our delight as we trailed wearily into the hotel to find Sydney waiting for us. Like a breath from home, Donald's brother Sydney, looking well and rugged, florid face and shining blue eyes like the skies of bonny Ireland, grinned at us from behind his full red beard.

'Welcome the travelers!' he greeted us with warmth.

'You're one day late. Did you have a good trip?'

'Don't mention this last lap,' Donald replied as he shook hands heartily with his brother. 'Good to see you, Syd!' then added: 'We were hoping you'd be here to meet us.' Sydney turned and asked: 'How's young Donny?' as he stroked the little fellow's head affectionately, 'My! What a splendid young lad he is!' Sydney had left Ireland before our son was born, this being his first introduction to him. Donny was in Mrs. Allen's arms and in very good spirits after his meal and a good sleep.

'This is Mrs. Allen,' I introduced her to Sydney.

'So this is Mrs. Allen, is it?' Sydney's eyes twinkled with delight. 'I'm glad to meet you. Hope you'll like it out here — it's perfectly delightful, y'know.'

Silvia Allen held out her free hand to him and smiled demurely: 'How do you do?'

Presently both Donald and Willy commanded his attention asking questions about the farm, the weather and the state of the roads. 'How's things in general?' his brother asked.

'Not bad, Donald, not bad at all. Of course we've had some dreadful weather these days, and a great deal of rain, but I think the worst is over now.' Thank heavens for that, I thought, I don't think I could stand much more bad weather.

'Evie and the child look fine,' I heard him comment. 'Tomorrow, after a good night's rest, they'll be able to go in the carriage to Las Palmas. The roads will be dryer and the going should be good. Plenty of mud, of course!'

Then Donald asked whether the river had flooded here in Mercedes.

'Oh yes, great floods as usual, and most of the people who live on the waterfront had to leave their homes and go up higher into the town,' Sydney replied. 'It's the same every year — but they won't learn. Once the water recedes they go directly back to their old homes on the river's banks.' He shook his head and then, 'Incidentally, it's past our bedtime...'

It was a very refreshed family that came down to breakfast the following morning.

'How long a drive to Las Palmas?' I asked.

'Roughly four hours,' Donald replied. 'If you get away before lunch, you'll be there much before dark and will be able to get a bit settled before nightfall.'

Sydney said: 'Somebody'll have to remain in Mercedes to wait for the luggage and I think it ought to be you Donald, as you know the stuff and all that.' Without more ado it was settled that Donald should stay and Sydney keep him company. I did not like the idea at all but there seemed no alternative if we wanted to get home at last.

'Will the road be all right?' I asked, trying to make the idea more plausible.

'Yes, it ought to be. In dry weather there's never any problem, but since these rains one can't be sure how much water has remained in the brooks. By the way, all brooks and streams are referred to as *cañadas* in this part of the world, so don't be surprised.'

We sat in silence for a short while digesting the unpleasant thought of going without Donald.

'Donald darling!' I suddenly exclaimed. 'Please come with us! I want to arrive at our new home together! Can't we leave Willy here instead?' I hugged him. 'Please, please, my love, come with me!' Yet in spite of all my begging I could not make him change his mind. 'Willy might have problems as he doesn't speak the language very well, and then there are the dogs...' he sighed, 'I signed for their quarantine the authorities will want my signature for their release. So don't make a fuss, you know I'll be home just as soon as I can.' He seemed so confident that I did not have the heart to continue with my entreaties. About half an hour before midday Willy, Mrs. Allen, Donny and I started in the carriage for Las Palmas. The day was good; a cool breeze blew across the fields as we continued our journey: the last lap.

The fields were beautifully green and fresh due to the recent rainfall. The road was far from perfect but at least dry enough to get out of town. How different the countryside was compared to the other I knew so well! Here it was flatter, the green different to the Irish green. The bushes and shrubs along the way were all unknown to me and the landscape much more sparse... no walls nor hedges like there were at home. This was plain open fields for miles; occasionally a clump of trees away in the distance or a dip in the road towards another *cañada*.

We drove along briskly, my excitement increasing with every kilometre travelled. At last Willy let out a complacent grunt.

'Ah-ha now! There you have it ladies, we're getting near!' He indicated to the right where another track suddenly appeared and we turned almost at a right-angle and entered it. Skirted by fields and a few eucalyptus trees that formed a small wood on one side. I closed my eyes for a second and let my mind drift. The tension of our recent journey now merged with this silent peace. I was drifting...

'Oh, for the touch of things that follow,
Pushed by circumstance into the morrow.
Hark! The silence is so great and still
The mist has lifted from yonder hill.'

We did get to the house eventually, and to say that I was disappointed would be putting it mildly. The rough plastered walls all were needing paint, and the plain flat roof showed no appeal save a low chimney with black smoke marks telling that at least the fireplace had once worked. As I dejectedly looked around the place, I noted that it was also dirty through and through. Plaster was flaking off the walls in the rooms, and as the Nursery seemed to be the worst of all, I decided Donny would sleep with me that first night. Things would have to be cleaned up in the morning.

I went into my bedroom where a large double-bed had been put up for Donald and me, and tried to settle for the night. At this point I discovered there was no lock to my door; an agonizing discovery with no solution, so we slept the night as though we were camping out in the bush, half expecting Indians to rush in and kill or rape, but of course nothing happened and our exhaustion gave way to sleep.

———

'Our luggage came from Mercedes' was an exciting entry in my Diary for that day. I often look back on those first days at Las Palmas with horror. The immense change of environment, coupled with the abrupt separation from my family and friends, made life almost unbearably hard.

Once Donald was there with our luggage, at least we had some material comforts with which to start turning this extraordinary place into a home. The boxes and trunks were all opened and the unpacking began. 'It's the most thrilling moment since we arrived!' I cried. 'We'll unpack all our things one by one and place them about the house. Our clock on the mantelpiece, the silver candlesticks on the dresser... table linen, towels and kitchen ware...' It was fascinating to bring out each object from its wrapping and place it as a part of our new home. I was beside myself with happiness!

'The rooms are already taking on a more homelike aspect. It's incredible the power these simple objects have, isn't it?' Donald had caught my excitement and was unpacking at a speed.

'My mirror!' I cried as it came out, a gift from my sisters for my wedding; fortunately, it had travelled well wrapped in the blankets. Soon the chamber pots and basins were brought out together with other familiar objects: silverware, ashtrays, tennis rackets and garments of all kinds. Thank God my sewing machine had arrived in good shape, and we soon got it up and into use. Seed bags for Sydney had to be made urgently for the on-coming harvest. Long evenings were spent sewing seed bags as well as making curtains to keep out the glaring sun.

There was much work, but perhaps the greatest concern during those first weeks was the lack of a cook, for I had no knowledge of cooking. My only experience of kitchen work had been one wet afternoon many years ago when my sisters and I were making a noise in the drawing-room while Papa was trying to rest. Mama had decided that it was a good moment, and just the sort of day, for the girls to go into the kitchen and get Cookie to teach us to make sponge cake. But now many years later, in the deep heart of South America, I saw that the gentlemen would not be satisfied with only sponge cake! Their demands were greater. So Donald applied himself to the kitchen, producing some meals, but the large old cooking stove was smoking badly.

'Something has to be done about this,' Willy said as he came out of the kitchen coughing and choking. The afternoon was spent cleaning the chimney which they found had a large abandoned hornet's nest in the upper section preventing it from drawing correctly. Once the nest was removed and the chimney swept, the stove began to work a treat and Donald found his work a deal more pleasant. Then good fortune sent us a cook a few days later; this quiet foreign man knew what he was about and we had meals served on time with tasty food.

Then there were the rats.

One night Mrs. Allen came knocking frantically on our bedroom door, shouting hysterically: 'Missus, come quickly!' Donald and I were up at once, fumbling to light a lamp and opened our door to find a very disheveled Mrs. Allen with Donny in her arms.

'What's the matter?' we demanded in chorus.

'There's rats in our bedroom!' Her usual quiet, controlled voice was rising to a scream. 'There I was lying awake in the dark, hearing scuffling noises as I always do before sleeping, when suddenly I felt a large rat jump on me!' She was shaking and I did not blame her. 'I rushed for baby and here I am!'

'How dreadful! But there, there now, don't worry, we'll do something about it in the morning.' I tried to calm her.

'I'm not going back to that terrible room!' she wailed.

'Of course not,' I assured her. 'Now don't get so upset. Leave Donny with me and finish your night's rest on the sofa in the drawing-room.' Donald illuminated her way in case there should be any more rats, and then he went into the Nursery armed with a great stick.

The following day was Operation Nursery. Everything was taken out and we discovered that the holes near the skirting-boards led to where the rats nested. Poison was put down and all the cavities cemented up and then various days were spent redecorating the room; the walls white washed and the floor waxed with the special wax we had brought from Ireland. The Nursery became the best room in the house. But rats were predominant all over the premises and so a great battle against them took place.

Immediately on our arrival the gentlemen started work; parting sheep, marking lambs and getting ready for the shearing which began in the month of October; the wool being an important sale, as very good money was paid for it, and when two men came asking for samples, Donald became excited and invited them into the drawing-room and offered them sherry while they discussed prices and quantity. They were buyers from Montevideo and when they eventually left, Donald wore a look of triumph. 'The wool's sold!' he announced happily. 'I got the price I wanted into the bargain!' He picked me up and twirled me around in delight. 'Now to make the bags and get it all ready to take away the day after tomorrow.'

The following evenings saw Donald and me sitting sewing wool bags late into the night. Two days later no less than nine carts drove into our patio and a great loading operation took place and soon the year's wool was taken away after being paid for. Our first sale!

I stood looking out over the wide patio which the men had graveled last week and I realized that things had improved since our arrival. One of the main changes was in the garden. The gentlemen had put in hours of work cutting away the overgrowth that had reached the edge of the veranda. Here some splendid rose bushes were discovered needing pruning, and various attractive shrubs of jasmine and syringa. The eternal job of watering each evening we took in turns and anybody who had a little energy left at the end of the day would give the grass its much needed moisture. The summer was hot and much dryer than any Irish summer I had ever known and I was shocked to find how much the plants suffered in consequence.

I turned around on the veranda — dreadful veranda which the rooms all opened onto; the worn-down bricks were difficult to keep clean for the dust gathered there in summer and the mud in winter. 'One day! One day soon,' I swore, 'we'll have a new veranda with tiles to be easily kept clean.'

But the greatest improvement was the interior of the house. The rooms were scrubbed out frequently, and soon all lime washed. Once the first was done, the difference was so great that even Willy got enthusiastic and offered to help with the dining-room and his own bedroom.

I found I was at peace except for the terrifying summer storms. Ever since I could remember I had been afraid of electric storms, the difference now being that they were more frequent in Uruguay than back home.

CHAPTER 2

When we were happily planning our emigration from Ireland late in 1873 and early 74, we were assured that Uruguay was now at last a country at peace.

In April 1872 the much longed-for peace came to the land, putting an end to two years of fierce civil wars. La Guerra Grande, the Great War, had ended at last and a peace treaty was signed with the revolutionaries and all military movements stopped and tranquility reigned once more.

D. Tomas Gomensoro was governing at the time. He was a good and honest man and his rule, though short, was very beneficial to the country. The farmers and land owners began to prosper and many small towns and villages were founded. Industry and Commerce took on new force and the Central Railway was extended to Villa Durazno in 1874. Two years previously Gomensoro had opened the Civil Register and fixed a date for the next elections.

In 1873 Dr. Jose Ellauri was elected President. He was a weak ruler but at the same time he was scrupulously honest with all monetary movements of the state. Unfortunately, his personality was not strong enough to confront the intense political passions which prevailed. Perhaps the most important feature during his rule was the inauguration of the National Telegraph which linked Montevideo with towns and villages in the interior, as well as with the South of Brazil.

This slow progress continued, sheltered by a peaceful period until some citizens began to conspire afresh instigated by the fact that the President was weak.

Therefore, late in 1874, exactly when we were going through our settling down period in Las Palmas, some military campaigns arose against the government but were suppressed. It was supposed then, that the soldiers who were meandering about the country at the time, of whom there were many, stealing cattle and produce from the unprotected farms such as ours, were remnants from the ranks of these military uprisings.

During my first summer in South America I found it difficult to accept the fact that we were soon approaching Christmas and the end of the year. It simply did not feel like it. Where Christmas had always meant the beginning of the snow, now I had to adjust to something quite different: a hot dry season filled with thistles, dust storms, field fires, heat waves and thunder storms, all very unChristmas-like, yet I had to accept that it was the season nevertheless.

The estancia work, from the shearing and wool sales in October and November, altered to a greater concentration on the farm itself. Divisions of paddocks, where the realization that fencing was an essential, made the gentlemen begin planning and looking into the price of wire and poles.

After Christmas it got hotter so that by eleven o'clock it was unbearable outside and we had to go indoors to shelter from the sun's burning rays. Inside the house it was only marginally cooler for there were parts where the sun filtered through the ill-fitting shutters and made the room like an oven.

We had all taken to wearing hats in protection from the sun; straw hats were easily purchased at the local *Pulperia* (local supply store and bar). The gentlemen had all brought felt hats with them from home but nobody had thought of bringing straw hats!

During this hot dry period, I felt sorry for the animals that clustered around the scanty trees or went into the *montes* (cluster of trees) where sometimes a *cañada* ran, to cool their burning hooves in the dampness of the undergrowth. Montes were of vital importance but unfortunately they were not plentiful on our land, so a tree planting programme was drawn up while adequate weather conditions were awaited. This would be a priority when the season changed.

This first summer was rainy with tremendous thunder storms assuring that the *cañadas* were well watered with no sign of drought. Likewise, we had nights without one bit of air moving, making it difficult to get to sleep unless one was as tired as I was. Occasionally Donald would drag out a mattress onto the veranda to sleep there; he said it was cooler and helped him to drop off. I suspected that Sydney and Willy did the same but I never got up to investigate — I was already sound asleep.

One evening at the end of February we thought for a moment that the very devil had been let loose over our land.

'Ooooops! Here comes the wind!' somebody yelled.

'Quick, fasten all the shutters! Hurry Willy, give a hand!' The wind got up before the rain began. 'Shut the doors onto the veranda before it rains too hard!' Everybody was rushing about calling orders, like a panic.

'Here it comes!' Great fat drops like giant tears began falling from the skies. We all huddled indoors.

A little later, 'It's become a tempest and sounds as if we lived on the edge of the ocean!' Sydney was laughing yet I couldn't see anything very amusing about it. At this point we realized our small house was far from waterproof.

'We need some basins and things to catch the drops in the dining-room. Hurry Evie! Where can we get some tubs from?'

'Here, try these.' Everybody was moving about the house in a desperate effort to keep things dry. 'Oh, quick! Here also! The drawing-room's getting flooded. Another bucket needed here!' We ran to the rescue.

'Something's going to have to be done to this blasted roof: it's just like a sieve!' Donald was looking cross when suddenly there was an ear-splitting crash out in the soaking wet darkness, followed by gigantic thuds, ending with a second crash as some object hit our roof somewhere in the vicinity of the dining-room. Donald and Sydney ran to see if there was any damage.

'Apart from a few pieces of plaster off the ceiling,' Donald told us, 'there seems to be no more damage.'

'Thank goodness!' exclaimed Willy who had been too lazy to have a look for himself. The storm was taking its time to abate; eventually it lessened and all that could be heard was the steady stream of rain which continued all night.

The following morning it had stopped and everybody tumbled out of bed and out of doors into the mud-splattered world. It was soaking wet and once people began moving about, there seemed to be more mud inside the house than out.

'I wonder what damage there's been?' Donald was sitting at his breakfast when Sydney came in: 'Well, the roof of the stables flew off and blew in this direction. The damage is here!' He pointed with his teaspoon directly above his head; it was where the bits of plaster had come down the night before. Big pools of dampness had appeared. Our dining-room roof was seriously damaged and the stables had no roof at all.

Between bites of thick bread and marmalade, Donald said: 'Have the horses been caught? We must go out and see what's happened.'

'Yes, they're tethered in the patio.'

'We'll spend the morning having a look around then,' he concluded as he stood ready to go. I knew I had many obligations in the house, including the churning, but the temptation of riding with the gentlemen was more than I could resist.

'Can I come too?' Donald turned and looked at me quizzically standing there in my working cotton dress. I read his thoughts — he was calculating how long it would take me to change into my riding habit and be up on my horse. Not very long. 'Hurry up!' he grinned.

Shortly we met on the patio and were mounting our horses and heading into the fields.

As the day progressed the weather improved, nothing as extreme as any sunshine but at least no more rain. On leaving the house we noticed two old eucalyptus trees had blown down blocking our avenue. Men and horses were at once called to clear this main entrance route. We took the track out towards the pass they had finished a few weeks ago. We trotted over the first crest of land to where we could see the lower lying field and the *cañada*, usually a tranquil trickle flowing gently. We stopped aghast. I could not believe my eyes! There in front of us was a wide expanse of water, rushing with force along a course to the lower land.

'My God!' exclaimed Willy, 'what a picture!' He was remembering all the long hours of work getting the pass firm across the slow dribbling water. It can't be the same place, I thought, as I took in the wild scene. Only one storm, one short night, and the change was absolutely unbelievable.

'Nothing can be done until the waters drop,' said Donald, 'so let's go and see the animals.' The rest of the morning we spent going round the paddocks, picking up sheep that had fallen down, their water-soaked coats preventing them from getting up. Between us we saved many lives by getting them on their feet again. The storm had also played havoc with the cattle on the further fields where we found two calves with their legs damaged and a cow that had got stuck in the mud and looked poorly. We brought the two calves up to the house for care.

The higher land had stood up to the tempest better, though some trees had come down in the *montes*. There was much to be attended to; the little calves were put into a small paddock beside the cook's room and we cared for them until they were strong enough to go back to their own herd.

Before lunch Donald and Sydney climbed up to the roof of the house to see the damage and later went to Mercedes to buy materials for the repair work.

Although there were these heavy rains and storms, let it not be thought that first summer at Las Palmas was not hot and dry also. There were endless pleasant summery days and they remain in my memory in particular as I went learning what this new land had in store.

'What's that strange strident noise that I keep hearing?' I questioned Donald as we sat out under the trees one of these summer days.

'That's the *chicharra*.' he said.

'What's that?'

'It's an insect, cicada type, that sits in the trees in the very hot weather, and if you were to look for one its sound will guide you to it. It's the male who calls to his mate, for only the male has the sound organ.' He paused to light his pipe, then through a cloud of smoke continued, 'it's very difficult to get a glimpse of them because they take on a protective coloration. Actually it looks like a locust and with its two wings spread out to their full, measures four or five centimetres.'

'Oh, not very big. Considering the amount of noise it makes, I'd have thought it was larger.' I said.

'It's shrill strident song is heard all the summer months. They sing mainly to attract their females by winding themselves up — you can actually hear them doing so — before letting forth their full-toned song.'

'What a funny little creature!' I cried. 'Does it do any harm?'

'No, absolutely harmless. Once the mating is over the female falls to the ground and perforates the roots of the tree she was in and there she lays her eggs.'

It seems that Pintos, our foremen, had told Donald all this, adding that the female *chicharra* lays about forty or fifty eggs which hatch in April or May, live among the roots of the trees and are totally different in aspect to the adult.

We sat outside that morning and listened to the shrill song which announced the beginning of the hot weather.

The separation from my horse in Ireland had been agony but once we had arrived and settled at Las Palmas I saw that there were many lovely horses and mares to replace the one left behind. Before long I chose Rosie as mine. She was a beautiful little chestnut mare, full of spirit. We took time to come to terms but soon she learned who was the boss when I was on board! I rode her daily, washed her down after her exercise and fed her special oats before letting her go into the fields. At first I rode with Donald or any of the gentlemen for fear of getting lost as the property was so vast and devoid of boundary fences, but soon I became independent and rode alone whenever I pleased. My dogs came with me...

My dogs. I remember a few weeks before leaving home when Donald came into my room and found me looking glum.

'Anything the matter, my love?' he asked. I looked at him in despair, wondering if he would understand my sadness.

'I was wishing I didn't have to part with all my animals when we leave.' I sighed. 'The pups...' I was almost in tears. Donald took my hand and pressed it gently to his lips.

'Perhaps we could arrange to take the pups with us. What do you think of that?'

'Oh, can we? Can we really?' I jumped up with joy. It had never occurred to me that this might be a possibility.

'I know of some families who've already taken their dogs with them,' he told me, 'so why not us?' I flung my arms around his neck and kissed him.

'Yes, yes, I want to take the puppies even if the older dogs have to stay.' I laughed, 'I'll be as good as gold and not complain of anything, if I can take them.'

'There'll be certain formalities which have to be gone through and maybe some quarantine time for them while on the trip, but it seems perfectly simple — I'll find out.' I rushed from the room to find my sisters to tell them the wonderful news, the puppies following at my heels. They were the Irish terriers that Donald had given me last Christmas. It was a few months before we were to be married and it was Christmas Day. I was expecting Donald to come over to Carriehall to spend the day with us.

I watched him turn in at the gateway; to my surprise he was on foot and carrying a basket in one hand. Whatever was he doing with that large basket on a cold Christmas morning, I wondered. Had he brought so many presents that he had to carry them in a basket? Suddenly he stopped and took a peek into the basket as if to assure himself that the contents were still all right. He continued his walk. I rushed down-stairs to meet him at the front door. He was looking splendid this morning: tall and handsome with his red-brown hair brushed to one side giving him a vague air of apology! The FitzPatrick colouring was very particular indeed and it predominated in all members of the family. Sydney, who was with us at Las Palmas, had identical colouring.

That Christmas morning Donald's overcoat was half open, he always looked as if he had dressed in a hurry. 'Darling, lovely Donald, how I love you!' With this song in my heart I sped down the steps into his arms.

'Happy Christmas!' I got it out first.

'Happy Christmas, darling!' he said as he handed me the basket. At once I knew that what was inside was alive. I stood transfixed.

'They're a Christmas present for you,' he said a little shyly, and there were two of the most adorable terrier pups that I had ever seen.

'Oh, how adorable!' I exclaimed as I stooped to pick one out. A little over one month old, they were curled up together as if drawing warmth from one another on an old rug.

'Thank you! Are they for me only?' half expecting to have to share them with my sisters.

'All yours.'

As they had arrived on Christmas Day as if brought by the jovial St. Nick, they were baptized Santa and Claus, names which remained for all their lives. During the first weeks I took great pains teaching them the etiquette of a household, and as they were intelligent little chaps, they soon grew to be obedient and house-trained. Santa and Claus became the joy of my heart; no wonder then, a year and a half later, when our emigration to South America was looming near that I was in a state of despondency until Donald came to my rescue. He spoke to the authorities and plans for taking the puppies were going ahead. And now we were here, dogs and all.

There was so much work during those first months at Las Palmas that I was permanently and incurably tired. There was a great deal to be done and hardly any money to do it with. One evening, tired and depressed, I decided it was time to write to Mama at home. I told her how my life had changed since arriving and that I was finding it particularly difficult to adjust. Not even did I find time to ride with my loved one in the evenings and this I found sad and frustrating, so I asked her how I could cope with such a situation. Mama would know; she always solved our problems.

Many weeks later Mama's reply reached me and it ran as follows:

My dearest Evie,

Your letter of... came like a cry of anguish into the very depths of my heart. How sorry I am that you are finding life in the new world hard. Don't despair! Having a good cry is not to be ashamed of. It's a safety valve that we have inside ourselves, that when things get too much for us, goes off and overflows in buckets of tears.

Now I want you to take things very gently. Rome was not built in a day, as the saying goes, and neither will Las Palmas be, and although you say your hard work goes unnoticed, I know you are wrong in saying this for in a letter from Willy he told me you have already done marvels in the house and your gentle touch with furniture and decoration is turning the place into a home.

I want to call your attention to one matter. You are making a mistake not riding with Donald in the evenings once work is done. You must take an hour when work stops and begin a relaxation period. You know that riding has always been a joy to you and anything one enjoys is relaxation. Therefore, you and Donald ought to ride together and this will become a tool to keep you united. It could also be a time when you talk things over.

Evie dear, you must work out your priorities and always keep that which is most important at the top of your list: riding with your husband is a priority with you.

If things are hard now, take comfort. Life offers compensations, they're all around you if you have the art of seeing them. Let me point out one or two: the song of the birds, the sound of music, the tie of friendship and of love, and like these, thousands more. Take comfort from them all.

Keep the faith; try reading Proverbs 3 and know that truly 'He shall direct thy paths'.

Your fond and loving,

Mama.

This letter was like a lifeline to me and once I had it with me I referred to it when things became difficult and Mama's beautiful words would pull me up once again, helping me through yet another period of loneliness and depression.

CHAPTER 3

Once the South American countries were discovered by adventurers like Solis, Magallanes and Gaboto, the King of Spain sent out further expeditions, this time to conquer and colonize.

I ought to have been afraid when we heard the hair-raising stories of killing and violence which had taken place between colonizers and the Indians of the land; we were assured, however, that the Indians had all been overcome and now, some three hundred years later, the inhabitants were mainly descendants of Europeans who'd come out to colonize. The majority were Spaniards but also many Portuguese, British, French and a smaller amount of Germans. Of the original Indians there remained but few and these now being civilized had lost all interest in resistance, having accepted with submission their new masters.

The manner in which this colonization by the Spaniards took place was fairly unique. The Spanish Government sent out adventurers of great courage, with large expeditions, with the understanding they would remain and govern the lands they'd conquered. These men were greatly trusted by the King, and four such adventurers came to the River Plate. They were known as *Los Adelantados* (the advanced ones).

Although it was over the course of nearly sixty years that the *Adelantados* were endeavouring to conquer, and a certain amount of ground-work had been done, they were still not completely successful, there being a great deal of resistance on the part of the Indians. When the last of the *Adelantados* gave in and returned to Spain, the people in the city of Asuncion del Paraguay, at that time the centre of the River Plate colonies, held their own elections and chose a local patriot called Hernando Arias de Saavedra, later known as Hernandarias, who was the first South American patriot to be raised as governor by public election.

Hernandarias, being a very valiant man, tried to overcome the Indians by force, constantly failing, until at last he realized the Christian religion would be the only way to make the Indians accept the Spanish dominion. Having obtained permission from Spain to make this change, he appealed to the Missionaries for help.

The first Missionaries to come to Uruguay (at the time called La Banda Oriental) were the Franciscan monks, who landed at the mouth of the Rio Negro and began their apostolic campaign. While the Franciscans civilized the south, the Jesuits were evangelizing the north, out of which arose the famous Paraguayan Missions.

This historical information was important to us for it told us what sort of people we were likely to be living amongst.

As I reviewed our first nine months at Las Palmas, the saying 'Come to South America and make your fortune' I saw was distinctly mythical. Perhaps one could make a fortune out here, but we'd not yet discovered how! This added to the fact that the gentlemen were not brilliant business men. Of course they were not. They were farmers. They had to be given time to learn the business side. Even as there was money coming in from cattle sales, rams, seeds and wool, there were also big expenses, not to be surprised when one remembered the sheer barren land and group of dreadful little rooms we'd originally come out to. Now the rooms were habitable and two more bedrooms had been added; the roof repaired after the terrible gale. Cattle had been purchased, workmen taken on, salaries paid and trees planted. The property was badly populated and trees were essential to ensure a good climate, moderate rainfall and shelter for our animals.

This was the year we started putting up fences. One morning Donald came back into the house and said: 'I've contracted an engineer from Mercedes to come to measure our land and indicate exactly where it begins and ends. We must put up boundary fences.'

'When's he coming?'

'Today.'

The engineer came with his young adult son and together with the gentlemen they went out all day measuring the land. When they returned at sundown I was told they'd be remaining the night for the job was intricate and was not finished.

'I'll look into some sleeping quarters for them,' I said, 'though I can't think where I'll put TWO men.'

Donald stopped short in his exit from the room. 'What do you mean? For one night? And nowhere for them to sleep? Don't be foolish!' I was surprised Donald was so sharp with me but presumed he was overtired and thought I'd easily solve the problem for him.

'Well...' I began, but he interrupted crossly: 'They can sleep in the outer rooms. There are a couple of camp beds down there, so that's fixed.' He left the room abruptly. Then later, when we were dressing for dinner he seemed more docile and began talking about the engineer and his family.

'They're nice people and the engineer is interested in seeing our son for he has two little girls, one's three and the baby sixteen months, same age as Donny.'

When we were assembled in the drawing-room before dinner Donald asked Mrs. Allen to bring Donny for the engineer to see.

'Sixteen months! He's enormous!' exclaimed the engineer, 'my little Maria is half the size,' he laughed, 'but she's a quick-witted one indeed.' Half the evening was spent discussing the children, and for the first time since our arrival at Las Palmas I was included in the conversation. It was good to speak to somebody whose interests were not entirely confined to the farmlands.

The engineer was earning a fee, of course, but when he finished the measuring of the boundaries, his instruction had been so excellent that Sydney and Donald had learned how to measure correctly, having no need in the future to contract a professional for the interior paddocks. There followed many long days of measuring and putting up stakes in strategic positions.

Then the wire. Hundreds of metres were purchased in the town at a high cost but fortunately the posts could be cut from our own trees, saving money there. Once the posts were ready, cut and loaded, on June 1st, 1875, the fencing began. This work was supported and encouraged by all for it was a fundamental advance on the estancia for efficient cattle raising.

Simultaneously the badly needed Quinta (kitchen garden) was beginning to take shape giving us weeks of work, and during the laying out we noticed a fence was fundamental here also to keep out roaming animals.

We had much to learn in those early days. I remember particularly one instance. Thousands of sheep skins had been prepared for sale and Sydney found a buyer in Mercedes and brought him to see the skins. We entertained him all morning and gave him lunch, but he did not buy the skins.

'He says they're not properly cured,' Donald commented. This failure to sell the skins made a big hole in our finances and the gentlemen went over to the Harrison's Santa Emiliana the following day to find out how to cure sheep skins correctly.

Even as 1875 began badly for us at Las Palmas, it also began badly for the country, principally in the governmental area, to the extent of being known as *El Ano Terrible* (The Terrible Year).

As well as constant revolts and battles, there came upon the land a tremendous financial crisis which ruined all industry and commerce. With the country in this condition The Terrible Year came to an end but simultaneously there'd been a long, cold winter for us at Las Palmas. It set in with no mercy; I felt the cold more at the estancia than ever before in Ireland.

There was little possibility of warming oneself except beside the log fire in the drawing-room, or else in the kitchen during the hours the old arguer was alight. But cooking to me was a bore, so my visits there were few, and I had to resort to the drawing-room. If I sat down anywhere else I felt the cold creeping up my legs and if I remained still reading or sewing, I'd gradually freeze until I was the most miserable of all creatures.

Over dinner one evening I first broached the subject of extra heating in the house.

'Baby Donny's constantly catching colds and chills and so is Mrs. Allen, so I feel we must add more warmth to their lives.' The gentlemen reacted in

different ways to this. Willy nodded his hearty approval. 'It's beastly cold.'
I heard him mutter. But Donald and Sydney didn't feel my arguments were
particularly authentic, so I went on: 'I know Mrs. Allen hates the cold and I
feel it would be a pity if she suddenly decided to leave us for this reason.' This
struck home and brought a favourable reaction from them.

'True, true.... Fireplaces will have to be built in the other rooms,' said
Sydney. 'How are they made?'

We were in the dining-room which all but had icicles hanging from the
ceiling while we ate our tepid meal. The food did not remain warm in these
temperatures; it was already cold before reaching the table.

'Making a fireplace is no easy matter, I know,' Donald told us. 'There's a
special technique in the shaping of the chimney; a certain angle to the elbow,
which only very specialized men can do. Sometimes it needs an engineer for
the job.'

'Can we get somebody from Mercedes, do you think?' I insisted, 'what
about the nice engineer who came for measuring?'

'I know the Harrisons had two fireplaces built last year, so they must know
of somebody.' It was arranged for us to ride over to the Harrison's to inquire
about these workmen.

I went to bed greatly enthused. The Harrisons would have a solution; they
were wonderful people who'd helped us many times over the recent months of
settling. Donald and I rode over the next afternoon to Santa Emiliana which
was on the way to the village of Dolores. It was a forty-minute ride and Donald
and I used to have bets we could do it in less time by keeping up a regular
gallop all the way. Nevertheless, we always found forty minutes had come
round as we rode into their well-kept entrance patio.

We trotted to the left where the wooden tethering bar for horses stood
along with a trough for them to drink on arrival. I noticed Rosie immediately
started nibbling the tender grass and Donald's *tordillo* (white horse) drank
thirstily like from a desert oasis.

'Hello, hello!' Margaret Harrison was glad to see us. She was weeding her
flower beds which were looking good even though it was mid-winter. She was

the sort of person who managed to have flowers in her garden all the year round, a virtue which I greatly admired and envied.

'Your lovely garden!' I exclaimed. 'How do you manage it?' She shrugged and laughed, 'I have a green thumb, you know.'

While the gentlemen went into the house, I watched her finish her job of weeding between jonquils in full bloom and pouring out a delicious scent.

'It's a good time to weed,' she said, 'because of the amount of rain.' Soon she took me into the sitting-room to join the gentlemen for tea. The fire was alight, throwing off a bounteous heat.

'We came to ask about the people who make fireplaces,' I said, but Donald and Bill Harrison had already got together on the subject and were looking up names and addresses.

The Harrisons had come out to Uruguay eight years before us and I wondered how this little gentlewoman managed to survive if her place had been half as barren as ours. Although she was tiny and frail-looking, she had a will of iron and they'd converted their estancia into a wonderful and comfortable home as well as a productive farm. Bill was older, fifty perhaps, had a great deal of working knowledge of farms, consequently we asked his advice often. I believe they were a little sorry for us in our struggle for survival.

This afternoon I looked admiringly around the large, airy room with its pretty chintz covered armchairs and large sofa. A beautiful English woolen carpet in tomes of green and brown covered the entire centre of the floor. I'd not seen a carpet since leaving home and looked at this one with envy. The room was furnished with much taste.

The sun was slanting through the wide bow-window and I thought of our rather dismal drawing-room with its easterly window. In this light and spacious room, the westerly view let in all the glory of the afternoon sun, and we saw the peaceful scene of the horses being brought up for the night.

'Let's go and take a stroll,' Mrs. Harrison said, 'while the gentlemen speak of fireplaces.' She led me out into the cold afternoon air, and I knew what was coming. She'd never let us go home without some produce from her kitchen garden.

'I want you to come and see the Quinta which Bill and our boy have been enlarging this week.'

I enthused at the suggestion. The dogs were soon at our heels; two sheep dogs and two terriers similar to ours. I stooped and patted them.

Immediately one could see the large expanse of ground recently added to the Quinta. It was freshly ploughed and turned over ready for planting, the earth was damp and jet black, as rich a soil as ours. The gardener Pedro was pulling up vegetables for the household consumption and the basket at his side was almost full.

'Pedro!' she called, 'please prepare something for the lady to take home.'

'Oh, please don't worry,' I hastened to say. 'You've given us so much already.' I knew my objection would make no difference and the vegetables looked good. Pedro, who was pulling up carrots, now set aside another basket for us. When full, he topped it with crisp cabbage and deep green lettuce.

On our way back to the house we saw a strange cage hanging from a tree branch near the kitchen door.

'What's that?' I asked.

'It's my *fiambrera*,' she replied as we drew level. 'It's a meat safe; much cooler out here under the trees than in the warm kitchen all day and night.' I noticed the *fiambrera* had two storeys on which there was food on platters.

'You'll notice it has one of the sides sliding up and down for access,' she demonstrated. 'It's been such a solution, especially in summer to preserve food,' she added.

'Our cook leaves the left-overs on the kitchen table,' I said, 'and they very often go bad during the night. When I go into the kitchen next morning, the sour smell of decomposed food strikes me like a cannonball!' I shuddered.

'Exactly,' she laughed, 'and then it has to be thrown away — such a waste.' She paused. 'You should have one made, Evie, I think you'll find it a great blessing and a saving.'

'I'll speak to Donald and have one made.'

We found the food lasted much longer out in the open air, so there was less waste. The one Donald had made for me had a roof for rainy days, and I soon learned why the netting was so important: the animals would devour it all if the protection were not there. Even so I often saw birds clinging to the sides, trying to peck a morsel.

Donald contracted the mason who'd made the Harrison's chimneys so well. The work began during the month of July and I was horrified to find what an amount of work and mess it entailed. They started in the Nursery one fine morning: all Mrs. Allen's and Donny's things were moved into Willy's room where they slept during the work period. Willy kindly moved into the little spare room behind the kitchen.

'How's the work?' Donald asked that evening.

'To have the masons is like having a minor hurricane blowing through the house all day, and I'm wishing we'd not chosen July in which to do it.' I sighed. 'Anybody with a grain of sense would've got it done in summer.'

'We didn't know it was going to be so cold, did we?'

As the days of work progressed, the house got colder and colder and the more we crunched in sand and cement. 'You must have the place open and airy,' we were told, 'then the plaster will dry quickly.'

The Nursery was finished in three days and our bedroom in another two, only the dining-room one left to be done.

Donald foresaw the extra consumption of wood. 'I've taken one of the workmen into the woods and made him chop wood to bring up to the house to dry out.' When at last even the dining-room was finished and the mason was packing up to leave, we lighted a small fire to try it out. The chimney drew well, so I went into my bedroom to dress and found the room full of smoke. From under the skirting-board adjacent to the dining-room there was a thin trail of smoke oozing out.

We caught the mason just in time. He had to remain until the following day to remedy the fault, so, after ten days we were able to light all three fires successfully.

———————

The Harrisons were not our only close neighbours. The Tomkins lived at *El Torrado* not very far from Las Palmas. Jim Tomkins was of a different calibre to Bill Harrison. We'd known Jim and his wife Emma in Ireland before coming out to S.A. but they were of a different school of thought, although the original reason for coming to Uruguay was the same for us all: to expand, to make big money, to enlarge our outlook, and finally create a solid future.

Jim was callous to a point of being lazy at times. He was a gentle soul, ponderous of the desires of the womenfolk. His greasy mouse-brown hair was worn slightly longer than necessary, giving the impression it was left long simply because he'd been too idle to have it cut. Yet he worked his farm and appeared to be keeping it afloat in spite of its slovenly aspect. Here there were constant signs of neglect, from the entrance drive where old branches blown down in recent gales were still lying about looking untidy, to the plain house of rough stucco badly in need of paint.

Nobody criticized, for old Jim was in Uruguay alone. His wife had refused to come out until the place was in working order and appropriate for a lady to live in. Unlike our case, I thought, where I'd packed my boxes and followed the man I loved to wherever he asked me. On thinking it over, perhaps Emma's attitude was more sensible, and might have spared me a lot of discomforts.

Recently Jim was over at our place and he told us he'd written to Emma telling her it was a good time to come as we were entering summer and everything was easier in the warm weather.

'The house is habitable enough, I think' he said, 'so it's time to end my solitude and the missus come to join me.' He smiled his slow smile, 'do you think she'll like it out here, Evie?'

What a question! I had no answer for him but was able to get by with a smile and a change of subject. Here one had to adjust, how long would Emma take to adjust? Time would tell. It was the end of October when we heard Emma was arriving the following Wednesday.

'It would be nice and friendly if you rode over to El Torrado, Evie dear, and put some flowers in the house in welcome,' Donald suggested, 'and possibly make them a cake too.' This would be a warm welcome for Emma and it was a good idea of Donald's.

On Tuesday I cut as many flowers as our garden afforded, tied them to the back of my saddle and rode over to the Tomkins. I didn't take a cake. I hated the thought of making another cake. I'd made one for our own table recently which had not been much of a success — a bit flat. The Tomkins would have to go without cake, perhaps their cook made cakes anyway.

So I got off with only the flowers in welcome.

By this time the long winter had drawn to an end and the trees were beginning to sprout. I was amazed how by August the willows bordering the *Aguila* river were already shooting. Spring did not come until the following month but the willows seemed to be anxious to welcome it.

On a beautiful evening at this time of year Donald came in from work and said: 'Come on, let's go for a ride.' He laughed, 'Race you! Bet I get off first!' he challenged me.

'Oh, you mean thing!' I cried. 'I have to get into my riding habit, so you're sure to win. Never mind!' I called, 'I'll take you on...' I dashed into my room on the pretext of changing, when all I did was to pick up my crop and, as swift as an arrow, I was running down the veranda into the patio, reaching the horses standing saddled and ready for riding.

'Hurry up, slow-coach!' I yelled as Rosie and I fled down the avenue. Donald heard my shout and saw my flying skirts as I galloped away at a speed. It didn't take him long to be up on his horse chasing me — fast, fast, faster... I could hear the pounding of hooves on the ground and knew he'd soon catch me up. The race was wildly exciting and we both laughed happily.

'You're a wild crazy girl!' he called as he drew near and we slowed down. 'Who's ever seen a distinguished lady — ahem — riding in a silk dress? You looked like a balloon as you took off from the patio with your skirts flying behind you.'

I laughed: 'I won the race, didn't I?'

'We'll say you won the race, but you don't qualify as a dignified lady of the manor.' He was jesting and I knew he loved me like this. It was like the old days when we first met in Ireland and we'd go jumping walls, galloping across fields and splashing over brooks. The very day we met was a bit like this. I remember how my sisters and I had been riding one morning after a very wet night and we saw the Fitzpatrick brothers riding in our direction. The two parties met exactly in the dip of a brook which was particularly muddy. The lads were galloping and arrived beside us with cheers and whoops of joy. I knew Hugh and Sydney, but not the other brother Donald.

'Hello girls!' they called to us, forgetting to draw rein before coming alongside us. The mud came up and splashed us mercilessly. I could feel the damp slime on my face and clothes. I was splashed to glory, and my new habit was ruined.

'Oh, sorry!' The boys, realizing their mistake too late, looked crestfallen at their carelessness. 'Didn't mean to dirty you so much.' I'd got the worst of it. Ada and Ethel only had a few specks on their garments, but me.... There was nothing to be done.

'Oh, Evie, your face!' shrieked Ethel.

'And your new habit!' gasped Ada.

Silence. Then I started to laugh.

It was such an impossible situation, the funny side suddenly struck me, and I began to laugh and laugh until tears started running down my dirty face. Soon everybody joined in and the tension eased. Donald told me, during our courting days, it was this episode which had convinced him that a girl who could laugh with such authentic mirth at her own misfortune, was very likely a girl worthwhile. A girl who'd laugh in all difficult situations all her way through life. A girl worth knowing better. A girl worth marrying perhaps?

At that point our courtship began.... And now, many years later, we were riding together swiftly over the fields, well-known to us already, in another country, on our way to see some new lands purchased recently.

'Where's the new property?'

'It's the piece which belonged to Bentos.'

'Beside the *Aguila*, do you mean?'

'Yep, that's right. Bentos needed cash so he offered it to us.' Strategically it seemed a good buy. It bordered where the new road would eventually run.

'I'll get Syd to come down with me tomorrow,' he said, 'to take measurements for the fence and get that started before the shearing when there's little time for anything else.'

Work, work, work, but rewarding work. I felt a surge of gladness and optimism welling up within me. I wished this wave of satisfaction would stay with me forever. We cantered gently home, with a glow inside us. I thought, Mama was right. Riding with Donald was vital in my life.

As we neared the homestead we saw we had guests. I recognized the Tomkins' trap and noticed figures on the veranda. They'd come to thank us for the flowers which I'd arranged on the day of Emma's arrival.

The Tomkins were swiftly making friends with Mrs. Allen who was acting hostess in my absence. This was good for I imagined Mrs. Allen was a lonely soul; the only person who held conversations with her was Sydney. They walked young Donny as far as the gate in the evenings and talked a great deal. I wondered what they could possibly have in common when seeming so different.

Silvia Allen with smooth white skin and full skirts. Dainty slippers barely peeped out from under her wide silk skirts. Her hands were soft and white, with well-kept nails perfectly rounded at the points. I knew she had a lovely manicure set with scissors, files, tiny tweezers and an assortment of creams. She was very vain about her hands and her hair. A long time was spent each day combing and plaiting her long black hair. She always wore her sun hat out of doors, of which she had many. They were pretty and fashionable and I sometimes envied her them. My hats were far more practical, and most of the time slipped off my head as I galloped over the fields after some animal. Mrs. Allen did not care for animals: 'They dirty my hands.' she once said, 'I prefer children.'

And Sydney? How could one describe Sydney? He was particularly unfathomable and very masculine like his brothers. He had the red-brown hair which curled in tight waves at the top of his head and turned over at the nape of his neck when left a little too long. He had an attractive habit of running his brown hand over the top of his head when embarrassed. Sydney's body was tough and sun-tanned for his work called for many hours in the sun giving him a weather-beaten appearance.

Sydney's main interest was the farm, with shooting and fishing for sport.

In later months the Tomkins' friendship with Mrs. Allen spread to Sydney also and he was often invited over to El Torrado. I think they'd have kept him there permanently had it not been for his commitments on our farm. When he went for an evening meal, he'd stay the night and return to Las Palmas in the morning, having had an evening of good food and wine. He'd have a beam on his face and a naughty twinkle in his eye after those evenings.

'Lots of booze?' I asked a bit cheekily once.

'Yep,' he answered with a grin. 'I drank old Jim under the table as usual!'

'And what did Emma say to that?' I couldn't perceive Emma's approval of her husband being 'drunk under the table' as Sydney termed it.

Emma was already in bed when we gents finally finished the bottle.' He laughed at the memory. 'Jim slumped over the table in a drunken stupor, so I let him sleep it off.' He shrugged: 'He went to bed much later.' As Sydney left me, grinning, he threw over his shoulder: 'He was up for breakfast this morning anyway.'

CHAPTER 4

Another year: 1876

'Soldiers came and took two horses,' entries such as this were frequent in my Diary during this year. Stealing took place regularly all through the year. It made me very indignant and I would have liked to go out and give the soldiers a piece of my mind when they came around, but Donald had forbidden me to have any contact at all with them.

'We don't know what sort of people they are, and if you rub them up the wrong way, they might get violent. Don't forget they're armed men and we don't want any serious problems.' He continued with his breakfast before going on: 'We've been told the best way to get rid of them is to give them what they ask and no comments.' These became everyone's instructions in the face of the nasty stealing soldiers. We were always careful to lock away our best riding horses at night. The poor cows and lesser animals had no more protection than being on our land but the soldiers did not respect this.

It was greatly upsetting, especially for me being well advanced in pregnancy, carrying my second child. Then one evening the big theft took place. Soldiers came again and this time took eighteen cows, the biggest haul yet, and it made me so angry I felt quite ill all day.

Willy was furious also: 'I don't think we should stand for this sort of treatment,' he grumbled, 'it's absolute highway robbery and they must be stopped.'

'How?'

The matter was discussed at great length, Donald was of a mind to let things go by and not do anything, not wishing to cause friction.

'The trouble with you Donald, is you're a pacifist.' And Willy was quite right. 'Pacific measures are not what an army of soldiers are used to. They're accustomed to harsh treatment, and if we let the thing ride as we always do, they'll steal more and more until there's nothing left.'

'I vote we go into Mercedes and find their Commander and report the theft.' It was Sydney who, after lengthy thought, proposed this.

'Yes, I agree,' I joined in, 'those dishonest pilfering men should be punished for their crimes!'

'Sh-sh-sh-sh, Evie dear.' Donald tried to hush me. 'You're in no fit state to be getting worried over men's matters. Why don't you go and lie down?'

I'd been lying down most of the day, feeling terrible, with slight discomforts in my stomach. I felt better sitting up.

'No, I don't want to lie down!' I declared hotly. 'I'm uncomfortable while lying down and I want something to be done about our cattle being pinched from under our noses. I agree with Sydney, somebody ought to go and put in a complaint about the thieving. Eighteen cows is too much for them to get away with.'

It was finally decided that one of the gentlemen would go into Mercedes the following day to report about the stolen cows.

After a very bad night with lots of pain, my little daughter was born early the following morning. She was a fine fat little child and Mrs. Allen said she was the image of Donald, but I thought she was merely a rosy bundle of pink flesh. We named her Ada Beatrice Margaret. Ada after my favourite sister, Beatrice after Granny Fitzpatrick and Margaret after my own mother.

Despite this joy, the imminent problem of the soldiers was uppermost in our minds, and Willy was chosen to go to put in the claim about the cows for Donald ought to remain near me as father of the new baby, and Sydney had much work on the farm.

Willy prepared for his trip and the gentlemen gave him instructions about the way in which he should proceed when facing the Commander. Willy's Spanish was reasonably good, at least we considered he knew enough to make himself understood. Donald taught him various tactful phrases to use with his petition, such as *'Le agradezco su atencion...'* (I thank you for your kindness)

'*Le pido disculpas...*' (forgive me for intruding) '*Espero que entienda...*' (I hope you understand) Willy wrote them in a little book to which he'd refer if necessary.

He left that morning.

'There's a possibility you may have to remain another day; you may not see the Commander at your first request, you do understand that Willy, don't you?'

'That's all right,' Willy grinned, 'I don't mind having a day off in Mercedes once in a while.'

'I wish I could go too,' Donald was anxious about the success of the mission.

'No, no,' Willy was emphatic. 'Your place is here with your family. I've no ties.'

Donald became resigned to his duties of father. They packed up a small case with a change of clothes for Willy and some food to help him through the day. 'What else might I need?' he asked. Sydney lent him his gun, partly in protection and partly in the event of him seeing something worth shooting on his way home.

'I hope to be back tonight with any luck, or if not tomorrow. Goodbye!'

'Goodbye Willy!' I called as he strode from the room; my anger being slightly appeased for something was going to be done about the stealing at last.

I was left alone with my baby. I heard voices on the veranda and soon the sound of the trap leaving. I sank back on my pillows wondering what made the soldiers act the way they did. Where were they going? What was their objective? We'd been told they were small groups of men, probably travelling from one point of the country to another, not being provided with food they had to take whatever was handy on the farms.

This sounded plausible — but eighteen cows? Some feast! That was more than nourishment for a small group of hungry men; it seemed as if they were making a business on the side. Under the cloak of patriotism, they were doing good business somewhere. It had to be stopped. Once their superiors were informed, we hoped for some control over the men, although we knew it was not only soldiers from the ranks who'd been on our land yesterday, for an officer's cap had been found in the field where the cows had been taken from.

With an officer in command of the group, one would have expected better behaviour.

As it was early I dozed a little until Mrs. Allen came into the room. 'How's baby this morning?' she asked as she bustled in. She always took on extra energy when I was laid up. She left aside her cool everyday manner and took command of the situation with both hands, to a point of becoming a little bossy.

'First we'll fix up Mum,' she informed me briskly, 'and then baby can have her meal.' She had firm experienced hands which felt good as she helped me out of bed for my toilet. Later those same hands were changing my baby into clean clothes and fitting her to the breast. My milk had not yet come in, but the child was sucking well and tomorrow...

Tomorrow... Willy ought to be back by tomorrow.

'I'm anxious to know how Willy's getting on, aren't you?' I commented when Donald was sitting with me later in the day.

'Willy's a likeable person and should cope, though I feel I'd have done better perhaps.'

'I hope he gets home tonight.'

'I doubt it. It's more likely he'll stay over and have a little spree, travelling home first thing in the morning.' But Willy didn't get home the following day. Nor the next.

'Something's gone wrong,' Sydney commented over dinner, 'it can't be taking so long.'

Donald's brow puckered. 'If there was a delay, why didn't he send a message to us?' he said, 'if he's not back in the morning one of us must go and find out what's up. I don't like this long silence. The army can be quite ruthless.'

They decided Sydney would go the next day, with the agreement he'd return the same evening with news.

It was a great relief to hear Sydney's return just after sundown while Donald and I were in the drawing-room. It was the first time out of my room since the birth; Donald had carried me for it was too soon for me to walk.

Sydney came in and sat down with a thump.

'What news?' we asked and then he told us the whole story. It seems Willy had arrived in Mercedes shortly after midday and had searched out the Commander's offices. Once these had been located he tried to get an interview. This was refused him.

'*El Comandante no atiende hasta la tarde.*' No interviews until the afternoon. Willy was told to return at five o'clock — after siesta. Nobody did anything without a refreshing siesta. So he ambled over to the nearby *boliche* (bar) and ordered a drink.

Eventually he had a good number of drinks. Before long the alcoholic beverages began circulating freely in the bar and Willy began telling stories. Soon the stories became more and more hilarious and he was in a frenzy of excitement. He was getting encouragement from all the *vecinos* (neighbours) and this was a change, they did not generally have an *ingles* (Englishman) making noise and banter in the bars of the town.

Willy was a very congenial person and word had got round the town of his exuberant presence and copious drinking, plus invitations to drink, and shortly the place was filled to capacity. There were stories and laughter and before very long Willy had all the townsfolk sympathizing and understanding his indignation at loosing eighteen cows in one night and he was encouraged to rehearse his forthcoming interview with the Commander.

Unbeknown to us Willy had taken the officer's cap found in our field and here he put it on at a jaunty angle while he rehearsed the interview, to the great amusement of his audience. He was egged on by his success, and as by nature he was rather a shy person, this unnatural state of affairs began to please him, his voice becoming louder and more boisterous as time went by.

'Another round of drinks!' he shouted when he saw his empty glass. Waves of mirth and many empty glasses were soon refilled by the delighted barman. Sales had not been so good for a long time. Willy found he was transforming a little gaiety into an ecstasy of delight and happiness; the tranquil townsfolk were not used to this sort of amusement in the middle of the working week.

Suddenly one of the gauchos turned to Willy and said: '*Son las cinco...*' Willy squinted drunkenly at his watch and saw it was almost five o'clock. Slowly he got to his feet in preparation for departure to find he could hardly stand. He even had difficulty in keeping his balance without support, so he made signs to the nearby gaucho to give him a hand, and together they were able to get out into the afternoon sunshine. This cleared Willy's head a fraction and swaying dangerously, singing lustily, the army cap perched on his head, he arrived at the offices of the Commander.

His appearance in this state at the official rooms was not received very favourably.

'What does the Señor Ingles want?' the Commander demanded coldly, observing the drunken figure with much distaste. Here Willy is said to have made various grave mistakes; firstly, he'd forgotten to remove the cap placed ridiculously on the top of his head, giving him an air of total disrespect for the army. Secondly he struck an air of superiority, abhorred by the authorities; his statuesque pose caused instant disapproval, and at the very same moment he forgot all his Spanish and could only blurt out phrases in half English.

'I wanna put a—' he started. 'I wanna puta-a—' he repeated, because unfortunately the word complaint refused to come to mind, so he repeated the fatal phrase once more: 'I wanna puta-a—' and these slurred words sounded to the Commander very like 'hijo de puta', son of a bitch, and this ended his patience. He told his orderlies to take hold of Willy while he made some decision as to what to do with him. The soldiers took hold of Willy in a firm military grasp, making him furious and his blood went to his head and he began struggling to get free.

'Lemme go, you bastards!' he yelled as he fought for freedom. There followed a vicious struggle as Willy was large and strong and the power of the alcohol he'd recently imbibed gave him some added strength, turning the tussle into a roaring fight. As fists flew many were the worse for it but Willy ended with a cudgel on his head laying him out cold on the office floor. He was then dragged to a nearby cell.

And this is where Sydney eventually found him two days later. He was in a poor state and extremely glad to see Sydney who was escorted into the cell by two armed soldiers.

'Get me out of this shit-hole, will you Syd?' Willy tried to get up from the bench, but didn't quite make it.

'Hold it. Hold it Willy!' urged Sydney. 'There are some formalities to go through before you can leave. I wanted you to know we've found you and we'll get you out as soon as possible.'

Sydney made various enquiries about Willy's release but nobody knew anything much.

'You must speak to the Comandante,' they always told him, but the Commander, in view of what had happened a few days ago, was not very keen on giving interviews to the *ingleses* (Englishmen) these days. Sydney remained in Mercedes talking to people and trying, unsuccessfully, to see the Commander. The latter was said to be interested and sympathetic but hardly helpful and an interview was impossible just now. The only information Sydney picked up by chance was from an old retainer sitting in the Plaza, who spent his days there watching the town's activities.

This old man was the one who told Sydney the whole yarn. His nephew had stayed in the *boliche* (bar) most of the afternoon — not that it was his usual habit, of course, but it was a special day when free drinks were being offered and stories told. His nephew had missed his work in the fields that afternoon, which he later regretted when his boss discounted the afternoon's wages from his pay packet. But at least he had the entire story and spent most of the remaining hours telling these details to curious townsfolk.

'The Señor Ingles has many charges against him,' the old man said as Sydney sat beside him on the park bench. He was drinking mate, a custom followed by many of the local people. The procedure was to fill up the bowl holding the yerba leaf with boiling water from a small kettle at his side, and with the metal *bombilla* (metal straw) draw up the hot tea into his mouth. The unhygienic habit of passing the bowl from person to person was customary, making all present to be '*mateando*' (drinking mate) together.

The old fellow handed Sydney the bowl recently filled with boiling water. 'Have one?' Somewhere in the back of Sydney's mind he remembered hearing that to refuse a mate was considered the height of discourtesy. Mortal offense could be taken, so Sydney accepted the bowl; he especially wanted to be on good terms with the people and most particularly with this old man who seemed to be well-known and respected, judging from the amount of passing pedestrians who stopped to shake his hand or have a word. If he was going to be able to do anything quickly for Willy, it was going to be through friends.

He smiled as he took the bowl and *bombilla* from the wrinkled hand and began sucking up the hot tea. BOILING!! Of course he burned his tongue and the roof of his mouth badly. The old man saw him wince and chuckled noting Sydney's inexperience in drinking mate.

'Don't hold the hot tea in your mouth. Suck hard and swallow instantly, then it won't burn you. He-he-he!!' He knew it took days of practice before one could drink from a *bombilla* and enjoy it. Sydney tried again. The stuff was cooler and he gulped it down as instructed and it was less painful. He handed it back to the old man who promptly began refilling it. God, thought Sydney, I hope he doesn't offer it to me again. His tongue felt rough and sore, he wanted no more for the present.

'What are the charges against our cousin?' Information was needed as fast as possible.

'Ah, let me see...' He began digging around with the *bombilla* into the bowl and slowly added more water. Once the beverage was ready again, he drank lengthily and slowly, savouring every drop. Sydney wondered if he would ever become so practiced as to enjoy drinking mate as the old man obviously did. The taste was pleasant enough, refreshing, but it was such a performance to get a couple of mouthfuls, it hardly seemed worthwhile.

'The charges against your cousin are various, for you see he used bad language to the Comandante and that is unforgiveable.'

'I can't believe he used bad language,' Sydney said, 'he's not in the habit of using bad language at home, much less to an Army officer. What did he say, do you know?' The old man rolled his eyes up to heaven. 'He made rude allusions to his ancestors, his mother in particular.' He shook his head in sorrow. Sydney had heard that to call anyone 'son of a bitch' in Spanish was asking for trouble. Why in heaven's name had Willy ever come to say this to the Commander? It was hard to believe, and it was days later we heard how it had come about.

'Carry on, what other charges are there?' 'Well, your cousin was in a bad alcoholic state: *ebrio*, we call it,' he sighed, 'not good to come before high authority like that.'

'All right,' acquiesced Sydney, 'that may be true, but it's not a major sin: there comes a time when the best of us gets a bit tight. We can work around that one surely?'

The old man continued without comment: 'He was disrespectful to the uniform of the Army — VERY BAD.'

Sydney's heart sank: 'What else?'

'He fought and made destruction in the official rooms. Broke chairs, spilled over ink-well and knocked out all the front teeth of a young soldier. Also very bad!' For a civilian to lay hands on a uniformed soldier was unwise, for the soldier, in the light of carrying out his duties, would always have the protection of the law.

Sydney groaned.

'You see,' the old man continued, 'it's very difficult indeed.' And Sydney saw how very serious Willy's case was. Not a thing one could hope to fix up in a day. Silly, stupid old Willy! Why the heck had he got himself into such a mess? Just like him, fumed Sydney silently, nothing much in the upper storey and no common sense at all had old Willy.

He thanked the old man profusely as he left the Plaza and tried again to convince the Commander to see him, without success. Finally, the door orderly advised him to leave it for the following day, when the Commander might possibly be in a better frame of mind. So Sydney came home to give us this discomforting news.

'What are we going to do?' Donald's mind was revolving around the possibilities of getting Willy free. 'We can't spend all our time going and coming to Mercedes in the hopes the damn Commander will speak to us.' He paused and began scratching his ear, a tick he had when extremely worried. 'It's a long drive to Mercedes and all hands are needed at Las Palmas, as it is we're one man short without Willy, and if someone has to go in every day, things are held up even more...'

Presently Sydney said: 'Willy's in need of clean clothes and food; he says he gets extremely bad food.'

I hated the thought of dear old Willy in jail. A solution had to be found rapidly. 'Why don't you go to Mercedes tomorrow Donald?' I suggested.

'Perhaps someone different will have more luck and make a good impression on the Army officials.'

'Are you well enough for me to go for the entire day?'

'Yes, I'm perfectly well and Mrs. Allen and Sydney will be here if I should need anything special. Nothing's going to happen in a mere day and Willy needs you more than I do at the moment.'

We packed up currant buns, oranges, apples and a meat pie for Donald to take to Willy, and some clean clothes.

These trips to Mercedes with clothes and food continued for weeks while a solution for Willy's predicament never came up. The judge was a slow-moving man and often, after a whole morning in discussion, he'd still not take a decision, leaving the thing pending for the following day. In this manner the days and weeks went by and Willy was confined in the revolting cell. By the end of the month he'd been pardoned his drunken appearance but the other charges remained.

Meanwhile it was dipping time on the farm and the work was intense. Willy was the one to oversee the sheep, and he was not here. One pair of hands less made the job seem twice as large, added to the fact that nearly every other day somebody went to Mercedes to deal with Willy's trials.

Work with the sheep was never ending. As one job finished it was time for the next. They were bred, moved from one field to another; they were shorn, dipped and cured and some of them slaughtered. Again life became complicated as everything organized now turned into chaos. The days were not long enough and when night came we fell into bed exhausted.

It was already four weeks since Willy had been jailed, and we were desperately worried for Donald and Sydney reported Willy was not wearing well in his confinement; signs of decay were appearing on his florid features and an enormous depression had settled on him. Although we sent him books and extra food constantly, his condition was steadily declining. He complained of terrible boredom and was becoming morbid from lack of activity. The sudden change from a healthy life with good food and exercise, to sudden seclusion in a dim little cell was ruining him.

The following week Donald had to remain at Las Palmas to attend to cattle buyers who had sent a message through the *Pulperia* to say they were coming today.

'It's my turn to go to Mercedes for we expect some reply from the Army about Willy,' said Donald, 'but could you go in my place Syd?'

'All right, I'll go, it's time I saw old Willy again and you should be here for the cattle buyers.'

As Sydney started off laden with extra comforts for Willy, I volunteered to go in the kitchen and make a tipsy cake for dessert as the buyers were sure to stay for lunch.

Two men arrived later and talked a long time with Donald, who presently took them into the fields to see the quality of the cattle. They were very smart gentlemen, who'd travelled in a brightly gleaming landeau, pulled by two fine black horses. Their appearance was one of affluence, so I changed from my rough working dress before lunch and went into the drawing-room to meet them. My cornflower blue dress with its deep neckline and extra full skirt helped me to look attractive to the gentlemen visitors, for it made a difference to sales surprisingly enough, Donald said.

No sooner did I enter the drawing-room I realized the sale must be already agreed upon for Donald's face was all abeam and the sherry was circulating freely.

'Gentlemen!' announced Donald with pride, 'this is my wife.' I gave a coy smile to both gentlemen while their bold stares complimented my appearance.

The meal was eaten with high spirits and the gentlemen, who'd been drinking before the meal, added wine to their fare, an extravagance Donald rarely encouraged but I supposed the occasion was special.

One of the gentlemen, Señor Fernandez, had a very smooth manner and held the conversation. 'You've come to Uruguay at a difficult time. Civil wars have been raging on and off, and this division is not good for our people. Have the soldiers troubled you at all?'

The atmosphere changed. Gone was the frivolous talk and a dark cloud covered the lunch table suddenly. I dropped my eyes to my plate while searching desperately for the right words to reply, when suddenly Donald cut in: 'We do get troops coming through our land, but have had no major problems with them.' So he's not going to mention poor old Willy, I thought. Had it been me replying to the gentlemen, I'm sure I'd not have been able to slide over the real truth with so much ability. My hot blood had already gone to my head with the very mention of the soldiers, I could never have said we had no major problems. There was a major problem sweating it out in a filthy cell in Mercedes right now.

Suddenly the second gentleman, the quiet observant one, spoke up: 'Perhaps the lady does not feel the same way about the soldiers as her husband?' It was a sort of question. He'd read my thoughts. 'I think she has something further to say about the soldiers who come silently to steal at night, eh?'

I dared not look at him. 'Excuse me.' I rose from the table and left the room in the pretext of giving orders in the kitchen, and by the time I got back the conversation had turned to other matters and the talkative Fernandez was holding the floor again. I sighed with relief. After all, it was nothing to do with these posh cattle buyers whether the soldiers treated us badly or not.

At mid-afternoon when they were leaving, the quiet gentleman bent over my hand to bid me farewell and whispered: 'If you ever need me, your husband has my name and address.' And they were gone. The cattle were sold. I flung my arms around Donald's neck and complimented him on his excellent sale.

'Thank you for looking so lovely at the table.' He pinched my cheek playfully. 'The men like it and it adds prestige to the estancia for future sales. These men are influential people and it's good to be well thought of.'

'Let's go for a walk, shall we?'

I felt I needed some fresh air and a little time to think. The quiet man's offer to help was tempting if associated with Willy's release. I'd wait and see what Sydney's news was before requesting this man's influence. I was reluctant, feeling it might be dangerous to get into debt with him; he'd more than likely demand payment from me...

Again it was dark before we heard the wheels of Sydney's trap coming into the yard. The sound of his heavy boots crunching on the gravel. Three steps up and he was on the veranda.

'Hello folks!' he called, 'I'll wash up and be with you in a second.'

Sydney's story:

When he was waiting for the Commander to see him, he took a stroll onto the Plaza opposite the offices and there he found the old retainer he'd spoken to some weeks ago.

'Hola amigo! (hello my friend)' he hailed Sydney as a long lost friend.

'Buenos dias! (good morning)' Sydney replied as he approached the bench.

'What news of your cousin today?' the old man asked, as he politely handed Sydney his bowl of mate. Sydney took it, of course, and had a drink. He told him he was still waiting to see the Commander.

'All these weeks and still no trial? No decisions?' he laughed. 'You're not using the right tactics for getting an audience then.'

'I'm damned if we know what the correct tactics are. Can you tell me?' Sydney asked.

A cunning look came on to the old man's face while he rubbed his first finger and thumb together in a smooth rotary movement. 'Money,' he whispered.

Sydney looked aghast. 'MONEY?'

'Oh yes. Those are the correct tactics for this Commander all right.'

'Bribery in high official places?' Sydney could not believe his ears. The sage old head nodded up and down in affirmation: 'Plenty money!' They sat in silence while this information sank in. 'Well,' the old man eventually continued, 'the Army pay is not very good and the man enjoys living well, and here's an opportunity of making something extra...' he shrugged, 'Who can blame him?'

After a long silence Sydney continued with his incredible story: 'He's given me the correct procedure of how to go about the bribery. It has to look like a payment for some service rendered. The Commander doesn't want anybody to get the idea of what's going on,' groaned Sydney, 'Oh Lord, the whole thing's so corrupt, it's hard to believe. Next time the Commander consents to see me or Donald, we must lay an envelope with the cash discreetly on his desk.'

'How much should one give the scoundrel?' Donald snapped in disgust.

'Well, the old man refused to mention any figures, but he said it had to be an important sum, you know, enough to make it interesting for him to start considering Willy's case. All the other business of trials was merely verbal formalities, a cover-up while he was waiting for the cash.'

'What amount?'

'I don't know.' Sydney said desperately.

'We must find out the figure before putting our foot in it by offering too little or too much. How can we discover this?'

We sat in silence, thinking.

'Our only hope is the old man in the Plaza,' Sydney mused. 'Although he wouldn't mention figures today, I think we can get it out of him eventually.'

Donald agreed: 'He's our only hope.'

The following morning shortly after Sydney's departure to Mercedes, we had soldiers once again on our farm. This time they came right up to the house in full daylight. There were about fifty men, mainly from the ranks but also three or four officers among them. The officers had a superior uniform and their caps were identical to the unfortunate one which Willy had taken. The cap which had, in the end, been the cause of so much trouble.

These soldiers seemed to be resting for they lay about the grass and in the shade of the trees. Donald remained on the premises in full command of the unusual situation and told us women to remain indoors and out of sight. He gave the cook instructions to make plenty of food, and if they demanded it, it was to be served them without comments. Inevitably it was what happened and we saw the cook making endless journeys to and from the kitchen with huge platters of steaming stew and vegetables which the soldiers ate with relish.

To our great relief they started making preparations to leave in the afternoon. They did a rapid sweep of the orchard, filling their pockets with fruit, but no beef was taken this time. The officers suddenly gave a sharp order and they all marched off briskly down the avenue towards the road.

Once they'd left we decided to have our tea on the veranda, feeling the need of fresh air after our enclosure.

'It's good to see how Donny loves dogs,' I commented, 'it'll soon be time for him to get up on a horse.'

Donald laughed: 'I wonder if he'll enjoy riding as much as his mother does?'

'Hope so...' I replied vaguely. I'd just noticed the buggy turning the bend of the avenue. I could distinguish two figures sitting up on it; one undoubtedly Sydney and the other... 'WILLY!' I cried as I rushed onto the patio where the buggy had already drawn up.

Willy's welcome was the warmest. People and dogs all gathered around him, clamouring for a view, a hand shake, a hug and a kiss. When I gathered him into my arms and pressed his hollow cheek to mine, I understood how much he'd suffered all this time. His appearance of dirt and decay was shattering; his garments hung loosely on his thin body and stank of rot and mould, as did his long dirty hair and full-grown beard.

The fine had been paid. I never found out how much his release had cost us, but I know it must have been a great deal for it remained a sealed secret forever.

CHAPTER 5

Willy's recovery was more rapid than we had imagined when we first caught sight of him climbing shakily down from the buggy. Once he had bathed, shaven and had his hair cut to its normal length he began to look more like himself, although a mere shadow of what he had been two months ago.

Now he woke each morning with the delicious, balmy surprise of finding himself under Las Palmas roof again, with seven thousand hectares of fertile land surrounding him, smiling in the morning sunshine. He felt happy but due to his loss of weight, he still felt weak.

'The food was completely inedible,' he told me as we sat out on the lawn in the morning sun. 'Even when I was at my hungriest I couldn't swallow the dreadful muck; it had no flavour at all, just grey and slimy.'

'We used to send you as much as we could,' I said rather lamely. On hearing these horror stories I wished we had sent him double.

'I know,' he nodded, 'the food you sent was what kept me alive. I'd ration it out and make it last until the next visit.' He laughed shakily. 'But the worst wasn't the hunger, the worst was the utter boredom and later the despair which got hold of.' He shook his head in grief and bit his lower lip controlling himself. 'There was a time when I thought I'd never get out again...' In his weakness his eyes filled with tears and he looked down at his feeble white hands lying limply in his lap.

Willy's hands! I took them in mine and pressed them to my equally damp cheek. Could these feeble things be the hands that had done so much work for us? Those hands which had sheared and cured hundreds of sheep, strong hands to mark cattle and drive the cart masterfully. The hands which had even cooked meals and gently cared for our little son.

Something stirred within me and filled me with indignation. This was unfair, and instantly I made a vow that those hands would be recuperated to their normal strength in a short time. Willy must have good nourishment, sufficient rest and lots of healthy sunshine.

I walked away from him with my baby daughter in her pram; we went to the top of the avenue where it met the road.

I knew Willy would recover but how long would it take?

It was pitiful to watch him in this frail state, sitting in the old rocking-chair with a small rug wrapped round his thin legs despite the late spring warmth with a look of tired resignation on his sallow face. How could I hurry things to make him look as I wanted to see him? The old Willy striding out of the house early, pipe in mouth, whistling to his old sheep dog and off to work. Large, slightly portly, he was always a picture of health.

He should have a tonic to pick him up.

Suddenly I remembered the tonic which Mama used to give the children when they lost weight after sickness. 'I'll make him an egg-nog!' It was an appetizing tonic: one raw egg, one tablespoon of sugar and one cup of milk all beaten together. Once fully incorporated, slightly frothy, it was to be poured into a large tumbler which already held one measure of port wine. One of these every mid-morning was a splendid pick-me-up and I was already on my way back to the house to make one for Willy.

He loved his egg-nog when I took it to him. The port wine gave it a special flavour and his eyes began to twinkle a little for the first time since his arrival.

'Thanks Evie, you're very thoughtful. I'll soon be myself again at this rate.'

Willy recovered quickly. Two weeks later he was walking about the premises, giving a hand with minor items and one morning I found him mending a fence which closed in the chickens. We had discovered various hens had escaped from their pen and been killed. Willy searched for the hole and with pieces of new wire mended the fence. Yet it was still noticeable that he did not go far afield, and that by eleven o'clock he was back in the house, generally sitting in the drawing-room, waiting.... Waiting for his egg-nog!

When I rode in the morning I always made a point of being back before eleven for Willy's tonic. The tonic was not only good for him physically, it also gave him a moral boost, a secure feeling that somebody cared enough for him to remember his tonic.

'Here's your egg-nog,' as I handed it to him while he sat reading in an armchair.

'Oh, thanks a lot!' he pretended to be surprised, 'I'd forgotten.'

'How are you feeling today?' It became a short period of conversation on the subject of his health.

'Fine,' he told me, 'better and better each day. I was thinking of riding a bit this afternoon, if there's anyone going out nearby.' That afternoon Willy and I rode over to the Pintos fields to watch the men gathering the sheep for curing. This was right in Willy's line of work.

'Most exhilarating!' he remarked as we rode back. 'I feel almost well enough to give a hand tomorrow.'

'Good idea — the pens are not far from the house, if you get tired, you can come back early. It'll be a help in any case.'

'Yes, I'll go out early before it's too hot and be back by eleven. What do you say?'

'Splendid!' Egg-nog time.

During this fantastic year of Colonel Lorenzo Latorre's rule three major incidents stand out as special for us at Las Palmas. Firstly, Willy's release and recovery; secondly building of our lawn tennis court and dipping bath, and thirdly our first locust invasion.

In 1876 Colonel Latorre became supreme governor and dictator of the land. He promised an honest rule and his first actions inspired confidence but soon his dictatorship deteriorated into cruel tyranny.

It is true there were no more revolts, this was because anybody suspected of conspiracy was instantly killed. Also any suspected opposition was terminated by arresting the leaders and sending them down to hard labour in the great prison called 'Taller de Adoquines' the Cobble Stones Workshop, where it is said that by 1878 there were about 400 prisoners, chained by their ankles, doing forced labour. Colonel Latorre used these prisoners to prepare the cobble-stones for the construction of roads to the interior of the country.

In spite of his cruelty Latorre did a lot of good in the country. With his strong rigid rule, he was able to remove from the interior the wandering vagabonds and gypsies known as '*matreros*'(cattle thieves) who infested the land, making it dangerous to travel or even to live.

He was constantly improving the city of Montevideo; the hideous old walls surrounding the city were demolished. These walls had been part of the great Fortress built by the Spaniards in 1724. The only thing saved from the demolition was the Doorway which was taken to another spot.

At all times Latorre favoured '*la industria pecuaria*' which was the livestock trade, and this helped all establishments like Las Palmas and others. Yet this was not his only interest. He reorganized the Education; he created a Bishopric in Montevideo and established the Civil Register which registered all births, deaths and marriages in the country, a great progress for the people of Uruguay.

Another important historical feature was the fencing of the estates which took place during the year of 1876, aided by a law which had been decreed one year previously exempting landowners from import taxes on wires and poles brought from abroad.

Even while improvements were taking place all over the country some changes were taking place at Las Palmas too.

There had been quite a lot of opposition to Donald's suggestion to make a lawn tennis court. Some members of the family considered there were other items which ought to have priority over a purely pleasure-giving device such as a tennis court. Yet after a great deal of debating, Donald finally made his decision: 'We SHALL have a tennis court! We have adequate space, nobody can deny it, and I maintain people like ourselves who are willing to work hard are entitled to have a reasonable amount of pleasure. The tennis court will be a great asset to our home. An estancia without any form of attraction, like a court or bowling green, is hardly considered an establishment at all. Through this acquisition we'll make new friends and be able to entertain them better.'

He smiled delightedly around the family circle. 'I repeat; we will make a tennis court.'

The following week the lawn tennis court was measured and laid out and was made far quicker and better than anything else before. It was a beautiful court and an all-round success. Unlike the sheep bath. This construction presented unexpected difficulties and it became hard, up-hill work. Frequently there was a whole day of exhausting labour but nothing much to show for it in the end. The gentlemen would meet again in the evening to plan the work for the next day.

Mr. Harrison was the greatest help with his inexhaustible store of ideas and knowledge. He spent many hours lending a hand and later they all came up for a meal, often depressed with their morning's toil but on other occasions optimistic. The optimism was usually evoked by Mr. Harrison's visit.

'Making a dipping bath is no joke; it's hard work.' he pronounced over the meal, 'but we can't give in, can we?' The gentlemen all gave him a 'hear, hear' in agreement and continued with their eating.

One particularly depressing day Donald turned to me and said: 'Evie, we've planned our afternoon differently to relieve the monotony, we're going off fishing to the *Aguila* river — we can't make Mr. Harrison work too hard, can we?'

After lunch the fishing tackle was brought out for inspection and immediately after a short siesta, they were off to the river. I had to admit it was a splendid day for fishing but what about the bath?

Eventually Mr. Harrison had to remain the night at Las Palmas because it was too late when they returned, triumphant with their catch and in high spirits. The bath forgotten for the present, I saw the importance of a time of relaxation for them; tomorrow would come around all too soon and the bath construction would go on.

Once it was finally erected and the last touches given, still some problems remained. They had thought the water was too cold for the sheep in mid-winter, so they unwisely built a fire at one end, with the idea of warming the water. Unfortunately, the bath was found leaking the following day, the flames having cracked the cement. Donald and Sydney, who were responsible for this error, were down there morning and afternoon for days until it was finally corrected and put to use.

Nowadays Willy was the first one up and out in the mornings, rounding up the flocks needing dipping. The sheep being his responsibility he worked them all day. There was always somebody to help with the dipping, but he was the authority, he was in charge, he made the decisions. Whether his decisions were the very best, we shall never know, but it was miraculous to see him so well again after his internment.

At the beginning of December there was a warning sign of locusts. A great swarm flew across the upper fields, settling for a while but leaving again. A sigh of relief from everybody, but we were not to be spared. Two days later they arrived in great clouds and kept on coming all day. They landed and began eating and the destruction was terrible. Some even settled on the trees near the house where they began their merciless ravaging. Nothing was spared from grass to garden plants; the kitchen garden was stripped bare and the alfalfa crop raised to the ground.

'Is there no way to combat this plague?' I asked.

'Nothing very efficient has been discovered,' Donald replied. 'In some places they go out banging tins and the noise frightens them off.'

'Let's have a try!' I said excitedly, 'we can get some of the young lads from the far-away *Puestos* (outlying farmhand dwellings) to come over and do some banging. Perhaps they will take fright and fly off.'

We brought some of these lads with tins and sticks and together we all spent the rest of the day walking around the garden and fields beating and rattling, making as much noise as possible but it was a disheartening job for only a few locusts rose and flew away.

Later I decided to ride and see what other damage had been done. I called the dogs; Santa and Claus were beside me instantly, always ready to go out. The big collie came slowly out of his box, stretch, yawned and stood watching the antics of the two smaller dogs, who were rushing about and yapping.

He was deciding whether or not to come.

'Come on Friday!' I called to him in encouragement. He wagged his tail in acknowledgement and, still a bit sleepy, trotted beside my horse. We were off!

I took the track up the avenue towards the road with the dogs in a particularly exhilarated mood, running and sniffing and falling over each other in excitement. Soon we crossed the road and into the field the other side, close to where maize had been planted. Everything was quiet but on looking closer I could see millions of little locusts which had hatched, now left by the main swarm. These were the dangerous ones, I knew, and when I told Donald of what I'd seen he said: 'Those are *saltones* (little jumpers) and must be destroyed otherwise in a few days we'll have another batch of locusts to contend with.' He smiled, 'Thanks for seeing them and reporting it.' Although it sounded a bit militarized, I smiled happily at his praise.

'More problems,' sighed Sydney, seeing himself in the destruction party. He was right.

'Syd, old man, we must lay hay along that area and set fire to it after tea; that'll kill the *saltones*; we must get it done while they're still on the ground.'

A strange entry in my Diary one day was: 'Burning parrots' nests'

'What are you going to do?' I questioned Sydney as he strode past me on the veranda, looking as if he was on a very extraordinary mission.

'We're going to burn parrots' nests,' he said as he fled past me.

'You're going to what?' I can't have heard correctly. He repeated the information. Burn parrots' nests. I'd never heard anything so outrageously cruel, a crime one would never consider committing for we had always been taught to be kind to the feathered friends. Granted there was the sport of shooting but it was different. The bird had a chance of escaping: there was a sporting chance for the bird but to deliberately creep up and set fire to the nest was criminal. When the dry hay and twigs began to roar up in flames, chaos would break out with smoke filling the wee home. I hated the thought.

I rushed to find Donald before it was too late.

'Sydney says you're going to burn parrots' nests,' I cried accusingly.

'We have to get rid of the nests in our avenue,' he said, 'they've become a plague and the parrots are doing more damage than we can afford.'

'What damage?'

by Heather Campbell

'They're eating all the ripe fruit; they've almost totally destroyed our peach crop. Have you been to the orchard recently? The loss is tremendous! Also the maize, they perch on the strong stalks and eat doing as much harm as the bloody locusts!' Donald must have been very angry indeed for him to use bad language. 'Nasty pests! Who eats the pears when they ripen? — Parrots. Who eats the seeds we plant? — Parrots. We can't afford to have a large colony living happily in our trees, swooping down daily to eat our produce. We CANNOT afford it and that's that!' he ended sharply.

'But-but-but— 'I really had no more argument.

The parrots' nests had to be destroyed. I turned into the house and let the men get on with it. Donald knew me well enough not to further the discussion. I felt ill. I had the same dreadful feeling when they had shot two dogs, culprits of sheep killing. Pintos had run them up to the house and Donald had very determinedly gone out with his gun. I heard the shots...

Poor parrots.... I remembered when last year we had brought up five little parrots found in a *monte* (clump of trees).

'Poor little things!' I had exclaimed when Donald and I had come across them beside their fallen nest. There were six baby parrots, barely grown their feathers and still not able to fly. One was dead and the others desperately hungry, were squawking and pushing against one another hoping to find food and warmth. Their parents were nowhere to be seen and on the floor their lives would soon come to an end.

'Can we take them home and care for them?' I asked timidly.

'Would you like to?' he laughed, 'I feel they'll be a bother to you for they have to be caged or else the dogs will kill them.' I agreed and together we picked up the wee mites and took them home.

We became very fond of these little parrots and enjoyed hearing their loud squawks and watching them grow pretty green I trained them to come out of the cage and sit on my finger and chortle.

Little Donny got much pleasure from them and he'd stay for hours watching their antics and laughing aloud. And now we were going to murder their families in cold blood.

I went into my room and slammed the door.

Take hold of yourself, my good woman, I said to myself. If you wish to be a good wife to the man you love, you're going to have to accept some things you don't like. Like burning parrots' nests.

The parrots in our avenue had become a plague; they had no association with the little ones we had as pets. The gentlemen's hard work was being destroyed. I recalled the days Donald and Sydney had been out all day long planting the peach trees. Donald had come in soaking wet, his hands blue with cold. 'We've planted fifty peach trees and fifty pear trees, so we ought to have a good crop this summer.' He dropped into a chair exhausted. The trees grew strong and tall... later came the grafting work... then they blossomed beautifully in spring and we rejoiced at the thought of the harvest. Then when each peach turned yellow-pink, the parrots swooped down and pecked them, smashing the tender fruit to the ground. This could not go on, the parrots had to be destroyed.

'Destroy their nests,' Pintos told us. 'It's the effective way of ridding yourselves of their young, their nests and their eggs. The birds which escape will fly away and feed on pastures anew.'

Oh Life, Life! What changes within me! Here am I the bird-watcher, the bird-lover, going to turn a deaf ear on the forthcoming slaughter. Surely life in this land was harsh and cruel. I sighed: 'Goodbye sweet protected girl of Bonnie Ireland! Enter a hard, cool-headed woman of the new world.'

CHAPTER 6

Some weeks later there dawned a lovely morning, fine and fresh after a night of rainfall.

While riding my favourite mare Rosie my spirits were high. The landscape was beautiful in a clean, freshly-washed way. The grass seemed to have grown up high over night, thanks to the downpour of the previous evening. The fields were still wet and parts of the track were muddy. If I galloped Rosie over the puddles, my riding habit would get splashed, yet I had to go fast to suit my buoyant mood this morning.

I could feel Rosie's strength beneath me, she was longing to go, go, go... and we went.

I felt the gorgeous sensation of freedom and release.

It was always like this after rain. I would get out into the fields riding furiously, madly free until reaching the house again where reality faced me and reminded me I was a respectable married woman, mother of two small children with much housework to do.

Horrible housework. Much more invigorating was a wild gallop over the fresh washed fields, alone with nature, the sky one's limit. Words came teaming into my head and I shouted them out for all the silent world to hear:

> In open fields and far beyond the meadow
> Grows thick the bracken, wild and ugly.
> In open fields began the journey of my life
> Where thistles covered every pathway.
> A cloudless morning when tender grass
> Springs forth upon the earth, as sunshine after rain.

I stopped, knowing the last words were biblical. The moment had passed. I turned my horse homeward — the journey was always swift and smooth.

Rosie snorted with delight as we turned into the patio, but my heart went down to my boots. Mr. Brown's small trap was under the big paraiso tree and his horse loosely tethered to the fence.

Ugh! I hated Mr. Brown. He was a fat, unpleasant little man who always found an excuse to stay for lunch or for the entire day if he saw the chance. I had told Donald many times I did not like him and would prefer not to entertain him, but Donald explained how important his visits were for he was our main ram buyer and a man of considerable means who always paid cash for the rams, so Donald begged me to be particularly 'nice' to Brown, encouraging him to come again.

I understood, so complied with Donald's wishes and was as civil as possible to the man.

The gentlemen were in the drawing-room as I approached the house, making it possible for me to slip into my room to change from my muddy riding habit into a dress before joining them for lunch.

'Ah-ha! There's the little lady of the house at last!' exclaimed Mr. Brown. 'As pretty as the wild flowers of the meadow!' He took my outstretched hand and gave it a damp little squeeze, holding it a fraction of a second too long.

'Nice to see you Mr. Brown,' I lied and slid swiftly past him to put an affectionate arm around Donald. Willy was in there also and they took their seats again after my entry. Donald seemed a bit nervous, I thought, as I listened to their talk about sheep, rams and sales. There seemed to be something slightly different this time to Brown's usual visits. The atmosphere was tense and Willy was puffing extra hard on his pipe which was making a particularly bad smell today, the room being already half full of smoke. Initially I could not think what the trouble was, but as the talk continued it appeared the price of the rams was the point under dispute.

The last time Mr. Brown had come there had been smiles and glasses of claret served before lunch. I had sat beside Mr. Brown at table as was my duty as mistress of the house and before the dessert was served I had felt the same slight pressure on my knee under the table from the porky leg on my right. Revolting little bastard, I thought, as I removed my knee out of reach.

I detested Brown's bad habits; hated the way he grew the nail on his smallest right-hand finger long and trimmed it into a point. With this nail he would occasionally pick his nose discreetly — filthy habit — and would use this same nail to clear out food remains from between his stubby brown teeth, then suck noisily through them to make sure nothing was left. Hardly table manners I complained to myself, but at that moment I caught Donald's amused glance — he understood — it was also a reminder of expecting me to tolerate these indecencies for the sake of the ram sale.

Still things were different today, no claret yet and the conversation slow, dragging on in boring fashion. Soon I went into the kitchen to order lunch and the meal was eaten with the same conversational difficulty; at last it was over and:' 'Like a bed for siesta, Sir?' Donald asked Mr. Brown politely.

'Thanks,' said Brown. In the privacy of our bedroom Donald explained how Mr. Brown was being difficult about the adjusted prices for the rams, so the sale session was prolonged into the afternoon.

I planned to get out of the house in the afternoon for I could not bear the thought of hours with Mr. Brown before me. After hitching the trap, I took Mrs. Allen and the children down to the brook to fish; under the cloak of devoted motherhood, I left the gentlemen to their business discussion.

This *cañada* (small stream) was not the very best fishing brook but today there was plenty of clear water after the rain and it was running well over the flat rocks. Here we spent a happy afternoon with nannie looking after the children and me fishing. There was a lot of little fish, not worth taking home, but eventually I caught two beautiful dorados, which I slipped happily into the pouch I had brought down with me. 'Tasty fish,' I mused on our way home. 'Cook does them very well in the oven. They'll be nice for supper tonight.'

The weight of Mr. Brown's visit had slipped from me until we reached the house again and saw his trap still in the patio. They were all sitting on the veranda and with pride I drew out my excellent catch of the afternoon.

'What beautiful dorados, madam!' exclaimed Mr. Brown. Donald sprang into action: 'Evie dear, how very kind of you to bring Mr. Brown such a charming present! They are for him, aren't they?'

I cast down my eyes in mortal grief and my whispered 'Yes' was barely audible. Good Lord forgive me this lie. Mr. Brown at once accepted the gift and the fishes were wrapped for him to take away.

I excused myself; the sun was already on its way to the west and soon the gentle twilight would settle over the land. It was dressing time before dinner and a special time once work was done. If only Brown would go home!

I opened my bedroom window wide to let in the final trail of golden sun. The room faced west and we were first row spectators to every beautiful sunset of the year. I knew I must now leave the window open too long for fear of mosquitos attracted by the light of the lamp, but the cool air touched my face and helped rid the sting of having had to give up my prize catch.

On my return to the veranda I found Mr. Brown had left. Oh joy! Spirits were high and the bottle of claret circulating freely.

'Mr. Brown seemed greatly touched with your gift and immediately closed the ram deal, agreeing to our new prices, promising to come and remove them tomorrow. Cash on delivery!' Donald bent and kissed me on the top of my head.

'You're wonderful,' he whispered. Compensating. The price of a ram sale was two fishes.

'We brought up a *guacho* lamb' This exciting entry in my Diary meant I would have a little animal to care for, for a '*guacho*' is an orphan needing special care.

Mid-morning. I was standing aimlessly in the middle of the warm, slightly smelly kitchen once the churn was done: the warmer the weather the longer it took to make the butter. Today I made rather soft butter, and I didn't know whether it was worthwhile salting to keep. I'd have to have somebody's advice on this subject.

Another cook had given notice. He was a horrid man and I wasn't sorry to see him leave. I wondered what was to be done about this situation considering the tremendous lack of cooks in the land.

'I'll be staying until the end of the week and then I'm off,' he informed me yesterday. Through mere routine I asked why he was leaving. To my horror he replied insolently: 'That's none of your business. I'm off because I chose to leave and that's all that matters to you!' His leaving, which had not come as a great surprise for we had various times felt his alienation towards us, was almost a relief now. Anyway the place was beginning to smell. It was dirty.

'Will you please scrub out the sink and take away the garbage after each meal, the kitchen is beginning to smell,' I'd ventured a few days ago. Complete silence had followed my request. I turned and left the room.

'It's quite useless Donald, I'm no good at giving orders in the kitchen. They know my inferiority and I hate the place, feeling at a disadvantage there!' I cried.

'Don't worry dear!' Donald tried to appease my anger with a hug and a conciliatory grin. 'You're admirable in other fields,' he laughed, 'I'll speak to the man myself.' I never knew whether he did or not for now the man had given notice.

I'd been sorry to see the other couple leave however. Gloria and Tito had been pleasant to have and although Gloria's cooking had much to be desired, at least she was good-natured and always willing. I never felt inferior when she was there. Sometimes she even asked my advice which was flattering.

'Does one put the sugar into the egg-whites before or after beating?' she asked once. Of course I had no idea which was correct.

I said: 'Try the whites alone and see how it works and if it's a mess, try the other way.' We'd had a good giggle over that one. The atmosphere was always pleasant, even if the food was dreadful.

Gloria's husband Tito did the garden for us. He was a lazy fellow and basket in the shadow of his pleasant, hard-working wife. We watched him raking the fallen leaves at the speed of a slug; every other step he took a rest and leaned a moment on his broom. A yawn, a shuffle into his pocket for some tobacco to begin rolling his own cigarette, lighting it and then leaving it hanging from his half parted lips while he made another half-hearted sweep before resting again. It was pitiful to see.

'It takes him longer to clean up the parkland than it'd take me to walk to Montevideo,' Sydney observed. Tito was never seen during the hours he considered his rightful resting time.

'This afternoon I want you to help bring up some young animals,' Willy told him one day. 'They have to be cared for up here by the house if we want them to live.' Tito looked sullen.

I'm a gardener and not a workhand,' he retorted crossly.

'I don't care what you consider yourself,' Willy continued, 'there are two or three little calves and a lamb which have to be fetched or they'll die.'

'I don't know how to look after animals,' Tito persisted. Willy continued as if he'd not heard the remark. 'We'll bring them up this afternoon straight after lunch, before it starts raining.' Tito showed strong disapproval and turned towards the kitchen.

'We'll leave directly after lunch,' Willy called after him. 'Be ready!'

After lunch Willy and I prepared to go into the fields and find the animals. There was a horse saddled for Tito also, but there was no Tito. We waited a few minutes. 'Lazy brute!' exclaimed Willy, 'I bet he's having a lie down.'

'I'll see if I can find him,' I volunteered and went to the kitchen hoping to find him finishing his lunch with Gloria. But she was alone, scrubbing the utensils. 'Tito?' I asked

'He's gone off for siesta,' she said.

'The Señor Willy told him this morning he had to be ready after lunch to bring up some little animals.' She looked at me apologetically.

'It's his siesta time, you know.'

'Go and get him up at once! The Señor is waiting.' She sighed and ran over to their room, returning shortly to the kitchen.

'Well?'

She dropped her eyes in shame. 'He's sleeping.'

'Gloria, you'd better get him up fast!' I warned her, 'it may cost him his job otherwise.' This would mean her job too and as we exchanged glances we were aware of this. 'Go and get him up!' I commanded, turning on my heel. 'We'll wait in the patio five minutes more.'

Tito did not appear so we brought up the young animals by ourselves and my cook and gardener were asked to leave the following day.

'We can't tolerate rank disobedience from the staff,' Donald said when I pleaded leniency for the couple.

'It's a pity to loose Gloria, she's such a nice girl.'

'It'll be a pity about Gloria, I admit,' he said, 'but her husband is impossible and yesterday afternoon was the absolute limit. He's a lousy gardener anyway.' He paused before going on: 'Actually Gloria is a rotten cook, so we'll be better off without them. They must go — sorry.'

It was directly after them this man had come and although his cooking was an improvement on Gloria's, his personality was most unpleasant, and now he was leaving too.

Donald had a trip to Fray Bentos planned for the next day and this left the kitchen totally unattended, but we discovered Willy was quite a good cook and willing to take over for the time being. 'Making pancakes is my long suit,' he announced once Donald left.

The calves and the little lamb we brought up to the house (without Tito's help) were put into a small paddock near the cook's quarters, but by the afternoon it was quite clear the lamb would not survive the night without his mama or any other of his kind, so I brought it near the kitchen and arranged for it to sleep in the porch where the flower table stood.

'This baby needs milk every few hours and protection from the early morning dews,' I tried to sound efficient and pretended to know all about bringing up little lambs, though really only common sense would save me. 'I propose bringing it into the kitchen porch to have it nearby during the night,' I continued briskly.

All went well; it took its late bottle and lay down on the sacking and for the first time that day, it stopped shivering.

The three calves were in good shape and would only need special care for a few days before going back into the herds again. 'I'll taken them over,' I quickly ventured. 'As there's no cook I'll be available for their care as well as the little lamb.'

'Will you have time for this extra work?' I felt that Donald's question was superfluous for he knew I would find time for animals, no matter what else I'd leave unattended. I'd sooner be found feeding the calves than cooking meals.

From that moment those animals were mine. The lamb kept me up most of the night, bleating, hungry or lonely and always making a noise. In the end I was so sleepy I brought it into the kitchen and curled up beside it on the floor, both sleeping better, though morning found me stiff from the hard floor and a headache from lack of sleep.

'How are the young animals today?' Donald asked cheerily when we met at breakfast.

'They're fine, thank you,' I replied hastily. 'The calves give no trouble at all.'

'But the lamb does?'

'Well, it's still very small and weak and we had a restless night,' I admitted. I wondered how many of the household had heard me traipsing about. I felt quite ill but dared not admit it lest they should take the lamb away from me.

I loved it dearly and was prepared to look after it until fully grown.

'The animals won't be any problem, you'll see,' I said.

'You're a funny girl,' Donald smiled. 'You'll stay up all night watching over a sick animal which is more than you'd do for your own children.'

'The children don't need me!' I cried sharply. 'The animals have nobody to fall back on, while the children have their nannie — it's different, don't you see?'

A ripple of mirth fluttered round the table among the gentlemen.

I felt offended at their criticism and their laughter, so I withdrew and remained silent for the rest of the meal while I pondered on my new and exciting responsibility.

I spent more time with my animals during the following days than with anything else. I was blissfully happy. While they were small the paddock beside the cook's quarters was good enough but later they'd need to go further afield.

This was where my problem began for I had no intention of allowing them to get mixed up with the estancia herds. They were mine, and how it was to remain.

During the first days I took them out leading them to the adjacent field where I tied them allowing them to pasture for some hours, always returning them at night. It was a temporary solution but not suitable for the rest of their lives.

I began making plans. A long, rather useless field which ran down to join with the dipping bath field, ought to be fenced to make a good field for my animals. Three calves and one small lamb would never justify the making of another fence. I remembered the amount of work entailed in fencing so I dared not ask them to consider it. I must bide my time.

A few weeks slipped by and we had some more torrential rains, filling some of the *cañadas* (small streams) to over-flowing and causing a lot of damage among the cattle and sheep.

Here arose my golden opportunity.

Over lunch Sydney was reporting what he had seen on his rounds that morning. Various calves had been left motherless and he was suggesting they be brought up to the house for care. Donald shot me a swift glance.

I was beaming: 'I'd be happy to take them with my others, if you like.' I tried to keep the excitement out of my voice but this was the chance I'd been waiting for to increase my herd. For no apparent reason this herd was becoming important to me.

That same afternoon Pintos brought up the calves for me and put them with the others. Six, that was a better number.

One cool autumn evening I was riding with Donny near the northern end of the farm. We had all the dogs with us for exercise and it was a beautiful serene evening like so many others this particular autumn. Donny was handling his horse like an expert and I fell in beside him in perfect harmony. The dogs were far ahead, the terriers yapping madly as usual and the others rushing after hares but never catching a thing.

The sun had almost set when we eventually turned towards home. Trotting along the upper slope by the new fence dividing our land with our neighbour's, we both caught sight of it at the same moment.

It was lying motionless in the grass just the other side of the fence. There was not a sign of any living thing for miles.

'Look Mummy!' cried Donny, 'it's a little calf and I think it's dead!' He was off his horse and slipping through the fence before I had time to say Jack Robinson. Gingerly he prodded it with his small boot. The calf moved slightly.

'It's alive!' he yelled with excitement. Without another thought I was beside him and together we lifted it into our land. To my horror I found it could not stand alone. It must have been there for hours and was badly in need of nourishment. If we were to leave it, it would surely die.

'Come on lad!' I called to Donny, 'give me a hand lifting the poor thing on to my saddle.' It was difficult and Rosie would not stand still. Eventually with the aid of a fence pole as a prop, we hauled it up. It remained still and limp as we rode home in the dusk. It was already dark as we entered the patio and half the household was out to meet us after some moments of anxiety at our delay.

Donald came down the three steps. 'Hullo, another baby?' he asked as he saw my load. Donny saved the day by explaining our difficulties in lifting him on to my saddle and it was not necessary to explain how the sick animal was found just the other side of our boundary fence. With all the scuttle of getting it some milk and deciding where it was to spend the night, the rest was left unexplained.

We had guests for dinner so I had to hurry to dress while Mrs. Allen took Donny into the pantry where his supper was and already getting cold.

The Tomkins had come over in the late afternoon and were sitting on the veranda before the gentlemen came up from work. They had been well entertained by Mrs. Allen. 'Evie and Donny are riding but will be back before sundown.' Donald had said. 'Do wait and see them; they'll be disappointed if you leave before.'

'Stay and have dinner with us.' Mrs. Allen never volunteered anything so precocious but she particularly liked the Tomkins and mustered enough courage to suggest this. Donald smiled; he agreed it would be nice if they remained. It was cool on the veranda already, so we came indoors and the children came in to say goodnight later.

'You must come earlier another day,' I suggested to the Tomkins, 'and we can have a game of tennis on the new court, it'll be fun.'

'That will be lovely.' Emma actually sounded enthusiastic, most of the time she spent complaining of her hard lot and giving long explanations of how difficult life was for her.

'It should be on a weekend, I think,' Jim said, 'because there's too much work during the week.'

'Agreed,' said Donald, 'but we have a break on Sundays. The Sabbath is still preserved here at Las Palmas.'

'Why don't you come next Sunday? It's a quiet time of year.' I could see Mrs. Allen nodding her approval.

Sydney had joined us. He looked quite different out of his course working *bombachas* (baggy pants) and rough shirt. He was sitting comfortably in the deep armchair, relaxed, in white trousers and a clean open necked-shirt. His ginger hair shone from scrubbing and I thought Sydney was looking attractive. He sipped his sherry with a slow smile, clearing his throat before making his first remark of the evening. 'We'll plan a tennis party for Sunday then, and perhaps the menfolk can do the cooking. We'll do an *asado*.'(cookout)

A barbecue was always popular. 'Good idea, Syd.' Donald agreed. 'It's time we showed the girls our cooking abilities on the open fire.' Before the Tomkins left, they said they'd be here in time for Morning Prayers and then the tennis would get underway.

Luckily Sunday dawned fine and warm; March being a beautiful month in this country. We were all up early in anticipation and after breakfast I was away feeding my calves and moving them to better pastures for the day. Sabbath or not, I could not neglect them. Donald and Sydney had also gone over early to the meat store to bring the adequate meat for the *asado*. All I did about the meal was to tell the new cook there would be little for him today because the gentlemen were doing the *asado*.

I went in search of Mrs. Allen for I wanted her to be as free as possible from her duties with the children, so as to be able to join us in the tennis games. I knew she played well and would be an asset, keeping the game interesting. She was a strong and capable tennis player despite her quiet nature and delicate appearance. I had seen her beat Donald many times, much to our amusement. She was nimble on the court and had an excellent backhand drive which always put her opponent at a disadvantage and made him lose vital points.

I found Mrs. Allen tidying the beds and folding clothes for putting away. Donny and Ada were all prepared for Sunday Prayers dressed in neat garments and they had been sent into the drawing-room to look at books and a 'no getting yourselves dirty before Prayers!' ringing in their ears.

I flung the window wide. Fresh air was necessary in the bedrooms each morning and as I had already been out in the fields, I found the Nursery stuffy. Mrs. Allen was not so fond of air blowing through the rooms for she had a theory it created draughts which were dangerous to the health.

'Let me help you with those clothes,' I offered taking a stack of small garments away from her. 'We must get things in order before Prayers for the Tomkins will be here soon and we want to enjoy ourselves.' We hurried with the work.

'Will you be playing tennis today?' I asked.

'Oh yes, I'd love to. Thank you!' she flushed with delight.

'You're a very good player, much better than I am, so we'll take the duties of the children in turns today, and you can be on the court as much as you like.' My generosity was genuine for I was not over-fond of tennis myself and this was an excellent opportunity for her to enjoy one day of sport.

The Tomkins arrived in good time for Morning Prayers which Donald read in his deep, sonorous voice, very appropriate for the head of the household. It was nice to see the drawing-room full of people and hear the 'Amen' response fill the air. Even the singing was improved by Jim's strong tenor voice which rang through the rooms and encouraged the rest of us to sing more heartily.

The tennis started immediately afterwards. The Tomkins took on Sydney and Mrs. Allen while the rest of us watched but soon Donald and Willy went to light the fire for the *asado*. It was important to have plenty of red hot coals glowing before putting on the meat so the fire had to be started early. The rest of us were being lazy and even the dogs felt the atmosphere of leisure and were sleeping happily in the sunshine. Santa under my chair, of course, he was never far from my side. He was a fine terrier with far more character than his brother Claus who was timid and slightly stupid. But they were excellent hunters and between them they kept the barns clear of rats.

My thoughts drifted to my animals doing well and increasing in numbers. Only the other day the gentlemen had brought four young cows from the *Aguila* field, and as they needed care I took them in. Beautiful animals, I mused as I watched the nimble actions of our governess as she leaped about the court, making incredible points in favour for her admiring partner.

'Thirty-love!' I heard her call as she took the service. Next moment after a roar of applause: 'Forty-love!' Some rapid smashing of the ball into her opponent's court and a second more, then: 'Game!' Echoes of clapping and laughter. I clapped loudly too, displaying interest which I truly did not feel. She had won another set.... Much more important to me were my cows which needed their own field now they were so many.

I had to ask Donald to put a fence where I needed it.

I strolled over to the fire where Donald and Willy were beginning to sweat with heat from the hot coals and the midday sun. 'Time to put the meat on.' Willy handled the red beef with expert hands.

I sat down snugly beside Donald on the bench and caressed his hot cheek with my cool hand. 'How clever you and Willy are to cook so well,' I cooed, 'it smells good and I'm working up an appetite.' We talked while the meat began to brown gently. After a moment more I plucked up courage to ask for what I wanted and was thrilled to receive an affirmative reply: 'Next week we'll get a fence out there, my love.'

New times were coming to Las Palmas. I was into cattle raising, and oddly enough it was the beginning of a certain form of prosperity.

CHAPTER 7

1876 - 1877

During this period all ranchers were encouraged by President Latorre to register their cattle, and for this he opened the Office of Marks and Signs, thus enforcing a little more order into the livestock raising on the estates. This registration was added to the new law of exemption of taxes for cattle breeders on the import of poles and wires, an encouragement to farmers to fence their fields. This does not mean that no fencing had been done before, quite the reverse, in 1875, in spite of all the calamities of the Terrible Year, many estancias had been fencing, ourselves included. Wire fences were first introduced in the River Plate countries by Richard B. Newton in 1845 thirty years before. One morning I was busy transplanting from the boxes on the windowsill to the flower beds, when I heard the sound of wheels on the gravel telling of somebody's arrival.

The gentlemen were out working and were not expected back until lunchtime. I got to my feet slowly and was surprised to see Willy. 'I've got myself a little job,' he told me with delight as he reached the veranda. 'The Dawson's, who live on the other side of the village, want me to do some carting for them.' He stretched up proudly, 'and I intend to charge them for my services. What do you think of that?'

It was some weeks now since Willy had bought himself a very smart new cart with which he had gradually become the family driver. When not using his own cart for moving heavy things, he'd use the carriage or pony trap for driving people about. He'd already built a coach-house being very meritorious considering Willy was not the best constructor but he'd been determined, only seeking advice from Sydney on a few matters.

Willy, who'd seemed to be taking a long time to adjust and become of any real use on the farm other than his sheep work, was at last taking an interest in something worthwhile. Transportation. A trade as worthy as any other.

'I think it's a good idea Willy, if you feel you'll enjoy it and make some cash on the side.' I said. 'Where have you to go for the Dawson's?'

'They want cereal bags taken to Dolores for the market this afternoon,' he smiled. 'It's not a very long run, is it? I should be home for dinner.'

His first mission was a success and the money he received was carefully stored away. 'The Dawson's have put me on to some other people who also need transport of this kind,' he announced at dinner. 'So I'll be over there in the morning finding out their requirements.'

'Good for you!' cried Donald encouragingly. We felt Willy needed a bit of a boost since his mishap in Mercedes and his span in jail. Sydney, however, was skeptical about this job which obviously would take Willy out of the estancia a lot and possibly affect his work at Las Palmas.

'Are you going to be able to manage the job as well as attending the sheep here?' he asked meaningfully.

'Of course yes,' Willy quickly affirmed. 'I'll only take on carting jobs when the sheep work is slack.'

'Hmmm,' murmured Sydney under his breath. 'I hope it'll work out for I never see many slack periods with the sheep. Most of the time the sheep are demanding and you can't expect your entire share of the wool proceeds if you've left all the dirty work to Donald and me,' he added a bit sourly.

'Oh, come on Syd.' Donald interrupted. 'Old Willy is aware of his obligations on the estancia, I'm sure.'

Willy threw Donald a grateful look and nodded happily into his soup plate. 'I'll manage, you'll see.' He was so delighted with his first carting mission and the prospect of further work, nothing could dampen his spirits.

Some time went by and he was successful in his new activity. If there was no carting, he spent the day looking after the sheep. With this new interest he showed signs of real recovery from his military internment and started putting on weight. Then, when the autumn was fully spent, the rain began to fall and this proved a serious handicap to the carting business for the roads were bad and the passes often flooded.

Willy at once rebuilt the low pass over the widest *cañada* on the farm. He managed to raise it considerably by bringing up rocks and stones from the quarry with a couple of men.

His orders for carting continued principally from the English-speaking settlers like ourselves in the district, but his trips to Mercedes were frequent and he took these times for bringing provisions for Las Palmas and on one special occasion he came back with a new shooting dog for Sydney. He was called Duke.

It was in the month of May the problems began. One afternoon when returning from Mercedes, heavily laden with posts for a neighbouring farm, his cart got stuck in a rut. Afterwards he told us he had worked for three hours with his horses trying to pull it out, to no avail. Eventually three gauchos on horseback rode up and came to the rescue; by attaching their horses to his team they were able to pull the cart out. This mishap made his return home very late and he was soaking wet. It was clear he was far from pleased with his misfortune, especially as he caught a cold and had to remain in bed for a couple of days.

'What a blithering idiot he is!' Sydney cried indignantly when he heard. I rushed to Willy's defense. 'Oh poor Willy, he can't have driven his cart into the rut on purpose. Nobody would do that.'

'Nobody but a blithering idiot.' repeated Sydney. 'It's about time he learned a few tricks of the trade if he wants to go 'carting' about the countryside in all weathers.' Sydney's disapproval was possibly shared by Donald but being kinder, he held his peace.

Later that year it was decided the new field required a fence. The main reason being it was a boundary with the road so the project went ahead. Sydney was designated to go to Concordia on the Argentine coast, slightly north along the Rio Uruguay, to purchase the posts. 'It's no longer good policy to cut down our own badly needed trees for the posts,' Donald explained, 'we've calculated it's better business to go to Concordia and buy them all ready for use. We're exempt from taxes anyway.'

'Right,' said Sydney, 'less work and expense.' I was delighted the gentlemen were understanding the business side of the work, and this time had even gone to some trouble in calculating which was the cheapest way to do the job.

'When will you go, Syd?' I asked enthusiastically.

'Early next week, I think, all being well.' He smiled at me and then went on: 'The idea being that Willy'll meet me on my return in Mercedes with his cart and we'll bring the posts home together.'

'Saving a carting fee,' put in Donald, 'unless old Willy decides to charge us!' There was laughter all round.

Sydney went off on Tuesday to Mercedes and on to Fray Bentos where he took a steamer across to Concordia in search of posts. In the meantime, Willy carted wire from Mercedes and once combined his trip to bring out the Romney Marsh ram we had purchased.

The new fence was going to be an extensive job and the fence men arrived the day after Sydney and Willy got back from Mercedes with the posts. It was the first time we were employing fence men, as up till now we had done it on our own, but as this was going to be long and tedious we decided a small group of fence men would save us days of hard labour.

The fence was started in July and took longer than anticipated for it was a wet month and rain often stopped the work. This was serious because while the fence men were working on our land they had to be fed regardless of the weather conditions. Rain stopped the work but they remained on our premises, eating us out of house and home, reducing the advantages of having them.

Willy encountered more problems with his carting and one day his horses took fright on the road and bolted. Over the ditch and on through the fields until Willy gave up trying to catch them and returned to Las Palmas on foot, hoping to enlist somebody to help him recover them.

I was the only person available at the moment for Donald and Sydney were still not back for lunch.

'Oh Willy!' I exclaimed when he told me of his plight.

'You're not going to be very popular when they get to hear about it.'

'Well, I can't manage the horses alone,' he said huffily, 'so the least they can do is give me a hand in catching them and bringing them home. I can't leave them and my cart out there in the unknown fields, can I?'

Donald went with him. Sydney flatly refused to have anything to do with it. Donald took one of the workmen with him, as well as two good riding horses, and plenty of rope. Mission completed, they were back at the house in a couple of hours and none the worse for wear, except for having their lunch very late.

This second accident of Willy's was looked upon with even less consideration than the previous and we began to wonder whether Willy's carting business was worthwhile during the winter months. We also feared for his safety for the evenings he did not return because darkness had overtaken him and he had to remain on another farm, caused a good deal of anxiety. I certainly was thankful when he appeared, hale and hearty, the following morning.

CHAPTER 8

The birth of our third child, plus lots of hard work and innumerable problems at Las Palmas during 1879, tended to make us overlook the prominent problems of the country at that time.

In February Colonel Latorre, wishing to go back to a Constitutional regime, handed the government over to Dr. Francisco Vidal, whom Latorre knew to be an easy candidate to overthrow, and in March Colonel Latorre was elected Constitutional President for four years.

This election did not lessen Latorre's opposition. His unpopularity increased steadily even as his cruelty did, until one year after his Constitutional election, Latorre resigned. He declared he considered his life was in danger.

Going back in history, during this year we were directly following the plan of production of that fine governor Hernandarias of two and a half centuries ago (1600-1609) when during his second government period he had introduced cattle raising into Uruguay, for his keen perceptive eye saw how very appropriate the lands of both Argentina and Uruguay were for this purpose. He noticed the cattle the first *Adelantado* had originally brought out to Buenos Aires had multiplied in an astonishing manner, so he took one hundred head of cattle and a certain amount of horses and mares to Uruguay. These animals were landed at the Arroyo de la Vacas (Colonia) where they spread and scattered into the fields and multiplied.

This was the origin of the livestock riches in the country and the beginning of our own flocks and herds of many years later.

At Las Palmas now there were three children: Donny, Ada and little Billy. This sweet child whom we baptized William Patrick George, had been born on New Year's Day and was already eight months old and could sit up alone. Billy was, with no doubt, the apple of Mrs. Allen's eye. She adored the child and would do anything to see him happy and for the first time since being in our service, I heard her telling stories and singing lullabies. Never having done this for the other children, she now seemed to have become more gentle and motherly.

'I suppose she's older so has become more tolerant,' I derived one day while chatting with Donald.

'Hey, she's not very old. You sound as if she was middle-aged. I don't believe she's reached thirty-five yet.' He laughed at me.

'Well,' I chuckled, 'you know what I mean, she's much kinder to Billy than she ever was with the others, don't you agree?'

'Surely, I agree. She's also put on a little weight recently and is looking the better for it.

'Hush Donald! You're not supposed to notice things like that in other women.' I chaffed him, 'you'll be making me jealous yet!' He put his arms around me lovingly and told me in his most endearing manner I was still his favourite.

On a miserably cold and damp September morning Willy was lighting a fire in the drawing-room straight after breakfast. An easy deduction would have been that he intended to spend the day sitting beside it. Willy had a cold and there was possibly not much work as it was so damp.

Donald and Sydney were preparing to go on business to Mercedes. It was needful they spend two days there and consequently would not be home tonight.

I detested the two-day trips I missed my darling. Meals were dull and I felt cold in bed at night. The house was quiet and somber when those two were away even though the children did play a small part in my life, the husband void was very evident. Today being the sort of day it was no doubt would see us closeted up indoors all day.

'Must you go for so long?' I asked Donald while we packed up a few things for him to take.

'I'm afraid so,' he replied. 'We must attend the Council meeting with all neighbours of the zone, and then place a request for the road from Palmitas village to run near our land.'

'But why two days?' I sounded miserable.

'You know how important it is for our future, otherwise I wouldn't go. The Council has to debate the matter today but only give their reply tomorrow. It's not worth our while coming back, then return tomorrow, especially in this weather, besides other bits of business to do there.' He hugged me. 'Don't look so despondent. Two days is not a life-time! Besides, you'll have Willy and the children to keep you company.'

I sighed: 'It's a depressing sort of day and we'll have to be indoors and not able to ride, will we?'

'No, don't attempt taking the horses out on a day like today. It's freezing cold and drizzling already.' He peered out. 'We must be off otherwise we shan't get away if it begins to rain hard.'

A kiss, and they were gone. The sound of the cart's wheels was the only thing left me and that soon faded too. They went in the cart because it needed soldering and it was an opportunity to take it to the blacksmith.

I turned from the window with a sigh. Boredom.

I could hear Mrs. Allen giving the children lessons. Poor Ada hated lessons. Her day had begun as badly as mine.

I'll do something useful, I thought, and as I had plenty of cloth and the sewing machine up on the table I soon got to work. The children needed nightgowns; they'd grown so much; last year's garments were no use.

We had packed up a big bundle of outgrown clothes recently and taken them to the Puestos where innumerable children lived, all freezing to death with inadequate clothing. Yet somehow those children seemed not to feel the cold as we did. Little bare legs and feet squelching in the icy cold mud, but big smiles and rosy cheeks and not a runny nose amongst them. The tough life they were subject to gave them extra defenses. Our children had fireplaces, warm garments and stout shoes, but they were constantly catching cold throughout the entire winter.

I took up my scissors and started cutting. I made good progress with the nightgowns. Soon the machining would be over, leaving only the hand sewing. I planned to take this into the drawing-room after lunch and sit by the fire with Willy, inviting Mrs. Allen and the children to come in, too. Perhaps Mrs. Allen would offer to help with the hemming and get it all done sooner.

In this manner the afternoon was progressing when suddenly we heard wheels on the gravel outside.

My heart gave a leap! Could it be the gentlemen back so soon? I picked up my skirts and ran onto the veranda. What horrors! It was Mr. Brown. How best could I turn him away tactfully I wondered, while I watched with little enthusiasm the grinning figure of Mr. Brown as he came striding arrogantly across the patio and onto the veranda. His resemblance to a small rodent was more accentuated than ever.

'What a delightful reception, my dear lady!' he exclaimed as he took my outstretched hand in his clammy one and gave it the usual squeeze.

'How are you, Mr. Brown?' I stepped back a couple of paces to enlarge the distance between us and in so doing I accidentally stepped on Santa's paw. 'Yowl, yowl!' I stooped down and patted him affectionately: 'I'm sorry old boy'... Santa was a real cry-baby and went on squeaking for a few moments but I was thankful for the distraction.

Mr. Brown soon ought to be telling me the reason for his visit, but he didn't and instead just stood there leering at me.

'My husband isn't home I'm afraid, in case you've come on business,' I began.

'Oh, what a pity!' he exclaimed and I detected a slight undercurrent of sarcasm. 'I'd hoped to find him in to talk about rams again.'

'Sorry you've come all this way on such a nasty day only to find him away.' A pause... I had to say it, Donald expected it of me, but the words came out reluctantly: 'Would you like to come in?'

'Thank you.'

He entered the drawing-room to find only Willy there because Mrs. Allen had removed the children and the sewing at the arrival of a guest.

Mr. Brown settled himself comfortably in the armchair near the fire opposite to Willy. I suspected we were in for a lengthy visit. It was nearly five o'clock and the day was getting darker and darker and soon the drizzle had turned into steady rainfall.

'Would you care for some tea?'

'Yes please, Evie,' said Willy. 'Will you bring it in here by the fire? I'm feeling a bit seedy and don't want to leave the warmth.' He coughed gently to emphasize his condition.

I agreed it would be better to have it in here; less formal than laying the long table. Perhaps Mr. Brown would be encouraged to leave early once he'd had his tea. But unfortunately the rain became torrential as we drank our tea.

'What rain!' exclaimed Willy. 'We certainly have had a wet year, haven't we?'

'Tremendous,' agreed Brown, and then: 'This is not encouraging my departure.' he chuckled with a little smirk at me. He must be reading my thoughts: if this rain continued he'd have to stay the night.

Nightfall came early so we arranged for his trap to be put under cover and his horse loosened to be taken to the stables for the night. He was beaming with satisfaction and he and Willy soon were happily drinking whiskey: 'Strictly medicinal. Good for my cold.' commented Willy.

I retired to my room after asking in the kitchen for an extra place at dinner. Luckily Mrs. Allen was with us at least making it four and helping the conversation. I took as long as possible at my toilet and change my dress. What to put on? I chose my very plainest and darkest dress, fitting my mood. I took out my violet velveteen which was the most sedate with a high neck and long sleeves. Donald had bought it in Buenos Aires last year when they had gone over to the Palermo Horse Show and I had used it little, but it seemed more than appropriate for this evening.

Eventually dinner was over and gone off well in spite of the tooth-picking interval with the long fingernail by Mr. Brown. He never omitted this revolting performance. Mrs. Allen retired when the meal finished for she never stayed up late because the children woke her early.

Willy's cold had increased considerably so, mumbling something about taking medicine, he made his excuses and trotted off to bed, leaving me to hold the fort with Mr. Brown alone.

'I hope Donald and Sydney will be back soon.' I pretended I expected them home this evening. 'It's a long drive from Mercedes.'

'My dear lady,' began Mr. Brown with a knowing look, 'if I can't get away due to heavy rain, your fond husband won't be able to reach here either.' He laughed. 'Be sensible, facts are facts.' I could not argue. Dropping my eyes to my lap I searched for conversation topics, luckily we had something in common and that was our sheep and cattle. I proceeded to draw him into lengthy discussions, asking endless questions for which he had ample replies and I found I was learning a lot from him.

'I see you're interested in the cattle.... Willy was telling me you have some cows of your own.' As we talked I even ventured to tell him hope of having a herd of my own.

'You're a very smart little woman, and I'm sure you'll have the greatest success. Unlike your husband, YOU seem to have your head screwed on the right way.' He lolled back in the chair over-confidently.

'I don't appreciate any criticisms of my husband.' I replied icily.

'Oh come on!' he cried, 'let's be frank with one another. You know as well as I do Donald is no businessman...' I stiffened in disgust yet tried to keep control.

'I'll thank you to keep your opinions to yourself!' I barked at him.

'My opinions are what is common knowledge around the vicinity and if you don't see this you must be partially blind. None of the Fitzpatrick family are any good at business transactions, being farmers and very hardworking, but most of their profits are lost by rotten negotiations.' I had to control myself and not give way to vulgar insults so I did my best to affect nonchalance. 'I've no idea what you're talking about,' I said stiffly.

'You should get out of here and start your own business, then you'd make a million.'

'What rubbish you're talking. Are you implying...'

'Yes, I'm suggesting you leave your husband and...' I cut him short. 'I'll have you know I'm happily married to Donald and won't dream of leaving him under any circumstances.' I found my voice rising in rage.

'Oh I know your silly old religion doesn't allow for changes of husband but what's the good of sticking to a man for better or for worse when the 'worse' is of his own making?' I had never felt my inexperience so much as at that moment. What could I do to deter him? Have him shown out? By whom when there was nobody about? He went directly on with his dialogue: 'Once you're away with somebody else, me for instance, you...' I jumped to my feet.

'Perhaps you'd like to retire to your bedroom now.' I said, 'this conversation displeases me and it's getting late.' But he'd also risen from his chair, stopping me from leaving the room. I turned and faced him. He was perfectly at ease: 'Your husband generally offers me a nightcap when he's here.'

'Ah, yes, I'll get you something.' It was a break, a pause, an evasion and a change of subject. I went to the cupboard where the drinks were stored. 'What'll you have? Brandy?' With his brandy glass in hand he reseated himself and crossed his legs comfortably, foreseeing an extension to our spirited discussion. He was enjoying it. I was not. 'It feels strange being in this room alone with you; I like it.' He eyed me craftily watching my reaction to this remark.

I said: 'Why do you bother to come so frequently to Las Palmas if you have such a low opinion of the gentlemen?'

'I come to buy their rotten quality rams so as to have a chance of seeing you.' I felt my colour rising in my face and I leaped to my feet again.

'I'll thank you to keep the conversation on a business level as it should be. I dislike your familiarity.' He grabbed my arm as I passed him on my way to the door, intending to leave the room.

'My, my, you're a real firebrand, aren't you? I like you more when your temper is roused! A good Irish temper at that! It makes your hair even redder — you're very attractive like this.' He pushed me back into my chair, not very gently.

'Mr. Brown—' I began but he held up his hand.

'Just call me Alfred.... We're getting on fine.' He was enjoying himself at my expense. I tried to keep calm, but my voice shook.

'Mr. Brown,' I began again ignoring his request of his first name. 'I'd appreciate it if you let me go to my room now.'

'It's not late and this conversation is amusing me and doing you a lot of good. For once you've met an equal: energetic and a good head on one's shoulders. Nobody has ever dared to speak to you like this before, have they?' When I started to object again, he merely waved a fat hand, demanding silence. 'As we've understood, your menfolk are fine farmers but weak in the business line. Soft, when making deals, and no idea how to manage a place like this successfully.' Again I tried to stop him. 'Please don't interrupt me!' he exclaimed as he swallowed another mouthful of brandy before continuing: 'You, inconspicuously, are the head of this place, so don't let the opportunity of success slip through your fingers. It's HERE! Don't be idle — form your own herd here, if you don't want to break away — buy cattle, sell cattle and you'll soon be a wealthy woman. But remember, keep it all apart from that of your menfolk, both cattle and cash. With them, it all slips away; they have no idea where it comes from nor where it goes to, I would—' At this point I could stand it no longer. This revolting creature had the audacity to sit in our drawing-room, under our roof, and voice these insolent opinions about what I ought to do and what not to do. He was the most obnoxious person with whom I had ever come into contact.

I made a dash for the door. Although he was small and fat he was nimble on his feet and he got there before me, barring my only means of escape. I stood and faced him. I felt better standing because we were at the same level being about the same height. I could feel my face burning; I lifted my head high; I would put an end to this.

'I won't allow you to speak like this about my family when they're not present.' I met his look with spirit. 'So you're a proud one too.' He stepped nearer to me and I smelled his alcoholic breath. 'Don't be proud, little lady, it's not good. Your own precious Bible says: 'Pride goes before a fall.' So get down off your high horse and accept what the real facts are. Stop living on your little pink cloud of love and romance with your hubby. Real life's not like that, and if you don't break away soon you'll have a fall and be dragged down with them all. It'll be a hard fall — Alfred Brown knows best.'

He was still in front of the door, the only one miserable door in our idiotic drawing-room.

I apprehended clearly and visibly all rooms should have at least two doors as a means of escape. ESCAPE! The only word racing through my mind; how could I escape?

He stood before me grinning; yes, actually leering, in his enjoyment of this situation. A red mist of wrath dimmed my eyes and I felt I could kill him. I'd scratch his eyes out happily, grab him by the head and dash it against the wall until his smirk disappeared and he was dead. Give me half a chance, I swore! I knew I was at a severe disadvantage, his strength must be double mine and there was nobody to help me, so I did nothing. Instead I lifted my head higher and glared at him. He continued just as if nothing had happened. 'You and I can make a good team together if you'd allow it.' A pause. 'What about it?' and he held out his hand as if to close a deal.

I ignored it. 'I refuse to listen to abominable suggestions any longer, I'm—'

He interrupted me by lunging forward and placing both his hands on my shoulders, but even as I twisted and struggled to free myself, I heard him saying: 'Ah, you're very beautiful when you're angry, I've said it before and I'll say it again!' A delighted chuckle rang out. 'Your eyes spit sparks of fire and your bosoms heave most appealingly. I'll bet you're fun in bed.'

A quick twist freed me from his grasp.

'I'll thank you not to be vulgar and keep your place as a guest in our house!' I cried hotly.

'No love-making? What a pity. A little business arrangement then?' he persisted.

'NO!' I shouted. 'I'll have nothing to do with you.' I slapped his face and he looked so astonished I took the opportunity to say: 'If you'll allow me, I'm going to leave the room.'

All of a sudden he was defeated, a tired expression crossed his face and he stepped back to allow me the way through the door. 'I wish you GOODNIGHT!' I flung at him as I finally slammed the door.

I heard him chuckle.

I locked the door of my bedroom firmly but did not sleep very well. The thought of Mr. Brown under my same roof, made me nervous. Fortunately, my door's lock was good for he was just the sort of person who would try to take advantage of a woman alone. He had implied intimacies a thousand times since we'd first met. Every time he came to the estancia the situation became worse. I simply did not know how to handle it. This evening he had become excited with his role as only male and totally over-stepped his position as guest. I found myself shaking with indignation under the blankets, instead of getting off to sleep peacefully. Damn Brown! His words about lack of administration and money control at Las Palmas kept whirling through my head. Sub-consciously I knew they coincided with some of my own thoughts occasionally. Could this nasty man be right? Hell, why can't I stop thinking and get to sleep?

Slowly, gradually I forced myself to begin thinking of Donald in a positive light and repeated my favourite Psalm: 'I will lift up my eyes unto the hills from whence cometh my help...' At last the peace of prayer began to have its effect and I drifted into a state of meditation... I slept.

It had cleared during the night and there was a cold wind blowing the clouds away at a great speed. Already there was enough blue sky to make a Dutchman a pair of trousers. Thankfully there was no more rain and Brown would be able to leave and Donald and Sydney get home.

I felt tired after last night and decided not to get up for breakfast. I called Mrs. Allen and asked her to bring the children to my room so I could play with them. In the meantime, I hoped Mr. Brown would breakfast and leave. I couldn't face him.

I knew I'd not tell Donald about last night's affair because he'd never deal with Brown again and he was a useful person. The scene the previous evening had left its mark on me. All the next day I was being reminded of certain remarks made the night before and I felt infuriated by them. I could not take this insult without hitting back.

The best solution would be never to allow him to set foot on Las Palmas soil again, but I knew this could not be for if I suddenly cut this easy flow of ram sales income I'd not be helping our farm. Quite the contrary, getting rid of Mr. Brown would create yet another problem of finding an honest ram buyer. Much as I disliked the man, I had to admit some of his remarks were accurate much as I hated criticizing my own family.

I wondered how much we really knew about Brown, except that he lived about thirty kilometres the other side of the Aguila river and he had a sheep farm, we knew little. He was a bachelor from England, had bought land, built a small house where he installed a housekeeper and gardener. His farm was large and his flocks enormous getting the very best out of his expanse of land. Rumour had it he had large bank accounts in England where he sent his fast made profits each year.

In the meantime, I was forming a nice little herd of my own. I had the field and put in a bull when the cows needed serving and now they were beginning to breed well. The herd had grown to double its original size and people respected it. Last spring when the gentlemen had been out marking cattle, I'd asked for my cattle to be done with a mark of my own and it was granted me.

It was about this time Alberto came to us. He was a hard-working lad, about nineteen years old, and had appeared at our place one rainy afternoon asking for shelter and work. His home was in Dolores but he'd not found work there. Somebody had told him of the *ingleses* (Englishmen) place where he might find work. Having no horse, he had walked from Dolores and remained the night in the workmen's quarters. The next day Donald offered him the job of gardener. He proved a very useful and willing lad, but his obvious love of animals drew him to my side and before long he was helping with the dogs and horses as well. He knew how to do a fine job of grooming and clipping, keeping my Rosie in meticulous condition. He also derived a great deal of pleasure from my little herd and we worked a lot together. As was only natural he got behind with his gardening duties by spending too much time with the animals.

My attention was drawn to this by the gentlemen, and a solution had to be found quickly; either I stopped his work amongst the animals or he would be replaced by another gardener.

'Personally,' remarked Donald, 'I don't feel it matters which he does but it's quite clear he can't do both.'

'He's excellent with the animals, you know.' I gave credit where it was due. 'Have you noticed the way he looks after Rosie for me?'

'Yes, impeccable,' Sydney commented, 'and he also grooms most of the other horses; he's a natural animal lover.'

'Let's try and get another gardener then,' I suggested, 'or is it a bit extravagant to pay two salaries?'

'Well, some things are essential, aren't they?' Quite casually Donald was accepting another member of staff in his matter of fact way. He lit his pipe, preparing to change the subject.

'If we've decided to take on a new gardener,' I put in 'and leave Alberto with the animals, I volunteer to pay him his wages out of my own money and be allowed to decide where and when he works.'

A poignant silence. The young Irish lassie was turning business-like. Were they going to accept this? I lifted my head in defiance.

Presently: 'Very well then, let's work it that way, shall we?' And with Donald's remark, the decision was made. Alberto was mine.

CHAPTER 9

The frightful weeks which followed our quiet month of April, commenced one afternoon when we had planned a picnic at the *Aguila* river to fish. In our customary style we had decided to take our tea to make a longer afternoon of it. Donald and Willy had gladly joined our party, never needing much encouragement to come fishing. They took over all the packing and preparing of the fishing tackle, they cut up bait packing it in small tins and sorted the lines. I was thankful for this help considering I had sufficient work with the sandwich making and the packing of the hamper.

I relished the thought of leaving the house for a whole afternoon and spending it on the banks of the river with the family. Donald and I had a special spot where we'd throw in our lines and await our first bite. The peace of the afternoon would surround us with romance of the past, we'd be young again, and snags and discomforts would fall away. The sound of the children's laughter a little away as they played with Mrs. Allen would be the only thing to break the stillness.

I was looking forward to this picnic and was surprised when Mrs. Allen suddenly approached me while we were loading the cart.

The children were dashing about and squealing with excitement and the dogs also had very astutely sensed an outing where they would be included. Santa kept leaping on the cart in anticipation, followed by Claus, then both were being dragged off by Donny who was trying to lift the hamper up. 'No Santa. I said NO, so don't get up!' he shouted at the dog. Next minute: 'Get down you silly stupid dog! No Claus, get DOWN!' Poor Donny was having a tough time with those two.

There was lots of noise and shouting and barking.

Mrs. Allen cleared her throat. 'I was wondering whether it would be all right if I didn't go with you this afternoon?' She dropped her eyes in embarrassment. 'I'm not feeling very well,' she concluded.

'Oh!' I was completely taken aback. I gazed at her in astonishment. 'Why? What's the matter with you?'

'I don't feel very well,' she repeated.

An afternoon's outing as we'd planned without a nannie was a completely different picture. It meant I had to attend and entertain the children instead of going off quietly to fish with my husband. I felt irked.

'Does your head ache?' I asked with asperity.

'No,' she said, 'I have a stomach-ache and I think I ought to remain near the house in case of emergencies.'

'I see,' I sighed, 'if that's the case you'd better stay at home.'

'Thank you, mam.' she made a hasty retreat into the house and her bedroom. Silly woman, I grumbled, she's spoilt my afternoon. It was unlike her I had to admit she never let us down in this manner. I went into the house to tell Donald of the change.

'We'll make do,' Donald assured me with a smile. 'We'll look after our own children for a change. It may be fun at that!' I loved his rapid acceptance of the inevitable and this happy disposition eased my ill humour and we were soon driving pleasantly in the cart with Willy and Donny trotting on horseback. Mrs. Allen's indisposition was falling further and further from our minds as the fresh breeze caught our faces and the sound of the horse hooves made music in our ears.

It had been a month since I'd stopped riding again for my fourth pregnancy had been confirmed. I was a passenger in the cart and Donald driving, with the two younger children by the side of their sedate and pregnant mother.

The afternoon was a success. The children in high spirits had found entertainment for themselves and the dogs had ended up bathing in the river. There was too much noise to fish and only Willy had walked upstream and caught a couple of little ones which he threw back.

When tea was over and the sun getting low on the horizon we started home again, singing happily some of the well-remembered Irish songs to accompany our good humour. Only as we entered the house did I wonder about Mrs. Allen. I was tired and wanted her to take over the children.

I knocked on her door and in response to her quiet 'Come in' I entered her room to find her lying on her bed fully dressed with a frightened look on her face.

'Any better?' I enquired pleasantly.

'No, I'm afraid not.'

'Come now,' I tried to encourage her to tell me what the trouble was, although I'd never seen her in such an apathetic state. 'What exactly are you feeling? Any pain?'

'The pain comes and goes, so I suppose it must be wind.' She rolled over languidly and closed her eyes. It was very clear she had no intention of getting up and helping with the children, so I slipped from the room, leaving her to her wind; if wind was all it was, she'd soon be better.

Once the children were bathed, fed and bedded, I joined the gentlemen in the drawing-room just before dinner.

'Have you discovered what the matter with Mrs. Allen is?' Donald enquired suddenly.

'She admits to pains in her stomach and thinks it's an attack of wind but I've never seen her looking so poorly in all these years.'

'How long has she been complaining of pain?' asked Sydney.

'Only since the early afternoon, just as we were preparing for our picnic.

'One has to be a bit careful with stomach pains for there is such a thing as appendicitis which needs an operation. I'm told it's dangerous to leave an appendix unattended.' Then he asked: 'Has she had her appendix out?'

'Gracious!' I exclaimed, 'I hadn't thought of that. Perhaps we ought to call Dr. Owens before it gets too late.'

'When you take her supper tray in, ask about her appendix and we'll act in accordance with what she says,' said Donald. 'It must be serious for she's not the type to drop into bed without a good reason.'

'That's true,' I agreed, 'she's not been ill since we came out other than a cold and cough, which make one wonder what's up now.'

On taking her meal in later on, I walked into her room as she was having some pain and it shocked me to see her gripping tightly, with white knuckles, the sides of her bed. I stood petrified holding the tray and a few moments later the pain seemed to have eased and she was almost herself again.

'How kind of you,' she breathed, 'not that I'm hungry.' She struggled to sit up, failed, and finally swung her legs off the bed and acquired a vertical position. All of a sudden she looked ugly, fat and cumbersome, gone was her usual suave manner and pleasant face. As she sipped the broth I asked her the dreaded question.

'Er... have you had your appendix removed?' I asked as gently as possible, not wishing to frighten her.

'No.' She waved her hand in a dismissal of the very thought.

'Anyway,' I continued, 'I think we ought to have Dr. Owens over to see you, don't you?' She remained silent.

'Well, I went on casually, 'finish your supper and think about it. I'll be in later, when we'll have to decide.' Something in her attitude, her resignation and reserve, stirred some memory in me yet remained undefined. She'd enclosed herself into a shell which was impenetrable so, with a good deal of impatience, I left her again.

By ten o'clock we were all tired and there were movements for going to bed. Donald had been yawning for the past hour and Willy had already turned in. Sydney was supposed to be reading but kept dropping off. It was bedtime.

'I'll look in on Mrs. Allen before going to bed,' I said. My gentle knock only provoked a muffled groan from within. She had changed from her afternoon dress and was in her nightie and had made preparations for the night. The untouched supper tray was in the corner of the room. She'd only sipped the broth while I was there out of politeness.

'What's the verdict about the doctor?' I asked, 'for the gentlemen are off to bed.' I wanted to emphasize the importance of making a hasty decision before they all turned in.

'Oh, I can't decide at the moment!' she gasped, 'let's leave it till morning.'

'Are you any better?' I asked.

'No.' Some pain was coming on and great beads of perspiration formed on her brow while she tried to cope with it and eventually when she was a little easier, I turned and said: 'I'm going to ask Donald or Sydney to bring Dr. Owens at once.'

'No... NO!' she cried harshly catching my hand in a strong grip. 'Please don't go away... don't leave me alone,' she sobbed. A great wave of pity welled up in me as I realized how terribly lonely she must be; she had absolutely nobody who cared for her at all. I often thought about my loneliness but it was nothing compared to what hers must be. Perhaps I was her closest friend although my feeling towards her was merely a cool acquaintance.

'Don't worry, I'll stay.' While I watched her steady breathing I thought back on these last few weeks with her in full activity; she'd been lively and pleasant but she did seem to tire more than before. She was doing less and less exercise and growing stouter in consequence. The gentlemen frequently invited her to play tennis but she invariably had some excuse to give: she had to take the children for a walk or was preparing their lessons, any excuse not to play. Surprising disinterest considering how much she enjoyed the game. Months ago she'd have dropped everything to get out on the court, now I'd condemn her by calling her sluggish. She was just the same except for this moment as she lay in an untidy heap on her bed; her hair rumpled and her face blotched. We MUST get Dr. Owens in the morning, I thought.

She seemed a bit calmer so I went and mopped her brow with a handkerchief.

'Better?' I whispered, terrified.

'Yes, it's easier now.' She sank back on her pillows.

'Would you like a glass of water?'

'No thanks, nothing.' She closed her eyes eliminating me from view. I considered it a good moment to go and get some rest myself as it was late into the night already.

When the grey dawn broke out in the east, I awoke and called Donald.

'I think we ought to get up and fetch Dr. Owens as soon as possible. I'm terrified Mrs. Allen's going to die of appendicitis. Her pains were very bad last night.'

'It sounds like a case for the doctor, so I'll be off.' He leaped out of bed and began dressing. He was so good and willing to help. Although I badly needed some more sleep, I feared Mrs. Allen might be needing something before the doctor arrived, so I went to the sick room with little enthusiasm.

The patient was no better, in fact I estimated her to be considerably worse; the pains more frequent and intense.

These pain sessions frightened me for I kept imagining her appendix suddenly bursting, and I'd be a witness to her dreadful death. The whole thing had become a nightmare of huge dimensions; the eerie glow from the dimming lamp now almost burnt out, the slightly grey hue of the new morning light, threw grotesque shadows on the wall making an ugly picture, and the odour of stale perspiration was foul.

'Let me sponge you down a bit before doctor comes,' I said as she opened her eyes a tiny slit. I hoped that for the first time she might condescend to do something helpful for herself.

'The doctor?' she cried and her eyes shot open in alarm. 'Have you sent for the doctor?' She sounded frightened.

'Yes, Donald must be reaching Dr. Owens' home already, so they won't be long in getting back.'

'Oh my God.' She covered her face with her hands. What was this strange refusal to see the doctor? I had to talk to her seriously about her illness.

'You know you can't remain like this much longer, I began. 'I think you're worse instead of better this morning, don't you?' She did not reply. 'You look dreadful and completely worn out.' I had to make her respond. The children would soon need attention and if I remained here I'd have to ask Willy to give them their breakfast. There was important cattle parting today and he and Sydney would be off early.

'Come on!' I coaxed her, 'let me wash you down and improve your ghastly appearance.' She looked at me with mortal offense, I might have accused her of resembling a decomposing leper. Again she gave me a negative headshake.

I rocked back and forth in the old rocker. One thing had come clear over the night hours, wind was not the trouble, it was much more serious. Nevertheless, I felt myself dropping asleep when suddenly the much longed for sound was heard. Thank God Donald was back and as I rushed onto the veranda I saw Dr. Owens was with him, his little black 'miracle' bag in his hand.

'They've arrived!' I cried excitedly on hurrying back into the sick room. I felt the responsibility slipping from me as a cloak from my careworn shoulders as the doctor walked into the room. Dr. Owens questioned Mrs. Allen about her symptoms and they talked quietly together then he turned to me.

'I'm going to examine the patient,' he said, 'so will you please leave us?' He smiled at me kindly noting my exhaustion.

'Have you been up all night?'

'Only partially.' Thankfully I left them and joined Donald at breakfast. He was already crunching toast and the contentment showed his early rising and hasty visit to the doctor's had taken no toll on him. He was happy... he was eating. Breakfast was an important meal to this family. At last he'd finished and wiped his mouth on his napkin when we heard the door of Mrs. Allen's room open and quick footsteps coming along the veranda.

'Dr. Owens!' I called, 'we're in here.' He wasted no time in entering the room, his expression one of calmness, no trace of anxiety nor alarm. So much for his profession, I thought, and asked: 'How is she?' We waited for the condemning verdict.

'Does she need an operation?'

Dr. Owens smiled: 'No. Mrs. Allen is not ill; she's having a baby.'

I felt contrasting emotions stampede through my body: disgust, indignation, hatred and then reluctant admiration for this woman who'd been able to keep her secret all these months. How had she managed it? Her ample skirts, artfully covered with an immaculate apron, had kept the secret from inquisitive eyes, but the long nine-month process without ever sharing it, was more than I could understand.

I stared at him in disbelief.

Dr. Owens continued: 'There's not much time, the child will be born soon. Don't look so shocked; you've had a number of children yourself, so you know what it entails.' He turned to leave the room. 'I'll need some help, please.'

Suddenly a great wave of exhaustion swept over me and the thought of what the impending moments would call for, made me feel faint and I dropped into a chair.

'Are you all right, darling?' Donald asked.

'I think Evie's too tired to assist in the delivery,' the doctor said, 'is there another woman who could step in and help?'

'Ummmm—' thought Donald. 'The Señora Pintos often assists in these matters, she's a sort of nurse.'

'Good.'

'I'll ride over to Pintos place and bring her back as fast as I can.' said Donald.

Dr. Owens turned to me: 'Can you make it a while longer till Señora Pintos arrives?' And after a second glance at my white face he asked: 'Have you had breakfast?'

'No, I wasn't very hungry.'

'Get the cook to make you a strong cup of coffee before you come back into the bedroom. Quick!' He left, directing his efficient strides swiftly into Mrs. Allen's room. In a few moments I reluctantly entered the sick room again but with a strong cup of coffee inside me I felt more apt to undertake my duties.

Quite surprisingly, the room I'd left about thirty minutes ago seeming to be in such a state of dirt and untidiness, was now miraculously converted into a plain labour room. The doctor in a spotless white coat transmitted an air of cool assurance and efficiency.

He had removed the superfluous quilts and blankets, leaving the patient lying on what looked like clean white sheets. Mrs. Allen was flat on her back and the sheet covering her was meticulously folded to reach her waist and she looked neat, only her face showed signs of anguish still. Her heavy breathing indicated there was another contraction. The doctor stood near her and placed his hand on her belly.

'Breathe deeply.' It was incredible how fear had flown out of the window so suddenly. All the night before's uncertainty and anguish had been converted into a normal childbirth.

I waited near the door, half in shadow, not wishing to disturb the natural rhythm of the birth. It was ironical: I knew what the pain and anguish of the night before had reminded me of: the birth of a baby and not appendicitis. My naive nature had not allowed me to consider the possibility of pregnancy in this unmarried woman. The blunt question leaped to mind: 'Who's the father of this child?'

The contractions were coming every two minutes now and although I had given birth to three children myself, I felt a cold revulsion at having to be at the opposite end of the delivery now. Dr. Owens turned to me: 'Have you some tiny garments we can dress the child in when it arrives? She tells me she's entirely unprepared for a baby.'

I left the room thinking: What a stupid bitch this woman must be. The arrival of Donald with the Señora Pintos mollified me slightly and I handed the little things to this woman as she hastened to the bedroom. Her large, overweight figure made her look middle-aged but I think she was only about forty and a happy eater. What a blessing she'd got here on time. I graciously accepted my dismissal, and Donald and I strolled into the lovely sunshine.

It was near ten o'clock and as the children were playing amongst the plants and high grass on the other side of the fence, we directed our steps over there. After seeing the little house they'd made, I told them they had to listen for the lunch bell.

'When it rings you must hurry up to the house, wash hands and be ready for lunch. You'll be eating at the big table today for Mrs. Allen's not getting up.'

'Yes Mummie!'

We walked to my cow field and circled the house and as we approached we heard the first wail of a new life: Mrs. Allen's child was born. I flopped into a chair and Donald beside me. He lit his pipe saying, 'It's a strange happening, isn't it? How did none of us ever suspect?'

'I want to know who the father is,' came stiffly from me. He said: 'I presume that'll come clear since the child is born.' Just then Willy and Sydney were seen coming into the patio on horseback having finished the morning work. After washing down the horses they came and joined us.

'What news?' Sydney enquired, indicating with his head Mrs. Allen's room. 'Did the doctor come?'

'Yes, and Mrs. Allen has just given birth to a child. Not wind, not an appendicitis, but a baby!' I peered keenly into their faces hoping for a sign of paternal recognition, but there was nothing save incredulous surprise on both faces.

'A baby? Not really!' exclaimed Willy, and as if strengthening my statement, the child started crying again.

'Who's the father?' No reply.

—————

The momentous and unexpected arrival of the child born of Mrs. Allen, produced a series of urgent problems which had to be solved rapidly. The major question being, which of the three gentlemen was responsible? The second thing was I had suddenly been left without any help with the children. Not only their care but also their schooling for they had begun lessons with the governess, and with her indisposition, I'd not only lost my nannie but also the teacher. The future looked black, especially as in about three months there would be another baby of mine added to the household.

If Mrs. Allen decided to remain at Las Palmas which I felt was unlikely, she'd have her hands full with two babies and three growing children to cope with. Contrariwise she might decide to leave Uruguay and return to Ireland. Her decision, I felt, would hinge entirely on who recognized the child as his. So far, twenty-four hours later, none of the gentlemen had claimed it.

When I had gone to see the mother and child just after birth, I found a very silent and subdued Mrs. Allen holding her infant son in a dejected fashion. He was tiny and pink with an unmistakable likeness to the Fitzpatrick family. He had their colouring. It eliminated Willy from suspicion.

I admired the new born babe and withheld from asking the prominent question for Mrs. Allen's expression did not encourage confidences, and knowing she must be worn out after approximately a whole day of hard labour, I decided to leave the topic untouched for now.

'*Es divino.*' (He's beautiful) breathed Señora Pintos as she approached the bed and gently lifted the tiny boy into her strong arms and rocked him to sleep.

'I expect you want to get some rest,' I said and left the room. I was also tired and furthermore upset.

The lunch meal with the three children at table which we were not used to, added to the gentlemen's lengthy conversation about the cattle parting, were getting on my nerves, and by the end of the meal I longed for my bed and some sleep.

Beautiful oblivion! A good Uruguayan *siesta* (afternoon nap).

———————

Like most of us Mrs. Allen had learned a certain amount of Spanish during her years at Las Palmas, so she was able to communicate with Señora Pintos who was remaining the rest of the day, nursing and helping with the new child. I was grateful, for this service allowed me to go off for my sleep. But tired though I was, I could not sleep. I lay on my bed in the semi-darkness of the warm room and tried to reason out the disturbing state of affairs so suddenly arisen.

Mrs. Allen has given birth to a baby looking like the Fitzpatrick's and there are only two members of that family for thousands of miles. It must be Sydney! It MUST be him! He was the one to sit beside her on the veranda steps in the summer evenings and chatted to her. Why did he not admit the fact he was the father, subsequently removing suspicion from his brother?

The incredible thing about the situation was the total unconcern of the three gentlemen. The question had been thrown out casually with no reply, so the subject was dropped. I could not let it stand like this. How could I live with the very slightest doubt about my husband. We'd all been living too innocently in close relationship together like a model family, never suspecting anything different. I certainly had never suspected any immorality; could it be Donald?

My thoughts flew back to the past; various little incidents where Donald smiled at her, spoken kindly or helped her with the children, thing he loved doing, came to my mind as I lay on my bed feigning sleep. Did the frankness in his glance, the clear smile or gentle attention have a double meaning?

The unborn child I was carrying stirred within me. I got up and went out into the sun and fresh air. Mid-siesta hour was a very silent time on the estancia; even the children had been taught to lay quietly in bed, if not asleep at least reading a book.

The sun was high as I walked quietly past the closed bedroom door; not a sound of the new infant either; it must've been born into his blood that it was not the time for crying.

The door opened silently and Señora Pintos came out with a jug in hand, in search of fresh water for her patient. I enquired: '*Como estan?*' (How are they?)

'*Muy bien.*' (very well) She wore a lovely expression. 'The baby and his mother are fast asleep; he's a lovely child.' I nodded, not fully trusting my voice. What was the matter with me? Was I jealous or bitter?

'*Señora,*' (Madam) she said, 'I want to talk.'

'Of course,' I hurriedly condescended. We sat on a bench under the nearby tree.

'I've been speaking to the mother of the child and she doesn't want to keep him; she says she did not know she was carrying him.'

'Oh, what rubbish!' I exclaimed indignantly.

'Well, whatever it is, she doesn't want him and has agreed I take him.' The Pintos had no children and this seemed like a solution.

She continued: "As I saw him born I've become very fond of him and would love to have him, if I have your permission.'

Things had moved too fast; I hardly knew what to think any longer. This unfortunate little child whose mother was single, was now being given away, casually, to a family of another race and culture. He was about to be deprived of his true nationality and birthright, and I was supposed to make this gigantic decision. I knew full well he would be better cared for with the Pintos than remaining with his mother who had disliked him from the start. She probably felt he was the cause of the change in her life which was inevitably going to take place if she kept him. Mrs. Allen was happy in her post and wished not to alter it. The result: she gives him away. What a cold-blooded woman!

I refused to take the responsibility at the moment of the switching of parents. Donald and Sydney would have to be consulted and make the final decision.

'We must speak to the Señor Donald about this,' I said to her gently.

'Yes, of course, I understand the boss must give his approval.' She smiled contentedly, as if already knowing he'd agree. 'There's no hurry to decide for I'm staying the night. I've greater interest now.' As she got up she said: 'When Pintos comes in from work to report, I'll tell him of my request.'

'Very well,' I said, 'we'll consult the gentlemen when they come in this afternoon.' Was this the correct thing to do, I wondered, but I knew it would largely depend on my handling of this tangled affair for the gentlemen seemed to be taking it very casually.

CHAPTER 10

The winter weeks went slowly by in a particularly dull and listless way; the end of May was already in sight and we were facing the coldest months of the year. Our fireplaces were a great blessing but there was little to relieve the monotony of the dark winter months, for me especially, as I became heavier with pregnancy. It was difficult to get out into the fields to watch over my cattle because of the constant mud through which the cart could make no headway. Riding was forbidden. I was handicapped.

Fortunately, I had Alberto. We understood each other and I trusted him. He was in charge, and as my herd grew in numbers his duties increased. He kept my animals apart from the others for he knew how zealous I was about this. As the bad weather prevailed there were constantly baby calves brought up to the house for me. None of these ever went back to their original herd, they remained as mine. The winter was a particularly wet one and about twelve little animals were brought along at intervals. The caring and feeding of these I could still manage as they were near the house.

In the weeks following the birth of Mrs. Allen's baby a change came over the household of Las Palmas.

It was unanimously agreed the child should be adopted by the Pintos family, who welcomed him with open and adoring arms. Three days after his birth, a proud and smiling Señora Pintos drove back to her humble home with a snug bundle of fine Irish flesh in her motherly arms, and nobody disputed this as the best and ideal solution for the unwanted child. Mrs. Allen seemed highly satisfied to be relieved of her burden. We were astonished at her cold indifference towards her offspring. The mystery of its paternal origin remained unsolved. Nobody claimed to be the father.

I liked this strange tension little but did not know how to confront it. I let it slide and watched with incredulous amazement how Mrs. Allen soon resumed her duties with our children. As my own confinement became more imminent, I was glad to have her taking the work of the children from me, but I found our relationship had altered and taken on a different course. I hated her. A slow and deep dislike had begun forming in my heart towards this woman who so skillfully hoodwinked us all for months. Her cool, satisfied face as she appeared each morning, added to my rage. Why should she have the privilege of quietly stepping back into her old position as if nothing had happened? 'Just like before... nothing has changed...' her smug face implied. Yet there had been a big change for I now had a Doubt and a Hate, and as the weeks went by I knew this feeling would not leave me.

It made me wonder what sort of feelings she honestly had towards me. All these years the sweet, calm smile had very likely been concealing something different. She probably considered me the biggest laughing-stock of all South America. I was the poor fool who fed her, housed her, clothed her and even paid her to remain in the family, while she was having her own way with the gentlemen. What a fool I had been.

Even though Donald assured me he had never had secret relations with her the time I openly asked him, I still had my unfortunate suspicions, but we never mentioned it again. My pride would not allow me to question him a second time, so the matter became a closed book between us. Previously I used to enjoy seeing Donald playing with the children while Mrs. Allen looked or joined in the fun but now I detested these moments and always shortened them by inventing different obligations for her.

I knew Sydney's relationship with her had nothing to do with me, but my dislike for the woman made me try to upset even their conversations together. I loathed seeing her as a success in anything and I never missed an opportunity of criticizing her. I spared her nothing.

'Why are the children making such a noise?' I demanded one day.

'They're only having a mock game of tennis with Mrs. Allen,' Donald replied in a disinterested fashion as he read his book.

'They should be in the house by now, it's getting cold outside.!' I exclaimed aggressively. 'Why has this stupid woman not brought them in yet?'

'They're just having a little fun on the court.'

'Their dinner'll be ready and getting cold before they've even washed their hands, if they don't come in soon. She's not sticking to timetables at all.'

'Donny and Ada are getting big now, so perhaps a little tennis will do them good.' Donald was trying to appease my ill-humour with favourable comments, then he sighed and gave me a sidelong glance. 'Are you feeling all right?' I nodded. I realized I was just being unpleasant, so tried to keep my mouth shut.

Sitting there I knew with firm certainty I wanted to be rid of Mrs. Allen but a substitute was essential. And where to find one? Somebody from the local people was, in all honesty, out of the question, due to the language barrier and the culture gap. We still wanted our children to be brought up as well-mannered Irish children even though we lived so many miles from Ireland. The breed and the homeland had strong influence still and I was sure Donald would never agree to one of the native women taking charge.

I'd write to Mama and ask her to look for somebody over there to fill the position. It was not difficult to engage Mrs. Allen seven or eight years ago and would possibly be equally easy to find somebody now.

I lay back on my pillows and relaxed. I could hardly believe my little daughter was born. Four weeks early, this tiny child had chosen to arrive. She was incredibly beautiful with far finer features than any of the others before her.

Mrs. Allen had taken her away to the Nursery to attend her while I supposedly got some rest.

Things had happened in such rapid succession the last two days, I could hardly sort out the details in my sleepy, fuddled mind.

I recalled a long argument with Donald in relation to my idea of getting rid of Mrs. Allen and writing a letter to Mama about engaging another woman in replacement. He had objected strongly to her dismissal, and the more he argued, the more suspicious I became of his motives of wanting her to remain.

The more he spoke in her favour, the more determined I was to be rid of her. His objections simply fanned the spark of suspicion which had been burning for weeks. I became firm. She must go.

This culminated in Donald giving way rather grudgingly because he considered we were being unjust to Mrs. Allen. He pointed out how she was a person who'd never failed in her duties, until this last unfortunate episode. I did not sway.

As soon as my letter to Mama was posted, I felt a balmy relief and a happy conviction that Mama would come up with a solution. I even began to feel slightly more tolerant towards Mrs. Allen as she went happily about her duties.

Before my baby was born, we'd had a spell of very warm weather for July, known as a 'veranillo', or little summer, and I'd decided to spend as much time as possible outdoors with the children. The morning we'd gone down to hunt for ferns for my winter garden, came clearly back to me now, as did the mud near the water's edge where the ferns grew thick, and where I fell flat on my belly. I still felt the mud sticking to my ankles, Donny's shriek as I landed and the difficult struggle to get up and regain my balance. The children had to help me on to the cart because of the pain in my back.

Donald's angry face when he was told, flashed across my mind now. I had to go to bed with the pain, and even though they put warm poultices on it all afternoon, the evening brought little relief. I could not get up; the only comfortable position was lying flat.

The unnatural heat of the afternoon was unbearable, and a huge storm began to form out west. The sun went down early as it reached the edge of the violet-black storm clouds which looked like an exotic mountain range rather than clouds. My window was open and the sultry hot wind blew in moving the curtains slightly. I could smell the odour of impending rain, and the first flashes of lightening were visible in the distance.

I hated these violent storms after unusual heat; they were frightening.

I had asked Willy to pull the blinds and fix the windows before the high wind started. I hoped Alberto had taken the baby animals and sheltered them in the shed. After the rain it was sure to get perishingly cold as July always was.

I saw the children's frightened faces as they came to say goodnight to me. Donny and Ada had been scolded on our return home that morning, for letting me get into trouble which I thought was very unfair. Little Billy cried and clung to me when he was brought into the room. 'There, there.' I tried to pacify him. 'Mummie'll be better in the morning.' He'd gone off sniffing, led by the hand.

I had dozed and woken at short intervals, hearing the distant sound of the gentlemen talking and dining. The dining-room window had not yet been closed as the heat would have been too much for them. Donald and Sydney had spent the day in the new field where they planted hundreds of little trees.

The lightning flashes were increasing... the storm approached. I was terrified... and more so tonight as I was helpless on my bed. I wished the meal would end and Donald come and sit with me; perhaps read to me to ease my mind. The child within me was uncommonly still; I hoped I'd not harmed it when I fell. I dozed. I woke suddenly.

The storm had broken, rain and wind together with tremendous fury. I cried out — Donald came into the room.

The noise of the storm was deafening for there were huge hail stones thrashing down on to the roof, each one sounding like a cannonball. The wind howled and seemed to discover every tiny crack to penetrate as our house shivered and shook.

It was impossible for Donald to read so he simply sat on the edge of my bed and held my hand. It seemed hours before the storm began to abate. It was one of the worst storms I could remember and my whole body was sore with tension. The rain was still coming down in sheets and the gutters belching out large waterfalls. It continued all night.

Towards morning I realized my labour pains had begun. Mrs. Allen was summoned. There was no hope of getting Dr. Owens for the *cañadas* would all be flooded and the passes washed away.

Preparations were made for delivery.

I was thankful it was not my first child. Despite the pain I knew I could keep the situation in hand. Only a little over two hours later my tiny daughter was born, and with her birth, the rain stopped and the first chill wind from the south started to blow. And the merciless, freezing cold south wind blew during the next two days as the temperatures dropped steadily and our house, which was never very airtight, gradually became colder and colder. Added to this we discovered some fireplaces could not be lighted because of the direction of the wind which drove the smoke straight down the chimney into the room. Neither my bedroom nor the Nursery could have the fires alight.

We did all we could to keep the children warm.

I made no attempt to get out of bed other than for elementary toilet measures, for fear of taking cold but our main worry was for our darling new born child. Premature babies had to be kept extra warm and our facilities for giving this comfort were nil.

We called her Celia Jane after my well-loved grandmother fitting for such a beautiful child. The other children were allowed into my room to welcome their pretty sister. Billy, with his affectionate nature, adored her and rushed to climb on the bed for a better view of the wee child resting in my arms. He smothered her with kisses and wanted to hold her.

'No, Billy dear.' I dissuaded him, 'Baby Celia is too small to be picked up by you, only big people can hold her.' In his sweet, docile manner he was satisfied to sit near us and sniff and sniff. His cold was very heavy.

Unhappily the following morning when we picked up the baby for her early feed, we noticed she had caught a cold and was breathing with difficulty. She cried constantly.

'We must send for the doctor at once,' I urged, 'it's dangerous for her to take cold as she's so small.'

Willy went for Dr. Owens once breakfast was over. He rode, for the flooding of the passes made it impossible for the cart to get through. When finally Dr. Owens arrived, he taught us to feed her little drops of sugared water because my milk had not come in. This was difficult and took half the day to give her just a few drops of nourishment. There was also a medicine which had to be dropped into her mouth every four hours. Donald took over the entertainment of the other children while Mrs. Allen and I fought for the life of the smallest one; to no avail.

My darling baby died during the night. With no reserves for fighting her cold, her breathing had become more and more difficult as the hours went by.

Dr. Owens had come again but in spite of his professional care, there was little to be done. He called for Donald and said: 'I'm sorry to say this infant won't live through the night. Will you baptize her?'

Donald agreed to read the Baptism Service himself. The whole family gathered around my bed; the adults in solemn silence, Sydney and Willy with clean hands and groomed hair were just in from work. Mrs. Allen in her spotless apron and sleek ebony hair, held little Billy who was desperately upset being ignorant as to what was taking place. Ada and Donny stood hand in hand with terrified faces, feeling the significance of the moment but not understanding it. The cook and Señora Pintos stood at a respectful distance near the door.

To this day I still hear Donald's beautiful and steady voice reading: 'Dearly Beloved... I beseech you to call upon God the Father, through our Lord Jesus Christ, that of His bounteous mercy He will grant this child that thing which by nature she cannot have — Let us pray...' The prayers were long and the room was getting darker as the evening drew in and the amount of people standing shuffling their feet, made the scene unreal. The baby lay still and limp in my arms. There were moments when I thought she had passed away already, but as I handed her over to Dr. Owens, who then passed her to Donald, I saw her little head move slightly and eyelids flutter. The pure water had been previously poured into the wide silver bowl given to us for our wedding by our great-aunt. I wished they'd hurry, I felt I could take little more. At last I heard the words:

'I baptize thee, Celia Jane, in the name of the Father,
and of the Son, and of the Holy Ghost. Amen.'

They were repeating the Lord's Prayer and then everyone left the room in silence. I began crying.

They took my baby away from me right at the end, and she passed away during the night.

There is little to compare to a mother's grief. The emotion I felt was so intense, my very chest felt as if it would burst. Even after the first downpour of tears, I lay in Donald's arms and sobbed for my lost child. Why had this sweet child been taken from us so soon? For some reason she had been born before her time with no strength to combat the difficulties of life here at Las Palmas. Goodbye baby Celia, may the Lord take you into His tender care.

———————

With the death of my baby, I found I could not face life as it was. I began thinking of our homeland, over a huge expanse of water, oceans and continents, where perhaps I really belonged. 'What am I doing here?' I asked myself time and again. Simply because a very young and foolish girl fell madly in love and married a man embedded in a pioneering scheme, and who came away to fulfil his ambitions, was I here at all. My love for this man made me break all ties with my country and had sent me flying into the unknown.

This unknown was a challenge that we were going to face together. Hand in hand we came 'for better, for worse' and it had worked up to this point. We had built in unison, supported each other in trials, established bonds and friendships, turned the virgin fields into a working farm and a living was being made. All had been well until the dark Doubt came into our existence. It pervaded all conversations, extending its somber cloud and laying in wait for any opportunity to make trouble. And how I hated that Doubt. I detested myself for doubting and everybody else for allowing it to exist. I hated its creation and every thought feeding it and maintaining it alive. I knew I was the chief doubter, so I had to get away from it for it was driving me mad.

Today I walked on and away from the house. The wind was bitingly cold as it lashed my face and forced its icy way down my neck. I shivered in misery. What shall I do?

Do I remain beside this man who's daily becoming a stranger? Do I stay tied to this country now my home for almost eight years? Do I abide under this shadow of doubt and allow circumstances to take over? No.

By this time, I'd reached the little knoll and I could see clearly the rolling fields sloping down to the brook. Well-known land often walked over, ridden over and driven over. Beautiful green open fields which have become so dear to me. The earth was jet black.

My torment went on…. If I leave now, taking my children and returning to Ireland, what consequences would there be? I'd go to the old home, parents, sisters.... There'd be enough backing to keep us from starvation but what would life consist of? How would the Irish folk whom I had walked away from receive me now? Three young children. Separation from the father. Foreign ideas. Restlessness. A failure! The picture was not attractive, and the worry of whether I'd find an occupation for what was I capable of doing other than breeding cattle? They'd laugh at me for this. Women did not do such things...

My freezing hand gripped my woolen jacket tightly on my neck as if in protection from further distress. I breathed deeply the cold, dry air as it lashed my face. A tear rolled down...

Again, if I go now leaving all this much loved land and the man I'd married, what would come of it all? Would the gentlemen merely shrug a shoulder and manage without a woman at all? Or would Mrs. Allen quietly slide into my position with her calm smile leading the way?

I had no replies to my questions. Possibly the only way out was to flee, yet was running away the base of a good future?

The intense silence made me reflect. Men and women of power never ran away from their problems, they faced them and fought them. Did Jesus run away from His temptations in the wilderness? No. He battled with them and gained a victory over His human nature. He stood and faced it all, right up to the Cross — He did not flee.

I stooped and picked up a handful of soft black earth and held it to my nose, smelling the strong earthy odour. It went to the very centre of my body and gave me strength.

One thing was clear, I loved this earth, the farm, this land which had opened its arms in hospitality to us when we arrived. A land with people all putting great efforts against difficulties and oppositions, striving to survive like ourselves, but with hope, expectancy and determination gaining a victory in the end. None of them had fled. They were all here still and when civil wars came and brother rose against brother, still they remained and fought.

I had two Uruguayan children now. This was their land and heritage. Was I going to take them to Ireland to try and make them Irish citizens? Never. They were part of our pioneering, the strongest hold on our lands. The roots. If you pull up a plant by the roots it dies. Was this what I planned?

I sniffed the earth again; it was rich and as cold as my face, and I knew I'd not leave it.

How to render battle against the prevailing evil then?

Pluck out the evil. Of course she must go.

CHAPTER 11

My recovery after childbirth was rapid as usual, the difference this time was my lack of acceptance that my baby was dead.

She had died on a Saturday and since then I went down every week with flowers for her grave, near the outhouses where they had laid her. At present there was only a small mound of earth to mark the place where she lay and a tiny wooden cross that Alberto had made, after he nailed together the small box to carry her wee body away in.

Although I knew it was ridiculous, I had wrapped her up in woolen clothes and lined her little coffin with the best quilt from baby's bed. She looked like a perfect china doll when we placed her there.

They'd not let me see them nail the top down. She was removed from my room once I'd kissed her freezing little face for the last time. The gentlemen and Pintos went over to the burial ground where kind Alberto had dug the grave, and they read the Burial Service.

Last night there'd been a hard frost. On opening our shutters this morning everything was white, reminding me of snowy mornings in Ireland. I decided I'd wait until the frost thawed before going down to the grave, for the frost was perishingly cold on the feet, and was a way of courting dreadful chilblains.

The fires were alight when I came in to breakfast and the gentlemen were tucking in. Mr. Harrison was also there for he'd spent the night at Las Palmas. We were happy to have him because of his cheerful manner and the way in which they secured useful tips from him on farm work. I'd often heard Donald saying, laughingly, 'Come and sit down Mr. Harrison. We want to pick your brains on a small matter!'

'Evie, my dear lady.' Mr. Harrison rose to his feet as soon as he saw me. 'Come and join us at our *desayuno*, (breakfast) we're miles ahead of you, very rude. I'm sorry. I'd understood you wouldn't be joining us on this cold and frosty morning,' he apologized.

'I'd planned to go out early, but on seeing the frost, I changed my mind.' I helped myself to tea and some toast. 'It IS a cold morning, isn't it?' I commented as I sat down. 'Did you sleep well?'

'Like a log.' he replied. Donald turned to him, as if my entry into the room had reminded him of the other man's wife. 'Will Mrs. Harrison be worried as you didn't return last night?'

'No,' he said. 'Margaret knows the rules: she's not to worry until at least twenty-four hours have gone by without a word.' He laughed. 'Years of this sort of a thing have hardened her, so she lives resigned to circumstances.' He wiped his mouth as he finished his tea. 'But I'll be off just as soon as the frost thaws a little.'

Soon Willy rose to his feet and, pulling on a warm jacket, went towards the stables where the cart was under repair, and Donald, Sydney and Mr. Harrison went into the office to discuss tax payments. Left alone I busied myself cleaning and filling the lamps and settling them for the evening. I could hear Mrs. Allen calling the children for their morning lessons. It was pathetic how her gentle voice grated on my nerves nowadays. She was so suave and self-assured, her footsteps light and silent as she glided about the house like a graceful swan. She'd matured with maternity and her natural slimness had returned and this irritated me even more.

I played with little Billy since he was too young for lessons. The thaw began after ten o'clock so I wrapped him up well, and together we started towards the burial ground with the flowers for the week. The dogs, taking it for a walking party, raced and yapped with excitement. Santa leaped and licked my hand and then kept close to Billy protectively — he was a good dog.

We walked slowly due to Billy's age and the damp, slippery ground. The day was beginning to open up and I heard Mr. Harrison calling his goodbyes as he made his way to the stables to saddle up.

Billy and the dogs were in their seventh heaven walking with me this morning, but I took little pleasure in it with my baby laying cold beneath the ground. Heaviness rose in my heart as I stooped to place the fresh blooms beside the cross. The dogs had no respect for the sad mound of earth and Billy stumbled and fell on his face in the heaped earth. I nearly cried, but understood his ignorance of heartbreak as yet, so why add my sadness to his innocent capering.

We continued past the milking sheds, passing the chicken coops where everything looked normal save the fowls looking cold were grouped in one small speck of sun which had reached their pen.

I walked slowly, thinking...

Poor darling little daughter. I felt very far away from home, and I became conscious of my aloneness. The gentlemen being constantly busy, as work on the farm was demanding in all seasons, were not a great company for me. Donald seemed to have recovered from our loss with incredible ease; as far as he was concerned there were plenty more children from where that one had come from. A masculine and insensitive way of seeing it and here lay the difference. A coolness had arisen in our marital life. The burning love for Donald had faded, and this left a huge void affecting my daily life. It was the centre of all my trouble and on grounds of suspicion and jealousy, my coolness towards him grew.

I knew I had to be rid of that woman. Our relationship towards one another had become cold to a point of freezing, only a distant respect remained which I clung to for the household, but I found the situation intolerable and longed for her replacement. Would Mama EVER find a suitable person?

Added to all this depression, another monstrous suspicion had lurked into the back of my mind, one which had been blown away almost before it was formed, but I realized it might well come back to stay. During my deepest depression it would press upwards and try to become a reality. Sometimes there was a struggle but until now it had not raised its satanic head, although occasionally it was dangerously near.

It was shocking how rapidly I'd been able to adapt to suspicion once the seed had been sown in my mind. Clearly I remembered how, soon after the birth of my wee daughter, Mrs. Allen had whisked her away to another room with the pretext of cleaning her up and dressing her. My previous babies had all been dressed in my bedroom where I lay recovering from labour. Why then, on the particularly bitter cold morning, had this woman removed her to another far colder room? Something deep inside me stirred. Its name was Suspicion. In the next weeks this was pushing to become a reality. I knew that if it did, I'd take immediate action against the woman, but there was a Doubt too. I had no proof of my suspicion being true.

I recalled Mrs. Allen's closed face when she returned with the baby, clothed but freezing cold, her little hands purple and her heart-rending cries of anguish reaching my heart. As she placed her by my side Mrs. Allen commented dryly: 'She's a one for making a fuss indeed.' However, once she'd been beside me for a while, and thawed out with the warmth of my body, she hushed and was soon asleep.

Ever since the birth of her own child Mrs. Allen had held the same hostility towards me as I had for her. She had become tight-lipped with resentment, while I was sharp and aggressive with her on every possible occasion. Critical of her work, a sharpness undisguisable in my voice with every command I gave her. At first she had responded with quiet submission, but later, as the weeks went by, she often had a sly little smirk on her lips, and an occasional fleeting look of satisfied superiority which I disliked intensely. What was giving her this confidence? Later I wondered whether she had decided on her revenge. What a macabre revenge too.

Days and weeks of this unspoken tension had taken its toll on me and I found myself in constant conflict with Mrs. Allen or my husband. I had nobody to turn and discuss the matter with.

Now we were approaching the fence separating the house grounds from the larger farmlands, and reaching a gate about thirty metres along the fence. We walked towards it planning to pass through it and walk towards El Palomar, a small abandoned tower housing thousands of pigeons and some other to birds about two hundred metres away. I loved El Palomar and sometimes went and sat in its shade and listened to the bird talk; the rich confidential sounds in the throats of the pigeons and the slight smell of their manure gave me a feeling of being very close to nature. It was rather far for Billy to walk today but if he tired I'd carry him.

Almost at the gate, I was suddenly halted.

I held back the child and called to the dogs.

I'd caught sight of two birds at work in the mud near the gate. Medium sized, rich brown birds. One flew up gracefully to the gatepost and deposited his little load of mud onto a small base already constructed. Could I be right? Yes! They were the well-known oven birds, called *horneros*, starting to build their mud nest on our very gatepost. What a thrill! I had seen countless finished nests in the fields, but never from close up. Now here was one under construction only a few metres from our front door. This was the most exciting thing which had happened in months. For fear of getting too near and frightening the birds, I took Billy by the hand and led him around the other side of the house. Later, I'll come and see how the job is progressing, I thought, without children or dogs.

The building of this simple nest represented very positive symbols to me. It gave me a sense of pleasure I'd not felt for ages. The beautiful oven bird had chosen our gatepost to erect his home. He trusted us. We were being honoured and I was going to be sure nothing would spoil this.

'The *hornero* is a well-known bird all over the country, and is particularly distinguished by its attractive mud nest,' Sydney said when I brought the subject up at lunch later.

'I've seen them out in the fields,' I said, 'but never at such close quarters.'

'Don't get too near while they're building,' Donald advised, 'or you may frighten them and discourage them from continuing their work.' I intended doing my bird-watching from a convenient distance unobserved, so there'd be no problem.

'You love birds, don't you?' Willy touched my hand lightly on the table. They were all delighted to see the change in me and encouraged the talk about birds. It was a relief from all the meals sat through in silent sorrow. A warm glow of sunshine was breaking through.

'Yes,' I replied, 'I adore birds. There's something in their freedom I admire and envy; they reach my soul and bring joy to my spirit.' I smiled around the table for the first time in weeks. 'How lucky to have these so near the house. Will they be safe there?'

'Perfectly safe,' Donald said. 'The *hornero* is a tame bird and an excellent architect. He constructs his nest sagely, economizing material and time, and when the mud is not the correct consistency he adds bits of straw or hay finally making a spherical oven with a curved partition inside.'

'They only use their nest once; did you know?' Sydney asked, 'they leave a comfortable living-place for other birds, such as sparrows, mistos and the likes.'

'I've seen many abandoned *hornero* nests,' said Donald. 'Pintos has one on a shelf in his kitchen.'

During my time of watching the *horneros* manufacture their splendid nest, I noticed my natural happiness returning. This magnificent nest was a material symbol representing the positiveness in our universe, and the birds' calm perseverance while they diligently worked was an example to be followed.

From my hiding place, a strategic position between wild periwinkles and a small cane wood, I watched their work unobserved, and began sorting out my mental condition.

I knew I was cured at last from my depression and I thought the cure had come from the birds' intrepid workmanship, but it was not so. My cure had come out of myself; it always did. At last I began to feel as if I really existed again — for a good purpose.

I could hear the sound of my cows mooing in the neighbouring field and I saw that giving birth and nursing my grief were not compatible with the work of a successful herdswoman, and had it not been for Alberto's constant care of my animals, I might have lost them.

The *hornero's* nest was at last finished, so I went to the field to see my animals. There was a little bull with a partly white face given to me some months ago by Mr. Brown together with two other cows, which I'd accepted without a backward glance or sign of gratitude, quickly removing them from his ownership. I marked them with my brand. Now I watched the little bull for a while and decided he was a fine specimen and would do for breeding in the near future.

Alberto came out of the barn smiling. His black crimpy hair thick on the top of his head, shining more than usual today. 'Buenos dias, Señora!' he saluted me cheerily, delighted to see me taking an interest again. He had questions to ask about the animals and their welfare, and I soon found myself in the grip of the business again.

When we were through I thought I ought to look at my horses and started hurrying towards the stables.

I stopped dead in my tracks.

Mr. Brown, none other than the repulsive Mr. Brown, was here. Already alighting from his trap, his toothy grin showing he had already seen me long before I caught sight of him. He had two more calves for me.

The manner in which this man showered me with gifts was really embarrassing. It had become a habit and now he never arrived at Las Palmas without something attractive for me. I could not refuse them; they were too tempting. I hurried forward to greet him with more warmth than I had ever shown him before. 'Mr. Brown, it's nice to see you!' I called across the patio, forgetting for a second whom I was addressing, my joy of feeling alive again was so acute. He looked at me with some surprise and suspicion. I'd hardly been civil to him since he had over-stepped the boundaries of politeness when he and I had experienced the unusual evening together. He'd also come over to offer his condolences when my baby had died, but I'd refused to see him. At this moment all constraint was gone and I found myself smiling at him authentically, not so much with my pleasure of seeing him but with the calves he brought. They were perfect and identical. He handed me the rope by which they were tied.

Their mother died giving birth. They're twins... for you,' he ended rather lamely.

'Thank you!' I cried, 'they're lovely.' I began leading them away to my paddock. Mr. Brown followed me. I'd hoped he'd take his usual route into the house seeking the gentlemen, but it was plain his intention was to come with me. I handed the new calves to Alberto, and told him to give them hay before turning them loose. My other animals, seen at a distance grazing on green grass, made a healthy picture. I did not want Brown to know the amount I had, but he was quick-witted and gave a little whistle under his breath.

'What a fine lot!' he exclaimed, then asked with sagacity, 'over a hundred?'

'Yes, over a hundred.' I replied inaudibly.

'Don't be ashamed, my dear, I always said you'd make a fine herdswoman. You must go into this in a big way.' His crafty eyes watched me slyly. Suddenly my thoughts were catapulted back to the evening of not so long ago when he'd been rude about Donald and I felt again my loathing for him.

Abruptly I turned on my heel. 'Come and see the gentlemen. They're sure to be back for lunch.' And together we walked towards the house. He sighed: 'You're SO stubborn!' he muttered half under his breath. 'Incidentally, there's a chap called Garcia from over my way who wants to buy fifty head of cattle, and I think he's offering a good price; are you interested?'

At first I was horrified at the thought of parting with any of my animals but I knew there would soon be too many in the field and this create a problem. I had to admit that the principal reason for breeding cattle was to eventually offer them up for sale and make money.

Here was my first offer. I hesitated as we approached the veranda where we could hear the soft droning of the gentlemen's voices as they sat sipping sherry before lunch. It was twelve o'clock.

Before entering the drawing-room I turned to Mr. Brown and said: 'Let me think about it.'

'All right, but don't think too long for good offers have a way of getting snapped up by somebody else.'

We joined the gentlemen.

CHAPTER 12

The anxiously awaited letter from Mama arrived at the end of September on a par with the early spring. Hand in hand with my elated spirits, spring was beginning to show her graces; the flowers were heralding the warmer weather and the birds, vociferous high in the trees, were dropping their twigs all over the place.

The *estancia* (farm) looked beautiful after the winter bleakness; the land now reaping the full benefit of all the rain.

Mama's letter was written on St Mary's Day, the 15th of August. It had taken the usual six weeks to reach us, but the crucial news it contained was to say she had at last located a woman who would satisfactorily replace Mrs. Allen. She said the new governess was a woman of about fifty with a great deal of experience with children. She was working in a local school and had decided she needed a change of environment and wished to settle in a good stable home. Leaving Ireland would be no problem for she had absolutely no ties there.

She sounded exactly what we needed.

I gripped the letter in delight and read it through and through before finally handing it to Donald. Once he'd read it, while I watched him closely, he raised his eyes to mine and remarked: 'Well, it's come. Our little Mrs. Allen will be leaving us now. Are you sure you want this change?'

'How can you even ask?' I cried. 'I've been longing for her to leave ever since she had the child, and you know this, don't you?'

'Yes, I've realized it, and I've often felt you've been very hard on her, and unforgiving.'

'Well, it's the way I feel about the whole situation, and I'm not going to change my mind at this late date. At last the new nannie will soon be here!' I cried.

Mama's words had been: 'Miss Daisy Hall will be leaving Ireland in a month's time (the middle of September) and not before, for she'll be giving notice in the school where she works. Once she gets her steamer, she ought to be in Uruguay four or five weeks later. Hope this suits you.'

As we sat with the letter between us, there was a strained silence. Then: 'Who's going to tell Mrs. Allen we no longer desire her services?' Donald asked tersely.

I thought for a moment. 'Perhaps both of us should be there when she's told, as we were when we first engaged her,' I said. 'We'll call her into the office tomorrow morning and officially inform her she's being replaced as from the end of the month. It shouldn't be too difficult.'

Donald grunted.

'You think she'll take it badly?' I asked.

'Yes, I do.' He wrinkled his brow in disapproval.

'She'll have to accept the change and there'll be ample time in which to find a new position. She can start writing letters as soon as she likes.' I found my voice rising. I was not finding Donald's displeasure at Mrs. Allen's departure at all gratifying. All my old suspicions came crowding back and it made me dismally unhappy. Aloud I said: 'The sooner she goes the better.'

'I'll be sorry to see her leave,' Donald remarked thoughtfully, 'she's become a friend and we're all fond of her in our different ways.'

'Oh yes, extremely fond of her!' I cried sarcastically.

'Come now, Evie love,' he said more graciously, 'let's not get nasty about it, it's nasty enough already I find.' And getting to his feet he left the room, leaving me alone.

I sat there letting the confused affair seep once more into my mind. Was I being unfair to her? No, just supposing she was to blame for our baby's death? My anger rose again to a point of being over-powering.

I jumped to my feet and ran out into the open air. The monster of Doubt would not oppress me.

As I dashed outside I almost collided with Alberto who'd come in search of me. There were three new calves and he needed my help. Thank God for this good, reliable lad. With deep gratitude for his devotion, I fell into step beside him and together we went into the field.

There was plenty of grass and the animals feeding well; since I'd sold my fifty head to Mr. Brown's friend Garcia, the field took on a better aspect. The money paid for the animals was mine.

I felt a surge of pride on thinking of this money. Never in all my life had I owned money of my own, so this was a strange sensation for me. I lovingly fingered the small money I'd made the same afternoon Garcia placed the peso notes in my hands. While feeling reluctant in letting my animals go, the feel of the paper notes and knowing their value was compensation enough.

I carried my money bag tied to my waist, under my garments, where I knew it was safe from idle hands. Some had been spent already, prudently, and the results were noticeable. The seeds and plants for the kitchen garden were growing. The splendour of that particular spring, I'll remember for the rest of my life. The farm was a spectacle of colour and abundance, enough to make a modest farmer feel proud of his lands. The fertile earth was yielding, the trees were growing and sprouting masses of leaves, the orchard was laden with good summer fruit crops and when one walked down the avenue there was scent of clover in the warm sunshine. Things were looking up...

We called Mrs. Allen into the office as planned and Donald informed her of her dismissal. I stood near to him in support and watched her face as she received the news. Not a muscle moved.

He told her she'd have adequate time in which to seek another position, whether in Uruguay or Ireland if she planned to return. She lowered her eyes and all the blood drained from her face. I thought she was going to faint, but she stood perfectly erect and said nothing. Donald paused then, 'Have you anything to comment?'

'No, Sir,' she whispered and left the room in silence.

At last that was over. I'd dreaded lest she make a scene, but she behaved like a perfect lady all through the interview. I respected her for this.

Two weeks later she came one morning with the news of her plan to leave Uruguay and return home for a holiday. The Tomkins had made all the arrangement and bookings for her passage on a steamer which was leaving Fray Bentos for Buenos Aires at the end of the week.

'We'll drive you in the carriage to Fray Bentos.' I graciously proposed being so delighted at the thought of her departure.

'Thank you, mam.' she murmured.

Friday morning, soon after breakfast Mrs. Allen with all her belongings packed into a trunk and a large portmanteau ready for loading on to the carriage, came onto the veranda.

Donald was giving the orders to the men for the day's work and all the family had assembled to bid her farewell. Donny and Ada looking a bit glum for they did not want a new governess. Little Billy, not knowing what was going on was romping wildly on the grass with the dogs.

Sydney and Willy came out of the house with Donald and we were ready to drive to Fray Bentos.

Mrs. Allen was looking pale but composed, dressed in a beautiful emerald green travelling gown setting off her dark, silky hair to perfection, and on her head she wore an attractive fawn-coloured straw hat, holding a sparkling red rose. She looked more like the mistress of the manor leaving for a holiday in London rather than the recently discharged governess departing from her ex-post.

Then the goodbyes started. She bent and gave each child a swift kiss and a demure handshake to the rest of the staff, until she reached Willy and Sydney. Here she flung her arms around Willy's neck and said in a strangled voice: 'Bye Willy dear.' (Had she been so fond of him?) and when attempting to do the same with Sydney, she suddenly collapsed into his arms and began to sob. They clung together desperately, forgetting for the moment the audience surrounding them.

'Take good care of yourself, darling.' Sydney whispered.

'I can't leave you, my love!' she sobbed between tears and kisses.

'You must.'

'I love you. Oh, how I love you!' she cried. Sydney tried to disentangle himself from her embrace. She continued crying.

'Keep a watch over our son... bring him to Ireland for his education... I'll look after him.... Oh, Syd!'

So she had it all craftily planned out, had she? Typical of her slyness, I thought. Sydney at last put an arm around her waist and walked her to the carriage where they kissed lengthily again, and eventually she climbed up, and we were off.

The cloud of uncertainty hanging over Las Palmas since April lifted. I gave Donald a swift hug which he richly deserved and he gave me that wide, warm smile of his and took up the reins masterfully, calling to the horses: 'Giddy up, me lads!'

SYDNEY. Why had he never confessed?

———————

Today Mrs. Allen was safely far away from us, on the steamer taking her back to her homeland, and I was blissfully happy having my husband back in the place he should never have been banished from. I wondered how I could have doubted him; my love had suffered while my jealousy had blinded me. As I hugged him passionately at night on our return from Fray Bentos, I prayed nothing would ever distance us again. I relaxed happily in his strong arms and we were united once more.

When the shearing was over and the new governess had arrived, there was a lot of settling down, but the children took a swift liking to Miss Daisy, and we became normal again with me delightedly pregnant.

Just when the lettuces were reaching their full size for picking, the French beans with full pods and the *zapallitos* (small squash) mostly ripe, the locusts arrived. A locust invasion is hard to describe considering all the emotions you live through and the desperate feeling of helplessness which dominates you as you watch the rapid and relentless destruction of everything you've worked at during the past months.

They were first noticed on a mild December evening when the gardener and I were in the Quinta gathering vegetables for the household. The sun was setting and there was a warm stillness reminding us summer was well on its majestic way.

I rushed into the house to advise the gentlemen but only found Willy. Donald and Sydney were over at Pintos place selling sheep and had very likely stopped to have a 'mate' drink with the Pintos family. Donald had learned to enjoy passing the bowl around while they talked. It was a relaxing time after a hard day's work, he said, and a habit he was beginning to develop, not that he'd ever prepared it for himself, nor did we possess the implements for it. Pintos was an expert and Sydney, after his experience with the old man in the Plaza in Mercedes years ago, considered himself a 'mate' drinker. And so they'd sit round the kitchen table, munching biscuit and talking, while the Señora Pintos boiled the kettle and rocked little Mario in her motherly arms.

When Willy came out to see the locust swarm settling, he said: 'We must light fires, for the smoke often chases them off.' He was already preparing a drum with paraffin oil to make fires in strategic positions, hoping the smoke would drift to where the locusts had settled. Some had already flown away by the time Donald and Sydney returned.

'We must keep the fires alight all night,' Donald explained, 'as this may dissuade new ones from coming our way.' It was a depressing evening and, 'Everybody up early, please,' he ordered as we went to bed. 'We must have all hands ready to fight the locusts as soon as it gets light.' The fully grown ones were not necessarily the biggest eaters, but they laid the eggs and when the 'saltones' (little jumpers) hatched, they ate everything.

The following morning was fine and much hotter. Breakfast was eaten in stoney silence, with no time wasted, and at its conclusion Donald commented: 'We'll go and see what the damage is and plan accordingly.'

Fires were rekindled all over the estancia and we saw the number of locusts which had subsequently arrived was terrifying. Donald sent for the young boys from the Pintos place to beat tins and drums, hoping the new waves of locusts might be discouraged from landing.

I very much wanted to help in this battle but Donald was not enthusiastic about my exerting myself due to my new pregnancy. So I took the children out riding at his suggestion going in our favourite direction, towards the Aquila river. Rich fields of grasslands spread before us, leading to the westward track before the final slope to the river. We did not get very far before we met swarms of locusts heading our way. In some places they were already thick on the ground making the horses' hooves slip, and the cart wheels made squelching noises as they were flattened.

After our morning of reconnoitering, the only news we returned with was that the creatures were everywhere. A desperate war began between man and flying insects! Large quantities of hay were taken from the near stacks, loaded onto the cart, and moved to the worst areas. The hay was lightly spread over metres and metres of fertile land fully planted with crops, then set fire to, in a dramatic effort to kill the *saltones* which were hatching daily. The battle continued...

It was the most despairing time and I felt like crying at the end of the first week, seeing the small impression made on our relentless invaders. What else could we do?

'Let's ride over to Harrisons' and ask their advice,' Donald suggested over lunch.   'The Harrisons are having the same trouble,' Sydney told us, 'Some gauchos passed by yesterday with this news.

They have no better mode nor equipment to fight them than we have.' Donald looked downcast, if the Harrisons had no better way of fighting the plague, no way existed.

There was already a scarcity of grass, the livestock were constantly seen hunting for food and I feared for mine too. It was clear that our enemy was winning the contest fast.

The only item saved from our yearly labours was the wool. The sheep had been sheared and a good sale made to the merchants from Montevideo again this year. Praise the Lord for this! I overheard Donald's comments one evening; 'If we'd not got the wool money, we'd be terribly in the red again this year.' We'd been planning to put on a new roof to the house and improve the old veranda; goodbye all hopes...

I stroked my money-bag fondly; at least I had a little reserve for emergencies tucked safely under my belt, and this gave me a sense of satisfaction. Now the vegetables had all been devoured we'd have to buy some in town. Only the underground roots such as carrots and potatoes were yet untouched. What horrors!

One afternoon we saw the Harrison carriage drawing up in our patio and both Mr. and Mrs. Harrison descending. They'd come to visit in spite of all their troubles. I was happy to see them.

'Come in!' I exclaimed in welcome. 'How lovely to see you.' Margaret Harrison rarely came over unlike her husband who was a constant visitor. She always said she had too much to do on the farm, but today she was here and looking well and serene. How did she manage it? Who would have thought their beautiful place had recently been ravaged down to their last blade of grass, looking at their quiet faces?

'Are you having the same fearful time as we are?' I asked as they crossed the veranda and settled in the drawing-room.

'Yes, they've been bad this year and there's little left for them to eat at home. So we decided to come and visit to cheer each other up.' she smiled.

'We thought a game of tennis would do the trick.' Bill Harrison glanced discreetly out of the window. 'By Jove! We'll have to do some clearing up before the court can be used.' The brown strip of ground which at one time had been our lovely green lawn tennis court was covered with locusts mostly dead. We walked out of the house to take a look and found it to be worse than from a distance but the gentlemen were enthusiastic about playing their game so we ordered a couple of lads to sweep it while we took a short walk up the avenue. We took the children with us, and the dogs came too. Even Trixie. She was a beautiful retriever bitch who'd adopted us some months ago. The Pintos had bought her in Mercedes but she insisted on coming to our farm with Pintos when he came for orders but it became harder and harder to make her go home with him in the evenings. Then one day she had, unbeknown to anybody, gone into the house and was quietly asleep in the drawing-room. When Pintos was leaving he called loudly and searched all over the grounds, getting no response before finally going home without her. 'She must've decided to go back alone,' he thought as he galloped off. That was the beginning of her change of address! Trixie had adopted us. Her great love was Donald and whenever he was in sight she was beside him. She'd taken up a firm position on the rug beside the fireplace at his feet and nobody could budge her from it.

We all took a quick liking to her; she was beautiful and her pale gold coat shone despite the fact she'd probably never been bathed in all her life. We estimated she was about three years old and she was as gentle as a lamb.

During my childhood our family had never owned a bitch, therefore I was not prepared for Trixie's first coming on heat. It became noticeable one day but by the time I was fully conscious of it all the dogs on the estancia were showing an interest in her. The garden was full of angry animals.

Willy came in first from work. 'What's up with all these ruddy dogs?' he asked crossly.

'It seems Trixie's on heat,' I said, 'and I don't know what to do about it.'

'You'll have to shut her in for the night, otherwise she'll be having puppies for sure.' We brought her into the house at night which was a solution, but the next day it was impossible to keep an eye on her all the time; so when I got up from siesta I was hardly surprised to find one of the workmen's dogs loving her ardently beside the barn. He was a medium sized mongrel, a 'yellow dog' and naturally only a few weeks later we saw Trixie was carrying pups.

Today as we walked with the Harrisons, Trixie was heavy and had little patience with the terriers and occasionally snapped at them. Perhaps her time was near, I thought, looking at her broad back.

'What a lovely dog!' exclaimed Mrs. Harrison. I'd like one of her puppies, if you're giving them away.'

'Yes of course,' I said, 'she'll have quite a number and we certainly won't be keeping more than one or two.'

'Well, please keep us in mind.' Trixie had got herself level with the gentlemen only a few inches from Donald's heel. Her adoring glances went swiftly to his unnoticing face as he walked and talked with Mr. Harrison.

We returned via the Quinta, or better said, what remained of it. 'Isn't it a disaster?' I wailed as we paused to look at the remains. This plague had done more damage than any other in our time.

Yet the children enjoyed the locusts. A locust is totally inoffensive to humans, so they felt free to pick them up to play with. I saw Sydney teaching Donny and Ada how to take hold of one so as to avoid being kicked hard by the back legs. The two elder children were entertained for hours playing with them, only Billy hated them. He'd scream if a locust came near him and Donny and Ada enjoyed teasing him by chasing him with one.

'Let's chase Billy with a locust.' I heard Ada enticing Donny into mischief. They ran after Billy thrusting the locusts near his face.

'Ah-ah-a-a-a!' yelled Billy in horror. 'Billy no like.' and he rushed indoors howling. I came upon the scene in the nick of time. 'Donny, Ada, you naughty, naughty children!' I scolded, 'stop teasing your little brother.'

'He's a sissy!' shouted Ada as she scampered out of my reach.

'He's only a baby yet so don't be cruel.' I defended the little one.

'Well, why doesn't he like to play with the locusts like we do?' Donny asked pertly. 'They're fun!'

He rushed again, locust in hand, at Billy who was taking refuge under my skirts, clinging frantically to my legs.

'Stop it Donny!' I cried as Billy's yells resumed. 'I'll beat you if I get you.' But Donny had darted off with Ada midst howls of glee.

'Now we don't know how to begin recuperating our losses,' I complained to Mrs. Harrison on that afternoon.

You'll do what all of us will do,' she was smiling again, 'and we'll forget the past and get our teeth into the future. A positive outlook will do the trick.'

A positive outlook. The very words Mama used in her letter long ago when trying to help me out of my depression. True words.

We dropped behind the gentlemen, so our conversation would be private, and she gave me a very thorough lecture about how to run a successful larder and kitchen. She made me see my priorities in the house and kitchen before those of the fields. She suggested I was using my energies incorrectly by dashing about the fields after my animals, instead of using all that vitality in my home, and ended by saying that a thrifty woman in the home is invaluable to her man.

'Your refusal to take this vital responsibility and make a success of it, is a very unfortunate matter. I believe Las Palmas will be a far greater estancia if it never lacked the essentials of diet. Your responsibility lies here.' She pointed to the house.

After a long pause she continued: 'I understand you're buying and selling cattle and making money, is this true?'

'Yes, yes,' I hurried to inform her, hoping to change the subject. 'I love the animals, and Alberto and I have quite a lot to handle. I've already made a sale.' She nodded: 'It's a man's job, isn't it?'

I'd never thought of it in that light. My animals were mine, most of them raised from babyhood. I saw no reason why a woman could not do this and said as much.

'Yes, it seems natural to you but it's a man's work,' she repeated. 'Think about what I've been saying and see my point. A woman's thrift in the home, is invaluable to her man.'

The gentlemen were changing ends of the court. It looked as if Donald and Willy were beating Mr. Harrison and Sydney, but the revenge match was going to be played before dark.

CHAPTER 13

March 1st, 1882

'Colonel Maximo Santos is the new President.' Sydney brought this news back after spending a whole day in the *Pulperia.* (supply store and bar) The object of his visit had been to inform Don Ignacio, the owner of the *Pulperia*, there was cattle for sale at Las Palmas. Don Ignacio had encouraged Sydney to stay so he might meet the *troperos* (cattle drovers) himself if they happened to come by today. A great deal of news and gossip circulated around the *Pulperia*, and at times it was prudent to remain several hours to hear what was going on in the vicinity, or in the country in general.

'Colonel Santos!' exclaimed Donald, 'another of these military tyrants?'

'He's said to be completely different to his predecessor Latorre, and although Dr. Vidal has held the position of Governor for the last two years since Latorre resigned, it's been Santos who's been doing the ruling.'

'Yep,' affirmed Donald, 'I'd heard that, too.'

Presently Sydney continued: 'And now, since the beginning of March, Colonel Santos has been elected Constitutional President; so he's here for the next four years at least.'

'Unless he's chucked out by some revolutionaries.' A sage observation by Willy.

Colonel Santos' rule and regime began. He did prove to be the complete opposite to Latorre. He was kind and friendly and surrounded himself with men of importance and renowned intelligence, but he was a rotten administrator. His love of wealth and splendour caused great expenses in the government and even though there were people living in poverty, he always had more than enough money for his own extravagancies.

One of the daily newspapers criticized him as being: 'a governor who squandered public money and who was surrounded by followers who took part in his lavish parties, while thousands of humble people were waiting for their salaries already nine months overdue.'

To sum up Santos' government was easy. Negative elements stood out: the squandering of public taxes, corruption, administrative disorders, autocracy, irresponsible actions, lack of definite plans and other abuses exasperated the people causing a lot of unrest. However, in spite of all this, Santos did manage to give the country back a certain renaissance in politics and press, and with this freedom the country emerged from the forced tyranny of the previous years.

These governmental alterations and difficulties caused little change in our small Las Palmas world and I often wondered why the gentlemen spent so much time with talk about all this, when there appeared more imminent problems on our own doorstep.

One afternoon early in the autumn of 1882, I was working in the garden when I heard the sound of hooves in the patio and knew we had company. By the way the dogs were barking, in a lazy sort of welcome, I knew the arrivals were friends. Even Trixie came out of her box where she'd been with her six new pups, already one month old, and trotted out to welcome the guests.

It was the Tomkins. I straightened up and waved a welcoming hand at Emma Tomkins who dismounted from the trap and came up to the house.

'Hello!' I called. 'How nice to see you!' I was honestly pleased to see them, for since Mrs. Allen's departure we'd seen little of these neighbours, and we felt the Tomkins had not been in agreement with our attitude towards her. Long, silent weeks had resulted and a consequent snubbing had taken place.

Emma smiled pleasantly at me, 'What are you doing down there?' she asked half-jokingly, implying I should not be working on the ground with my maternity swell.

I replied: 'Since we had those wonderful rains, I felt I should take advantage of the soft soil to do a bit of weeding. All the plants are sprouting, even if a little late in season; but it's the locusts' fault, isn't it?'

'Oh, no mention of the locusts to us!' she cried. 'We had SUCH a bad time of it; they say ours was the WORST zone; how we SUFFERED! What about you?'

'Beastly,' I affirmed. I reached the veranda and welcomed Jim who was looking well, in summer clothes and his sleeves rolled up to his elbows. He was a person who felt the heat greatly, and was mopping his brow with his hanky, while his mousey hair hung lankly over his ears and onto the nape of his neck.

'Nice to see you, Jim,' I said. 'You've arrived at an opportune moment for we were going to have tea as soon as the gentlemen come in.' As I said this, we saw horses arriving with the workmen and Donald and Willy bringing up the rear.

Emma was smiling, 'Let's have a look at your pretty garden before we go in, shall we?' We walked by the flower beds which had recuperated in the late summer after the locust plague. My zinnias were doing best having grown tall and had flowered over and over again, and my coreopsis had spread wild amongst the nasturtiums together making a colourful array.

She said: 'A pretty garden needs a lot of undivided attention I realize, whether one likes it or not.' She sighed and then added: 'I can't be bothered.'

I walked further away: 'Here are the shrubs which, apart from an annual pruning, look after themselves, and passed the tennis court the periwinkles and violets grow wild — I never have to bother about them.'

While the gentlemen came and washed up, Miss Daisy removed the children and we went in to tea.

'Oh, what a pretty table!' exclaimed Emma as we entered. There was an air of wanting-to-please about both the Tomkins this afternoon which was difficult to understand. However, it was pleasant to have one's work praised.

'Don't get a shock.' I laughed, 'but I've recently learned to make good cakes and scones, so our tea table has improved.'

'How wonderful of you! Where do you find the time and recipes?'

'I've made myself a very useful Recipe Book and most of its contents came from Mrs. Harrison.'

'Ah, no wonder they're so good.' She was helping herself lavishly of the peach jam. I'd taken Mrs. Harrison's advice about getting into my kitchen and found I could even tolerate the drudgery and enjoyed seeing the family benefit from my efforts.

'You're becoming quite a personality, aren't you?' Jim grinned at me over his teacup. 'Cattle raising, I hear, as well as child-bearing again. What next?' He beamed complimentarily at me. I didn't know how to reply to his flattery, he'd never been so attentive before, so I simply shrugged and offered his wife some more tea. It certainly seemed as if we'd been forgiven for our past sins. I was glad. I hated having hard feelings amongst the English speaking people of the district; there were few enough of us and a rupture was keenly felt.

Donald opened a new line of conversation by asking: 'How are things at El Torrado?'

We all knew their farm was far from being a show place but they seemed to keep it going despite all the dirt and squalor. As Emma never got out of bed before noon, she had no time for work, and there had been few improvements since she came out. We differed. We tried to reform or build on every year, and from the original row of austere little rooms we had at first found, we now had a reasonable house with some new bedrooms. There had been improvements outside also, a milking shed, stables and quarters for the workmen to sleep — and a lawn tennis court. We might not have much ready cash, but we had it in property.

Jim was answering: 'We're doing relatively well, trying to keep afloat after the damn locusts' destruction.' He stopped and looked pathetic, but when he got no sympathy from anyone, he went on: 'We're to have some radical changes soon. Have you heard we're expecting a young couple to come and work for us at El Torrado? We're hoping to expand a bit, aren't we Emma?' He handed the conversation over to her, but she remained silent, her eyes fixed on her plate.

'Where are they coming from?' I asked.

'Ireland, of course.'

'How exciting!' I cried. 'Do we know them?'

'They are Colleen and Edward O'Brian. Quite young, early twenties, wanting to emigrate, and Silvia Allen spoke to them about us when she got back.' A chilly pause but then he went on. 'We've been corresponding, of course, and they plan to leave Ireland sometime in the spring, our autumn. We're looking forward to having them, aren't we Emma?' Again he tried to include her but she seemed to have drifted off. She suddenly cleared her throat nervously. 'Oh yes, we ARE looking forward to having Colleen and Edward with us.'

'Good!' cried Sydney suddenly, rubbing his hands together in delight. 'Some more possible tennis opponents for us,' he laughed.

'Hey, wait a minute!' cried Jim. 'The idea of bringing them out is for them to do some work, not only play tennis on your magnificent court,' he rejoined jokingly.

Magnificent court. Another compliment. They were being more than courteous, perhaps making up for the weeks of silent snubbing.

Various questions sprang to mind. Where were the new people going to sleep? Their house was small with only one bedroom, a dining/drawing-room and little else. Whenever Sydney went over and spent the night, he slept on the sofa, but this would not accommodate a new couple.

The gentlemen were speaking lengthily of the many links with farm work that Edward had already experienced in Ireland, and all things considered, he sounded like a particularly useful person. Needless to say it was for me to ask the one painful question: 'Where will they live?'

The Tomkins both started answering together, then broke off and remained silent, hoping the other would go on. At last Jim said: 'We'll have to build them a bedroom as there's nowhere for them to sleep at present.' He paused disconcertedly... 'and now we come to the crucial point.' He stopped and filled his mouth with huge bites of cake, hindering him from further speech. We sat in stupefied silence, waiting for his next words, wondering what the crucial point was.

At last he swallowed and resumed his laborious explanations. 'The problem is we have no money with which to build, but we must make a proper bricks and mortar room with adequate connections with the main house.' Here he stopped again and fidgeted with the food on his plate. 'What do you think, Donald?'

Gradually the impact of what he was driving at, the real reason for their friendly visit, became clear to me. The Tomkins had an economic problem and they'd come over to ask us to lend them a hand. They wanted to borrow the money to build the new room. Borrow off us of all people! Ironic.

I gasped and looked at the gentlemen. Donald's mouth was slightly open which meant incomprehension; Sydney and Willy were obviously more interested in the meal than the conversation, so the shattering implication of Jim's last words were lost on them.

'What do I think of what?' Donald asked.

'What do you think of us building on another room?'

'Umph! You'll have to offer them somewhere decent to sleep,' he replied pensively.

'Of course, and what I thought of asking you, old chap, is whether you can make us a small loan for this purpose?', He cleared his throat, grunted and looked sheepish all at the same time. 'It must be built soon, while the weather is dry.'

'My dear good fellow!' exclaimed Donald in astonishment, 'do you know what you're asking?'

'Well, we thought.... Since you're always.... It's really quite difficult to...' Jim broke off in despair.

I saw the discussion was going to be very complex, and thought it might go off better without the intervention of the ladies. 'Let's go into the garden before nightfall, Emma,' I said rising from the table, 'and allow the gentlemen to speak freely about money matters.' I'd make myself the perfect idiot on this point and let Donald tell the Tomkins we had no spare cash for their improvements.

Our finances were usually precarious but although we'd had a bumper price for the wool this year, it did not mean we had anything extra for generous loans to our less-favoured neighbours. Besides, our excellent wool profit had its reasons. We'd increased our quantity of sheep by almost a third and we'd raised the quality, thanks to some priceless advice from Mr. Brown, making the wool of the best. Hours had been dedicated to sheep this year, and my thoughts went back to all those days when Donald and Willy were out early, rounding up flocks, bringing them up for dipping, and then dosing against worms, before finally returning them to the fields and starting on the next lot. Long days of hard work which had to be multiplied by the hours of hand-curing also done. No wonder there was a consciousness among us at Las Palmas that the wool money was extra precious this year. We'd talked about buying a holiday house in Fray Bentos because of the excellent fishing in the river, but nothing was decided yet.

As Emma and I walked to see my animals, she exclaimed: 'What beautiful animals!' when she saw the four young Jersey calves born about a month ago. Alberto was bringing them up to the shed for their extra evening feed. 'How do you manage to breed such beauties?'

'We have an excellent bull,' I replied, 'and Alberto does a lot of hard work in the fields, especially when I'm pregnant.'

'You're lucky to have him.'

I looked at the dark-haired, stocky man, the Alberto of today, and I mentally compared him to the slight lad who'd come to our estancia asking for work so many years ago.

'How many animals have you?' Emma seemed interested in my work for the first time. She used to rather sneer at me before.

'I've well over three hundred,' I said, 'and next week we're going to rodeo to buy some more for fattening. I'll sell them when they're just right.'

'Who tells you when they're just right?' she laughed. 'I'd never know.'

'I can see for myself when an animal is fat and healthy and will bring in a good price.' I retorted rather briskly. 'Don't forget I've been raising cattle for a number of years now.'

She glanced at me slyly. 'Clever girl.' We strolled back to the house and were just in time to see a beautiful red cardinal perched precariously on our *fiambrera* (meat safe) trying to pick a morsel. The low afternoon sun caught his bright red crest giving him regal brilliancy. Next I led Emma on a tour of the nearby farm and watched her face as she surveyed with speechless admiration the plough land, the hayfield, the orchard (very bare after the locusts) the sheep bath and eventually, as it was getting dusk, we went into the stables and ended our little tour where we were joined by Donny. I asked him about the other children and Miss Daisy and he replied: 'Miss Daisy told me she was going to read them a stupid old Fairy Tale, so I asked if I could come out and find you. She said I was old enough.' He slid his hand into mine and together we stepped inside the quiet stable interior. There was a smell of fresh straw and the sound of low whinnies reached us as we approached the stalls. Rosie raised her beautiful head from her feeding-box and attempted to push herself out of the stall, until I reached and touched her velvety nose and talked to her quietly. It was weeks since I'd ridden and I longed to do so. We heard the sound of soft blowing through wide nostrils and munching of loose hay, but largely the stables were silent. The three of us walked quietly and soon reached the door and pulled the bolt, retracing our steps to the house.

The gentlemen had moved from the dining-room to the veranda and were sipping sherry. At our approach Jim emptied his glass and said: 'Come on, Emma, we ought to be making the long road shorter. As it is we'll have to drive home in the dark.' He placed a kindly arm about her shoulders and beamed at her. 'Never mind, never mind, it's been a good day.'

I sensed he was a little too happy for a man who'd recently received a negative reply to his petition. What agreement had they come to, to make him so cheerful? I dared not think, although I strongly suspected that most of our precious wool money was being carried away in Jim Tomkins' deep and well-lined pockets.

'I can't understand you men!' I flared up when the Tomkins left and I was officially told of the incredible loan, whereby we remained almost penniless and the Tomkins drove off with our precious cash.

Donald took my hand and pressed it to his lips. 'You know how much in need the Tomkins are, and their plan to expand is a good one. Anyway, he's promised to let us have it back just as soon as things start working better for them.' The arrangement could hardly have been vaguer. Although we argued continually over the matter, there existed a frigid finality about it for the money was gone. I was silenced in disgust, until three weeks later I was shown the picture from another angle.

Donald and I drove over to El Torrado to see the building. It had been started immediately; the masons were contracted the day after the visit to Las Palmas.

The Tomkins greeted us with intense pleasure and we were shown the progress in the building. Emma displayed excitement as she directed us over planks of wood and cement heaps. The walls were already up and the roof was to go on the next week.

The difference seen in this couple, their tremendous transfiguration, made me feel better about the loan. At least the money was not going to waste. As Donald and I alighted from the cart and found this spectacular change in Jim and Emma, the ethical correctness of our action rose up before me like a huge and beautiful flower, reaching such positive dimensions, it was difficult to remember us as the prejudiced party.

How had Donald had the foresight? I chuckled, well knowing Donald had no foresight at all; he acted on impulse. He was a man with no guile nor speculation for himself, so he'd given it all away. To him, others came first. I loved him for this beauty of soul and wanted to learn from him how to be the same.

CHAPTER 14

It was an unusual sound for the time of day. It was hard to discern what was so different about the sound of swift horse hooves in the patio at ten o'clock in the morning. A feeling of urgency reached me and I hastily put aside the fruit I was about to peel for the fruit salad, when I heard the unexpected arrival.

I hurried onto the veranda and watched the woodman's cart draw up to the fence, and saw it being tethered with speedy skill. Donald was climbing awkwardly down, helped by the strong hand of Sydney.

They'd gone off early this morning, with the woodman on horseback, to the *montes* (clump of trees) to mark the trees to be felled for firewood. They'd been away about two hours already but I'd not expected them back until lunch time.

The estancia had been quiet in a mid-morning routine with the children in the schoolroom, having lessons with Miss Daisy, and me in the kitchen planning some quick cooking before going to see my animals.

My heart leaped with fear — there was something wrong. Donald was limping and as they reached the house I saw he could hardly climb the three steps which raised the veranda from the level of the patio.

I rushed forward: 'What's happened?'

'It's all right. Don't worry.' Donald raised an arm in a gesture of dismissal while Sydney helped him by the other arm. Donald was suffering great pain; his colour was ashen and great beads of perspiration formed on his forehead. Neither of them said another word, and they made their way into the bedroom where Sydney placed Donald on the bed and began unlacing his boots. I followed closely, my presentiment of something serious clinging to my mind.

'Is he hurt?' I asked Sydney as he came out of the room. He frowned anxiously and put a firm hand on my shoulder, turning me away from the door and pushing me onto the veranda again.

'It's all right, Evie. It'll be all right, I expect,' he said unconvincingly. 'Don't go in there... we must get a doctor as quickly as possible... he's very bad...' He was speaking in rushed, short sentences and gave me another little push.

'But what's wrong with him?' I shouted

'Don't ask so many damn questions!' he shouted back. 'Go and get Dr. Owens — QUICK!' He turned back into the room leaving me alone with my terror. I had to act and I ran towards the stables in the hope of finding the cart but I was more than lucky for Pintos was saddling up to go out.

'Bring Dr. Owens!' I cried as he jumped into the saddle.

'Si, Señora.' He waved as he galloped swiftly in the direction of the village where the doctor attended patients in the mornings. A wave of strangeness swept over me as I watched our foreman galloping rapidly away as if he already knew of the emergency. Had he been with the men when the accident had happened? How did he know? I cursed myself for not having asked him about it seeing that Sydney was so secretive.

The children were coming out of the schoolroom when I returned to the house.

'Mummie!' they called, 'may we go for a ride before lunch?' I caught Miss Daisy's eye and she smiled.

'They've been very good at their lessons today and I feel they deserve a little change, don't you?'

'Yes,' I agreed. 'Perhaps you'd go with them. The cart's in the stables, if you'd like to take it.'

'Let's go in the cart!' cried Donny, 'then we can take Billy too! Let's go to the river and fish.' The idea was attractive and soon there were scampering feet all over the place.

'Be back for lunch!' I heard myself calling. My voice sounded hollow with an echo in my ears. My whole attention was centred on the bedroom door which was still closed.

I don't know how long I was rooted there but eventually I heard the blessed sound of hooves in the patio again.

'Dr. Owens, Dr. Owens!' I heard my far away voice calling. In spite of all the urgency, Dr. Owens appeared calm as he strode in the direction of the bedroom, his 'miracle' bag in hand. He disappeared inside.

I waited dejectedly. What seemed like an eternity went by as I strained my ears to hear something but the only sound was soft medical murmurs, pierced occasionally by cries of pain from Donald, cries no longer loud and strong for his voice had lost its initial strength.

Later I heard that Dr. Owens had not wasted one second before making his dismal diagnosis, and telling Sydney and Willy nothing could be done for him and only a miracle could save him from death.

Here Sydney lost control of himself. His most loved brother lying prostrate, groaning in agony and the doctor telling him there was absolutely no hope of survival, triggered off bitter emotions in Sydney, not to be contended with in a closed room. He dashed out, almost colliding with me, his face contorted with unshed tears. I grabbed him: 'Sydney!' I cried and didn't let him go. He collapsed against me and then, weeping bitterly, the story came out.

While walking through the long grasses in the monte, a snake had suddenly risen up and bitten Donald just above his boot top. Although the vile creature had been beaten off speedily, the damage was done and the poison in his leg. There followed a desperate race back to the house in the hopes of finding an antidote but Dr. Owens said there was nothing in the present day medicine to help, except that of making a deep gash to suck the poison out. This he'd done but to no avail for the poison was already travelling up his leg; the hideous red line was reaching his groin.

'*Madre querida!*' (Dear woman) exclaimed Pintos who'd joined us. 'What a tragedy!' As we looked at one another helplessly, Pintos got an idea and with renewed strength said: 'Our only hope is a *curandera*.' (healer) He spoke with urgency.

'A what?' we choroused.

'A woman of the spiritual world, who does curing by witchcraft — they often cure where the medical man fails.' While he explained this the door of the

142

bedroom opened and Dr. Owens came out and as if by telepathy he asked: 'Do you know of a *curandera*, Pintos?' Medical men usually despised *curanderas* because they were often successful where the doctors failed.

Pintos nodded.

'Go and bring one as fast as possible.' urged the doctor, 'it's our only hope.' The urgency in his voice made Pintos start running for his horse. He went in the direction of his home knowing his wife would find the right person; she knew everything; she'd save the master. Fast, fast, fast, he drove his horse.

With this terrible news spinning in my head, I could no longer remain as a spectator. I had to see Donald and be at his side. 'I must see my husband!' I declared as I pushed past into the room. Nobody stopped me but Dr. Owens touched my arm as I went by and said: 'I won't have any scenes which might upset him. You must be very brave and not let him see how anxious you are. Understand?' I nodded and he continued: 'I've just given him a shot of morphine to ease the pain. Perhaps he'll rest...'

The room was warm and slightly dusk as the curtains were drawn and Willy was standing on the other side of the bed looking gaunt. Dr. Owens need not have feared about my possible indiscretion for Donald was lying with his eyes closed. My terror increased. He looked.... I refused to accept the gruesome reality. I called him by name 'Donald, my love.' There was absolutely no response and when I got near to him I noticed he was breathing in short little gasps.

Willy moved towards me and soon I was resting my anguished head on his kind shoulder. 'Don't worry, Evie, don't worry.' Words failed him. Together we knelt beside the bed and began to pray: 'Our Father, which art in heaven...' My elbows shook as I rested them on my own bed. The bed where for seven years Donald and I had shared the intimacy of married life. The bed where we'd rested, recuperated from sickness, and where our children had been conceived and born. The big grandfather bed we'd brought all the way from Ireland was a noble bed. I loved my bed. I lifted my head and looked about me. The bright brass knobs at each corner of the bed seemed to be smiling at me, giving me hope and courage. They shone and twinkled for they seemed to have been polished recently. Because of their oval shape they reflected in grotesque form.

The children would stand in front of one and stick out their tongues at their own misshapen image and rush away howling with laughter. I'd caught Donny doing this many times; it was a joke on himself.

Now we had something different on the bed. The figure of a man, head of the household, father of the children, leader of all, lying on the bed fighting between life and death.

A snake. How could this be? I knew there were poisonous snakes, only a few in this country, yet the exception had caught Donald. Tears started running down my face and Willy heard my sobs.

'Let's get out of the room,' he suggested and as we reached the veranda we saw arrivals in the patio.

Suddenly it was all confusion. Our dogs reacted disfavourably and tried to attack the strangers. Santa had reached the main wagon, bristles up, growling, he made an inspection of everything. The workmen's dogs were all barking wildly from the rooms down below and even Trixie was stalking aggressively about, sniffing and growling with disapproval.

Pintos and his wife descended from the covered wagon, followed by three gypsy-looking individuals: two women and one man. The man was lean with very dark features. His black hair fell on his grimy shirt and he wore a sullen expression. He disliked the dogs and their unfriendly reception. Any time one of them neared him, he let out sharp and dangerous little kicks.

An elderly woman walked ahead of everybody, afraid of nothing, head held high. She was absolutely circumferential, as wide as she was high and her dark hair was drawn back in a huge bun, pierced with long wooden needles that crossed and looked like a fallen crucifix. She was the *curandera*.

'*Adonde esta el enfermo*?' (Where is the sick person?) she asked on reaching us. Willy and Sydney immediately led her to Donald. Through the half open door, I saw her rip off the covers from his still body and then turned to address her helpers in sharp, rapid terms. Soon they had all the packages inside the room and they closed the door.

I jumped forward with an exclamation of disagreement but the Señora Pintos held me back saying softly: 'You must leave the *curandera* to do exactly as she wishes, if not she won't work,' and she led me gently by the hand to the other part of the house where Dr. Owens had retired to. He knew the *curandera* did not appreciate men of his profession so he'd tactfully hidden in the drawing-room on their arrival.

We all sat down together. The time was half past one and the middle of the day.

The children had long since come back with Miss Daisy from the river but I'd not been aware of their return. Miss Daisy had tactfully given them their lunch in the Nursery and they were having their afternoon rest. A heavy, sultry silence reigned over the house.

I tried to eat the food they brought me but it stuck in my throat, so I went outside again. The air was cooler out here and I could see the door of the bedroom and I edged my way a little closer hoping to hear something. Not a sound, so I crouched on the floor close to the door and here began my vigil.

'How do I find consolation, if there's only desolation?

'There's no more solace to be found...

'Just bent submissive on the ground.'

A long time had gone by when suddenly the bedroom door flew open and the gypsy man came out and babbled something excitedly, totally incomprehensive to me, and he seemed to be wanting some sort of reply. At the sound of his raised voice, Pintos came out of the house and listened to the complaint. He nodded his head which calmed the gypsy considerably. Pintos explained to me the *curandera's* difficulty in getting the spirits to work due to some hindering spirit within the household and until it was removed they would not proceed.

Astounded, I could not imagine which one of us could be the obstruction. Pintos nodded and went into the drawing-room while the gypsy became slightly mollified.

Next moment all the gentlemen came outside and I noticed Dr. Owens was preparing to leave for he had his case in his hand. Pintos drove him home. I heard later the witchcraft did not work while there was a professional doctor on the premises — he'd been the obstruction.

Shortly after his departure a low chant started in the room. It was not a song for it had no tune, yet it had a steady rhythm and soon one found oneself chanting the same thing. I rocked to and fro to this miserable sound.

There was some occasional movement to and from the room, and each time they opened the door I got a glimpse of the interior, which was almost dark as sunset approached. I saw Donald still on the bed, stark naked and uncovered. He had poultices on his upper leg and groin where the poison was making its deadly way. Later they lighted a candle and began brewing some foul-smelling liquid which the poultices were soaked in. When the door opened the next time, with difficulty I understood they wanted some soft material belonging to the woman who shared Donald's bed at night. That was me. I started for the house to comply with their wishes but the hand holding me back was firm and strong: 'The cloth must be of the very best.' I hesitated for a moment; one of my petticoats was in the laundry, my other clothes were in the wardrobe in the bedroom. I returned to the veranda with the plain petticoat in my hand but the woman began shaking her head negatively. Not good enough.

If Donald's life was in play I'd sacrifice anything, so I told her my better clothes were in the bedroom; she guided me inside.

The foul stench of boiling herbs hit me and made me reel and I almost fainted, but when I looked at Donald on the bed he looked terrible and hardly human any more. Rapidly I went to the wardrobe and found my beautiful silk petticoat embroidered with so much love by my darling mother. I placed it in the grimy brown hands of the *curandera* who smiled satisfied when she felt the smooth texture and saw the lovely lace edge.

I was immediately pushed out of the room and at once the sound of ripping could be heard. It was going to be used as poultices for Donald.

Hours went by slowly, painfully, and although Sydney and Willy tried to make me go into the house and rest, I refused and kept my vigil.

I waited. I was determined to be the first witness to news from the room: good or bad. The gentlemen, after eating, settled in the drawing-room to doze. Willy brought me a small blanket and draped it over my shoulders as it got cold at night.

146

Unreality drifted over me the more tired I became. What were they doing to Donald, curing him or killing him? I saw dizzily that Donald was dying. The terrible vision of his coffin being carried out of the room drifted before my eyes. In a fit of terror, I scrambled to my feet and ran wildly into the house.

'They're killing him!' I heard myself screaming. Poor Willy and Sydney woke with a jerk from their light slumber. 'They're killing him!' I yelled over and over again. Sydney gripped me firmly around the shoulders hushing my cries of anguish, similar to what I'd done for him some hours ago.

'They're doing the best they can,' he assured me.

'We simply must give this woman a chance to cure him,' said Willy. 'She's our only hope... we must have faith.' Once I was a little calmer the Señora Pintos came forward and rested her hand on my forearm while she explained: 'This *curandera* has done some wonderful cures. I know her, she's a very strong woman. She must be given a chance to cure him. You know he was on his death bed when she arrived and we must give her our support. She has powers unknown to us. It's our only hope...'

I looked at her in a daze.

'The more you doubt, the harder it is for her to work. Come.' She took my arm and led me to the little table and poured me a strong cup of tea and then we left the room together. She whispered: 'Be brave. Think well of the *curandera* and have patience.

The night goes by...' And she left me alone.

Alone. Not even the dogs kept me company tonight.

———————

As the first grey streak of dawn broke out in the east, a change was noted. Trixie came out of her box and went to the bedroom door and flopped down against it with a sigh. I fondled her ears. It was a good sign; a dog always flees from the presence of death.

Shortly after sunrise I saw the *curandera* standing in the frame of the door. She was smiling in a friendly manner, as if we'd invited her to lunch and she was accepting happily. 'Ven.' she bid me and stretched out her hand to help me up from the floor. The child I was carrying gave a leap inside me. She led me cautiously up to Donald's bed. They'd covered his lower torso with a sheet. His hands lay comfortably at his sides; his eyes were closed. I saw he was merely asleep for his breathing was deep and regular.

The *curandera* smiled as I turned to look at her wonderingly. '*Esta bien.*' (He's alright) she explained, his fever had raged until the early hours of the morning when suddenly he'd broken into a violent sweat and this had eliminated the poison from his body. Then he'd fallen into a deep sleep.

They'd not moved him nor cleaned him up but I could not criticize this extraordinary woman. I felt respect for her: she'd saved Donald.

Seized by a sudden impulse, I stepped forward and kissed her on the cheek in gratitude.

The arrival of the O'Brian's at El Torrado coincided with Donald's convalescence. Emma and Jim had come one Sunday to enquire after his health and were pleased to find him up and sitting out in the sunshine.

'We're expecting the O'Brian's to arrive this week,' Jim told us.

'Oh, is the house finished then?'

'Yes, just about. There are one or two small items of paintwork to be finished but another day will see it done.'

'I expect the place is looking wonderful,' remarked Donald.

'Absolutely lovely.' Jim grinned. 'You must get a little stronger and come and see it for yourself. We hardly know ourselves with so much space — it's a treat.'

The money we'd lent them had evidently been more than ample for their needs, and they'd taken advantage of every peso by adding yet another room apart from the bedroom for the O'Brian's. The house now seemed spacious compared to the little hovel it was before.

I suddenly understood how great were the workings of God, where an accident such as Donald's, with acute worry and drama, could completely erase the antagonism I'd felt about the loan. I wondered how I could have ever attached so much importance to a mere money loan when there was so much else of importance in life. Not long ago I'd been outraged at the Tomkins' cool acceptance of the amount offered them, but now I felt only gladness that they had a decent home to live in. What did I care about the money so long as I had my darling still at my side?

CHAPTER 15

Our fourth surviving child was born shortly after Donald's recovery from snake bite and she was a beautiful baby girl whom we decided to name Celia Jane in memory of her little sister who had not lived more than a few short days.

This little Celia was a strong child with flaxen colouring different to any of our other children who had the unmistakable ginger tinge of the Fitzpatrick's. We decided Celia's blond whiteness must be a throw-back to my grandmother who'd been frequently known as 'Goldilocks' for her golden curls had been similar to those that Celia was fast growing.

Celia being the first baby born since Miss Daisy's arrival, was her favourite from the beginning and I was glad of this extra incentive for her to remain with us. Billy and baby Celia slept in the Nursery with her, while Donny and Ada had gained their independence when the sleeping quarters were enlarged, now having a bedroom of their own.

The subject of their education was frequently on our lips. Although Miss Daisy was capable of teaching elementary reading and writing, and introducing simple arithmetic, history and geography, we knew this would not be sufficient for a lad nearly ten as Donny was. It was clear he'd sooner or later have to go to Ireland to be educated. The old homestead Carriehall was still there and my single sister Ethel lived there with our parents, so it ought to be easy for Donny to go and join the family and attend school nearby.

Then, to disrupt this happy domestic scene, we received the sad news of the death of darling Papa. He'd been ailing for over a month after his initial stroke which had left him half paralyzed. Mama had written telling us how he was now disabled and they had to get some nursing help during the day. Papa was not resigned to this situation and seemed constantly unhappy. One month later the telegram telling us of his death reached us.

During 1883 we built our big hay *galpon* (barn). To economize in the cost, the gentlemen built it themselves. They sought advice from people in the village as well as from Mr. Harrison who came over frequently during the construction helping with his ready experience. Every spare moment from the working day was spent building the hay *galpon*.

Donald and Sydney were chief constructors, while Willy took over more animal care but he also put in hours of work when necessary. After weeks of toil, we had a splendid barn. The day the roof was put on called for great celebrations as was the custom in this country.

They built a huge open fire and cooked meat for everyone on the establishment to enjoy. Wine flowed like water and we all became very merry, but the roof was on and the barn almost finished — lots of cause for celebration. Even the women and children were included in the festivities and the entire day was spent eating and drinking.

As usual Miss Daisy was a great help with the baby, who we'd brought down to the site in her pram during the morning. Later, however, as she did not settle for her siesta under the trees Miss Daisy removed her into the house where she slept quietly.

Some weeks after this day of celebrations, the hay *galpon* was completed and a busy time took place with the work of filling it. The hay had to be brought in before the rain.

That Monday it was fine and dry with the temperature rising and by midday Tuesday it became fairly obvious a storm was forming, so we had to increase the tempo of the work if it was to be in before the rain. All hands were put to the job, including the animal people: Willy, Alberto and myself. We worked hard for the next two days; a lunch break and short siesta were the only pauses from sunrise to sunset. Every moveable object, from the woodman's cart to the garden wheelbarrow, was put to transport the hay into the new premises. The cart went into the far fields with one of the gentlemen and two workmen, while the rest of us laboured in the near fields and paddocks. Sydney and Willy did most of the stacking in the barn.

Alberto and I worked together. He would push the empty wheelbarrow to the hay field and then together we'd fork it up until the barrow was full. I was amazed to see how strong Alberto was, as he pitched the fork I watched his arm muscles contract and he did the work with remarkable ease. It embarrassed me to find I could not lift a quarter of what he picked up and after five minutes of work I was sweating and panting, while he was still cool and energetic. I laughed: 'How strong you are, Alberto.'

'Señora, I work all day with my hands and arms, it's not surprising I've developed strength.'

'Of course,' I said as I looked at him in a different light from the habitual. The young lad who'd come to us many years ago, thin and slight, had since become a full-grown man of twenty-five. The hard work had afforded him a beautifully formed body, muscular and sun-tanned. His black curly hair which he kept clipped very short, shone like a crown on his head. I idly wondered who cut his hair — it might be fun to clip those dark curls, so different to cutting the gentlemen's hair which was one of my constant jobs. With these thoughts, I had stopped working and was lazily watching his virile movements. He became aware of this suddenly and turned and smiled at me.

The smile was dangerously dazzling. For the first time I noticed his beautifully even white teeth and a wee dimple at the side of his broad mouth. Our eyes met for a brief second but I turned quickly away and began lifting hay into the barrow again. What I'd read in his eyes could in no way be allowed.

Presently we made our way back to the hay *galpon* in poignant silence.

It was drawing near the end of the day and an opportune moment to stop work. I'd be in time to see the children before they went to bed. I'd read them a bed-time story.... Basically I was looking for excuses to be far away from Alberto. I wanted to quench the fire I'd seen in his eyes; I wanted to pretend I'd never seen it.

Right now Alberto should go to the animals, so I told him briefly to stop working the hay. We both left the hay *galpon* in different directions.

'Goodnight, Alberto!'

'Goodnight, Señora!'

The hay *galpon* became a tremendous asset once it was finished and well stocked. We made less and less use of the little shed beside my field. Alberto had complete command of this shed, and I suspected he slept his siesta in the coolness of its interior, though I'd never been down to find out.

The new *galpon* had great attractions being cool in summer and the scent of fresh hay mingled well with the smell of new wood from beams and rafters. I loved this barn and often found myself going down there for some peaceful moments. The children also enjoyed it for here they were allowed to run wild, climb the stacks of clean hay and jump daringly from one level to another. Our trips there became more and more frequent and these visits often replaced a cold damp walk which we'd otherwise have taken.

My success as a herdswoman increased. My cattle had my special mark on them now and were easily distinguishable. The gentlemen still considered my work a capricious whim and always humoured me with my requests. Only one person approved wholeheartedly and that was the detestable Mr. Brown.

Naturally I enjoyed my success and loved the work. I had Alberto to do the hard labour and I made a lot of money. One day there'd be enough to build a new house. I was tired of the rain dripping into most of our rooms. We needed a new roof but if a new house was possible, so much the better.

After the O'Brian's arrival at El Torrado they became frequent visitors at Las Palmas. A charming couple, they met with approval by all members of our family. Colleen was lovely, tall and willowy and when she walked her slender form swayed as if caught in a breeze. She was blessed with the typical colouring of the finest Irish beauty: hair as black as ebony and eyes a mid-ocean green. Her lively face suggested a sweet nature and Edward had a spark of joviality which made his rather ordinary hazel eyes shine when he spoke. He was also tall and thin and younger looking than his twenty-four years while Colleen might have passed for the same age instead of her mere twenty-one.

'How are you settling down?' I asked Colleen one afternoon they had come over to play tennis. The gentlemen had made up a foursome and a hard and exciting game was in full swing, while she and I sat under the trees. The dogs sprawled on the soft rugs we'd brought outside.

'Quite well, thank you,' she replied. 'Edward has his duties and is busy from sunrise to sunset but I'm the one lacking an occupation. I find the days endlessly long.'

'Don't you like gardening?' I asked. 'In homes like these there's always plenty to do in the garden, so you might fill in some morning hours making a flower garden.'

'I've spoken about this and Mrs. Tomkins agrees. It's pretty barren just now since the builders left cement remains which have to be cleared away.' She paused and gave me a small sidelong glance, wondering if she dared say what was uppermost in her mind. She took courage and went on: 'You must know nothing gets done rapidly over there and it's made worse with Mrs. Tomkins sleeping all morning.'

'You're right there!' I exclaimed. 'I can't understand anybody being able to lie in bed all morning when the weather's good.' I watched her face as I rocked the baby's pram gently to and fro hoping she'd sleep again. 'What's stopping you from beginning a flower garden then?'

'Well, we must get some of the men to shovel away the rubble left by the builders before we can start anything. But none of them have volunteered to do the job and that's three weeks ago already.' She sighed, 'it'll be Christmas before we even get started.'

I thought a bit: 'Perhaps I might go over with Alberto. He'd not mind taking a little time off from the animals and giving us girls a hand — he's so strong.' I smiled, remembering his recent work with the hay. I was sure he'd be more than delighted to ride over and lend a hand there.

'Oh, I couldn't dream of asking you to help, you have enough on your hands here.'

'No need to ask,' I replied, 'I'm offering!' While it did seem absurd for us to go and shovel rubble to get the Tomkins garden looking decent.

The tennis was over and 'Game, Set Match!' was called. Baby Celia began to cry as we sprang to our feet, clapping the winners and simultaneously pushing the pram into the house.

The subject of the Tomkins garden was reopened over the tea table and was finally decided we all go over to El Torrado after tea and do the job.

What a success it was! Actually there was not very much to be moved away, the cement was a mere thin coating and once broken up, it was easy to carry away to the dump. Everyone put their hands to the picks, hoes and spades and before the hour chimed it was clear and fresh earth brought up. We left the planning of the garden to Colleen.

We were offered cool lemonade on the porch once the work was done and Emma, having served the drinks, reclined in the rocking chair as if thoroughly exhausted and sighed: 'I always tell Jim the Fitzpatrick's are like tornados; only mention the job and zoom... it's done!' She beamed around the group. 'Thank you for coming and helping clear up. We were going to do it, but...' her words trailed away.

The arrival of the young O'Brian's in our area marked a new period in our lives for it coincided with the tenth anniversary of our residence here. These two facts had a strange effect on us at Las Palmas. Up to now we'd been the youngest settlers in the region. People respected us for our ambitions and showed us kindness and friendliness always. They were willing to help in all circumstances because we were the young 'gringos' who'd come to make good in their land. Our presence was an honour to their country and we were popular and attractive to them.

The men who owned the *Pulperias* (General Stores) were generally most respectable persons. The *Pulperias* extending throughout the length and breadth of the country and for a lapse of more than a century before our arrival, were also known as places of trade and supply houses.

In the very primitive days the *Pulperias* were the only places where social conviviality existed. Here raw brandy or wine was drunk as a form of 'killing time' while waiting for a friend or client. Many a long day Donald and Sydney had spent at the *Pulperia*, talking business, haggling over prices and later buying provisions.

The shelves of the *Pulperias* were well stocked and neighbours and travelers found everything to satisfy their elementary needs. There was, naturally, a greater concentration of *Pulperias* around a church or a new village, but it's equally true that *Pulperias* appeared in strategic points as the territory opened up: on river banks, at cross roads or on small hills. Often in the melancholy loneliness of the open fields, one might have seen a flag flying on the end of a cane stick, indicating to passing travelers the tempting presence of a *Pulperia*.

The Uruguayan *Pulperia* was transformed long after the Guerra Grande. The dangers and risks of that war period obliged the store-keeper to assure not only his capital and work, but his very life, behind a protecting grille, sometimes reinforced by a wire screen. Clients were attended to through vertical iron bars also reinforced with two or three transversal metal plates.

The *Pulperia* nearest to our farm and the one most frequented by the gentlemen, had a thatched roof shelter for the horses a little distance away from the main building, as a protection from the weather conditions. Here then, in the interior of these very picturesque *Pulperias*, was virtually the only point of contact between men. Here friends or foes were made, horse races discussed, the local market talked of, messages received and songs sung. Only by the charm of a guitar were voices hushed and the noise of glasses silenced, card games postponed and dangerous knives put away.

It was not altogether surprising therefore that Donald, Sydney and Willy were, after so many years, well-known and respected clients at Don Ignacio's *Pulperia*. On our arrival the owner of the place had been extremely protective towards our gentlemen, giving good advice against dishonest transactions.

The change came when Edward O'Brian first went to the *Pulperia* representing El Torrado in a cattle sale. Over the course of the years the Las Palmas people had learned the tricks of the trade so Don Ignacio had gradually flagged his protection but when Edward first walked in there, the full attention was centred on him.

'It took me back to our first visits there,' Donald remarked. 'Don Ignacio dropped what he was doing and came to meet the new arrival.'

'How did Edward take this rather suffocating attention?' I asked.

'He took it well and found it as helpful as we did.' Don Ignacio had protected us from all dishonest dealers until we found our feet. History was now repeating itself with Edward and so it would run its course, we knew full well only the very best would come of advice given by Don Ignacio. He was the middle man. He granted us favours in exchange for our faithfulness as clients at his store.

Jim Tomkins had never done much about his cattle sales but now Edward had different ideas and saw that a few trips to the *Pulperia* were going to make changes in favour of El Torrado's production. He'd pointed this out to Jim, who'd agreed, on condition all extra work involved was done by Edward. The O'Brian's, young and dynamic, were bringing improvements not only to the house and gardens but also in the farm with consequent financial gains.

No more boredom for Colleen; her flower garden had taken shape. It was discovered she had special gifts where plants were concerned, and even as I had originally given her seeds and shrubs to get started, soon it was she who was providing me with new and pretty plants.

CHAPTER 16

When the mail came in from Ireland the following month I received word that Mama would not be coming out to visit us. Her letter was full of love and apologies and she said: 'You must remember I'm now an elderly lady and the thought of such a long journey terrifies me.' She went on to explain how busy she was going to be in the near future for the sale of Carriehall was being considered. She and Ethel were finding it too large and because it badly needed repair, they knew they were not able to put up large sums of money for this.

They'd already reduced their quarters by shutting off the entire upper floor, the ground floor alone was still too big, dark and cold for them alone. What was my opinion?

How strange it all sounded, not having lived there for ten years. My memories were of a house of great comfort, rooms ringing with laughter and little feet constantly thumping up and down the stairs, more fun and warmth had never been found in any other house.

How distant it seemed now being called cold and dark. How could any of my family possibly want to be rid of the darling place?

I knew time had gone by and all members had gone away. Caroline and Papa had died within its walls. Flo and Ada and Hubert had married and gone to their own homes, I had left the country and so there only remained Mama and Ethel. I supposed it must be different now but I wanted to remember it as it had been when I was a child.

The house, standing gracefully in its own parkland, called in welcome as one drove up the winding drive. The two storeys of walls were covered generously with creepers which drooped languidly over the windows, dimming the rooms in some cases. The small windows at ground level, seemed to wink when the lights were on: the lights from the scullery, basement and box-rooms. Forbidden rooms for the children, but the mystery of these chambers was eventually revealed when I'd finally selected and removed my travelling trunks for my emigration to South America.

Suddenly everything was to change.

The house was being ranked as old, cold and dark. I could never imagine it described in those terms. Was our beautiful homestead going to be turned over to some unknown buyer for cold cash? Mama had said we ought to be practical and now was the time to sell the property and buy another smaller one. The money left over would be distributed equally among the children to use as they thought best.

Mama wrote: 'You are all adults now; I feel this will be a way in which to help you in your different spheres of life.' She reminded me Ada and Flo had money needs with their growing families. 'I suppose you, with all your wonderful acres of fertile land, are the one to need the Legacy money least,' she said. I laughed ironically. How distant and unknowing we were of each other. Neither of us fundamentally understood each other's situation. She thought I didn't need any money to live in Uruguay and I felt she had no need to sell our beautiful old home just because it was partially empty. The gap was widening. Years of separation were beginning to tell. I had to give it a lot of thought before replying.

Memories came flooding back.... Smoke curling from the chimney as I rode home in the trap from school and the delicious smell of fresh toast as I pushed open the kitchen door to find Cookie standing patiently by the stove making our toast for tea. Hungry and cold, here was the haven I'd been looking forward to all day long. Something warm to drink and eat and my own family around me. Mama's soft footfall on the stair, the rustle of her gown as she came from her bedroom where she'd been resting while we were at school. Her lovely warm smile and gentle hands as she stroked my hair and laughed: 'My goodness Evie! What a mess you do get into at school, dear!' she'd gently chaff me while she cuddled me. This was the warmest and dearest moment of my early school days: my mother and my home to come back to after the long and tedious hours facing the teacher.

And now, more than two decades later... 'Mama, oh Mama darling. How little you understand us here. How surprised and shocked you'd be if you saw the tubs and pans out catching the rain drops in our house in bad weather. What would you think of our rough old veranda I've never been able to renew as I swore I would when we first arrived? What would you say when you found we have to walk thirty yards to our nearest latrine in all weather? Would you still say we had no need of money?

We need a new house and only hard cash can build it. I think we are the ones in most need of the money. The amount of pounds sterling, whatever it was, would turn into many thousands of pesos and enable us to build. Great though our need was, I still held back from approving the sale of our Irish home. To me with all my happy memories, it seemed a crime to get rid of it.

The miles between us spread before me like an entire world. A world of obstacles and difficulties, and of no solution.

I found myself sobbing into my pillow at night when everybody was asleep, my thoughts still whirling in my tired head. I knew morning would bring nothing new and my family was waiting for my approval of the sale. They'd never sell it without my written approval. In the morning I had to write the letter for it was my decision which would finally deliver my beloved Carriehall into the hands of strangers. A voice within me said: 'Grow up, Evie, grow up! It's time for change. Part of the money will come to the new continent and make a home for those of us here.

Las Palmas will benefit from this sale. Part of Carriehall will be transported over here and will continue to shelter the same family.'

I made my decision.

The new Las Palmas would be similar to our old Irish home. We'd construct a place worthy of the graceful old beauty which is to provide the money.

As the dawn broke I sat down and wrote my letter to Mama, giving my approval of the sale. Tears ran down my cheeks as I wrote (I felt like a traitor) yet I knew it was the only practical solution.

The sale would not be a help as far as our children's education was concerned but the possibility of boarding schools was also in consideration. They'd go down to the new cottage for their holidays. I could not hinder my mother's life in order to benefit my children. This sale concerned many young lives, the decision had to be magnanimous...

Houses, houses, houses.... Contrary to what one would have thought of people living among fields, hills and vales, the importance of houses was immense and the emphasis placed on housing was as great as that placed on life itself. I was counting the days when we'd have enough money to build a new house. The Tomkins had a partially new house and a great deal of importance had been given to it as we all knew. There was also the question of a house to rent in Fray Bentos for our holidays...

When Donald came back from a day in Mercedes, early autumn after the particularly hot and dry summer, he told me he was planning a short holiday in Fray Bentos, the charming little town on the coast of the Rio Uruguay, just the other side of Mercedes. I had not visited Fray Bentos often but it was where we'd landed many years ago.

'Why Fray Bentos?' I asked.

'In Mercedes today I met an old acquaintance, Peter Miles, and we stopped for a quick drink together before taking the road home.' He paused and smiled mischievously. 'Peter was telling me about the excellent fishing in the river there.'

'Really?'

'Yep, they live in Fray Bentos and often go on the river to fish. He suggested we go for a few days to see about renting a house for next year. He told me there are many British families working for the *Anglo Frigorifico* (cattle slaughterhouse) so we'll have a chance of making new friends.'

'Oh Donald, how lovely!' I cried, 'it's a gorgeous idea!' I flung myself onto his lap and my arms encircled his neck. 'Fishing or no fishing, it's still a wonderful place for a holiday.' I kissed him and tweaked his nose.

'Hey, gently now!' He warded me off, 'it's the only nose I have, you know.' But his arms were around me in happy reception of this sudden joyful outburst of mine. It had been a long time that I'd been wanting a holiday and change of scene.

'Yes, yes, duckie!' I squealed, 'we need a change.'

Soon we began making plans and eventually decided to go without the children, making it easier to find lodgings and discover the prospects for the coming year. When the entire thing had been discussed fully we included Willy while Sydney remained at home in charge. Sydney agreed to this and Miss Daisy was to manage the children.

We left on Wednesday by cart with an air of holiday spirit among us, so we sang some of the old favourite songs as we drove along. It was good to be away, bounding along the rough road in the uncomfortable old cart with prospects of entertainment ahead.

I took an instant liking to Fray Bentos. It was an open and fresh town built on the banks of the wide Rio Uruguay with its port, adding some important activity to the town.

We found rooms in a hotel without difficulty and the gentlemen were up early next morning to fish. It had been arranged that Peter Miles and his wife were coming to have dinner with us at the hotel later.

'This is my wife Evie and this our cousin Willy.' Introductions were speedily being made once they arrived. 'My wife Margaret, but we always call her Maggie.' Peter was a pleasant forty-fiver and Maggie slightly less in years but much more in weight. We made friends instantly and before long we felt as if we'd known each other for ever.

Peter ran a hardware store which was his full-time occupation and this was why they lived in Fray Bentos. Maggie kept house for her husband and three large children who went to the local Uruguayan school where they'd learned Spanish quickly and read and wrote it correctly. Their English had been handicapped a little but this was not a problem to their parents.

Peter and Maggie were the most happy-go-lucky people I'd ever met. Most of our time with them was spent laughing, and although sometimes I felt they had their priorities mixed, it was very refreshing to be in their company and we soon found ourselves immersed in their good humour.

When asked what I'd spent the morning doing, I replied: 'After getting up a little late, a change from my usual routine at home, I walked into the heart of the town to see the shops and do some shopping.'

'What did you buy?' Maggie asked.

'I got some nice flannel shirts for the children.' I stopped, hesitating while wondering how my next confession would be taken by the present company, but I decided to go on: 'I was looking for corsets, but couldn't find anything approaching what I wanted.'

Maggie let out a bellow of laughter which caused more than one head to turn in our direction in the lounge. 'Did you hear that one Peter?' she boomed, 'this young lady was out looking for corsets!' All heads were turned towards me and for an instant I wished the floor would swallow me up but there was pure amusement in their faces. Peter looked me up and down.

'My dear lady, if you're ever successful in finding corsets, please send them over to our house — they're badly needed here.' Maggie took no offense at this impolite insinuation and roared with laughter herself.

In Fray Bentos with the Miles nobody ever was in a hurry, few time-tables kept to and we came and went in a tranquil fashion and still things always worked out.

Willy was fascinated with Maggie and when they were together they laughed and joked in a manner I'd never seen in Willy before. He drank more spirits than he normally did at home which cheered him and made him witty. I was equally surprised to find he had a store of funny, and slightly naughty stories he could run off at a moment's notice.

'Have you ever heard this one?' he asked Maggie and he began telling the tale: 'A friend of ours had just finished playing tennis at his Club, and he had to dash away to catch his train home, with no time to even change. Once on the train he noticed he still had a couple of tennis balls in his hands, so he stuffed them into his pockets. As he sat on the seat in the train, the tennis balls became uncomfortable putting his hands into his pockets he tried to accommodate them. Soon he noticed the lady opposite him in the railway carriage was absolutely intrigued with his antics, and could not take her eyes off him; so much so he felt he ought to offer her an explanation. He smiled nervously and said: 'My tennis balls!' She raised her eyebrows and looked surprised then said: 'Oh, I'd heard of tennis elbow, but never tennis balls!!'

Donald and Peter Miles became close friends very quickly. They spoke on all sorts of incredible subjects and Donald was getting some important tips on life in Fray Bentos. He learned, for instance, it was practical to travel to Buenos Aires from Fray Bentos because the steamers went over every other day, making it simple to get passages and visit the city.

'Everything is available in B.A.' he told us, 'from prize bulls at the Palermo Show to kitchen knives, clothes for the family, furniture, exotic foods, and perhaps even corsets!' I'd still not been forgiven for my confession. Donald and I made a mental note of paying Buenos Aires a visit in the near future to do some shopping.

The week in Fray Bentos sped by and before we knew what was happening, it was time to return to Las Palmas.

One thing we learned was that the catch from a boat was far more plentiful, so Donald looked into the possibility of buying a boat but was put off by the high prices.

'Why don't you make one for yourself?' asked Peter. 'There must be plenty of space for such a construction at your estancia, so why not try it?'

Donald's face brightened. 'That's a good idea!' he exclaimed. Discussions on the lines of how long it might take Donald to fabricate such a vessel, what dimensions it would have, what materials would be needed and where to buy them, followed this suggestion. The main bulk of materials would come from Peter's store it was decided, and Maggie became excited. Rubbing her hands together delightedly, she said laughingly: 'This is one of the best arrangements I've heard for years. We'll sell them the merchandize and we'll take it out to their farm and spend some days with them. Business and pleasure combined!' she cried.

These initial plans were made for the boat's construction, but before long it was realized none of them knew much about sizes and materials, so very sensibly they got the boatman from the riverside to assist. When all details were affirmed, Peter made price estimates and Donald placed our first order before leaving Fray Bentos.

CHAPTER 17

By the end of May of 1882 the weather had turned bitterly cold and exceedingly wet. I didn't remember so much rain so early in the winter before.

As the year advanced, the country was struggling under the erratic rule of General Santos who, in his extravagant and excessive way, managed to achieve only some few things. There was little progress made in the country for he continued squandering public money to such an extent making the people exasperated and consequently four small revolutions broke out.

Even as we cursed the excess of rain and lamented the country's instability and unrest, we were thankful for our well stocked hay *galpon.* (barn) Our work of the past months was being rewarded and we had reserves for our livestock.

The riding horses were being totally fed on hay from the barn. Alberto was constantly seen carting barrowful's over to the stables, a heavy job which everybody thankfully left in his capable hands.

The hay *galpon* continued to be my great place of peace, and sometimes when I felt a little low I'd sneak off for a few hours there to read. Towards evening I knew Alberto would come in and we'd have a chance of discussing cattle movements for the following day.

Sometimes Alberto called a young lad from the milkman's post to come and lend a hand due to the large quantity of animals now. 'It's good for these boys to begin working,' he said one day. 'Sooner or later they're going to be sent into the fields by their parents, and they won't know where to begin. Coming here they'll gain experience, working beside me.' He smiled his wide, clean smile and added: 'And they are a help.'

'Do you find the work too much?' I asked, astonished. It was the first time I'd ever heard him insinuate there was too much to do. 'Would you like a permanent help?'

'Oh no, Señora!' he exclaimed. 'It's only that I want to help the boys. They'll begin to like the work and then they can get a job on another estancia and start earning their own money.'

'You're training them?'

'Yes.' He stopped and looked away, out of the window, as if seeing the past again. 'I want them to have some abilities of their own and know how to work the animals and not start from the bottom as I had to.'

'But Alberto!' I exclaimed, 'you seemed so experienced, as if you'd worked all your life with cows and horses.' I thought back and remembered how decisive he'd always been and I'd taken it for granted that he knew.

He laughed: 'It may have seemed like it to you but it was not really so.'

––––––––––

Two weeks later Sydney came back for lunch with three new born calves found motherless. It was drizzling and extremely cold. The little animals were in poor shape and could barely make the long trek home; the smallest collapsed as it entered the patio and refused to get to its feet again. The other two were led into the shed near my field and I called Alberto to decide what to do with the wee one on the ground.

'It needs special attention; perhaps we can leave it in the hay *galpon*?' he questioned Sydney, as it was not a normal procedure. The little shed was half under water by now and this calf had to be kept dry if it was to survive.

'That's all right,' said Sydney after a moment's hesitation. 'He can be in there until he can stand alone.'

Alberto picked it up bodily and strode away to the barn. I'd have liked to go with him but lunch was going to be served and I knew Donald preferred me attending to the family instead of caring for a new calf.

'What a filthy morning,' Donald commented between mouthfuls of Irish stew which the present cook had at last learned to make well. I'd spent many patient mornings teaching her and eventually she realized Irish stew, made correctly, was a delicious dish.

'Did you see the calves I brought up for Evie?' Sydney asked.

'Yes, where are they from?'

'From where the big *cañada* (small stream) runs through. All of them had lost their mothers — hopeless cases. The smallest looks very weak to me, I doubt whether it'll survive.' Sydney reached for some bread and began mopping up his gravy. I wished they'd hurry so I could go to the hay *galpon* and see for myself how the patient was doing.

Presently the meat plates were taken out and the dessert brought in. This girl even waited nicely at table. She was from the village and was working out well; she was gentle in her movements, yet quick and neat, and she soon disappeared quietly through the door into the kitchen but not before Santa had slipped between her ankles and rushed under my chair. He hated the rain and usually found his way into the house in damp weather. I suspected this maid of having let him into the kitchen. The convenience of the connecting door between dining-room and kitchen had been a recent addition; the food now reached us hotter than when it was brought in via the veranda for so many years.

The gentlemen were still talking and eating bread and cheese, a custom they'd acquired when the food had been particularly scarce. I'd often heard one of them saying: 'Come on, fill up on bread and cheese!' jokingly but as a solution for satisfying their hunger too. The habit had remained even though they had no need to 'fill up' on anything now.

After what seemed to me an eternity the meal ended and we stopped forlornly on the veranda to look at the weather before siesta. When there was sunshine we'd roam about the grass or sit while digesting our meal but today we stayed under cover as the rain persisted. Donald put his arm around my shoulders and kissed my cheek: 'Siesta?' he asked.

'I want to go down to the hay barn and have a look at the baby calf before I lie down. You go ahead. I'll join you later.' I pulled a thick shawl over my shoulders and ran across the patio and into the hay *galpon*.

The hay *galpon*. It had its usual instant effect on me and I stood perfectly still and listened to the wonderful sound of nothing and breathed its special scent. Where had Alberto put the poor little thing?

I walked the length of the barn between the bales and heaps of dry hay until I reached the wall opposite, and there, slightly to the right, was a small space; from here we'd been taking hay for the horses daily. The space was no longer so small and an alcove had formed where I found the calf. It was alone; Alberto must have gone out to lunch and siesta. I knelt down and felt the calf. It was very thin and it trembled slightly. I wondered if Alberto had given it anything to drink... I had to do something for I didn't want it to die.

I went and got milk and fed it. It did take some but on the whole it was not a successful feed. It was breathing with difficulty: I sat with legs crossed under my skirts and watched. No change. The shivering continued. Perhaps it was cold and I was busy pulling bits of hay to cover it when I heard a step. It was Alberto.

'No, no,' he shook his head, 'that's not enough, we need something warmer... some sacking perhaps?' Then I remembered there was some in the little shed tucked onto the rafter.

'I'll go and get it.' I pulled my shawl over my head and was gone before he could argue. I preferred action to sitting miserably feeling useless.

My short boots made squelching noises as I plodded to the back of the silent house. The door of the shed stood slightly ajar so I pushed my way in with ease. The two calves I'd seen briefly on their arrival were huddled together. They looked quite well, there'd be no problem with these two — our problem was in the hay *galpon*. I'd struggle for its life.

The roll of sacking was tucked on the rafter as I'd remembered so I reached for it and left the shed.

Alberto covered it cautiously with the sacking and then laid dry hay on top of it, leaving only its head uncovered. It looked like something out of another world.

Alberto squatted down beside the calf and I sat a little way away. It was comfortable like this and having Alberto there it was no longer tedious to remain. We didn't speak and after some time he went to get some more warm milk. I waited. Siesta time must be over I thought, for I could hear people walking about and voices in the distance. Donald came into the barn together with Alberto and the milk; between them they managed to get the calf to drink more than half the bottle, which was heartening.

Donald turned to me: 'You missed your siesta...'

'I'm worried about this animal.'

'Syd and I are riding to the fence again as it's stopped raining, would you like to come?' There was little I enjoyed more than riding with the gentlemen, so I decided to abandon my little calf and go with them. 'I'll be ready soon.' The drizzle had stopped but it was not a nice day. We came in late for tea.

The calf showed no change even though Alberto had fed it again. I remained a long spell in the *galpon* until the evening sounds filled the air. Trixie had come in with me and was sitting a respectable distance away. Donald and Sydney came in on their way up to the house.

'Don't be long, dear,' Donald said as they left, 'there's nothing you can do.' The door slammed behind them and their footsteps echoed across the patio. It was going to be a long night, I thought, and regretted not having put the calf nearer the house.

Evening was setting in when I heard the barn door again. Alberto had washed and changed before returning; he looked tired.

'Did you get the cows parted for tomorrow?' I asked.

'Si, Señora; everything's in order out there.' He sat on the hay. 'How's the baby?' He pushed away the coverings and touched it lightly, shaking his head.

'There's milk in the kitchen,' I told him as I got up to leave.

'I'll stay and feed it during the night hours, it's our only hope.'

'Oh, thank you Alberto, that's very good of you!' I went away with a strong desire to remain, but my duty was with the family and I remembered that Mr. Dawson, from a neighbouring estancia, was spending the night so I was expected to play hostess.

The Dawson's were new neighbours, and so as to entertain Mr. Dawson we played Whist after dinner. Luckily he seemed happy to go to bed at ten o'clock when the game was over, and indeed we all went to bed then and the house stood silent in the cold May night, but sleep refused to come to me rapidly as it normally did, and I found myself tossing and turning, unable to shut an eye beside Donald already fast asleep.

The minutes ticked by...

It was extraordinary how wide awake I felt. My brain was buzzing away and my thoughts unique. I thought of my family in Ireland and the sale of Carriehall. Then I thought about the education of our children. Donny would go to a boarding school in Ireland, and the idea troubled me. The separation from our eldest son would make a wrench in our lives, yet away he must go.... This unpleasant thought woke me more and I then began wondering how the little calf was faring through the night. Alberto might at this very moment be struggling for the life of the calf. It had been unfair of me to cast this responsibility on Alberto, for if the calf died there'd be instant criticism.

Suddenly I decided it might be a better idea for me to go to the hay *galpon* and see how things were. Silently I slipped from the bed, groping in the darkness for my dress, stockings and shoes. My thick shawl was in the drawing-room where I'd left it earlier. Fortunately, I knew the house like the palm of my hand, so I walked silently out of the bedroom onto the veranda. Donald had not moved, his breathing was strong and even; I closed the door behind me. With my shawl and a lamp to light my way across the patio, otherwise the shadows menaced too tangibly, I kept a steady footfall as I went across the gravel to the barn.

The door was unlocked, naturally, as Alberto was inside. I let it swing open and stepped inside the sweet-smelling interior. As I closed it the latch snapped back with a sharp 'click'. A figure moved where the little calf was laid, and I saw it was Alberto. He had his hand on his knife which was in its sheath at his waist, but when he saw me his hand dropped to his side and he smiled.

I felt a fool as I approached him, though he showed no surprise: 'I wondered how the calf... I mean, I couldn't sleep so...' I tried to explain my sudden appearance.

'It's very bad and has little life left.' We crouched together beside the unfortunate sick animal and I thought it looked dead already as it lay so still.

'If you lift its head off the ground, perhaps we can make it drink as it's not had anything for a long time,' he said.

I rolled up my sleeves and reached for the calf's head. In doing so my arm brushed Alberto's bare arm as he drew near with the milk and I felt a strong electrical excitement run through me with the accidental touch. Our efforts at making the calf were completely useless, so we sat side by side on the hay and watched its life end.

Once it was dead Alberto covered it totally and pulled it slightly away. I put my hands over my face and started to cry silently. He came and put his arm around my shoulders.

'*Pobrecito*,' (Poor little thing) he whispered, '*esta muerto*.' (He's dead)

Alberto let himself slide slowly onto the hay beside me and I felt the same electric excitement of a few moments ago. I felt some pressure on my shoulder and I turned my face up to meet his.

We kissed. I shut my eyes and began swirling deep into the most delightful and exciting pathway of translucid new sensations that I'd never experienced before. He lifted my body into his arms without stopping the burning kiss. It went on and on, impossible to break away. I felt his strong teeth grip my tongue in a gentle yet possessive caress, while I began half-heartedly to struggle to free myself. But it was too late; we'd gone too far. His burning lips held mine and he seemed to be drinking from a long-forbidden fount. Something he'd been waiting for, for a long time.

Gradually he loosened his hold on me and released my lips completely. I took advantage and pushed with my hands against his strong muscular chest, but his face was only an inch away from mine and his smouldering black eyes were very demanding.

I was standing locked in his arms as he kissed my face and neck and shoulders hungrily, while his hands fondled my body. In the tumult of emotions sweeping over me, I knew this man wanted me more than life itself. He was willing to give up all for me.

My head fell back and his fierce tugging ripped my dress and the whole bodice fell apart, torn open by the violence of his eager hands. Suddenly I was half naked. He stared and then he began caressing my bare breasts and I knew there was no turning back; no holding his furious attack. When his soft dark lips travelled down my neck and caught my nipple, I felt my entire being existed only for this purpose. This longing and this desire I'd never felt before. I had no thoughts, no reasoning, only a deep longing for this man who was making love to me. He was no person in particular; he was Sex and Desire mixed together.

As my passion increased, so did his, and we were down on the floor and I felt the hot flesh of his hairy legs against mine: possessive, hard and cruel and soon we were rolling frantically about in the hay, reaching for each other, pulling away to make it more intense and lasting, rocking, until at last we came to the summit and we lay together in the soft hay in total submission. Panting, exhausted, yet completely satisfied. I never knew it could be like this.

He remained sprawled on top of me for a long time, perfectly still, knowing if either of us moved it would break the spell of our incredible encounter, and then would come the shame, the guilt, the explanations…. I shut my eyes and began drifting into a light sleep with a sensation of having reached perfect contentment. I think he slept too, because at the first sound of crackling, burning hay, we were both instantly on our feet.

Somehow, sometime, we must have accidentally knocked over the paraffin lamp I'd brought with me from the house and by the time we noticed, there was fire in the hay barn.

'Hurry!' he shouted, 'we must get water.' The nearest water available was in the well in the patio but it had to be pumped from the depths.

Alberto dashed for the door while I frantically tried to button my dress with one or two of its remaining buttons, not sufficient to cover my bosoms decently, but I had no time for appearances; the fire had to be quenched at all costs. He and I fought it alone for a few minutes but the dryness of the hay made it spread wildly. We needed help.

I dashed into the house and woke the gentlemen while Alberto ran for the workmen sleeping in their rooms down below.

Soon all hands were out fighting the flames.

––––––––––

Once everybody had been rudely shaken out of their peaceful sleep, a scene of incredible confusion and chaos took place. Men dashing against one another in the darkness, some calling orders, but everybody in disorder not knowing what to do.

The pitch darkness prevailing when I crossed the patio on my way to see my calf, was no longer there. In its stead the whole landscape soon became lighted with a violent orange blaze coming from the *galpon,* and the stillness of the frosty night was interrupted by the roar of burning hay inside the barn, which sounded like the thundering of lava from an erupting volcano or perhaps the rolling of a tidal wave coming swiftly.

Figures, indistinguishable in their hasty attires, ran from one point to another. Shouts, orders and yells of distress filled the air over and beyond the fire's fierce burning sound.

I kept bumping into Mr. Dawson who was completely at a loss as to what to do, and I wondered what he was doing at Las Palmas in the middle of the night, until I remembered he was our guest for the night. He was making me nervous, his uncontrolled rushing about, his startled look at my bodice, inadequately dragged together, now smudged with black and my skirt ripped to glory. I must've looked a freak to him considering the only lady of the house he knew was demure and white freckled skin. Could this fiendish half-devil he kept meeting be that same person?

Now the strong voice of Donald could be heard, calling directions, shouting advice and yelling for Sydney's help, as he organized a water-chain which went from the well to the entrance of the hay *galpon.* Mr. Dawson, I noticed, joined this water-chain and then I thankfully lost sight of him.

Sweating figures swiftly passed bucket after bucket to the person in front of him, returning the empties with his other hand. It was quick and efficient once it was underway but it was too late. The flames inside the barn where whipping up high setting fire to the rafters. The heat in the doorway was so intense that the water evaporated even before it reached the flames. Sometime during this action, I tripped and fell and hurt my ankle but I still went on despite the pain.

When finally, the futility of our efforts struck us and Donald realized every pail of water merely sizzled before evaporating and fresh hay was catching on, he ordered the water-chain to be stopped and everybody stood back, away from the flying sparks.

All movement ceased. I took my pail forlornly back to the kitchen, limping, now fully aware of the intense pain in my ankle. I went and stood close to Donald and Sydney who were standing together watching the disastrous scene in tight-lipped fury.

Dawn broke some minutes later, grey and sullen, over the smouldering ruins of our beautiful hay *galpon*.

During the weeks that followed I had to remain in bed because of my sprained ankle, and due to this I had more than plenty of time to think things over.

What have I done? This question revolved constantly in my mind, finding no satisfactory answer. What had I done? I had, indisputably, been the cause of the fire in our lovely hay barn. Nobody else was to blame. If I had remained sensibly in bed and not gone to the barn, supposedly to see my calf, this horrible accident with the paraffin lamp would never have happened. But I'd chosen to act differently; I'd not summed up the possible consequences of meeting Alberto in the dead of the night, alone.... I hadn't thought of the flame it might spark off.

Pertinently it had become a furious and impetuous spark of passion culminating in something unthought-of of. Even as I hated myself for having allowed it to happen, I did not entirely regret it for I knew that in some way it had contributed to my life's experience as a woman. I'd never known anything like that. Disgraceful as it may seem to anybody, I knew I'd never, in the depth of my soul, have any regrets. I'd matured. Alberto had taught me what love-making was really like, something utterly consuming, something one could crave for. The sad part was the involvement of other parties innocently brought into it, and here I did feel guilty.

The remorse and pain caused by the guilt which I carried, would be with me for the rest of my life; I'd committed the unforgivable sin most abhorred by me in persons bound in matrimony to another. I'd done what I'd so harshly accused Donald of when a doubt existed as to the father of Mrs. Allen's baby, to find it had been my own misjudgment. Oh bitter, bitter remorse! How could I have done this to him now?

Additionally, I'd burned down our wonderful hay *galpon*. No explanations had potentially been needed; the truth, with one or two vital facts omitted, was told. When the calf died, the lamp I'd taken to light my way, had rolled over unnoticed by either of us and the fire had kindled with the spilling of the paraffin.

My grief at its destruction was perhaps the greatest for I knew I'd been the cause and also because of my love for the place. The gentlemen were mortified because of the work, the time and money spent on it. Its use had been relatively short.

'Perhaps we were too confident about the fire situation,' Sydney commented kindly, 'there was so much dry hay all in one place.'

My sprained ankle had been a sort of buffer to the original fury of the gentlemen when they realized the barn could not be saved. I'd limped to their sides and we stood in the filthy, churned up patio, with the stench of burned hay and wood in our nostrils.

The dogs were frightened. Santa whined and came and sat at my feet followed by Claus, who tried to get close to Donald but was kicked away with an angry foot. It was by this particularly unkind act towards our dog, I first saw exactly how angry Donald was.

Later I'd been laid on the sofa while we waited for the water for a bath to warm. I lay back, frightened and shaken, and tried to accept what had happened. Nobody had accused me, but the unspoken word was sometimes worse.

In the morning they'd called the doctor. 'It might be broken,' Donald remarked as he looked at the enormous swelling on my ankle. Dr. Owens told us, after some painful examinations, it was not broken but I should not put it to the ground for two weeks. The first week in bed for he found me very fatigued, and the following I could get up with help.

'This foot should not be put to the ground for fifteen days,' he ordered. I lay back on my pillows, and again: 'What have I done?'

I tried to justify myself but it always returned to the same end: I'd burned down our hay *galpon* and broken my marriage vows. I found little consolation in those blunt facts. I dozed a little.

I woke with Donald coming into the room just before lunch. He was washed and ready for the meal. He sat on the edge of my bed silently. There was something further amiss, I felt it when I saw his tense face. 'What's the matter?' I reached for his hand, but he withdrew it.

'I have some news you're not going to like,' he paused dramatically.

'What?' I asked, not daring to imagine what it might be.

'I've had words with Alberto. I've just now fired him.'

For a few seconds I was struck dumb; my throat went dry and I didn't trust my voice. Eventually: 'Why?' I whispered.

'I'm surprised you should ask that!' he cried, 'after what happened last night!' I froze. How much did he know? How much did he guess?

'Oh Donald, it wasn't his fault, it was mine!' I cried in dismay. 'Don't punish him...'

'It's not that I particularly want to punish anybody, I simply feel it'll be impossible to have him on our farm any longer,' he said. 'To have him in our midst would be unwise, so I told him to go. He's packing his things at the moment and I'll pay him after lunch.'

'What am I to do with my animals without him?' I wailed, very upset. Life without Alberto would be difficult to say the least. Donald shrugged.

'You know I can't manage without him,' I went on sulkily, 'he does everything. All the hard work. I can't do it alone!' I winged my words tactfully, hoping they'd reach the depths of his stoney heart. 'Go and call him back, please darling! Be an angel and don't let him go!' Donald's face remained impassive.

Oh dear, it was all so difficult.

'Please let's give him another chance.' I begged.

'It's too late, my dear,' he said, 'I've already fired him, as I told you.'

'But, but...' My last hope was this: 'You really had no right to do this, he was my employee, and when he left the gardens you told me I could do as I wished with him, and now...'

'Times have changed, haven't they?' he replied, 'and Alberto is no longer the skinny little lad of seventeen badly needing work; he's now a fully grown man and a fool to have let things reach this point. We've now lost our hay *galpon*, thanks to him, as well as other things.'

I gulped and turned my head to the wall.

Those first days were the blackest of all. I was distraught, on edge, confined to my bed; facing problems over and over; waking in the night with starts of fear; sinking back on my pillows in resignation; controlling my mind; working out plans of how to face the new situation; how to pay back what we'd lost; and worst of all the thought of a new man for my cattle.

I could not consider life at Las Palmas without Alberto. He'd been part of it for eight years and I'd come to rely on him for everything and consequently could not accept the void.

I was torn between two opposing forces: Donald whom I loved and trusted and Alberto for whom I'd now found was a fierce fascination to me. Lying there on my bed I knew the puzzle that needed joining together was still in hundreds of pieces.

'How's the leg?' Willy was the kindest, and he'd stay and converse with me. Perhaps he remembered his own illness after imprisonment and the one who had helped him pull through; the one who'd made the egg-nogs for weeks. After a week in bed I could truthfully say: 'My ankle's better, thank you Willy. Tomorrow I can get up and sit in a chair.'

'Well, that's an improvement,' he smiled affectionately and squeezed my toe sticking up under the bed clothes. Perhaps Willy was not a very great brain, but he was kind.

CHAPTER 18

Time had elapsed since the loss of the hay *galpon*, (barn) and Alberto. We were in the month of October and the days were showing summer splendour and the estancia was preparing for the shearing. A team of men had been taken on for the job, but the gentlemen were particularly busy rounding up the flocks, separating and generally preparing for the event. So much had taken place in my life during those five months, it seemed unreal.

Donald would get up and be out early each morning, with a hasty good-morning peck on my cheek. Cool and distant, he'd be off for the morning and sometimes the whole day. I detested these long absences and felt neglected, yet dared not say one word.

Once my ankle was better and I could walk again, I took time to become fully incorporated into the affairs of the farm. There was such an enormous void where the care and attention of my animals was concerned now Alberto was no longer there, that my interest flagged and I made excuses to remain in the house instead of going into the fields as I used to when Alberto was there.

Another change in myself was my frequenting of the tennis court more than ever before. I enjoyed tennis only partially and would skillfully organize games among the others, leaving myself out, then quietly retire to see my animals. But now had come the time when I wished my children to learn the game. With Mrs. Allen no longer with us, and Miss Daisy no athlete, the job of teaching them was mine. Donny already ten and going to boarding school next year was at an age when it was important for him to be encouraged to learn. He and I went out after breakfast most mornings and had a game.

There's a magic in the cool early morning when time hangs in suspension and the day does not reveal what it will do in the next few hours. I loved these early mornings, especially in springtime, before the great heat.

On some very infrequent occasions, we'd been able to persuade two others to come and make a foursome.

'Yes, please, please, Daddy!' Once Donny had begged his father while still at breakfast. 'Come and play with Mummie and me. I'll get Uncle Willy; I know he'll play if you do.'

'I've work to do, son,' Donald replied slowly, 'the farm doesn't run by itself.' But at Donny's crestfallen face he'd reconsidered and added: 'Perhaps just for a moment I can join you this morning.'

'Hurray!' yelled Donny as he pursued Willy down to the wool shed. 'I'll get Uncle Willy!' he threw over his shoulder as he raced away.

Our young son played better than I'd ever seen him play before, and I smiled my thanks to Donald when the game was over. He returned me a cool, distant smile as he was want these days. How I wished I could get close to him again. Our personal relationship had been breached and I was to blame and was not forgiven.

During the month of July, I'd become aware of another pregnancy, but this time I had serious misgivings as to whose child it was. It might just as easily have been Donald's as Alberto's.

Worry, worry, worry... if the winter was cold and cruel, this worry was more cruel. I began having terrible nightmares and I dreamed I'd given birth to a tiny black boy with curls like Alberto's and when Donald had come in to see me he said: 'What's this?' Repeating it again and again, his voice was violent and accusing, then I'd wake up in a bath of perspiration to find it to be only a dream. I kept this pregnancy to myself, not daring to tell Donald in case he'd ask me about its origin.

One thing I decided was not to give up riding, I had no intention to stop the moments of fun on horseback I was having with the children every day. Ada was still the better horsewoman by far, but Donny held his own and liked to feel he could sometimes beat his sister in a race. They were learning to jump. The gentlemen had put up some low jumps in the near field and I was instructing them. Great progress was being made and one special day, in spite of the high wind and approaching storm, the class was going well. I could feel the nervous tension in my mare, probably because I was not allowing her to jump. She was very fresh and she picked and shied and the howling wind did its worst for us both.

I rode her up and down beside the jumps as I instructed the children. Donny was galloping, approaching one of the level bars, when his horse hoof caught the bar and sent it flying. Rosie took fright at the flying plank and reared suddenly and threw me off.

The children had never seen me take a fall; their own accidents had been taken lightly and laughingly we'd lift them from the floor and put them in the saddle again, in case they took fright and never wanted to ride again. Now they came up to me with whoops of glee as I slowly got to my feet. 'Oh Mummie, you looked so funny!' cried Ada as she rode up laughing.

'Did you hurt yourself?' asked Donny, the kinder of the two.

'No,' I called to them. 'Don't worry, I only got a bump on my bottom.' But I felt quite shaken and decided not to get into the saddle again. My back was hurting.

I stayed in bed for the rest of the day, hoping to ease the pain, but it increased steadily. The following day Dr. Owens was called, who prescribed some medicine and told me to remain in bed for two days. They had to call him back in the middle of the night when I became much worse and suspected the beginning of a miscarriage. This was confirmed by Dr. Owens who told me I had to go to Mercedes to have proper attention in the morning.

'Willy will drive us as soon as it gets light,' Donald told me. I'll have to be away for about two weeks, so we must pack up some clothes; can you do it for me?' I asked him.

'Of course; what shall I put them in?'

'There's a small portmanteau in the bottom of the wardrobe; perhaps that'll be the thing as it's not too large.' Then I added: 'What about your things?' Donald did all the packing immediately, in the middle of the night, so as to be ready to leave at the crack of dawn.

It was the most uncomfortable drive I'd ever taken although Willy came up in the best carriage and horses and they lined my seat with pillows and cushions but still I could not get comfortable. My back ached and I felt ill. We had to stop various times during the trip because I thought I was going to heave up, only to go on again in unlimited agony.

'How much further is there to go?' I kept asking as if I'd never done the journey before, it seemed so long and painful, I thought we'd never get there.

Eventually we did get there and it had taken us half the day for Willy had been driving carefully, trying not to cause me undue pain. The doctor who attended this sort of thing had gone to Fray Bentos for the day, so we had to decide whether we'd wait for him or follow him into Fray Bentos. The gentlemen asked me what I wanted to do.

We went directly to Fray Bentos. At least there we had friends... the sooner I saw the doctor the better. And eventually he confirmed I was miscarrying a two-month pregnancy. He performed the necessary intervention and told me I had to stay in Fray Bentos for two weeks to recuperate. Donald remained with me while Willy went back to Las Palmas.

We stayed with the Miles', so I was comfortable and not alone. Maggie was kindness itself and while I had to lie in the following days she stayed with me while Donald and Peter went off fishing.

One day Maggie said: 'You've lost a baby, are you sorry?' Then when she saw my grieved expression she added: 'I thought you might not want another as you already have four.'

'I always want children,' I said, 'I adore them and there's something so special about the maternity months which I love.' I paused and sighed, 'Yet this one was different, perhaps it's best for it not have been born.' She looked at me strangely, not understanding. Here was the perfect opportunity to confide in her and tell her of my distress, but I'd kept my secret so long I thought it best not to reopen the wound since fate had kindly taken care of things.

We rarely spoke of serious topics with Maggie so we dropped the subject. She always looked on the optimistic or amusing side of things and this was catching. It was her nature which helped me recover during those days otherwise I know I'd have mourned my unborn child. With Maggie beside me, it was impossible to be depressed.

Once back at Las Palmas, completely recovered, it was the month of August and Donald had brought back a lot of material for the building of his boat. It took up a lot of his time and kept him out of the house more than I liked. Yet he looked so happy while working on it I felt I had no right to interfere. During the boat construction, after his siesta, he'd not return to the fields but go down to the shed and spend the rest of the day there, sometimes skipping tea. On these occasions I'd pack up a small basket and take it to him. He was extremely polite, thanking me for the trouble, but with a coldness in his manner not enjoyable.

'That's very good of you,' he said one afternoon as he wiped his mouth on his sleeve.

'Did you like the fruit buns? I made them myself.' I said coyly.

'Very nice indeed,' he replied dryly, returning to his woodwork without further comment. I stood there a little despondently, watching. His hands moved about the wood, measuring and planning with much skill. Donald had nice hands, sort of warm and dry and a bit hairy. I always loved the feel of his hands. I needed to feel those hands touch me in the old affectionate way again.

Suddenly I wanted to put my arms around him, hug him close and say 'I'm sorry' but I dared not lest he turn and ask me, in that cold way, what I was sorry about. I'd never confess. So I remained standing beside him, feeling unwanted, hoping a small spark of affection would flare up.

Presently I said: 'It's a beautiful evening, let's go for a ride together!'

'Mmmm... I'd rather get this planning done today because I won't be working on it tomorrow as we've planned a shooting spree after lunch.'

I turned and left him to his work for I knew there was no way of convincing him to come out with me.

Little Billy had been poorly during the day; he had a bad cold and his eyes looked heavy when he went down to siesta. In the Nursery Miss Daisy was putting away clothes as the washing had come in. Billy was in bed and she said he had a temperature.

'I believe he's in for a bout of flu,' she said. I sat for a minute on the edge of Billy's bed and felt his pulse. Racing with fever. 'Poor darling' I said soothingly, 'you'll be better in the morning.' To Miss Daisy I said: 'Give him plenty of barley water and keep a damp cloth on his head. I'll come in and see him later.'

Donny and Ada were going riding so I went with them.

'What's the matter with Billy?' Donny asked.

'He has a heavy cold and must stay in bed,' I told him. 'It's not serious but he must keep warm.'

At the moment I did not know that Billy was the first of our family to come down with influenza, a part of the tremendous epidemic which swept the country that year. We became concerned when Billy did not shake it off in the predicted time and then when Donny and Ada both came down with it in the following few days. The Nursery suddenly had to be transformed into a small sanatorium. The sick children were bedded down in semi isolation, in the hopes the sickness would not spread any further. Our hopes were not fulfilled for another week saw Miss Daisy coughing and sneezing all day and by evening she was feeling terrible.

'My body aches all over,' she admitted.

'Then go to bed at once,' I ordered her, 'to avoid complications setting in. I'll bring you your supper shortly.' I wondered how I was to cope with all the sick people.

The gentlemen had just come in from another shooting expedition which had kept them away all day; Mr. Dawson came with them.

I went to the kitchen and ordered various trays of light food for the sick rooms.

'Dinner will be an hour later than usual,' I said once the gentlemen were settled in the drawing-room having their evening drink.

'Why ever?' asked Sydney rather curtly.

'Miss Daisy has also gone down with flu. I can't do everything by the usual time.' I explained slightly exasperated.

'Good heavens!' exclaimed Donald. 'Miss Daisy down too? What an epidemic! The people at the *Pulperia* (general store) said almost every household has at least a couple of cases.' He shrugged. 'Hope ours remains in the Nursery.'

As dinner was going to be late, they settled down to a round of Whist before dinner while I got on with the nursing.

The epidemic raged through the country in relentless fashion striking down young and old, male and female, without distinction. The adults of our family did not escape: Sydney one day and Donald the next, and Miss Daisy still not well enough to get up. Willy took over the nursing of the gentlemen while I remained with the rest.

Dr. Owens came to check lungs for fear of pneumonia complications and he ordered they remain in bed until he gave permission to get up. 'They must sweat it out!' he ordered.

As a precaution I moved out of our double bed and went to sleep elsewhere. The epidemic gave no signs of abating neither in the country, nor in our home. It was not long before the workhands also collapsed and the work on the farm slowed down. One morning Señora Pintos came to tell us her husband was also down with the illness.

If the estancia work was being neglected because of Donald and Sydney's sickness now it was much worse without our splendid foreman Pintos.

Donald had been down a week and with this news of Pintos' illness, he felt he should get up and start working again. However, Dr. Owens was firm and refused to allow him to leave his bed until his cough had lessened. The same applied to Sydney.

'This type of flu often leaves lung complications,' he said. 'One has to be careful. The relapse is ten times more dangerous than the original illness. Be patient! See you tomorrow.'

The days crept by... The sound of coughing and nose-blowing was constantly heard throughout the house. The weather was cold, wet and cloudy and we lighted the fires in all the rooms. Our roof still leaked when the rain was torrential — pots and basins often decorated the rooms. How I longed for a new house. I must've sent up thousands of silent prayers for one, until one day my prayers were answered.

When September came in, things took on a better aspect. The children were all better and also Miss Daisy; she was even strong enough to start some schooling again.

The weather also began improving, more sunshine, trees sprouting and bulbs shooting.

Donald and Sydney had permission from the doctor to get up, but with strict instructions to remain indoors for a few days. We were beginning to rejoice in our victory over the wretched illness, when one morning I woke with a bad sore throat. Only a few hours later I collapsed with high fever.

Dr. Owens prescribed the same as for the others, but I heard him saying to Donald as he left: 'Be extra careful with her, she's delicate. She's had a lot of sickness and stress recently and she's been weakened.' He lifted his long, boney finger and shook it at Donald, emphasizing his warning. 'Extra care, please! Call me if you need me in a hurry.'

Immediately I was put into the double bed and I was thankful to be there and relaxed gently onto my beautiful feather pillows. At night I began coughing and was not able to sleep due to the high temperature and the trembling that shook my body. By the following morning I was in a state of semi-consciousness and my thoughts no longer coordinated. Nothing focused... my mind kept drifting and I knew I had something worrying me but could not remember what it was. It was a terrible feeling... I wanted Donald to love me again... Why was he going away from me? 'Donald, Donald!' I heard myself calling, but never was there any reply.

I was constantly aware of Dr. Owens in the room, listening to my chest, looking in my throat or making hasty comments to somebody else. Whispering figures; frightened faces... I slipped away again to unconsciousness.

I woke and it was morning by the angle of the sun. There was a lot of chirruping of sparrows outside my window; they were making their nests in the ivy which covered most of the house now. Thank heaven my throat and head felt better. I thought I was alone in the room but when I let out an involuntary sigh somebody moved quickly towards the bed. I turned my head slowly and looked into the kind face of Señora Pintos. What's she doing in my bedroom in the morning? I wondered. She leaned over me and asked: 'How are you?' All I could do was whisper 'Better' and closed my eyes again.

'O gracias a Dios!' she exclaimed. 'I must call the Señor Donald at once. He's so worried,' and she left the room.

Donald was with me in an instant. He must have been eating breakfast by the faint aroma of toast and coffee on his breath as he bent to kiss me. All he said was: 'My darling!' and held my limp body in his strong arms, then straightened and put both hands over his face. I saw tears squeezing between his fingers and he sniffed a big drop about to fall off his nose. Donald crying... I'd never seen him cry before and I didn't understand. I shut my eyes again and reached for his tear-splashed hand. We sat together like this for some time until I asked: 'How long have I been ill?'

'You were partially unconscious for four weeks. The fever would not go down even though we tried everything. Dr. Owens has been wonderful coming two and three times a day.' I felt weak at the thought of such frequent visits from the doctor.

'You nearly died,' he whispered. I remained silent, wondering.

'Wasn't it only flu?' I asked faintly.

'It started as flu, yes, but after a few days you got steadily worse.' He frowned as the long, anxious days and nights came back to him. 'It became pneumonia and you were very ill.' They'd fought for my life during the following weeks, the doctor visiting frequently and constant nursing. Poultices for my lungs were applied by the doctor himself and somebody sat in my room all twenty-four hours of the day, attending to my needs and watching for signs of recovery. The Señora Pintos took over night duties for Donald had to have his night's rest.

'When I went out to work' Donald went on, 'Different neighbours came to sit with you. Mrs. Harrison stayed many hours.'

'I never saw her.'

'The fever never left you and sometimes you became very agitated, calling for help and naming me.'

'How long?'

'You've been unconscious for four weeks,' he said.

'Two or three visits a day from the doctor,' I whispered, 'He might have almost brought his bed and remained.'

'He did spend some nights here...' No wonder his thin anxious face always seemed to be in front of me.

'We thought you weren't going to live,' he said shakily, 'and I couldn't face life without you. You know how much I love you.'

All the pain of my recent sickness was suddenly taken from me by those wonderful words. The anguish of blurred recollections of the fear of losing Donald faded, and the wonder of having him sitting by me, holding my hand and telling me he loved me, gave me the peace I needed. I wanted to hold this moment for ever, carry it into the future, it was so sacred and precious.

Then it was I who was crying. I knew Donald had forgiven me; the moment you are forgiven; you feel forgiven as I felt then. My tears were of gratitude and joy.

My convalescence was lengthy but steady. Some days later when I was able to sit up in bed, the mail accumulated for me during my sickness was brought to me by Sydney. 'I think it's time you read these,' he said as he placed the small pile of letters and magazines into my hands. 'You have letters from home.' He sat down on the rocking-chair and began lighting his pipe. Sydney was not the constant pipe smoker as Donald and Willy were, but he often lit one when he intended to communicate...

'Thanks, Syd,' as I took the letters. 'Where's Donald?' I asked, tearing open the first family letter from Ethel, sending news of Mama I was sure.

Sydney replied: 'He's tidying up some accounts of the cattle sale before coming to see you.'

The day was almost over and the farm work finished. I began reading Ethel's letter through and then I read it again. It had come at last; the family was selling Carriehall. I felt a huge lump form in my throat but swallowed it and refused to cry. Instead I turned to Sydney: 'Did you know they're selling Carriehall?'

'I'd heard something to that effect,' he said gently, 'has confirmation come?'

I nodded. A step on the veranda told us Donald was approaching; he came in and kissed me fondly 'How's it going?' and then he caught sight of the mail: 'Good news?'

'Ethel confirms the sale of Carriehall,' I told him.

'Ah! What a pity! We'd hoped Donny might live there when he goes to school next year...' He sat on the bed and reached for my hand and squeezed it. That helped.

Presently: 'Ethel says there's a notification in this mail from the Solicitors telling me about my part of the legacy.' I sorted aimlessly through the other envelopes until I found an official-looking one addressed to me very formally in over-perfect handwriting.

My legacy had arrived, and much to everybody's surprise it amounted to a lot of money.

At last we could build the long awaited new house.

CHAPTER 19

The household was quiet and the sun high in the sky, it was siesta time. Even the dogs were all napping under trees or in some deftly sought out cool corner.

The intruder was unobserved, so either from curiosity or by mistake, it had found its way on to the veranda. As I came out of our bedroom door with the intention of saddling up and going for a ride before tea, I had to stop dead. There it was before me, only a few yards away; it saw me immediately and our eyes met and fixed. I began to retreat very slowly, tiny steps, like a shuffle, hopefully unnoticed by the animal until I reached the bedroom door again. I slipped inside.

'Donald, Donald!' I whispered urgently. 'There's a small skunk on the veranda and I don't know what to do.'

'Drat!' he exclaimed. 'We've got to get rid of it without frightening it, otherwise it'll stink us out!'

'How?' I asked, 'it's already seen me and looked alarmed.'

'I must think.' Swiftly he was into his pants and opening the shutters of the window.

'Our only hope is to make it leave the veranda unfrightened.' He was over the sill jumping down lightly. 'You stay there until I give you the all-clear.'

Complete silence followed. I sat down and waited... then I faintly heard a 'cu-cu-cu' the particular call of the skunk. Gracious! I thought, have others invaded our veranda?

I heard the throaty call again 'cu-cu-cu-cu'...

Eventually Donald lured it off and he soon came back to me, triumphant. 'I made skunky noises just around the corner of the house, and as they're curious animals, it followed me away. I don't expect it'll return.'

But it did return. Exactly at siesta time the following day, our visitor appeared again on the veranda. Donald had to use identical tactics to get rid of it as the day before. It repeated the visits so often in the end we baptized it the Two O'Clock Skunk.

'Seems as if they live nearby, as their visits are so regular; they toddle off over there,' Sydney pointed to a small coppice nearby. 'One day we'll have to hunt them out.'

It must have been a very particular year for skunks for it was soon afterwards Emma Tomkins acquired her own pet skunk.

We'd ridden for two hours and a half one evening returning to Las Palmas at dusk and we found the Tomkins sitting comfortably in our drawing-room, being entertained by Willy who'd not been out. Donald and I became speechless with horror when Emma introduced us to her new pet.

'I got him when he was just born,' she explained, 'and I've trained him to be very domesticated, like a dog or cat. Don't you think he's beautiful?' she cried.

'Nice shiny coat,' said Donald stiffly.

'Oh, he's as clean as can be,' she continued with praise for the animal as she stroked the white stripe from head to tail, while it sat complacently on her lap. We wanted no more skunk problems and here was Emma presenting us with a risk we'd rather not take. The little skunk watched me with his beady, black eyes from his strong position.

'Where did you get it from?' My question seemed reasonable for, after all, baby skunks were not easily found nor were they common pets.

'The milkman brought it to me. He said they'd killed the big ones and this little thing had been overlooked.'

'I don't know how you have the courage to have him; I'd be terrified.' I said.

She laughed: 'I have to keep an eye on it lest the dogs get it, of course, so it's with me all the time. I've become terribly fond of it as of any pet.'

'What do the O'Brian's say?'

'I haven't asked their opinion. Why should I? The house is ours, isn't it Jim?' Jim kept on looking attentively at his boots. Emma laughed again: 'Jim's taking time getting fond of it, aren't you Jim?'

Donald and I exchanged glances while Jim remained silent. Their visit dragged on in an unnatural manner but eventually we were glad to see their backs.

'I refuse to have that filthy animal in my house again!' Donald cried out crossly once they'd gone.

'I totally agree,' said Willy, 'it's horrible, and stinks even without pissing at us.'

'Yes, but it'll be difficult for future visits if she brings the skunk along too.' I said.

'We must make it quite clear,' went on Donald, 'the skunk is NOT welcome here and if she wishes to visit, she must leave it behind.'

'She ought to be told to let it go now it's old enough.'

'Somebody should quietly do away with it one night,' said Sydney. 'I suspect old Jim might have a hand in that!' We all laughed having noticed Jim's aversion. 'I must say he didn't look very enthusiastic about the brute.'

We heard from the O'Brian's sometime later that it was causing disagreement in the home. Nobody liked it, save Emma, nor was it trusted. Constant arguments arose and Colleen told Emma very pointedly how she disliked being in the same room with it. But the skunk remained. The time came when the Tomkins were being excluded from different social events because of it.

One Sunday afternoon the gentlemen decided it was time to go and hunt out our Two O'Clock Skunk's whereabouts. They searched all through the little coppice but found no evidence of skunks so returned to the house.

'We have to take some of the dogs to smell 'em out.' said Donald.

'But darling!' I protested, 'they get so smelly; can't you manage without them?'

'No, we've already been out there without results. The terriers will smell them out.' He whistled. 'Come on dogs!'

We'd planned to go visiting later but with this mishap, it would very likely mean staying to wash the terriers when they returned.

Presently we heard shots at irregular intervals and the afternoon dragged by; it had become a dull Sunday until we heard the sound of an approaching carriage in the avenue.

The Miles family. A flutter of hands from the interior showed they'd all come but Peter was alone up on the driver's seat. He sat there in solitude, proud and majestically covered with dust; the drive from Fray Bentos was long.

Immediately all was movement and activity as the children and I rushed out to welcome them as they tumbled out of the carriage.

'At last we're here!' cried Maggie, 'we seem to have been travelling forever.' Their children were already out and shaking dust from their clothes. Their hair was bleached to tow and dry from the scorching summer sun; our children looked more cared for, compared to these others who had a look of running wild about them. Peter was climbing down from his authoritive position, the dust sticking to him everywhere, making his eyebrows white but his smile wide and genuine. We were all so happy to see each other.

'Come in and freshen up,' I said. 'Donald and Sydney are out hunting skunks but should be back soon.'

Their eldest son was quick to detect some excitement: 'Hunting skunks?' he whooped, 'Can I go out too?' He was dissuaded with promises of tea and we were able to attend to his father.

'Peter, you look done in!' I cried.

He grinned at me through the dust. 'There's a dry pungent smell in the air,' he said, 'as of dry vegetation and of distant wood smoke.' He inhaled deeply. 'I love it and it's good to be here.'

Later we told them endless stories of our Two O'Clock Skunk's visits to our veranda. The Miles children were fascinated and were impatient for the gentlemen's return. I think they imagined they'd bring back armfuls of dead skunks, while in reality what they did bring back were some excellent pheasants. The skunk hunt was not a success, even with the terriers, so they'd gone shooting birds instead.

The Miles' visit lasted one week. I'd never known people with such a capacity for enjoying themselves. They were up early every morning, walking, riding or playing tennis even before breakfast. The tennis court was in constant use with games going on all day; never was there so much noise and movement on the farm. The gentlemen went shooting and we went fishing, taking picnics near the *Aguila* river, where we bathed when it was hot enough. It seemed like holiday time, but there was something so infectious in this family's delight in living that soon we were all behaving the same way, quite oblivious of our work commitments.

'Will you and the family be joining us for Prayers?' I asked Maggie early on Sunday morning. She looked a bit taken aback, but they did come in to Morning Service with us, but it was a meek and subdued family which grouped at the back of the room, respectfully silent.

Billy was impatient this morning and he could just reach the leg of Ada's chair with the tip of his shoe, so he began kicking a steady rhythm. This annoyed Ada and she turned various times with a scowl but the kicking continued. Finally, Miss Daisy tapped Billy sharply with her fan and gave him a loud 'sh-sh-sh-sh' just as the Lord's Prayer was about to begin and Donald looked up from the Prayer Book and directed a stern gaze upon Billy.

The service over, Peter was all smiles.

'By jove, I admire you people for maintaining family traditions and having Sunday Prayers like this. It took me back to my childhood when we used to go to Church every Sunday.'

The children were all running and tumbling about on the grass and shouting to one another; it was all fun these days. Suddenly their youngest came rushing up to his father crying: 'We want to see a skunk!'

Sydney began shaking with laughter: 'We'll have to pay the Tomkins a visit this afternoon.'

'Oh, my goodness!' exclaimed Donald.

'What's all this about?' asked Peter.

'The Tomkins, whom I believe you don't know, keep a pet skunk.'

'Not really?'

'Cross my heart!' said Sydney, 'Emma doesn't leave it alone for fear the dogs will get it.'

'Let's drive to El Torrado this afternoon and the children can see a real live skunk.'

The visit to El Torrado was a mistake from the beginning, from the moment the large Miles children and our two eldest rushed to the house demanding to see the skunk, to the time in which we left, it was all wrong.

The skunk was sitting placidly on Emma's lap under a small tree and Jim was beside them when the sound of our carriage wheels brought Jim to his feet, and he came out in welcome.

Maggie and I and the seven children had travelled in the carriage with Peter driving and Donald and Sydney were on horseback.

'Where's the skunk?' yelled James as he flung himself from the carriage interior. He was closely followed by his two brothers and our two, all disappearing in the direction of the house.

Then we heard the shrieks.

They'd run unrestrictedly up to where Emma and her pet were sitting. 'There it is! LOOK!' shouted the children. This was more than the skunk could tolerate, so it leaped out of Emma's lap landing on the ground, turned, squirting the approaching avalanche of children with its fiercest ejection. It caught Donny and one of the Miles on their clothes. Emma screamed.

The skunk, utterly stunned, stood its ground for a few tense seconds, before turning and throwing up its tail again with a fresh squirt, and then rushed into the furthest corner of the garden.

Pandemonium broke out. Howls from Donny and James who stank and a weeping Emma who started in the direction the skunk had fled. There were apologies from us all and 'Oh, it doesn't really matter!' from a grinning Jim.

The gentlemen began roaring with laughter, while Maggie and I dashed frantically about in search of Emma's pet. I don't know what we'd have done had we found it but luckily it was never seen again.

The smelly children were stripped of their clothes and donned some old shirts of Jim's which were more like robes on them but served the purpose.

'Let's remain outside,' I suggested and Emma, only partially resigned to the loss of her skunk, sank into a chair and exclaimed: 'What a multitude of children! Wherever have they all come from?' looking bewildered.

'We had to bring them all for its Miss Daisy's afternoon off.' I explained.

'Of course, of course...' she sounded totally unconvinced. 'What a sad day it's turned into. I wonder where my darling Scooter can be...'

The gentlemen had grouped together near the house and were in happy conversation. I'd not seen Jim look so chirpy in weeks and I strongly suspected the disappearance of Scooter the Skunk was the cause of his good humour.

The Miles left Las Palmas on Tuesday and we were sorry to see them go, they were such a 'fun' family that one could do nothing but enjoy oneself when they were about.

CHAPTER 20

'It's a disgrace that you've been in Uruguay for ten years and still don't know the capital city,' Sydney said to me one November afternoon of 1884. 'Donald and I are planning a short visit there soon and suggest you come with us. What do you think?'

'Oh, I'd love it!' The idea delighted me. 'It's not absolutely true that I don't know Montevideo,' I said, 'I passed through it on our arrival ten years ago; we spent some hours there before taking the riverboat that night.'

'True, I'd forgotten,' he said, 'but it can't be considered a visit to the city. If you come with us, we'll take you sight-seeing.'

Donald agreed to the plans to go by steamer, via Fray Bentos, for travelling overland was not considered advisable as there were no good roads to Montevideo.

Willy drove us to Mercedes in the carriage with our luggage strapped on the back, and we took a stagecoach over to Fray Bentos. We had a brief encounter with the Miles family before finally taking the riverboat 'Silex' to Buenos Aires, where we remained a few days, sufficient to do some excellent shopping.

The shop attendants were extremely kind and we were glad to find we could make ourselves understood even in that city. The best of our stay in the huge city was when we took a tram ride out to Flores to visit some friends the gentlemen knew from a previous visit. I met the Blake's and the Courtland's, both such noble families and so well esteemed by the gentlemen.

We sailed on the 'Silex' for Montevideo and spent seven days there. On arrival we went to the Oriental Hotel where the gentlemen had stayed before. Our rooms were on the top storey, up a flight of rickety stairs. The whole place was dark and had a damp musky odour despite the summer season, and when we opened the door of our room and peered into the gloomy interior, the smell was much worse. The proprietor must have noted our disgust because he ran to throw open the window, which did little to relieve either light or odour.

'You have a good view of La Catedral!' he exclaimed cheerily, as though one lived solely on views, while he pushed the grimy shutters open.

'Thank you,' said Donald without much enthusiasm. 'What time's lunch?'

Donald and I rested in this unattractive room for we'd docked very early. Sydney slept soundly in his room next door until we woke him for lunch, for he'd sat up in the Silex saloon nearly all night playing *Truco.* (card game) He'd not wanted to hand it in for his luck was running well and he'd won a lot of money. It was only as dawn broke and the Uruguayan coastline was well in sight that he went and threw himself down on his bunk for a couple of hours' sleep.

Before eleven o'clock Donald and I could stand the musky enclosure no more. 'Let's go out and take a walk,' I suggested as I bounced off the bed.

'Good idea, the day's beautiful.'

'Which way?' I laughed as we stepped into the street. Neither of us had any idea of where to go, but automatically turned towards the waterfront and the Port. The sea being always fascinating.

The Port of Montevideo was in a very antiquated condition, with wooden piers jutting out where embarkations tied up on arrival. Each pier had a crane and a certain amount of service material, but largely it was an outdated port. Recently there'd been great talks and projects with the British firm Cutbill Son & Delungo to build a new and modern port worthy of a town such as Montevideo, but severe complications with the negotiations between this firm and the present Santos government hindered the final decisions.

Today there was a salty freshness in the air and we could hear the running swell of the sea as it broke against the rocks fringing the bay. It was cool on the water-front despite the warm December sun and we felt a congenial love for this city as we strolled arm-in-arm along the jetty and looked at the steamers in dock.

After lunch we decided we'd find a better hotel, so we took a stroll and relatively nearby we found the Paris Hotel much more to our liking.

The proprietor was most helpful when we told him we wanted to see some important sights of the town.

'Well,' he began, 'you being British will want to see La Brecha, where the English forces penetrated the great walls of our Fortress and conquered the town. This was back in 1807. At the foot of this street (it's now a street, you see) you'll find the Olitriniti.'

'The what?' asked Donald.

'The Olitriniti,' he repeated. 'The English call it that. They arrive and they ask where it is; and I tell them.' he smiled and then as an afterthought added: 'They go there on Sunday.'

'Is it a sort of Church?'

'Yes, it's the English people's *templo*. (church) Of course,' he lowered his voice and his eyes, 'I've not been inside. It's the English who go there on Sunday — we have our own Catedral.'.

Early in the century the English invaded this country and after fifteen days of heavy bombarding from the sea of the great walls of the fortress, they made a small 'breach' ten metres wide near the *Porton de San Juan*, and came into the city by this gap taking over for seven months.

We saw the street Brecha only had historical value, but on the seafront with waves breaking against the southern walls, stood the church. Magnificent in the afternoon sunshine with emerald sea in the background, its huge red granite columns stood as pillars of a vast temple, and printed above the columns were the words HOLY TRINITY CHURCH of MONTEVIDEO; 1844.

At last we knew what the proprietor had meant by Olitriniti, it was as any Spanish speaking person would have pronounced it. We began to giggle and soon were bellowing with laughter.

'Let's try and see it, shall we?' said Donald. We were lucky to find a very pleasant caretaker who let us in to see the interior. It was a large church with a wide aisle up to the chancel steps, and on past the choir stalls to the alter. Beautiful stained-glass windows lined the walls above the altar and along the side walls.

'How old is the church?' I asked him.

'We're having our 40th birthday next month. The foundation stone was laid on January 1st, 1844.' He smiled proudly, 'it's the second oldest Anglican Church in South America. St. John's in Buenos Aires is older; do you know it?' None of us knew St. John's Pro-Cathedral in Buenos Aires, but it made our visit to Holy Trinity Church none the less attractive, and we decided to come to Morning Matins on Sunday.

Next morning, I woke early, yawned, stretched and woke Donald. 'It's another beautiful day!' I cried. 'Wake up, sleepy-head and get out of bed; we don't want to sleep away all our holiday.'

We spent the morning shopping and found some attractive stores where we bought Christmas presents for the children. Later as Donald and I were lounging on our beds in the hotel once again when Sydney's firm rapid knock came to our door.

Sydney had been out reconnoitering: 'We must go to the Plaza Constitucion,' he said excitedly. 'It's the Plaza where they had the battle in '75 when President Ellauri was overthrown. Do you remember hearing of this massacre shortly after you'd arrived in the country?'

'Yes,' reflected Donald, 'and we were terrified the whole country might become involved in civil war.'

Sydney went on: 'A provisional government was set up and the following March of 1876, the strong man, Colonel Lorenzo Latorre took over as Dictator.'

'We must see this Plaza, and let's look for bullet holes!' I exclaimed, 'but let's have lunch first.' It was agreed that the meal was as important as a historical tour. After a substantial lunch we went to the Plaza Constitucion.

It was kept clean and there were few people about. The Cathedral of Montevideo, built in 1733, looks on to the Plaza and is decorative with its two main spires and three large arches framing the entrance doors. Across the Plaza, opposite to the Cathedral was the fine El Cabildo building, the seat of the Parliament.

On our return to the hotel we asked the proprietor about the Port Market for Donald wanted to go to the *Cigarreria* to buy some English tobacco for his pipe.

'The site chosen for the market,' said the proprietor, 'was the area known as the Baños de los Padres, named like this because it was the spot where the Franciscan monks from the nearby convent used to bathe. A bit before this, in the same zone, the Aduana Vieja was made, so the new market's in a strategic position facilitating the entry of produce from the interior. But what stands out most in the building is the magnificent roof! Go and see it!' he urged us. 'Take a walk inside the walls and look up at ROOF!' he gestured in adoration. 'I saw it being built; every brick, every stone, each pane of glass — I saw them all placed.... I love the Port Market!' he ended dramatically.

Naturally, in the late afternoon, we went to see the Market and its beautiful roof, quite as lovely as it had been said to be, and we bought Donald's tobacco too.

The next morning the proprietor was helpful again: 'Today you must go to our main Plaza and walk on Avenida 18 de Julio which begins at the foot of the Plaza Independencia which was laid to commemorate the country's independence. There's a magnificent mansion, the Palacio Estevez, which has recently been bought by the government and will become Government House.' He paused. 'Take a good look at it for the architecture is worth seeing. No expense was spared, it's all luxury and perfection.'

The Palacio Estevez proved to be quite as exquisite as our friend had announced, and even though we were not architecture experts, we did appreciate its beauty and enjoyed seeing the exterior.

'What a beautiful building!' I cried excitedly.

Donald linked his arm through mine: 'Are you enjoying it?'

'Yes, tremendously!' I replied. 'I love this city, it has so much charm. It's fresh and clean smelling, due to its proximity to the sea.'

We passed by a large, and evidently popular cafe, judging by the amount of people inside and the sound of music drifting out. It stood on the corner of the Plaza and Avenida 18 de Julio and here we began walking along the main avenue.

Avenida 18 de Julio was paved with cobble-stones and today lined with carts carrying merchandise to the many stores. Two-storey buildings, correctly patterned, gave it an aspect of neatness, added to the elegant lamp-posts on every corner which illuminated the avenue during the night watches. We noticed the illumination was far better here than in the old city where we were staying.

The Avenida was light and sunny with trees flanking the sidewalks, adding a green flare to the pleasant thoroughfare. As we stood on the corner of Calle Arapey, looking south, we could see the towers of the Cathedral dominating the city. As we walked back we looked at the shops and compared them to those of Buenos Aires and despite them being on a smaller scale, they were none the less pleasant and prosperous. I also enjoyed watching the people who, being a weekday, were all busy about their work. We were not noticed, only when the foreign language was heard did they turn their heads to stare.

Soon we reached the Plaza Independencia again and after another quick look at the Palacio Estevez, found ourselves beside the untidy open market which cluttered the edge of the Plaza and led to another cobble-stoned street called Buenos Aires. This brought us practically onto the steps of the Solis Theatre. Being almost midday, the beautiful theatre was closed but Donald promised to bring me to the evening performance of Faust which was announced on the noticeboard.

We made preparations for going to Church the following day as it was Sunday.

'What shall I wear?'

'Something cool,' said Donald, 'it feels hot to me.'

'Something cool, but what? My new pink dress? My white two-piece, or is it too dressy? Oh, I don't know what to put on!' I cried as I stood in my under-clothes in the middle of the room while Donald was already fully dressed and wanting his breakfast. He stepped to the window and threw it open.

'It's hot,' he repeated, 'wear something cool.' Frowning impatiently, he sat down on the bed. I quickly grabbed my blue silk and slipped into it.

As it was the hottest day of all our holiday, we planned to go to Pocitos beach for a bathe after Church.

'You go to Olitrinity?' our friend asked us at breakfast.

'Yes, we're going to church.' We burst out laughing and the unfortunate man looked abashed.

Once we were inside the great walls of the church sitting on some extremely English and grossly uncomfortably erect pews, we suddenly felt as if we were somewhere in England. The service was slightly dull and the singing poor and to make it worse they sang the Psalms as well as the Venite and Te Deum. The sermon was far too long and I could not concentrate on what was being said for our forthcoming bathe was foremost in my mind.

We took a tram from the centre and bought tickets for Pocitos. The tram was comfortably equipped with rush seats and we had vision out of the windows, soon entering the suburb of Pocitos and we got down at the end of the line.

The air seemed fresh and sweet when we were off the tram, with a faint salty savour suggesting the closeness of the sea. We were only a few yards from the coast and the well-known waterfront. The air was delightful and bracing, very different to the dry country air we'd been used to these last ten years.

The light surface of the water glistened as we approached the beach and a little later we'd booked bathing-machines of which there were many. After a lovely bathe which removed all the discomfort of the hot day, I cried: 'Let's come again tomorrow!' to which Donald agreed.

'We'll come again but we must get back to town before it gets dark.

We arrived in town just as the sun was setting over the pleasant Montevidean bay with a good view of the Cerro; the same hill we'd seen by night when we were first making our way to Las Palmas. The perilous trip across to Buenos Aires, never to be forgotten — it all seemed so long ago now; we'd been so young and full of hope.

The Cerro was picturesque at sunset. A Portuguese sailor is said to have once climbed to the top and on reaching the flattened surface together with some other expeditionaries, added this footnote in his diary: 'One cannot describe the beauty of this land.'

Tonight we stood and watched the first flashes from the light-house coming across the bay.

———————

'Today you must go a little out of town,' the proprietor called when he saw us the next morning.

'I know you're appreciative of our beautiful buildings, so today you must see La Quinta de Berro; it's a bit out of town but not inaccessible for it's near the Prado Oriental which is one of the best neighbourhoods.'

The carriage provided for us with a friend called Pancho in the driver's seat, had seen better days with the leather seats worn and shabby but the two beautiful chestnuts in harness were a treat to be seen and after getting used to the creaking of the old woodwork, we began to enjoy the drive.

La Quinta de Berro was impressive. The style was slightly Gothic and it stood in an exquisite parkland with abundant orange, tangerine, lemon and mimosa trees together with many eucalyptuses.

A regal aspect was displayed by the wide, exterior marble stairway leading to the first floor. At this level an extensive gallery served as entrance hall and was sometimes used as a ballroom. The dining-room was separated from the other chambers by a delightful interior patio, with a fountain in its centre and many exotic plants.

A fully equipped theatre hall gave the ground floor its own character. Wide doors showed how the parklands opened up into avenues to the back of the castle and ran down to the edge of the bay.

We spent a long time roaming about the beautiful grounds and admiring this lovely place, until we returned to the carriage and Pancho, who proved to be a most obliging person, offering to take us further to see El Prado and the Plaza de Toros (Bullring) on our way back to town.

'Thank you, Pancho,' Donald said as he paid him his fee when back at the hotel.

'Tomorrow?' he asked gullibly.

'No, Pancho,' Donald was firm, 'we're getting to the end of our holiday and can't afford any more.'

'We ought to go and have another swim,' said Sydney, mopping his brow.

The difference to our first tram trip to Pocitos was our getting off at the great Ombu tree with its own history. It is said that Artigas, the national hero, used to sit in the shade of its inviting branches.

The water was bluer this morning and the bathing more delicious. I stayed in too long and got very cold, having to come out and sit in the sun to warm up. The fine white sand spreading all around me, helped me to dream about a future holiday here where we could bathe once or twice a day. We'd take long walks along the prom and breathe in the rich air. I could see us, with the children, coming down to the beach, making sandcastles, collecting shells, hunting crabs.... What a lovely holiday; but soon my dreams vanished as distant clouds began drifting up. Donald and Sydney were also out of the water declaring they were hungry.

We found an Italian bar where they served pastas and red wine. It was a particularly cheerful lunch and we laughed a lot, then deciding to take our frivolous mood with us on a stroll along the coast. Eventually we reached another beach — a far more fashionable one — where the ladies came down to bathe and to take the air. We saw the long wooden bridge on which the *tranvia de caballitos* (horse tram) stopped to pick up passengers who wished to go home.

'We must do the business we came for initially,' said Donald across the breakfast table next morning, 'it's our last day for we're booked on this evening's riverboat.'

'We'll do the shops this morning and the banks in the afternoon,' suggested Sydney. 'Do you mind being left alone?' he asked me.

'Not in the least,' I replied. 'I'll spend the morning packing and settling our things. Will you be back for lunch?'

'Oh yes! And siesta too!'

I was downstairs in the lounge by midday. The kind proprietor came to keep me company.

'Have you seen our stores with imported cloth and other lovely articles?' he asked.

'No,' I said, 'where are they?'

'On Sarandi Street, on the short stretch between the two Plazas is where the high quality stores are located.' Then he went on to tell me: 'In the late afternoons the grand ladies go down there to have a look around, not always to buy but it is considered chic to be seen there at that time of day. The gentlemen take part and wait on the sidewalks to get a glimpse of their favourite lady'. He went on to tell me how it was the time of brief encounters, gallantries, bold stares from the gentlemen and soft blushes by the ladies.

'Every day?' I asked.

'Oh yes.' I liked the idea of being a witness to this, if only as a fly on the wall.

'I'll walk over this afternoon,' I murmured barely audibly, but he must've heard for he leaned forward and touched my arm. 'Dear lady, you cannot possibly go alone.'

'Why not?'

'It's considered the height of ill manners for a lady to go alone. There must be a mother, a husband, an aunt or somebody to accompany the beautiful young lady...'

I burst out laughing: 'I'm not a young lady! I have four children!' He rose to his feet and cleared his throat. 'You don't understand the Latin mind...' He broke off. I still didn't understand his fear of my getting out there alone, but I realized he was serious about his warning. Pity. I'd have to wait for Donald and Sydney. It was not hard to persuade them especially once they'd had a good cup of tea.

The shops were splendid and full of gorgeous imported items but what I was more on the outlook for were the people since the proprietor had told me the social event which it involved. There were ladies dressed in the latest exotic fashions and elegant gentlemen.... I caught his eye suddenly! He was on the other side of the street and his stare was bold and admiring. It embarrassed me to look into those naked eyes; my heart gave a leap. They reminded me of somebody long ago. Alberto, whom I'd never seen again. I looked away swiftly yet he was attractive so I gave him a tiny side-long glance before continuing down the street. He followed us, his eyes fixed on me, and I made a pretext of looking a little longer in one window.

My admirer advanced slightly towards me, wishing to get into conversation, but I knew it was impossible. I lowered my head, rejecting his approach, and just then I caught a glimpse of Donald's impatient face a few yards along. I peeped again at the tall handsome gentleman who was smiling at me as if he understood my dilemma.

I realized why coming alone would have been a mistake.

———————

I thought a lot about Montevideo in the weeks that followed. When we arrived, before us had spread a pleasant town, open and airy, its principal attraction being its situation on the coast. A balmy little peninsular full of sunshine and sea breezes and people of goodwill.

The visit had given me the power of renewal. I'd almost forgotten what it was like to live in civilization, I'd been so long in the bush I'd lost touch with community living, with people and culture.

The noise of the city, the movement of carriages and carts and the crowded streets, had often tired me. At night there'd been the sound of voices and music coming from the bars and cafes, such a contrast to the immense silence of the country where, once the sun sets, the only sound is the rustle of the wind in the trees or the hooting of an owl.

The city had been different. We'd seen beautiful buildings, green parks, seen the sea and even bathed. These things were important to us for we hoped to make this land our home and that of our children. Could it be that some grandson might be heard to say: 'I am Uruguayan!' with a hint of pride in his voice? I'd be content to hear it for it would stamp the seal of success on our mission.

CHAPTER 21

For the first time in ten years we were to have a real Christmas party. Perhaps it'd have been better to wait until we had our new house, but the mood took us to celebrate our tenth year at Las Palmas, small house or beautiful new one.

Christmas in this part of the world comes in the middle of summer which assisted our space problem for the amount of guests we hoped to invite. The party would be outside, just off the veranda on the grass which was looking smooth and green thanks to the extravagant care the gentlemen gave to it. The gardener kept it cut but the gentlemen, in their spare moments, carried out the weeding at the beginning of each spring.

'It rarely rains on Christmas Day,' Donald remarked one afternoon when we were first planning the party, 'but it might be our bad luck to have a wet evening this year.'

'Oh, don't be pessimistic, darling!' I chipped in. 'If we should be so unlucky as to have a bad evening on Christmas Eve, we'll just squeeze into the rooms — it'll be lots of fun anyway!'

The thought of rain for that evening worried Donald and persisted in his mind, until finally he and Sydney decided to have a big marquee erected, which would enlarge the premises and subsequently make provision in case of rain. They spoke to people in Mercedes and eventually found what they wanted.

As the weather was so hot we were planning a Christmas Eve party with a cold buffet supper. We invited everyone we knew and soon the list of guests was longer than imagined in the wilds of Uruguay.

Christmas Eve dawned fine and hot. No sign of rain. Nevertheless, there was great activity about the house and grounds when the men arrived to erect the marquee shortly after eight. They dug in large poles to hold this enormous covering.

The cooking was underway when I went into the kitchen to look for vases for the flowers. There were two extra women from the village to help for most of the cooking had to be done on this very day because of the heat.

A little pine tree had been found near to Dolores and Donald had brought it back in the trap a few days ago and after some discussion we decided to place it at the end of the veranda where it was perfectly visible to everybody.

At this time of the year it did not get dark until about eight o'clock, so to give people time to arrive before sundown as they mainly came in traps or carts or on horseback, we invited for seven. Those from far away would have travelled half the afternoon and would be hot and dusty, so we prepared a bedroom as a rest room and a long trestle table was put up and laid with cool drinks at which people stopped to wet their parched lips on arrival.

I wore white this evening and my dress stood out and away from my body, fitting only at my waist, while my bare shoulders felt deliciously cool. I'd drawn my unruly hair into a very smooth and fashionable roll which had been taught me by a hairdresser in Fray Bentos. As I took a final look at myself in the mirror, I thought it made me look a fraction older.

The other women's dresses were like full-blown flowers dotted about the grass and the party was gathering impetus as more and more friends arrived and the conversation swelled in volume. When I thought everybody was here, I went to where Donald was standing, glass in hand, talking animatedly to the O'Brian's. His eyes were fixed on Colleen's face as he talked and laughed. She was looking lovely. Her pale yellow dress looked like a daffodil which was about to be blown away. Her dark hair fell in soft waves over her bare shoulders as she swayed slightly with delicate grace and I felt a moment of envy at her youth. As I approached, Donald caught sight of me and held out his hand to welcome me into the group, his free arm encircled my waist. 'My gorgeous wife!' he exclaimed in rather a higher tone than his usual voice, showing he'd already had his fill of wine.

'Do you think it's time to serve the food?' I asked.

'Yes!' he cried. 'Yes, yes, yes, it's time to start eating.' I disentangled myself and started for the kitchen. I almost collided with Mr. Brown as I turned into the house. It was slightly dark in the passage where he was, and at first I did not see him. He put out his hand and touched me.

'Ah! The lady of the house, I believe.' His piggy eyes glinted at me through the dusk.

'Hello, Mr. Brown,' I greeted him and held out my hand. He took it but did not let it go, the old trick of his.

'I've asked you to call me Alfred: won't you?'

'Oh sorry: I always forget.' I was able to snatch my hand free. 'I'm going to order dinner.' I began edging past him. 'I'll meet you again outside. Please make yourself at home.' Once again I felt the revulsion towards this man, yet he so obviously adored me, always being incredibly generous in the past with gifts of animals. Indeed, one of my favourite breeding bulls had originally come as a calf from Mr. Brown. Besides, I had to be polite, he was our best ram buyer.

'I always feel at home here, dear lady, and I certainly will see you again!' He made a little bow as I slipped past him: a sour smell of wine hung in the air.

Soon the food was circulating; the talk started up again with the clattering of knives and forks against the china plates. The kitchen had done us well, never in my memory of Christmas had I seen such a feast. Roast lamb, finely sliced beef, turkey and chicken, pies and pastry bulging with dried fruits, added to unlimited amount of salads. I watched the platters being carried off to different corners of the gardens where guests settled to eat and drink. Smiles of satisfaction, and of greed, on their faces as they hastened to find a convenient spot to devour the meal.

The noise was deafening. Loud laughter and animated talk made a continual crescendo and soon we had to shout at the top of our voices to be heard at all. But everybody was enjoying themselves.... I could see Pintos propped against one of the veranda columns, surely not trusting himself to stand alone. He normally was no drinker, but Christmas was, after all, Christmas which comes but once a year. His wife was sitting demurely a few yards from him, smiling in her tranquil manner, keeping a close eye on young

Mario who was playing happily with our children. With his rusty, close-curling hair, Mario had a strong likeness to his cousins.

I wondered what Sydney was thinking as he watched his little son. I wondered if he ever went over to Pintos' place purposely to see him. Did he take him a present on his birthday? Tonight, did he remember the child's mother spending her Christmas so many miles away?

Soon the greasy platters were being cleared away and it was time to light the candles on the tree and distribute the presents. Everybody moved closer to the tree while Donald and I handed out a gift for each person. This took much longer than we'd anticipated, and there were lots of 'Oooohs" and Ahhhhs' as the little parcels were opened. Mrs. Harrison sat down at the piano and began playing soft music and gradually the soft tunes turned into polkas and waltzes and some of the guests began to dance and naturally it did not take long for the dancing to become general. I found myself dancing wildly with Edward O'Brian over the grass. It gave one's steps a weird bouncy feeling unlike a ballroom, but it did not hinder the dancers.

Later on when the dancing was at its height I saw, out of the corner of my eye, the shadow of a couple strolling off into the dark night. Was it Colleen? The slim figure, swaying slightly, was not easily mistaken, yet here was Edward still dancing madly: a waltz this time with Maggie Miles whooping and hooting with laughter as she rocked and swayed in young Edward's arms. Next I was dancing with Donald and we stopped to rest by the edge of the lawn.

'People are enjoying themselves,' Donald commented.

'What luck it's a success!' I laughed happily into his face, 'and we've had a perfect night for it.'

I looked towards the house, all noise and movement. Even Jim and Emma Tomkins were seen to kick up their heels and join in the fun. Skunks and debts had been left aside for this magical evening.

It gave me great pleasure to see Dr. Owens with his tiny wife for once in our home on an unofficial visit, eating, drinking and laughing as any other person present. I recalled all his past visits — rushed — urgent — so many fears and so much distress — then his calm professional presence smoothing it all out.

Tonight, with all barriers down and all sickness forgotten, he was laughing as Willy told him a joke.

In the meantime, it was distressing to me that I could never raise my eyes without meeting the bold stare of Mr. Brown. His little eyes were permanently fixed on me; I could not shake them off. I watched him briefly as he strutted about and spoke to different people. Everybody knew him. His sheep flocks were well known over all the countryside as being the best. The name of his farm was respected by the proudest landowner — they went over and shook his hand. They talked and asked his advice. He grinned and showed his brown stub teeth but his eyes always flitted back to me. All at once he bowed to the company he was in and made movements to come over in my direction. I hid behind Donald, looking for a way of escape. The big eucalyptus tree was near, spreading its haughty branches to the star-spangled summer sky. I slipped behind it, but he'd seen me...

'Will you dance, madam?' He reached for my waist and I couldn't refuse. I was in his arms and we mingled with the rest of the crowd, his breath hot on my cheek. I turned my head away and hoped the jingle would end and release me from my torture.

'You're beautiful in white!' he whispered in my ear. 'I've been watching you all evening, you know.' He gripped me tighter and tighter until I could hardly breathe.

'Mr. Brown!' I gasped, 'will you please...'

'Ah, again Mr. Brown. Call me Alfred, I tell you...'

'It's not easy for me to call you Alfred, I always think of you as Mr. Brown.'

'Do you always think of me? That's good. Do you think of me often?' I realized my mistake or his misinterpretation of my words.

'Sometimes...' I broke off vaguely, conversation was difficult being held so tightly.

'Good, good, you should think of me always as I do of you! We'd make a wonderful team; a business team to start with.' He was at it again. I shook my head and tried to turn away. 'Why are you so negative about my idea of a partnership?' He feigned a look of deep hurt. 'You know you need a man at your side to help and advise you about your cattle.' He paused and a crafty look came on to his face. 'Especially now your precious Alberto has been given the push, eh?' He felt me stiffen and I tried to wriggle out of his arms. 'Ah!' he continued, 'so there was something in the relationship between you two. I often wondered.' He gave a dry, mirthless laugh.

'Will you please loosen your grip on my waist? You're hurting me!' I panted. I wanted so much to get away.

'Come now,' he grinned, quite restored to good humour. 'Don't start getting coy and prudish. Don't forget we understand each other — there's not much you can hide from Alfred Brown, you know.'

'I don't know what you're insinuating!' I cried in my haughtiest manner.

'I'm not insinuating anything, my dear, I'm telling you straight that your smutty affair with your cowhand was no secret. Oh, don't get vexed! Your guests will wonder what you're upset about and you might have to explain!' He twirled me around expertly in tune to the music. I had no alternative but to follow on. There was no escape and he was enjoying himself at my expense as usual. Why did he always seem to have the upper hand over me?

'I won't have you speaking of Alberto in that way. He was a very useful person and...'

'In more ways than one, no doubt.' he broke in. His sarcastic double-meaning made me wince.

'Mr. Brown...'

'Alfred,' he reminded me.

'Alfred,' I repeated absently, 'I wish to stop dancing, I'm exhausted.' He skillfully led me to a fallen tree trunk we had as an ornamental bench, just outside the range of lighting. Thankfully I sat down, glad to be away from his grasp. It was also cooler away from the marquee and I tried to collect my wits.

'I repeat,' he continued, 'your affair with Alberto was no secret to anyone with a spark of observation at all. One only had to see the way he looked at you to know of his burning desire! Only the simple-minded and the blind refused to notice it, until it was too late. What happened in the hay *galpon* (barn) that night?'

My mouth went dry and words failed me yet I opened my mouth to give him a curt reply, but he held me back and laughed: 'You've no idea how attractive you are when you are roused!' He chuckled under his breath. 'Don't worry, your secret is safe with me. I shan't let on.' With this last slight I jumped to my feet preparing to leave his company, but he drew me down to the log again.

'Wait!' he ordered, 'I've very few opportunities of talking to you alone, and even though I don't give a sausage about your illicit activities of the past, I do have a serious proposition to make you.' He stopped and looked seriously at me. 'It's a business proposition. I've said it once before and you turned it down very emphatically, but I'm hoping the years have made you reconsider it, so I'll repeat it now.'

'Not a hope,' I pouted sulkily, still smarting from his recent attack on Alberto.

'Ah madam, you're such a lovely woman, with so much potential all going to waste here on this badly run farm, which gives little compared to what it should.' He shook his head.

'I can't conceive any sort of business you and I could possibly undertake together.' I declared irritably. 'No matter what you have in mind, my answer will be negative.'

'How foolish you sound. I thought better of you. You've not even heard my proposal yet. That's no way to do good business, is it?' He paused, 'I'm sure deep in your innermost heart you're bursting with curiosity to know what it's all about.' He regarded me slyly, hoping to find a breach in my armour, before going on: 'It's a good idea, easy to carry out and very profitable.' He brought his face close to mine, emphasizing the money angle of the bargain. He knew how to capture my interest, damn him! The temptation to slap his insolent face was almost irresistible, and he was near enough too. Yet it would not be the thing for a Christmas party, so I controlled myself and held my peace, thinking how much my cattle business had suffered since Alberto left. My animals were there, an occasional calf added, a few sales to cattle buyers in the vicinity but little else. My money bag was getting thinner, I had few reserves now and this might be an opportunity to make an improvement. Brown was always very generous with me.... I should at least listen. He noticed my hesitation and gave a knowing grin. 'Behold! A spark of interest at last!' he cried.

'Tell me what you have in mind and stop beating about the bush!' I cried impatiently.

'Not until you say 'please', dear lady,' he laughed. Now he was teasing me and prolonging the conversation on purpose. I rose to my feet again intending to end it all but he caught the edge of my gown and pulled. I sat.

'Say 'Please Alfred', then I'll begin.' He was revoltingly cruel; now he had my curiosity aroused he was taking his time to tell me what he had in mind. I turned the tables on him and lisped in baby language: 'Pleeese Alfwed' He laughed again, satisfied.

'My idea for the present is very simple. You know my line of animals is mainly sheep, but I have a small amount of cattle and I'd like to have more but my land is too small for this. Yours is large. I propose buying steers to fatten on your land. You will rear them — you've already proved yourself extremely successful at this, and when the correct time comes, you'll sell them. The profits we'll divide between us; it'll be a joint affair. Your lands will be better populated, and,' he added craftily, 'your pockets will be filled more abundantly.

'Do you honestly imagine Donald approving such a thing?' I asked indignantly.

'Not at first perhaps,' he said, 'but I have every confidence you'd be able to convince him of the benefits, if you really wanted to. Am I right?' He stopped talking and looked at me a long time as my thoughts raced around my head. 'What do you say?'

I had no ready reply so 'I have to think about it' was all that came out, and here I rose to my feet slowly, repeating 'I'll think about it. Excuse me, I must attend to my other guests.'

I made my way to the centre of the party again, smiling and chatting, but Mr. Brown's words had left me disturbed. His business was worth thinking about but his other insinuations had awoken all sorts of emotions I had long since filed away in the back of my mind. He'd spoilt my Christmas party! Hateful, horrid man!

'What's the matter? You look so vexed.' It was Donald at my side and I thankfully slid into his arms to dance.

'It's that nasty Mr. Brown, who always seems to spoil my evening. I hope he'll go home soon.' It was not the moment to talk about business deals with Donald. It was nearly Christmas Day and this was our wonderful party.

The clock was nearing the hour — twelve o'clock — and more cider was being poured in preparation for the toast of the great day.

Raising his glass high, Donald called out at the very top of his voice 'MERRY CHRISTMAS' and everybody responded.

Presently guests were coming up to us with outstretched hands and words of thanks and then departing to their homes. 'It's been the best Christmas Eve we've ever had.'

'Come again next year!' Donald had enjoyed his evening. We were standing together on the edge of the veranda, looking onto the patio where all the vehicles and horses had been tethered. I thought I saw some moving shadows sliding among the trees, making their way back to the house from somewhere out there. One was Colleen and the other... Sydney! His hand decorously under her elbow, guiding her return across the rough gravel. They had enjoyed their stroll and everything was in order, except for the tell-tale wisps of straw hanging in her hair.

CHAPTER 22

Our new house was in the process of construction but somehow it was not being built as fast as we'd anticipated. There were drawbacks: slack workmen had to be dismissed and new men taken on. The weather had been wet, forcing the work to be frequently stopped.

Although we had extensive problems and also a great deal to do, we could not be totally oblivious of the country's situation at this particular time, early in 1886.

'They say there's another blasted revolution in the offing.' Sydney had returned from Mercedes where he'd spent two days on cattle business and purchasing materials for the house, with this news.

'How did you hear?' asked Donald.

'In the town it's pretty common knowledge, though it's only commented on behind closed doors. The people are fed up with the military oppression, and this revolt is said to be the real thing.'

'What's so different about it?'

'It seems to be a final movement planned to overthrow General Santos and his government. It's to be a national intent, neither Colorado nor Blanco party alone, but everybody in one great revolution to save the country from the political crisis, and the disgraceful administrative disorders which threaten to ruin us completely,' Sydney went on.

Donald looked concerned and then asked: 'Who's at the head?'

'Not sure, it's being organized in the Argentine.' Historical accounts maintain Dr. Joaquin Requena y Garcia was the alma mater of this revolution which was eventually known as La Revolucion del Quebracho.

The people initiating this attack wanted to place an outstanding officer to lead it. The most appropriate person was Lieutenant General Enrique Castro and he took the appointment, leaving Montevideo for Entre Rios, Argentina, in February to join the legions assembling there.

I hated these discussions and comments on revolutions and wars as much as the gentlemen seemed to enjoy them. I let the others converse and mourn over all this trouble; they were completely helpless anyway; I didn't worry over matters I was not capable of controlling.

There's absolutely no doubt that the building of our new house embraced the centre of our lives entirely for the following months, despite the country's problems.

Our return from Montevideo was marked by two major events. One, Herbert, Donald's youngest brother, was travelling out to visit us and two, he was bringing my Legacy money with him. The solicitors had written months ago informing me about the money being available whenever desired. At first we did not know how to get it out here, trusting neither Bank Money Orders nor Drafts, and then we heard of Herbert's possible trip and decided this was the best way for it to come. Letters were written and a formal authorization signed granting Herbert the power to withdraw these funds.

We were looking forward to seeing Herbert; he was ten years younger than Donald's thirty-five. 'He was a mere child when we left,' said Sydney, 'it'll be marvelous to have him here as a young adult.'

'Let's hope he's sufficiently mature and responsible to bring my money,' I said. 'It would be the end of the world if it were to go astray after so much time.'

'Don't worry, my pet,' put in Donald. 'Herbert's a Fitzpatrick and I'd trust him with my own life.'

'Surely,' I agreed, 'but he'll have his hands full with all the bits and pieces coming out under his care as well.'

Carriehall had been sold and the vast contents divided as the money had been. Ethel had written letters explaining in what manner the furniture and other objects were being split up as fairly as possible. I made no claims, but I'd told Mama of my particular fondness of the lovely Welsh dresser which stood in the dining-room and if this was in no special demand, I'd like to have it. They'd not replied to this request, so when we went to meet Herbert in Mercedes, I'd no idea what he was bringing.

While we were away in Montevideo Willy had not done well with the farm work, he seemed to have done more carting business, taking advantage of the good weather. All the sheep needed bringing up for dipping and curing and he'd not even started this.

'Willy's an old bastard!' Sydney declared shortly after the neglect was noticeable. One can see he's been bumming about with his own carting instead of getting on with things here.'

'Let's not get worked up about it,' said Donald, acting as placater as usual. 'He'll have to move his ass as of Monday when we start the dipping.'

'We'll jolly well see that he does.'

Yet it was Sydney who remained to work the sheep and Willy drove the carriage to meet Herbert the following week.

Herbert had grown tall and he was now half a head taller than his brothers. He was smiling happily as he approached us.

Fresh news from home. We kept him talking late into the night until he eventually told me: 'Your mother is ailing,' he said gently. 'They don't know what's causing her sickness but suspect something serious.' He must've seen my shocked face for he reached and pressed my hand affectionately.

I went to bed with this agonizing news gripping my heart. I did not sleep, instead I went over every beautiful moment I'd spent with my mother and there were many.

'Oh Mama! Darling Mama!' my soul cried.

———————

All the previous year we'd spent talking and calculating prices of the exciting project for the new house. We could hardly wait to receive the cash. Now the moment had arrived.... There was a binding feature with us in the house project; we wanted the very best.

Donald was at the head of the construction. Sydney the purchaser of materials; he knew the market best, was well informed by *Pulperia* (general store) people and had a slight knowledge of building. He engaged the constructor and took on workhands. Willy, since he'd built his own coach-house so well, was to give advice on woodwork, tiles, floors and other such luxuries we hoped to have.

I was the principal designer for it was generally understood that the woman knew more about the interior as she spent the most time there. Whether this, in all honesty, could be applied to me I'm not altogether sure, but being the only woman the job was designated to me.

Predominant in my mind was the feature of the house being as much like Carriehall as possible, which had been the source of the financial aid. I adored the idea of it being transported in some way from Ireland to South America to be the home of many Fitzpatrick generations.

Having Herbert with us was a great help and his opinions were valued. He'd delivered the Legacy money safely into our hands as well as many lovely pieces of furniture from Carriehall. The beautiful Welsh dresser was amongst them.

Herbert proved strong and agile, and through his love of animals he was allowing Willy, almost unperceived, to do less and less work. Herbert could always take his place. Willy had put on a lot of weight recently, and I noted his physical movements had become increasingly cumbersome. He much preferred sitting up on the cart to being out on horseback working the sheep. Herbert filled in admirably and soon became part of the estancia and its workings.

Despite political revolts and revolutions, we noticed the country, at least in the interior, was developing well. Two years ago a committee had been formed in an attempt to combat the locusts, now a national plague. An obligation to attend the meetings had been imposed on all landowners, with a fine of 10 pesos to those in neglect. The idea was to exterminate all locusts, caterpillars and small alligators by a simultaneous action on the part of all inhabitants. Farmers were instructed to light fires at nightfall, feeding them and keeping them alight for several hours. Las Palmas complied with the regulations to the last letter and Donald and Sydney had taken turns in attending the meetings to avoid the fine.

Another sensible law enforced by the government was the controlling of abusive tree felling for posts and 'piques' for export going on. 'If nothing is done

to stop this abusive felling,' said the governor, 'all our woods will soon
be terminated. The tree felling must be controlled and the planting of
trees fostered.'

If anybody had complied with the planting it was Donald who'd put in
thousands of eucalyptus trees on our land. The authorities could not criticize
Las Palmas on these grounds.

April was a sad and memorable month for we learned two very important
things. First, that my mother had died in a Dublin hospital, and second, that
the defeat of the Revolution was consummated.

I knew I ought to be rejoicing at this grand triumph for the government,
but all I could feel those early days was an enormous void where thoughts of
Mama used to dwell, and sadness was my constant companion.

Yet the Revolution had been fought with outstanding heroism, in spite
of inferior numbers, inadequate arms and the advanced knowledge of their
movements by the opponents. At last the government flag was raised and the
firing ceased. The battle had only lasted seventy-two hours. Six hundred men
surrendered to the government forces as prisoners and the rest retreated in
different directions. No doubt the group sighted at Las Palmas were some of
these men.

The children were practicing their horseback jumping when they suddenly
left their horses and came rushing into the house shouting 'Soldiers, soldiers!'
in fear. None of the gentlemen were on the premises so I called Miss Daisy
to come and give a hand with horses and terrified children. Our horses had
to be got out of sight quickly for the straggling soldiers always stole horses. I
padlocked the stables door rapidly once they were inside, and ran for the house.

Miss Daisy had the children inside. 'Don't let them out until you have my
permission!' I called nervously.

I saw the soldiers marching along the upper road, not yet reaching our gate.
The trees along the avenue obstructed our view; I'd have to wait before knowing
whether they'd turned into our estancia or not.

I waited riveted to the veranda. If they came in, what should I do? Donald
always told me I should hide during the soldiers visits, yet who could take the
responsibility of talking to them today?

A few more minutes and I'd know our destiny.... I gripped the riding crop I had in my hand tightly and at the same time realized it was Ada's and a tell-tale object. One would not have a riding crop in one's hands if there were no horses as I was about to make them believe.

My throat went dry; the first uniforms came into view. I rushed inside and slammed the door. I was shaking.

Marta, the cleaning girl, was dusting the furniture.

'What's the matter, madam?' she asked when she saw my face. '*Que pasa?*' (What's up?)

Soldiers coming up the avenue!' I gasped. She peeped out of the window calmly.

'Oh, soldiers,' she turned to me smiling widely. 'Are they coming to the estancia?' What a foolish question!

Then I remembered Marta was only sixteen and she'd not been frightened as we had. Ten years ago she was a mere child of six, living quietly away in the hovel she came from in Palmitas. Our children were apprehensive about soldiers but Marta did not fear them, and an idea was forming in my mind.

'I'm not afraid of soldiers; my father says they're young men doing their duty. They could be my brothers.' 'If you're not afraid of them Marta,' I said, 'will you go on the veranda and ask what they want?'

'Yes, of course,' she replied with superiority, 'I'm not afraid of my own brothers.'

The men were entering the gravel patio and went directly to the well to drink. There were ten or twelve of them and one in particular was having a look around after his drink.

It was all quiet and as nobody had come out to intercept them, he started walking towards the house. I felt my knees begin to tremble. I gave Marta a short push on to the veranda. It felt like sending a lamb to slaughter but there was no time to change anything.

'Buenos dias!' (Good morning) I heard them exchanging greetings. From my cowardly position behind the drawing-room curtains I watched the scene. There seemed something different about these lads to the ones of years ago, these clearly showed exhaustion.

The man in charge and Marta were carrying on a conversation which I could not hear. I began to lose my fear when I saw the entire contingent was docile and depressed. Even my knees began to feel stronger.

Marta stood her ground valiantly while the conversation continued to which she constantly repeated 'No, no, no!' until another soldier drew up level and he began speaking in harsher terms. Then, after another of Marta's negatives, he flung out a hand and gave her an abrupt push.

That was enough for me. I reached for Donald's rifle, though I knew it was not loaded, opened the door and faced the mob.

A deep hush fell and they all turned to look at me, rifle in hand, standing framed in the doorway. I straightened my spine and raised my head up high. Nobody was going to guess how terrified I was. I looked directly into the face of the leader and called Marta to my side. 'What do they want?

Another short pause before the laughter broke out. I must've cut a comic figure. The rifle I was holding could not harm a hair on their heads, even if it had been loaded. These men had been faced with real artillery fire these past days, and the presence of an air rifle in the hands of a young woman was highly amusing. They laughed loud and long.

It sort of broke the ice and I lowered the rifle and soon Marta and I had joined the laughter. They wanted food, of course, and once it was arranged for them to eat in the workmen's quarters, they left our estancia with polite thanks.

I asked them if they were part of the Revolution and they admitted they were. They hoped to reach Colonia to get a vessel for the Argentine.

Now I knew why they were a different sort of soldier; they were not regular like the ones of ten years ago, they were merely young men who wished to liberate the country from the tyrant's rule. I was sorry for them, no defeat is pleasant, and most of them seemed educated lads. I might have had them eat at my own table but for Donald's inevitable reproach.

CHAPTER 23

The desire to have our new house finished became an obsession during 1886. It became the hub, the corona and the circumference of our thoughts and conversations. We'd hoped for it to be completed by the twelfth month but we'd not accounted for the countless hindrances to arise.

The weeks rolled into months, the seasons came and went. Autumn saw the foundations and cellar dug and the walls started, but the bricks were delayed three weeks in arriving and it was our first frustration. Then the winter was wet slowing down brick-laying as rainy days were stop days. Only in spring did we begin to feel it was really going ahead; two storeys up and the roof on before the spring was over, but the finishing touches took longer than the actual building.

The carpenters were utterly uncontrollable. Willy was supposed to be in charge of the woodwork but they were so sly they hoodwinked him at every other turn. There was lots of wood, beginning with the innumerable floors which were to be made from some beautiful boards Sydney had ordered from the south of Brazil. Here Willy refused to take the responsibility of cutting them, and handed the job ostentatiously to the chief carpenter, claiming he had no time to do this work.

When the shipment of planks arrived at Las Palmas we all stood back in awesome wonder at their magnificence. The cutting was to be a very specialized job. In my opinion, Willy was not prepared to take such a heavy responsibility, more especially after Sydney's remark once the boards arrived. 'They're beautiful AND expensive, but in my opinion worth buying.' He narrowed his eyes and went on: 'Now it only needs some blatant idiot to cut them wrong and ruin the lot!'

'Don't be pessimistic, Syd,' Herbert chipped in, 'all will be well.' But the shot had struck home with Willy and shortly afterwards we were told the carpenters were going to do the cutting, not Willy.

Willy took a great deal of interest in the banisters once he was freed of the floor work, and he cut and carved the supporting pillars with the workmen. It took what seemed an eternity; the work was slow and meticulous, but the results good.

Then came the day when Willy made a secretive trip into Mercedes alone, leaving early in the morning and merely saying he'd be back before sundown — and he was gone.

'What d'you suppose old Willy's up to in Mercedes?' Donald laughed during lunch.

'He never said one word about what he was going to do,' I said. 'He's never so secretive, is he?'

'Hope he doesn't get into mischief as he's done before once he's had a drink too many in the pub.' Sydney had never fully forgiven Willy for his initial mishap with the Army so many years ago.

'Oh Sydney, don't be mean; it's time we forgot poor old Willy's disgrace of so long ago.' I said, 'he'll be all right today and be back by sundown.'

When Willy got back towards evening he brought with him a large parcel of old newspaper wrappings and he asked us to assemble in the drawing-room to hear the secret of his trip. I was speechless with curiosity and nobody said a word.

As he spoke he began unwrapping his parcel: 'For a long time I've known of its existence, and from the moment I first set eyes on it, dominating the shabby little *Pulperia*, (general store) I knew I must have it. It was utterly wasted in the poor environment. It had to be brought here where people can see its magnificence and appreciate its beauty.' He was struggling with the final covering and I wished he'd hurry for the suspense was killing me.

At last it came into view. The head of a splendid lion carved in wood appeared.

'Willy! How did you get hold of this?' I exclaimed as he handed it to me; its weight told me it was solid. 'It's lovely!' I passed it on to Donald.

'Whew!' he whistled, 'this is a masterpiece!' he declared while inspecting it. Even Sydney admitted the carving was perfect, so he asked Willy what he proposed doing with it.

Very grandly, very deliberately and slowly, Willy got to his feet and held his trophy up high. 'I've brought it to stand on the first pillar of the staircase,' he announced with pride, beaming as he did so. None of us had the heart to tell him the majestic lion's head was more relative to a mansion in Africa than in our Las Palmas home, in modest Uruguay. There was no doubt the carving was perfect and the beast looked almost alive; he had a glint in his eye giving a suspicious feeling he was merely tarrying before the exact moment when he'd spring and devour us all.

Willy constructed an appropriate column on which to set the lion's head and finally it decorated our entrance hall. It was immediately known as Willy's Lion and through the years it kept a stately guard on our home. It saw everybody who came into the house; it was stroked and patted by most of us as we mounted the stairs. The invigilation of the ample drawing-room door on the left, in which the bow-window facing west was a witness to every sunset, was Willy's Lion's task as he watched all intruders in there. He was also a spectator to everybody who came in and out of the room on the left called El Boliche (The Pub) where all drinks were imbibed before and after meals. It was a cozy little sitting-room concealing the entrance to the wine cellar. A subtly hidden trapdoor could be found hidden under a rug opposite the fireplace. With time it took on a slightly sour odour of old spirits matured and tobacco smoke still present. Willy's Lion kept an account of everybody's condition as they came out of El Boliche before lunch and wended their way to the dining-room facing east and the graceful slope to the dipping bath, no longer visible because of the trees grown in between.

―――――

Another baby on the way had an instantaneous acceptance by everybody for in September Donny had gone off to school in Ireland, creating a void in family life. The prospect of a new baby was a blessing from heaven and ought to fill this gap.

Donny wrote happily having made friends quickly and learned to play Cricket. The game seemed to be the centre point of his days, being more important than Maths, Latin or French in his estimation

'I hate French,' he wrote, 'it'd be much better if I learned Spanish, which would be a continuation of what I already know, but nobody speaks Spanish here, they're complete fools!' And so his letters went on...

The person who missed Donny most was Ada for he'd been her constant companion and playmate since birth, and suddenly this person was taken from her. There was Billy, of course, but Billy was three years younger and not fond of riding. I often heard her calling: 'Come on Billy, come for a ride!' But Billy's reply was always negative: 'No, it's too hot' or 'It's lesson time', Billy invariably unearthed a plausible excuse why not to accompany her.

'Oh blast you!' she'd blurt out furiously, 'you're a sissy!' The result, Ada had to find another companion for riding or stay in the house and sulk. The person she found was young Mario from Pintos place for his father used to bring him over every day with the pretext of finding him some work, but he and Ada sought each other's company and off they'd go on horseback. The rules were the same as when Donny was here: the main road was out of bounds as well as all deep woods. No bathing in the rivers or *cañadas* was allowed no matter how hot it was. They had to be back in good time for lunch, or well before dark, and the Pintos applauded these rules.

Today I was waiting for them to come in for lunch. It was a bit late and they'd not have time to wash up before coming to table.

The gentlemen were awaiting their meal.

'Hungry?' I asked as I passed through the room on my way to the veranda to watch for the late riders.

'You bet!' exclaimed Willy emphatically. Willy was becoming more and more lazy with his extra weight. I worried about this and its cause and inconvenience in the estancia work, for although at present his place was ably filled by Herbert this would not hold forever.

I could hear the sound of galloping hooves and soon the children were in sight. Wind-blown and wild Ada was the perfect picture of Girl and Horse in Nature — she and the horse were one.

'You're late,' said Donald as Ada rushed into the dining-room and hastily took her place with uncombed hair and grubby hands.

'Sorry,' she chirped, unconcerned.

'And why are you late?' he asked, 'haven't you got a watch? You know the rules.'

'No, I have no watch; it fell in the river last month,' she replied. 'Today it got late while we were over at Pintos place looking at the piglets born today.' She started eating and then asked eagerly: 'Mario's given me one of the piglets. Can I bring it home?' Animals, always animals. What would Ada and I do without any animals?

As the two storey house grew in height and in beauty, it dwarfed the original house which appeared to have shrunk as the other grew, the only redeeming feature being the ivy and other creepers which totally covered it now. The heavy scented jasmine creeper spread and arched its green arms over our bedroom window and perfumed the room during its flowering season. The vermillion Santa Rita had climbed relentlessly up the kitchen walls and was beginning to grip the chimney. Gone indeed was the austere row of white-washed rooms I had first come out to, and in its place stood a quaint bungalow with rustic veranda and heavy foliage, some windows barely visible through the drooping leaves. Even as I'd detested the brick-floored veranda then, I saw it now as something unusual, pleasing by virtue of its strangeness, with singular attraction to the casual observer.

'When we move to the new house,' asked Sydney as we sat out one summer evening, 'what's to become of this place?' There was a profound silence. 'Are we prepared to pull it down? Or if it's left, what use will it have?'

'Dunno.' replied Donald, turning to me and asking: 'I've never thought much about it, have you?'

'It would be a pity to pull it down, the rooms can be made use of, I'm sure.' I said.

Thoughtfully Donald said: 'It'll remain for now, but it gets in the way and obstructs the entrance to the new house.' This was true but nobody commented before he went on: 'It puts the big house in a minor position... if it were pulled down, a fine entrance drive could be made in its stead and some good trees would form a stately avenue.

As the talk revolved around the demolition of the old premises the more I felt averse to having it destroyed. It had become part of my life and much as I'd longed for a better home, I'd learned to love this one and was nostalgic about it.

We'd not pull it down; no, no, no!

Then Donald asked: 'What do you think, Syd?'

'It'd take a lot of the gilt off the gingerbread to bring guests through the old premises before getting to the new house, wouldn't it?'

'I know,' I assented, 'but there must be a way round...' With these words an idea came to mind, 'why not make the entrance drive to run another way round? It shouldn't be too difficult. We'd have a fine front gate, wide enough for carriages, and a stately drive circling to the front door, over that way.' I indicated where I meant. I could see the idea had caught on for the gentlemen were nodding their approval.

'And these rooms empty and abandoned?' asked Willy.

'There'll be uses found for them.' I said.

'Yes, to accumulate junk in!'

I ignored Willy and went on: 'Donald could have the first room as his office, by making a window to over-look the patio, he'd have command of all who came and went.' I smiled at Donald's happy face. 'You'd have a strong safe and a new desk where you can pay the salaries sitting in dignity and attend to buyers and sellers too. A decent office adds prestige to an estancia and here's an opportunity of having one without much extra expense.'

By this time, I saw I'd won the day. Donald's eyes were gleaming and Sydney was beginning to light his pipe, a sign he had something on mind. Only Willy sat silent and looked a bit out of sorts.

'Very well,' said Sydney, 'suppose we decide to keep the old house; one room the office, and the others?' Silently I begged for time to think, something MUST come to mind. There! I had it!

'Another of the rooms will be converted into a bathroom.'

'A bathroom? Whatever for? We'll have two in the new house, another out here will be superfluous surely?'

'She's gone bathroom crazy.' Willy chipped in again.

'Yes!' I cried hastily, 'a bathroom out here will be a blessing when visiting buyers come for the day. They'll have no need to go messing up our own bathroom.'

'That's a good idea!' applauded Donald, 'a guest's bathroom.'

While we planned and schemed in this manner for improvements in our small Las Palmas world, the Uruguayan government changed hands once more.

Although the Santist government were the victors over the Revolucion del Quebracho, General Santos felt insecure especially after an attempt on his life had been made. He was entering the Teatro Cibils one evening to see the show there, when a shot rang out and a bullet went into one of his cheeks, throwing him to the ground.

Santos partially recovered his health but resigned from power. General Maximo Tajes took over and began working hard for reconciliation after the Revolution. His words were: 'We shall work in peace to the interest of the country.'

Although a military man, Tajes changed the government from the military regime existing back to the civil regime, and with him in power a very prosperous era began. Industry and commerce developed greatly and a building fever followed. Principally in the city of Montevideo many important edifices were constructed.

The roof of our house went on in mid-October and there was great rejoicing at Las Palmas. I tried to join in the festivity but I could not understand why I was feeling so heavy and impatient in my pregnancy only six months gone. I knew what nature required to grow and mature a baby in the womb, so what was the reason for my impatience this time?

I was enormous in size and thought I must be carrying a lovely fat boy. Yet why this impatience? I was impatient with everything; with the men working the house and their delays; impatient with Willy who was not pulling his weight on the farm; impatient with the domestic staff which seemed worse than usual; often impatient with the children during their hours with me, but above all I was exhaustedly impatient with my large abdomen which seemed to be at its fullest expansion. It hindered all my movements, handicapping my activities, so when November came in with no relief, I decided to go and see Dr. Owens in his surgery one morning to hear his version of it all.

He was kindness personified as usual and looked cheered when he saw me. 'Come in, good lady, come in and sit down,' he ushered me into his consulting room. I edged myself laboriously into the chair he offered me, hoping it would hold my weight, trusting I'd not disgrace myself by breaking what seemed to be the only chair for patients.

'How are you keeping?' he asked, 'what's brought you here this morning?'

I tried not to sound too dissatisfied with everything as I told him the purpose of my visit.

'Well, well,' was his only comment. 'Let's have a look at you.' He helped me onto the couch to be examined. Soon his deft fingers were prodding my abdomen. 'Umph!' he grunted once or twice before reaching for his little wooden ear-piece to listen to the baby's heartbeats. He leaned over and placed his ear carefully on the small apparatus and listened and listened, constantly changing position of the small instrument. He listened a long time... until I became exasperated with impatience and cried out: 'What's the matter?' and then: 'Is there anything wrong?'

He was smiling when he eventually raised his flushed face from the listening position. I marveled he could lift his head and straighten up at all, he'd been down so long.

'There's nothing the matter,' he assured me, 'the reason for your extra weight is that you're carrying twins and I wanted to be sure there were not any more than two!'

CHAPTER 24

Near the house there was a feeding table for the birds on which twice a day I placed bread crumbs and other scraps of food. On it clustered the sparrows, getting more than their share, but also the gold-brown oven birds and '*venteveos*' (bird) with their yellow breasts aglow. We watched them with never failing interest and our excitement grew when a cardinal honoured us with a visit.

Five years had gone by since the birth of our twin sons. Simon Percival Lewis and Paul Thomas Jonathan were fine healthy lads from the moment of their birth to this day, five years later as I watched them take out the crusts of bread for the bird-table.

I'd never suffered so much as at their birth. They were both lying incorrectly, consequently there'd been hours of agony before they were both safely delivered and my body free from them at last. As I lay limp and exhausted while people attended to the babies, Donald came to my bedside.

'Darling,' he breathed, 'how wonderful they are! Two big beautiful boys! I can't believe it!' He stroked my listless hand laying on the counterpane. I turned my head away and whispered: 'I don't want to have another child ever.' He looked startled for a fleeting second, and then he smiled.

'You've had a tough time of it, my love, and TWO... what an achievement!' and as an afterthought: 'You'll get over it.'

'Whether I get over it or not, I don't want any more babies, is that clear?' As Donald made to leave the room, he said: 'What a pair they're going to be!'

His foresight had been correct, they were a wonderful pair, but I made a vow they were not going to handicap me by making me become a martyr, or turn me into a fat old mum with nothing better to do than produce and raise children.

I recovered quickly as usual and was soon strong enough to start tackling the many problems and demands of Las Palmas. I took on extra help to care for the twins, a young girl from the village came to help Miss Daisy with them allowing me my freedom. I weaned them very early with the pretext that feeding two was too much for my strength but in reality it was to free myself from timetables. There was an abundance of rich milk brought up to the house each morning from the milk shed, and at the milkman's suggestion they brought up one particular cow and her calf to live near the house, and the babies drank milk only from her. She was fed with the very best fodder and consequently the twins thrived and grew fat and strong.

My main concern was to get the big house finished. The workmen had got into the bad habit of doing things at their own speed for there'd been nobody to order them otherwise. They'd become slack... the woodwork, the papering, the painting, the kitchen and the bathrooms were still unfinished. But things started moving when I went in every morning to organize and supervise the work, yet this progress created new expenses.

'There's not a great deal of money left, you know.' Donald admitted one day as I was asking for funds to buy the bathroom fittings.

'Sydney's going into Mercedes today,' I said, 'and it seems a splendid opportunity for him to buy what we need.'

'I know,' he said, 'but if I let him have what he's asking for it cleans us out of Legacy money.'

The Legacy money finished! And the house was not. I realized what had happened: we had, as they say, bitten off more than we could chew. We'd planned a house beyond our Legacy means. None of us had the slightest idea as to what a house such as we'd planned would cost. Now, too late, we found its total cost was more than we had.

Debts began mounting up; we'd overstepped the mark and run into debt in various areas in a desperate attempt to finish the work. In the end, I lent the money out of my cattle fund to buy the bathroom fittings but similar to this incident there arose many others.

I approached Donald at this point about going into business with Mr. Brown who was constantly repeating his offer for business. I'm fully convinced it was the many accumulated debts which made Donald agree to the association.

Mr. Brown came to lunch on Sunday, with the idea of discussing the business, not over lunch because of the children, but after the meal.

On receiving our invitation, Mr. Brown had become euphoric, suspecting the reason. He'd been waiting a long time for this association, never giving up hope.

He bowed politely over my hand when I entered the room and enquired after the twins. His eyes were gleaming triumphantly. How I disliked being close to him! But as he was our only loop-hole to get out of this financial mess, everything had to be tolerated.

The sherry was flowing perhaps a little too freely, to Brown's utter satisfaction. When at the table and the meal underway, I noticed the long finger nail, longer than ever; did he ever cut it? Would he begin picking his teeth with it?

The gentlemen were discussing the effects of last year's Revolution, getting distinctly worked up with their arguments. Why did they always discuss politics with every male guest?

'Why can't these ridiculous people understand they can't have a military man at the head of the civil government?' expounded Donald loudly.

'Jesus Christ!' Brown burst out furiously, thumping on the table. A deathly silence followed. We were not accustomed to take the name of the Lord in vain. Ada looked up sharply from her plate, her eyes darting to her father.

Brown wondered what he'd said wrong.

Tactfully I rang the bell for Celeste to come and take away the plates.

Mr. Brown cleared his throat and started again, this time without evoking the Almighty. 'What I meant to say was that military men make good soldiers but should leave politics to the civilians. I agree with what you said Donald.'

'At least President Tajes seems to be a better chap and has returned to civil constitutional policies.'

'Yes, and that's good,' agreed Brown. 'Last time I was in Montevideo I heard the electric light system was being connected soon. The first power house is being built.'

'How wonderful to have electric light at home!' I exclaimed, hoping to veer the conversation on to lighter lines. 'Do you think it'll be long before we get electricity here?' My idiotic question was ignored though it had interrupted the political talk and we moved to our business meeting which lasted barely a few minutes, both parties being desirous of the arrangement. Mr. Brown would bring cattle to fatten on our land and there'd be a fifty percent profit for me when sold.

'Incredibly generous.' The gentlemen applauded the terms laid down by Brown.

Almost immediately the cattle business was in full swing and during the following two years' extra cash was flowing in from this source. It was astoundingly easy, every time another batch of animals was taken to market, large sums of money were handed to me at the end of the day.

We gradually started emerging from our debts.

The house was finished and fires were lighted in the rooms many days before we moved to dry out and warm the walls. We moved during August of 1887.

Donald and I went to Montevideo for a short visit the following spring with a view of looking into girls' schools. Ada was twelve and the age Donny had been when he left for Ireland. It'd been easy, for Donny was perfectly docile about leaving Las Palmas, but we were finding it different with Ada.

'I don't want to go away to school,' she stated emphatically the first time I broached the subject.

'Ada darling,' I tried to sooth her, 'you know how important schooling is.'

'I've been doing lessons with Miss Daisy ever since I can remember, so why should I go away now?'

'You're already twelve and we feel you're at the age when you need something more than your childhood nannie's teaching.'

'Miss Daisy is very intelligent and I like her. She's most understanding: for instance, if I do my lessons well and keep quiet, she'll let me out early for a ride.' Ada's tone implied she was being very patient with me. 'She's a very considerate person, you see.'

'That's exactly what's wrong,' I explained, 'it's time you had a stricter discipline and some higher studies.'

'I don't need anyone more strict than Miss Daisy, and I'd HATE to go away.'

'There comes a time in life when one needs new teachers and new friends. Look what nice friends Donny has made.'

'Oh, Donny's an old softie and everybody loves him, but they'd hate me and fight me and I'd be miserable!'

'Now you're inventing things. Be sensible and start thinking about going to school, like Donny.'

'No, I won't!' I felt at a loss, she was so stubborn.

'It won't be forever, you'll come home in a few years very much the better for it.' I got out a pamphlet advertising a girls' school quite near to where Donny was. 'Look what a beautiful building you'd be working in.' I handed her the sheet which she studied for a moment then handed it back.

'No!' she shouted and shook her head fiercely, 'it looks nice from the outside but it's full of horrid things like blackboards and desks and mean old teachers who are always punishing the girls.' She stopped. 'No, I don't like it.'

'Ada be sensible, please. Why are you being so difficult?'

'Because I don't want to go away to school and you're insisting.' She pouted. 'I love Las Palmas and its animals: my horse, the dogs and my pigs, so why should I go away, especially when we have a new house and I have a bedroom all to myself at last?'

We were, undoubtedly, back where we started and I dared not go through the arguments again, it would drive me crazy, so I dropped the matter and Ada went up the stairs, patting Willy's Lion as she went.

I stood watching her athletic figure receding as she leaped easily to the upper floor, two steps at a time. I found it so hard to understand her, she was so willful and totally out of reach. Donald would have to speak to her and convince her about her future schooling.

But Donald was as equally unsuccessful as I'd been and before much argument had ensued, they were both in tears and Donald was promising never to send her away. That settled it, in their estimation, but I was not so convinced and it was then I began looking into schools in Montevideo.

When we were there we were assured there were no boarding schools in the city and we should consider Buenos Aires. I decided to write to schools in Buenos Aires requesting a prospectus.

The biggest drought on record in the land began that summer. It started with an important lack of rainfall and the dry hot weather continued steadily from late September, over the New Year, and on through February and March without a drop of rain. The drought stretched all over the land and cattle and sheep were dying by the hundreds, as well as crops withering under the scorching summer sun. The brooks dried up as did the provisional water holes.

We did what we could for our own livestock but it soon got out of hand and eventually it was considered a national disaster.

I'll never forget those parched days and nights when we longed for some relief from the endless heat. There'd been incessant field fires, some of which proved dangerous. We lost thousands of fence poles and half our old monte was destroyed. The men were constantly being called out for firefighting with an endeavour to keep things under control.

Standing on the front porch at nights one could see, far in the distance, the dreaded red glow of another fire. There was so much destruction, so much waste, and so many deaths among the animals. It was cruel to see, as the weeks rolled by, the animals in their final state of dehydration standing among the hundreds already dead and the sour odour of rotting flesh. It was a depressing time for man and beast.

During this unfortunate year and subsequent economic crisis, Dr. Julio Herrera y Obes was elected as new President. He was faced with one of the worst eras: the country's income did not cover the expenses of expansion.

The recuperation from these disasters was a slow process and only began once the regularization of the rain occurred and the land received its rightful due. With this taking place, our lives were restored to normality. Our friends paid calls and we saw our neighbours with regularity. Tennis parties at Las Palmas became popular and we found ourselves being selected as hosts to social gatherings and parties. It happened the year the twins turned five, 1892, we were chosen to be hosts to the Bishop of the Diocese. No doubt it was a courtesy to Donald, staunch Anglican as he was, and the Church wished to honour him with a visit from His Grace.

It was astonishing how this visit was adding prestige to our estancia, to our family name and particularly to Donald, head of the family.

Donald at the top at last.

He had a beautiful homestead, standing in the heart of a prosperous farm...

Willy's change was greatest perhaps. He no longer worked and therefore never climbed into the carts any more. He complained of pains in his legs and after a great deal of opposition, I convinced him to see Dr. Owens about this. The doctor's diagnosis was worrying. Willy's arteries were going through a process of hardening and his walking abilities would decrease as the days went by. Despite suggestions that he should go back to Ireland to have himself seen to, Willy refused. 'I'm perfectly happy here, so why must I go?' And on this basis, he remained where he was.

Preparations for the Bishop's visit were many and varied. The guest room was aired and decorated and then redecorated many times.

'I think a shade of blue is the most indicated,' I said, indirectly asking Miss Daisy's opinion in my total inability to decide. 'Blue is sort of celestial and in keeping, don't you think?'

Miss Daisy smiled. Her blue eyes twinkled mischievously, perhaps she knew me better than I realized. 'Or wouldn't yellow-gold be more fitting for a Prince of the Church?' she asked.

'Gold?' I gasped, falling headlong into her trap. We had no curtains nor bedspreads in gold, it would mean.... Or was Miss Daisy pulling my leg? I turned and faced her in desperation and she laughed. 'Madam, if I may say so, I think you're being over-concerned about the decoration of his room. After all, he's a human being as well as a Bishop and he'll be delighted with this lovely new room and its exquisite view over the fields, no matter what colour the draperies are.'

'Oh!' a little abashed, 'do you think so?'

'I'm sure of it.'

'Then I'll put blue colouring...' but I wavered still, 'or should it be gold?'

Similar to this incident there were others, with enigmas about meals, guests to be invited and entertainments to be thought of. I was in a frenzy the day before he arrived, while Donald, on the other hand, showed no alarm, having already met the Bishop on a visit to Fray Bentos and liked him enormously. Donald agreed with almost everything I suggested, nodding and smiling his approval. 'That'll be fine, my love, don't worry.' He was repetitive in his encouragement and commendations not to worry.

'There are too many flowers in this room!' I cried in an impetuous outburst the evening before he arrived. I'd spent nearly all afternoon picking, cutting and settling these flowers. Now they seemed too many.

'I think they look lovely,' Donald said, looking up quickly from his book. 'Don't worry.'

'Don't keep telling me not to worry!' I exclaimed. 'It's got to look nice and fresh and not look like an undertaker's office! It's positively funereal like this!' and I sprang up to remove a vase.

'Now, now, Evie!' Donald's voice of authority arose suddenly. 'You're working yourself up into a panic quite unnecessarily — please go to bed and rest and tomorrow you'll see what a charming man the Bishop is, and now there's no need to worry.' He took me by the arm gently and led me to the staircase. Willy's Lion eyed me suspiciously and seemed to whisper: 'You're a fraud.' as Donald gave me a soft pat on my backside.

This week I'd begun to doubt myself in every respect, from my outward capacity towards guests to the manner in which I'd brought up the children.

How could I cope with a Bishop guest? It was bound to be difficult; I'd want to leave the formalities and rush outside and romp with the dogs or go for a wild gallop. Yet how could this be done when being constantly watched by a high ecclesiastical Christian.

Now I mounted the stairs on my way to bed with misgivings going round in my head. I went to the window and knelt down on the old ottoman which stood beneath it. It was a beautiful night, but I didn't notice it at first. It was cold and frosty but never a gust of wind to rustle the trees in their lonely nightly vigil. I began to rest as I prayed.

On opening my eyes, I let them take in the beauty of the cold still night. Multitudes of stars decked the black sky and peace reached me at last. I remained in this position of prayer before the closed, uncurtained window until I felt Donald put his arms around me.

'Not in bed yet?' he asked softly. 'You'll be getting cold, my dearest, the fire is a small glow.' I turned and smiled as he raised me to my feet. I adored him when he was gentle, I allowed myself to be led to the bedside and he unbuttoned my dress. My love for him surged up within me and I knew he was the only person who had taught me to recite the verb to love.

CHAPTER 25

The following morning dawned cold but clear and the everyday sounds of an estancia at work came to my ears as I opened my sleepy eyes. Donald's place in the bed was already empty and cold, which meant he'd been up for some time. The sheep's 'ba-a-a-a, ba-a-a-a' came clearly into my room and the sound of small hooves trotting on the hard ground near the pens told me they were up for curing and clipping. The balm of a good night's sleep which began with Donald's closeness and the giving of myself in complete abandon, was still with me. I felt happy for a few gorgeous moments until my mind began functioning again and I remembered the Bishop's impending visit.

Before I'd carried out half my daily chores a very fine carriage had drawn up at our front door. The Bishop had arrived.

The gentlemen were out to meet him, even Willy staggered out too. I pinned up an unruly lock of hair as I went primly out. They were getting his luggage down from the carriage and he was smiling pleasantly. It came as quite a shock to find he was wearing a simple grey suit, dog-collar, and a huge overcoat, looking like any English gentleman coming to call. I was looking at a rather short man whose brown eyes were about level with my own; the eyes were both kindly and amused with a depth to them which was fathomless. But he was ugly; eyebrows too bushy and nose too large, his hair sparse on top and going grey at the temples. He looked about fifty to me.

'I'm so delighted to be here at last,' he smiled at us. 'What a charming place you have here.' I'd planned the children should come and meet him a little later to avoid the arrival hassle but I'd overlooked the dogs. Our young sheepdog, Sandy, having heard the excitement came dashing round from the back of the house and leaped up at the Bishop in welcome.

I gasped.

'Well, hullo, hullo, young fellow.' He stooped to pat the euphoric hound while removing his dusty paws from his trousers. 'Is he a sheepdog?'

'Get down Sandy!' I called him off, embarrassed. Sandy kept up his wild attentions to the newcomer who laughed as he patted the dog again.

'I seem to have made a friend,' he said, 'I love dogs.' First point in his favour... the uncomfortable moment slipped by.

The Bishop went directly to his room with his valet, the only person travelling with him. He had an enormous amount of luggage for a few days stay, I thought. He walked up the stairs at the precise moment Ada chose to dash downstairs, singing lustily, causing a near collision. She'd forgotten the Bishop was arriving she confessed afterwards.

'Oh, sorry!' she exclaimed breezily and stopped one stair below him. She held out her hand in an unaffected act of friendship: 'I'm Ada, are you the Bish?' she asked.

'Hullo Ada,' the Bishop greeted her cordially as if nothing had happened. 'You're in a hurry?'

'Not particularly,' she replied, 'but I always take two steps at a time — makes it more exciting.'

'Ah, of course!' they grinned at each other in complete understanding.

'Well, 'bye for now!' called Ada, 'see you later!' and she was off and away like a gust in spring. I caught the Bishop's amused eye as he turned to continue upstairs.

The other children came in to meet him with Miss Daisy before lunch with Miss Daisy, all cleaned up and subdued. Billy's hair parted in the middle was flattened like a pancake, making him look more timid than usual. Then Celia, soft and pink as a peach, her golden curls had been brought into submission by a diligent Miss Daisy and a pink satin bandeau. The twins brought up the rear in their sailor suits, somehow resembling Tweedle Dee and Tweedle Dum though they were not fat.

Simon sat himself as close as he dared to the Bishop and stared unblinkingly at him as if he was a museum piece. I tried to distract him elsewhere but he was oblivious of anyone else's presence. It was a little embarrassing but the Bishop seemed at ease having Simon hanging on every word and soon Simon found his voice and asked: 'Do you like being a Bishop? Or would you prefer to be the President?'

In spite of one or two uncomfortable moments such as this, the children behaved well and were allowed to come to the lunch table for this one meal, for otherwise it was only Ada and Billy who ate with the adults. The Bishop understood children having two sons of his own and we learned he'd lost his wife recently and had left his two boys of fifteen and thirteen at school in England so as to carry out his diocesan work unhindered.

'Why did you leave them alone in England, poor things?' Ada asked swiftly being totally at ease.

'They're not altogether alone, you know, for I have a very good sister and her family who keep a close watch on them and their needs, and anyway, they're in school.'

I could see it coming by Ada's face. 'So beastly and stuffy to be in boarding school!' she declared.

'Now Ada,' I intervened, 'that's not everybody's opinion as you know.' The Bishop held up his hand to halt me, not Ada, before he replied:

'Schools are very necessary because we have so much to learn,' he smiled at her. 'There comes a time in the life of the young adult when they need a certain discipline of study and there's no better place than a school in which to get it.' From that moment I began to love the Bishop. He was echoing my words to Ada some time ago. He was on my side.

'I'd HATE to go to school!'

'Why Ada, I'm surprised at you.' he said, 'you strike me as a very intelligent girl and would have thought differently of you. Tell me, why do you think you'd hate school?'

'Because I'd be separated from my animals, and our farm, and everything and everybody whom I love. I'd be alone, far away, unhappy, miserable!' She drew in her breath. 'I'd hate it.' she repeated firmly.

'Of course I understand you, having this wonderful place to grow up in, but sadly it's different for my boys as they have no mother.'

We read sorrow in his kind face, and then I said: 'We have our eldest son at present at school in Ireland.' He turned to me.

'So you also know what it's like to feel the sadness of separation, yet sometimes it's so necessary...' He paused gravely for a moment. 'Yet we grow with tribulations, did you know that, Ada?'

She dropped her eyes to her lap and remained silent; she and her future had been shelved for the moment, but nobody was going to change her opinion of schools. Though we tried hard to displace Ada as the central figure of conversation during the meal, she constantly came back as the heart of the matter. Soon she was talking and laughing happily with our guest, at one point getting so excited while telling him about her family of pigs, she dropped a spoonful of her pudding into her lap. She cried: 'Oh, I'm such a filthy eater!' causing a great deal of merriment and the Bishop roared with laughter. Her frank spontaneous nature enchanted him.

'She's so refreshing,' he whispered to me as a stage-aside.

———————

The Bishop's visit turned out to be the exact opposite to what I'd imagined it would be. There was no need for me to take wings to my sanctuary of horse and field. We all rode together. He was an excellent horseman, having taken riding lessons for years when he was a boy. When he'd asked to be shown around the farm, I presumed he'd want to do it in the coach, and was surprised when they suddenly invited me to join them on horseback.

We saddled up: Donald, Sydney, the Bishop, Mr. Harrison (who'd come over to help in the entertaining) and Ada and I. Billy chose to remain at the house and practice the piano, so we made a party of six.

The Bishop's elegant attire was also a surprise; perfectly cut riding breeches and gleamingly polished boots, topped by a scarlet jacket and cap like a British hunter.

'Sorry there's no organized fox,' smiled Sydney when he saw him, 'but we may run across one by chance. Let's take the dogs.'

And we were off. Ada leading the party was always miles ahead. Donald kept abreast with the Bishop and explained points of interest as they came along. The Bishop wanted to know everything, from how the oven bird made his nest, to the breeding of cattle and sheep. We couldn't tell him enough as he lapped up the information, and we loved telling him.

We dismounted at the *Aguila* river and as he stooped to drink the crystal clear water from his hands, the Bishop asked about fishing. He confessed it was one of his favourite sports, so I guessed how the afternoon would be spent.

The gentlemen went off fishing without us, Ada and I remained to prepare the house for the next day, Sunday, when Morning Service was to be held at Las Palmas with all neighbours invited and refreshments served on the lawn afterwards.

We attempted to convert our large drawing-room into a church hall for the service. We were expecting roughly thirty people, so chairs were brought in from all the rooms and placed in rows to seat the guests and the children would sit on cushions on the floor.

People began arriving shortly after nine although the service was called for ten, but the journey always brought tired travelers, hungry ones, or some requiring a wash or rest. The Miles were very hungry by the time they arrived, having travelled for hours, and Ada took them into the kitchen and gave them their second breakfast. Colleen's baby unexpectedly needed changing so I took her upstairs to find a bed on which to do this. I watched Colleen's lovely slim hands move about gently as she attended her little daughter now three months old and growing a fine shock of ginger hair. Had Sydney had something to do with this sweet little child also?

Now there were voices all over the house and I became anxious because the Bishop had not yet come down though it was already past nine. Donald had knocked on his door at seven as he'd requested and he'd called out in reply Donald affirmed as I expressed concern.

'Should we knock again?' I asked.

'No, he shouldn't be disturbed a second time.'

Emma Tomkins had a bad cough and I visualized her barking loudly during the entire service, so I suggested she take some hot milk and honey before the service, which she thankfully drank down and I also filled her pocket with menthol sweeties, hoping that would do the trick.

It was a quarter to ten and the room full of people without any sign of the Bishop, but at five minutes to, his bedroom door opened and he started his way downstairs slowly. He was in full clerical regalia, all white cassock and surplice, his staff in his hand and mitre on his head, making an imposing figure, altogether another person to the man who went fishing in our old river and came back with soaking wet feet and rumpled trousers, or to the man who came riding with the family. This attire gave him a theatrical appearance whereby a total hush fell upon the congregation assembled as he descended the stairs. Donald was waiting for him at the foot and led him to the drawing-room where the service took place.

As the service proceeded, it seemed unreal having a Bishop reading Matins as Donald did every Sunday, with now Donald second in command. Completely at ease, they might have been serving together for tens of years to all appearances. Donald read the Lessons and during the reading I thought how good it sounded from his lips and I saw how easily he could have been a parson instead of a farmer, it all came so naturally to him. After a short address and once the last hymn was sung, the Bishop raised his hand in a final blessing.

Drinks were served on the front lawn despite the rather cold day. We placed Willy in his chair under the shelter of the porch allowing him to feel he was partaking of the event with a rug over his knees protecting his useless legs. Once or twice I noticed the Bishop stopping by his chair drawing him into conversation and attending to his needs.

'A beautiful service,' remarked Mrs. Harrison, 'and we certainly will be back in the evening for Holy Communion with your kind permission.'

Most people left for their homes shortly except the Miles family for it was too long a trip to Fray Bentos to do twice in a day and Peter very much wanted to attend the evening service. After lunch there was tennis, where turns had to be taken because of the amount of players. Donald organized a short eliminatory tournament which included all guests and I pleaded out by exaggerating my duties as hostess for in truth I had no desire to participate.

We were surprised to find the Bishop did not play either for we had labeled him as such an accomplished person. Therefore, when Donald and Sydney began a set against Mr. Harrison and Peter Miles, I found myself alone with him. It was much too cold to sit and watch the game so 'Would you care to take a short walk?' I asked him.

He smiled: 'A charming idea and much more my type of exercise than a hard game of tennis.'

Gently taking my arm, he led me away walking in the direction of the workman's quarters which would never have been my choice had I been consulted, but we simply walked.

'You know I'm very concerned about your cousin Willy and his health,' the Bishop suddenly said.

'So am I!' I exclaimed

'I had a talk with him yesterday and tried to get to the bottom of what's really wrong with him.' He stooped to pick a lonely dandelion growing on the side of the patio. 'He told me his condition has been advancing slowly, standing or walking too much makes his legs ache consequently he moves as little as possible not to cause himself pain.'

'For many months we've been noticing how reduced Willy's activities have become and now he's so fat, it makes walking even harder,' I said.

'Quite, quite,' he assented and added that he was shocked to hear Willy was doing nothing about his health.

'He refuses to see another doctor after seeing Dr. Owens some time ago.' I told him. 'He's very obstinate, you know.'

The Bishop continued: 'If the illness is progressing, as you suggest, the only prospect for his future is the loss of the use of his legs — he'll become a cripple and that's terrible!'

'Oh, poor Willy; what's the solution, do you think?'

'He must consult a professional as soon as possible, before it's too late.' Then he added more cheerfully: 'It's wonderful what medicine can do nowadays.' I suggested he speak to Willy, hoping he'd have more success.

My walk with the Bishop ended on happier lines; we circled the pig-sty and saw Ada's piglets, causing us great amusement to see the twelve of them feeding from their mother at the same time, before we cut across the field to see the sheep bath and inspect the new trees planted in its vicinity.

There was no indication of work on the estancia as it was Sunday but we could hear voices and singing to the accompaniment of guitars in the men's quarters. They were singing around an open fireplace; even siestas had been postponed today. We stopped at the rear of the building and listened to the end of the song:

'Otra revolucion habia estallado, y el caudillo...

andaba combatiendo, en los pagos del Perdido.

La rendicion o la lucha... por unica respuesta tuvo,

la voz de algun balazo!'

'What a pity,' commented the Bishop, 'they only think of their revolutions in this country. It's time they forgot the past and began living for the future.' We continued on our way. 'I'd hoped they might be doing a '*payada*', where one man begins his song asking a question and the other replies in tune and in rhyme. They're very clever and highly amusing. I often hear some well-known '*payadores*' (improvised gaucho folksingers) in Fray Bentos where I visit regularly; they get together in the *Pulperia* (general store) and they're well worth staying to hear.

We reached the house again and our presence was being claimed for the tennis was over with a victory for Ada.

I went indoors to see about tea for our guests. Ah, youth, youth, I thought, she's worn them all out and won the tournament. She followed me inside and remarked: 'They're a lot of old fossils and easy to beat,' she laughed. 'One has to place the ball where they always have to run for it and they soon tire! Then the game's won!'

I peeped into the drawing-room and Willy was already installed in a chair by the fireside. He'd slept a good siesta and now he'd got himself up and was reading in front of a cheery blaze. I was thankful he could still do this much for himself, but what were the prospects for the future?

Ada and I helped Celeste lay out a long tea table. The players were more thirsty than hungry at first but eventually did justice to the goodies and large chocolate cake we'd prepared. As I mounted the stairs later going to my room, I observed the Bishop lingering in the drawing-room and settling down in the armchair opposite Willy.

Perhaps it was the moment to speak to Willy about his health.

———————

Much to our regret, the Bishop left on Tuesday morning after his five-day visit to Las Palmas.

I had been awake for hours on Sunday night worrying about Willy, searching mentally for a solution for him and with the approach of the gentle dawn I'd got out of bed and gone downstairs, surprised to find all the gentlemen, including the Bishop, already downstairs beginning breakfast. I joined them at the table and here I heard the good news about Willy having conceded to go and see a doctor in Fray Bentos.

'I know Dr. Whiteoak personally,' said the Bishop, 'and I've offered to take Willy myself to see him. He'll be travelling with me tomorrow.'

My relief was immense and I smiled at him gratefully.

'Don't worry too much about Willy,' he commended kindly, 'he needs your prayers as well as the loving care I know you give him.'

'Yes, of course.'

'Always remember he's in the hands of the Lord, and He will supply all Willy's needs.'

At this point Donald and Sydney returned to the dining-room with shooting rifles in hand, ready for the morning's entertainment, and I understood what the early rising was all about.

'Wrap up well, Sir,' Sydney advised, 'it's very cold this morning and frosty underfoot.'

'Right-oh!' and he was away to his room, returning shortly with a splendid leather jacket, stout boots and a warm tweed cap. He looked so smart, I wondered how I'd ever thought him ugly. His attire and the serene expression he always wore, made him as handsome as a prince.

They were off in a jiffy. 'We'll be back for lunch!' Donald called over his shoulder.

I turned and went to prepare Willy's things for his trip tomorrow. What hopes for Willy! I felt deep gratitude towards our splendid guest. It made my work in the house, usually so tedious, joyful and rapid this morning.

CHAPTER 26

We were saying goodbye to our friend the Bishop and there was a foolish lump in my throat — no matter how much I swallowed, it would not go down. One and all we'd have happily had him stay for there'd been so much happiness while he was here.

Now he came up to me and drew me very slightly aside: 'Thank you for all your hospitality. I've had a wonderful five days.'

'My pleasure.' I replied.

'You don't know how much I've enjoyed this visit to Las Palmas,' he went on, 'it's been a long time since I've been in the heart of such a charming family, who made me feel so welcome at once. People tend to be afraid of a bishop and are stiff and unnatural in consequence, but I found none of it here, thank goodness.' Little do you know, I thought, how terrified I was before you arrived.

'I'm glad you enjoyed yourself,' I breathed, 'I was afraid it might seem a little dull to you.'

'No,' he smiled. 'Quite the reverse. I discovered, as the Psalmist said: '...how wonderful it is, how pleasant, when brothers live in harmony...' and this had made my visit well worthwhile. I'm leaving refreshed and the better for my stay, taking memories of great value.' He let his eyes stray away into the open fields before continuing: The faint scent of eucalyptus wood-smoke... waking to the sound of sheep calling to one another in a distant field... the lowing of cattle and other things have all become very special to me, for with them comes a peace never found in a town.'

'I'm glad you're going away with a little something of our farm,' I murmured.

'Ah, but there are other things too which will remain in my memory: a Blyth girl's laughter and the soft voice of a woman about the house, constantly attending to other's needs, the voice of a good woman. The last Proverb reminds me a little of you where it says: 'She watches carefully all that goes on throughout the household, and is never lazy.' 'Oh, you're flattering me!' I said, embarrassed by the beautiful compliment.

'No,' he said, 'it's the absolute truth, and I thank you for all these things that have made my stay so happy. Particular thanks for allowing me to know your children. Ada's freshness, with her tenderness for animals and weak helpless things, and Celia's sweetness, just to begin with.'

'I hope you'll be able to come again soon,' I said, struggling again with the lump in my throat which was likely to overflow in tears.

'Yes, my dear,' and he kissed me on the forehead, 'I'll return one day. God bless you.' He shook hands affectionately with Sydney and hastily took his seat in the carriage beside Willy. Donald was following in our coach in which to bring Willy back.

Great grey clouds were gathering and suddenly the rain began to patter against the carriage window as it drove away.

––––––––––

1892

The months sped by as they always have done, with never a regret for the season gone. The Las Palmas household slipped back into the old routine of an estancia hard at work.

The intense rains during most of the winter following the Bishop's visit, played havoc with a great many of our fences, taking the gentlemen out constantly to repair them once spring came in. I regretted they had to do this hard work, especially now they were both having minor health problems. Certainly Sydney should not be out in the damp fields since he'd had bronchial influenza. He'd been laid up for three weeks with bronchitis which refused to leave him. Dr. Owens strongly recommended he give up his pipe smoking and take special care of himself during the cold winter. Donald seemed the strongest of the two brothers, but even he had a slight problem. He'd been complaining recently of acute pains in his arms and shoulders, and there were certain movements which were difficult for him to make. This malady was referred to as 'rheumatism' by Dr. Owens for which he had no remedy.

As there were few fence men in the vicinity, and those there dedicated their time to the erection of new fences only, never taking on repair work, it fell to the landowners to do the repairs. We considered our fences essentials, and the business I had with Mr. Brown demanded strict order with the cattle.

The business with Mr. Brown was doing well — too well. It seemed unbelievable when so much money was handed to me. I worked very little at the job for there were workmen whom I ordered to do the necessary with the animals and I finally decided when they should go up for sale. I had little love for these steers, knowing they were part Brown's and this was allowing him to be about our home constantly. Of course there were occasional small animals which I separated and joined with my herd for special care and feeding, often leaving them there for good. These were the only redeeming feature of the whole business. But Brown, with greater interests on our land, took full advantage of this to come regularly.

It was Thursday and there he was again. His trap which he whipped about the countryside in, was tethered in our patio. I was returning from a ride with the children which Ada had instigated.

'You hardly ever go out with the children,' she reprimanded me.

'They're supposed to be in school with Miss Daisy at this hour.' I retorted swiftly.

'Oh, stuffy old lessons! They'd all be better off riding with us this beautiful morning. Blow some of their cobwebs away.' I stopped and looked at her, abashed at the possible truth in her words. Could she be right? She noted my hesitation and took quick advantage of it. 'Shall I call them while you saddle up the extra horses?'

'All right. Tell Miss Daisy it's with my approval. They'll have some lessons in the afternoon perhaps.'

Ada had won again. She won every battle nowadays. I'd noticed that with maturity she was imposing her will over mine more and more. She was a delightful person, but what a strong will!

The children came tumbling out of the schoolroom with loud whoops of joy: Thank you, Mum, for letting us ride!' yelled Simon as he fled past me to the saddle room, intent on getting the 'cowboy saddle' which had a leather handpiece like the cowboys in the pictures of North America. Normally the children rode on simple sheep skins but one day Simon had discovered the 'cowboy saddle' and from then on he'd use none other.

Celia had delayed coming out for she had to change into her riding habit but soon her golden curls were dancing in the sunlight as she rushed to take possession of her favourite steed.

'Where's Billy?' I asked when we were almost ready to leave. Ada shrugged. 'He said he had some lessons to read over with Miss Daisy and preferred to remain — he's crazy!' and she was off at full speed, calling to the twins: 'Come on boys; race you to the gate!' I felt it was a pity Billy hated riding; he never came out with us nowadays; I couldn't even remember the last time he'd come.

Celia and I followed at a respectable canter in conversation; it was heartening to find Celia coming out of her usual reserve, talking and laughing as she'd never do in the confinement of the house. The freedom of air, horse and sky released her tongue and she told me all about her schoolroom activities and musical accomplishments on the piano, leaving her shyness completely to one side. There was no doubt Ada was right, I should get out with the children more often.

I kept a keen eye on Paul for he was young to be handling the large horse he'd been allotted, but he was having no problems and much enjoyment.

We arrived back shortly before lunch-time — and there was Brown's trap.

'Brown!'

'Blast his hide!' exclaimed Ada.

'Ada, please control your language.' I commanded as we washed down the horses and allowed them a drink.

'He's such an old bastard!' she cried, 'and you know you detest him too.'

'Ada!' I cried, indignant to find she knew such a strong word and had the audacity to use it so boldly. She started laughing at my shocked face and put her arm around my shoulder. It gave me a slightly inferior feeling to find she was already taller than me.

'Don't be shocked, darling Mum. He IS a bastard and you know it, so why pretend?

Come on, I'm starving... hope lunch won't be long.'

We walked along the old veranda towards the new house, past the remodeled office where Donald had his desk and the gentlemen did accounts and bookwork, on past the next room now converted into the billiard room since the beautiful table had been bought, past a spacious bathroom and then the storerooms, altered since the new house was in use.

Smoke was curling from El Boliche chimney, the gentlemen had already built a fire and must be entertaining Brown with sherry. I wondered what his excuse for coming today was, and would he stay for lunch? I changed and tidied up before joining them, stopping by the kitchen to see whether lunch was underway. Celeste was very good but slightly vague about timetables, yet the old cook Grippy was more conscious of the clock, her ample stomach was as good as an alarm.

The gentlemen rose as I entered and I held out my hand to Mr. Brown.

'Hullo, Mr. Brown, lovely morning, isn't it?'

'Not half as lovely as your good self,' he replied promptly. I was startled at his brazen outspokenness in front of the gentlemen. He was smirking and making me feel uneasy. What was he scheming now?

'Lunch'll be served in a few minutes,' I tried to sound casual. 'Will you stay for lunch, Mr. Brown?'

'Thanks, I'd love to. But Alfred, PLEASE!' He was very much at ease and over-confident.

Ada buried herself in a book and the conversation remained in the sphere of cattle breeding with the gentlemen. But Brown tried to keep it general and was slightly impertinent when addressing me. He was such a loathsome creature; I wished he'd go home soon. But I was not to be spared. After lunch he cornered me and said he wanted me to go into the fields with him. There was something about his attitude I did not like.

'Right,' I agreed briefly. 'I'll see if Donald will come out now before his siesta.'

'I want you to come alone,' he said testily, and when he saw my face he added: 'It's important.'

Donald and Sydney were toddling off with siestas in mind and Willy was already in his bed. I had to decide quickly. Brown's attitude disturbed me and I knew I'd not rest, so I might as well go.

'I'll be out with Mr. Brown for a few moments,' I told Donald, and at his raised eyebrows, I explained: 'He's asked me to see some of the animals with him.'

We drove in Brown's trap to avoid saddling up again. He held the reins well in his fat, short-fingered hands, I'd give him credit for that. We drove in silence for some time until I wondered what was coming when he asked: 'Do you keep my animals apart from your herd?'

'Yes, mine are down in the field near the bath and out that way,' I indicated, 'while yours are higher up here, it generally depends where the pastures are best, as yours have to fatten fast.'

'Never get them mixed up?' I turned the full blaze of my eyes on him in indignation. He remained perfectly cool. 'It's that I have reason to suspect you're doing me out of some animals belonging to me.'

'Are you accusing me of stealing from you?' I cried hotly.

'Yes, sort of,' he laughed gently.

'Then our business relationship is over!' I cried. 'You can take your wretched cattle away this very day!'

'Woa, woa; not so fast!' He laid a hand intimately on my forearm. I snatched my arm free, while he went on: 'All I want is for you to be aware that I HAVE noticed your little bit of er — pilfering?'

'I don't know what you're talking about!' I snapped at him. I didn't want to delve too deeply into the matter. If he was referring to the few pretty little cows I'd taken into my herd the other day for special care, I was not going to admit it and then have him accusing me of stealing.

'You know perfectly well what I'm referring to, young lady, so don't get on your high-horse and act innocent when you know you're guilty through and through.'

'I don't know what you're talking about,' I repeated to gain a bit of time.

'I always knew you were a fast one with the illicit 'taking over' of young animals during the course of the years, but I didn't think you'd dare try to pull the wool over MY eyes.'

'Those little cows I moved on Monday are being given special care because they were small and weak,' I said.

'Yes, my dear, I don't doubt it,' he put in sarcastically, 'but they'll never be put back with mine, will they?'

'You're being particularly vile today, aren't you?' I cried.

'Don't try and talk yourself out of this little fraud. I merely wanted it to be made perfectly clear that I'm aware of it and warn you not to let your hand run too free. I've decided to tolerate the past because it's you.' I inclined my head in acceptance of his consideration with as much grace as I could muster under the circumstances.

'Let's go back, please,' I murmured, hoping the incident was now over. At this point the only thing I wanted to do was to get down from his wretched trap and walk home, but we were travelling at a snappy speed.

'We'll go back, dear lady, once we've come to some amicable agreement for the future on this matter,' he went on calmly, turning the trap deftly into the road and heading in the direction of his own farm.

'What agreement do you propose now?' I asked sulkily. I had no intention of returning the young animals which had reached my hands in bad shape and were now, after weeks of special care and feeding, looking fat and healthy. No way was he going to get them back. Over my dead body! I'd have to play my cards carefully.

'To begin with, I could demand you return them immediately.' He must've seen my face so he continued: 'but... as I know you so well, this would hurt your precious pride and you'd not want to part with the twelve or fifteen lovely healthy animals now grazing peacefully on your pastures, and have them sent up for sale, would you?' Damn him, he'd been aware of my skillful manipulation right from the start. I tried to smile, to soften his heart.

'So, in return,' he said, 'I'd like a little more of your personal attention.' I opened my mouth to shout out some curt reply but he held up his hand to silence me.

'Sh-sh-sh-sh, don't start shouting in your usual Irish rage. Just be quiet and listen. I want an occasional visit from you at my home; somewhere I could have you on my own without the stupid gaping family around you. Some private hours where we could talk and...'

'Mr. Brown, don't you dare...'

'Alfred,' he reminded me.

'Your suggestion is completely out of the question.' I hoped it sounded final. 'Please turn this wretched trap around and take me home. We'll have to fix this up another way.'

He didn't draw rein and the horse trotted on. Brown's farm was already in sight over the next rise of land. I began to get panicky, when his voice got very low: 'I've been extremely patient over the years, haven't I?' He paused. 'It's been a long time I've been wanting this, as you know, so here's the moment when you can repay me for some of my generosity to you. What do you say?'

'No!' I cried.

'Your refusal is no agreement, is it? We must go further into the matter.'

We were almost at the gate of his farm and other than flinging myself bodily out of the trap, I saw no way out. Perhaps I should change my tactics...

Suddenly I threw my head back and began to laugh, 'you really are a very persistent man!' I cried, 'I'd have thought after all these years you'd have accepted my repeated refusals.' I peeped coyly at him sideways, sufficient for him to notice. I felt sorry for him, in spite of my disgust, and I knew a little bit of flattery from me would make him melt. 'Come now, I'm sure you're not really so angry with me as all that, are you?' His face had softened. 'I've never led you to suppose there'd be anything more than a business deal between us, have I?'

I smiled up at him again and he lowered his eyes.

'Come, come, Alfred,' I went on sweetly sensing I was gaining ground, 'you know you enjoy coming over to Las Palmas and eating with the family and spending the day in our midst. Don't spoil it by demanding more. If you do, our relationship will have to end completely.' I saw his attitude change, he was being taken over by my words and I smiled happily into his face at my partial triumph.

We stopped at the gate of his farm.

'You're the most winning creature I've ever known.' And as he began swinging the trap around in the direction we'd come, he muttered: 'I adore you and I'll get you one day.'

We both broke out laughing at this point: myself in relief that the tense moment had passed, and he?

'What a blackguard you are!' he accused me.

'And so are you!' I threw at him, laughter bubbling within me. I knew I'd won.

Presently he began to sing and I joined in. The old Irish ballad sounded good in the soft afternoon air:

> 'When Irish hearts are happy,
>
> All the world is bright and gay,
>
> And when Irish eyes are smiling
>
> Sure they'll steal your heart away!'

Out of this absurd incident between Alfred Brown and me there sprung up a different relationship. At least one could say we'd become friends. Until now he'd virtually been an enemy, a person I disliked to an extreme, and although we were constantly being thrown together by circumstance, I'd hated every encounter, every contact. Then had come the business relationship, which I'd taken full advantage of, coining in money, filling my money-bag to bulging, increasing my own herd with more of his good beasts, all thanks to him. I had lots of cash on me permanently, the estancia was constantly borrowing from me, and still more was coming in. No second thought had I given this situation, I'd accepted Brown's generosity without thanks or gratitude. My only punishment was when he came over and stayed for a meal. Today he'd made me see it in a slightly different light; he knew he had the upper hand especially since he'd found me out and noticed the animals I'd disposed of so artfully, never imagining he'd notice this little maneuver of mine. But he did know, and had known all along, and still he forgave me and allowed my disgraceful behaviour. I had to feel differently about him, even if it was only pity for this unattractive, unwanted, horrid little bastard, as Ada would say.

A slight feeling of conspiracy had arisen between us because of the things we knew about each other, yet would never dare to defraud one another in the face of others. Now we were friends.

When we reached Las Palmas, as he helped me down from the trap, he said: 'Don't ever take animals from me again! Promise?'

'Promise.' I said, 'at any rate not until the next time!' I walked triumphantly into the house.

CHAPTER 27

1896

Even though the military regime was over and *civilismo* (civilian rule) in force now under the Presidency of Dr. Juan Idiarte Borda, there was still unrest in the country.

Donald sighed: 'I wonder when all this fighting will cease and the people will be allowed to live in peace, don't you?'

'Listen Donald,' Willy lifted his arms in despair, 'I'm beginning to think the people of this land actually enjoy a good bloody battle.'

'Let's change the subject,' I suggested, 'and go in to dinner. We've much to celebrate and look forward to since Donny will soon be home again.' The letter had arrived last month and we'd still not got over the excitement of seeing Donny again. Ten years since he'd gone away as a youth, he was now a man of twenty-two, and how would he look?

'He'll probably have a big black beard!' exclaimed Ada.

'Oh no!' I cried, 'he's never mentioned having grown a beard.' I felt hurt at the thought until I realized Ada was teasing me. Yet I knew Donny must have changed; grown tall and matured. He'd completed his schooling five years ago, after which he'd been invited to further his training by working in a farm belonging to a cousin before finally returning to Las Palmas. We'd allowed him to take the path he wished to follow and he'd never mentioned his return until now.

The steamer bringing him from Buenos Aires where he'd spent some days visiting friends, was due in Fray Bentos at midday, so we left the estancia early, giving ourselves plenty of time. It was an important event and everybody wanted to meet him, each with his own particular reason.

'I shall go to meet my brother,' stated Ada, 'because I was always closest to him.'

'He doesn't even know us,' declared the twins, 'so we must be there to greet him.'

'What rubbish!' piped up Celia, 'I was always his little pet so he'll want to see me first. He sent me a doll for my fifth birthday and I still have it, don't I Mummie?'

I looked at Donald across the sea of anxious faces wondering how we were going to sort this one out without hurting too many feelings.

'We'll go in two vehicles,' Donald said serenely, 'then everyone can come.'

'Hurray!'

On the way to Mercedes we passed the little farms which had sprung up in the last few years. One solitary house in the middle of the open fields, perhaps one old 'ombu' tree, a little barn, a field of maize, sometimes a well and windmill, a few fences with a remote gate and nothing more.

How alone. I'd always thought Las Palmas was alone and isolated but with our establishment as it was today, it must seem like a regular city to some.

The carriage covered the distance from Las Palmas to Mercedes in half the time it had taken a few years ago, for the new road had been completed at last. The achievement was, after all, something of a triumph.

Donny would notice these changes, there was much for him to see.

Dinner that night had the aura of a great feast and the children were allowed to stay up. Extra candles and lamps were lighted all over the house to make it look festive.

'By Jove! What a splendid place we have here now.' Donny admired everything he saw.

I drew back a little and watched him standing beside Ada as he remained rooted in the middle of the great drawing-room in admiration. He was tall, taller than his father; very slender, perhaps almost too thin. His features had sharpened somewhat, yet he still had the strong Fitzpatrick cut about his face and his colouring was not to be mistaken. Surprisingly he was wearing his hair much longer than the other gentlemen of the establishment.

'You need a haircut,' Donald said rather abruptly during the meal.

'Father, all the lads wear it like this nowadays over there, and even longer, I may tell you,' he laughed.

'I'd remind you you're no longer over there, and it would be advisable to have it cut while you're here.'

'It's worn longer in Buenos Aires too, so the fashion will soon be reaching you.'

'Goodie!' popped in Simon who hated having his hair cut. 'I'll be letting mine grow long too.' But his father's frown quietened the lad quickly.

'Tell us about your stay in Buenos Aires,' I diverted the conversation.

Donny smiled: 'My visit there was good. The Courtland's are a splendid family, as large as ours, but the children are all adults now, of course. I got on famously with them but I liked Bob, the eldest, most of all. We talk the same language, if you follow me.'

'Did you see anything of the city?' Ada enquired.

'You bet! It's magnificent by night. You must come and see it, sister, it's an education in itself — you'll love it.'

'Oh yes, I'd love to go!' she cried.

My goodness, I thought, my children visiting the city of Buenos Aires by night. What horrors! What dangers!

'Don't look so crestfallen, Mum,' Donny had read my thoughts, 'it's not all murders and rape, you know, it's a beautiful city filled with light and entertainments, with good places to go and eat, theatres to visit, fun fairs, there's SO much!'

'And what about Palermo and the horse shows?' asked Ada. 'I'd love to go for the Cattle Show in August.'

'Right, we'll take you to Buenos Aires in August and you'll see it all.'

'Why are you going away again so soon?' asked Paul, who'd not fully understood.

Donny reached for his little nine-year-old brother and made room for him on the sofa beside him.

'No Paul, I'm not going away too soon, but we must take Ada to see the sights before she becomes a cabbage here.'

'Can I go too?' asked Paul.

'You're too young yet but your time will come, don't worry.'

Presently Ada said: 'I didn't like your remark about my becoming a cabbage, I'm not a bit...'

Donny chipped in: 'You're absolutely gorgeous, darling Sister, but you need a little new scenery and ideas, new people to meet, to get the full benefit of your ravishing beauty. It's going a bit to waste here amongst your horses and pigs!'

Donny brought new and fresh ideas into our home; he made us realize how the outside world was moving on, developing and progressing rapidly, and how we were being left gently aside.

'You have to get out and about,' he said, "Uruguay is delightful as it always was and always will be, but the young generation has to move about. Travel, expand their thoughts, learn new techniques and bring them home to be put into action.'

'You must show your father and Sydney some of the things they do and use on farms in Ireland and on the Continent,' I said.

'The main advancement needed here is to go into planting in a big way: agriculture,' he said.

'Planting?' echoed Willy, horrified.

'Yes, planting. Our land is wonderfully fertile; this good black earth will produce splendid crops — you'll make a fortune in no time.'

Donald and Sydney remained silent. They knew he was very likely right, but who was going to discover all this? Their generation was getting on in years and if Donny did not intend to remain to carry out these ideas, who was?

A spark of admiration shone in Donald's eyes suggesting approval of his son's ideas while Donny soon continued:

'There's a great deal of agriculture in Europe now on small and larger scales. The world is extending, the world population increasing consequently more food is going to be needed, and the farmers are the ones to produce it.' He was enthusiastic. 'Machinery is coming in to help farmers sow and reap; it's tremendous! They have harvesters which you'd never dream of here.'

'Yes, of course,' agreed Sydney, 'but those things are far off across the waters and will take ages before they come out to this backwater here.'

'It'll be difficult to get this modern equipment here,' Willy said pessimistically.

'Nonsense!' cried Donny, 'you're just too set in your old-fashioned ways of working the place. It's time for change and expansion!'

This continual talk of progress, modernization and expansion came as rather a shock to us at Las Palmas, but after some time we did begin to see how we were in a comfortable little rut, with blinkers on, assuming blindness to what was going on in other parts of the world. All we did at keeping up to date was to upgrade our livestock constantly, importing rams and bulls from England, but little else.

'It's all very well, Donny, for you to bring suggestions to us 'on paper',' commented Donald, 'but it'll not be easy to carry them out in practice. Still, we'll have to look into things,' he condescended.

From his comfortable armchair Willy put in:' These things are for the new generation, not for us. We're too old to start now.'

'I don't agree,' argued Donny. 'You must always push forward for there are younger people coming behind to be thought of. There's money in the land — expansion is important. We'll have the railway out this way soon. Palmitas will grow automatically, especially if the neighbouring estancias collaborate by growing also. The pioneering era is over; don't you see? Real prosperity is at hand! You must look into buying some machinery to help with harvests. The machines are called threshers and are used for separating small seeds like oats, wheat, linseed, from the chaff and straw. At present they're still drawn by horses but soon machines will be made for pulling the threshers and it'll be marvelous! Steam power is being used all over the world, as you know, and soon there'll be motors run by gasoline out here as in Europe and the United States. The automobile is already in the streets of those continents and will soon be here.' He gazed out of the window as if already one of these machines were running around the house of Las Palmas.

This kind of talk went on and on during the entire spring Donny was home but shortly after his arrival I'd also spoken of other matters such as: 'What news of Billy?'

'I saw Billy just before leaving. We met for lunch,' Donny replied, 'he's extremely well and happy. You know what Billy's like; he lives among his books and his music and is blissfully happy. He's a real bookworm and getting worse as the years go by,' he laughed, 'he's not even learned to play Cricket yet and he's been there three years. He never will, he's just not interested. What a waste! When there are so many wonderful opportunities over there of getting a game. Such matches every weekend from sunrise to sunset, they ran me into the ground — splendid! But not old Billy, he's the intellectual type and will do well in college. But don't ask him to walk ten metres or play a game or ride a horse!' We all laughed, remembering darling Billy always making excuses not to ride.

So...' continued Donny with a grin, 'he's put on weight, lots of weight, in fact he's now a fatty.'

'Oh, how dreadful!' exclaimed Ada.

'Billy can never be dreadful!' I cried in swift defense of my son. A roar of laughter broke forth.

'Mummie's little darling could never be dreadful, could he?' Ada's sarcasm caused more amusement.

'Well,' put in Donny, 'he's not dreadful but he's extremely portly. And he's wearing glasses, as I expect you already know.'

First-hand news of Billy at last.

He was a scholar and a very fine pianist. I wondered how a lad with so much talent had come out of a family such as ours where horses, cows and sheep were of primary value.

Unexpectedly then one morning at breakfast Donny and Ada announced their visit to Buenos Aires to show Ada the big city lights and introduce her to the Courtland's. Letters had been sent announcing their intended visit and a positive reply had arrived. The trip was arranged.

They were away ten days and came home with vigorous excitement about all they'd done but equally ready to plunge into farm life again. They were inseparable and tremendously energetic making me feel my age at times.

Often I thought Donny would give up his plans of returning to Europe to complete courses on vines in Bordeaux. His enthusiasm was so great about everything involving work at Las Palmas, I didn't see how he'd break away from it all again. Those days he reminded me greatly of his father and how he used to talk about pioneering into this land so many years ago. They had the same enthusiasm. Donny and Ada discussed farm business at great length and made elaborate plans for the future; but vines were in Donny's future and he finally returned to Europe to learn about their growth and care. His plan was to return to Las Palmas to plant an enormous vineyard and make a fortune selling grapes for wine.

He left before Christmas of 1896, therefore we were surprised to receive word from Bob Courtland saying he was coming to spend Christmas with us. Since Donny's departure Bob would have no contemporary for he was a man of thirty.

Nevertheless, we were glad to be able to return hospitality and welcomed him warmly.

I immediately perceived why Donny had said he was so likeable and easy to get on with. He was very tall and handsome, with an open face and piercing blue eyes.

'I wanted to come and see this paradise your children speak of so lovingly,' Bob explained as we sat out on the porch before dinner the evening he arrived.

Donald laughed: 'It's no paradise, as you can see, but they all love Las Palmas especially Ada which is natural, considering everybody loves the place where they're born. I've a great nostalgia for my own homeland recently,' he ended.

'Of course,' said Bob, 'yet it is beautiful here.'

The sun was going down to its resting place and tinted everything with its own hue and we were facing the impeccable scene. It was warm and windless, absolutely perfect for sitting out.

The gentlemen had bathed and changed from their working clothes as was our custom and the women also dressed. I felt refreshed and relaxed and incredibly happy, indeed the happiest since Donny had gone away.

Here was Bob, gallant and suave, of Donny's generation, at once becoming the centre of attraction Donny had been. It had become important to me to have younger people surrounding me; the gentlemen were getting on.... Willy disabled despite Dr. Whiteoak's treatment, he was now an old man. The Fitzpatrick brothers had their problems of age.

With these few handicaps in our midst, the difference between our generation and the younger blood was easily detected. Bob was in the land in between, with his ten years ahead of our children yet in his prime. He looked marvelous as he sprawled gracefully in the low Morris chair we'd dragged out. Everything about him was attractive, even the clothing worn with such grace.

Unconsciously we were lamenting Donny's recent departure when Bob intervened: 'I think Donny was perfectly within his rights to go back to specialize in vines. Don's a plant man and will make good. Don't hinder his success.'

'True,' said Donald, 'he always preferred plants and trees to the animals; you're right there.'

'However, you have a young lady,' Bob smiled across at Ada who was sitting a little out of the circle, balancing on a fallen tree trunk. 'She's the animal lover like her mother.' With keen alacrity, he'd summed us all up. 'I've heard all about your success as a herdswoman and I admire you for it.' He leaned very slightly towards me, his warm personality extending all over me. I was glad I'd taken a bit of extra care with my dress this evening.

Bob soon became a favourite with us all. Good company for the gentlemen, he helped and turned a hand where necessary, and there was no doubt he was a success with the ladies. Ada and I were delighted to have his company on any of our chores. He became speechless when he heard about my business deal with Mr. Brown and even though he had the tact not to make any premature comment, I felt he liked the arrangement very little.

The younger children openly adored him. The twins became his constant shadow whenever they were allowed, and even Celia, in her pretty shy manner, showed her admiration by the way her eyes followed him from place to place.

Ada took him down to see her pigs and asked his opinion on the construction of a new pig-sty she had in mind.

'There are so many full grown pigs and the fences not very strong, we'll soon have them all escaping,' she said. And now he was sitting cross-legged on the grass with the twins on either side of him, watching the sketches he was making for the new sty. But in the end it was not the pigs which escaped, it was a *jabali* (wild boar) that broke into the pigs' pen only a few nights later, much to Ada's disgust.

'The beast must've served my beautiful female pig!' she wailed in the morning when one of the workmen came to inform us what had happened.

Simon snorted: 'What a fuss! What does it matter anyway?'

Ada turned on him fiercely. 'You stupid boy! Of course it matters! Now the baby piglets will be half wild pig and no use for sale, don't you see?'

'No, I don't see!' Simon shouted back stubbornly. Gently Bob took the lad aside and said: 'See here, Simon, if the father of the baby pigs was a *jabali*, then the piglets will have his blood, won't they? Children have the same blood as their parents, understand?'

Simon nodded. Whether he understood or not was unknown, but he was satisfied with the explanation he received from Bob and they went off together to inspect the damage to the sty.

Once the news of a *jabali* on the grounds got out, it was immediately decided to go and hunt it. The gentlemen, all armed with rifles, left on horseback very shortly after breakfast and naturally Bob went with them. They thought the beast was living in the thick copse full of brambles and undergrowth around a small stream running through it.

Ada had wanted to go on the hunt too but her father was very firm. 'It's no place for a lady!' he said with a grin as he patted her cheek affectionately.

I tried to go about my morning chores in the normal way but I was apprehensive about the hunt and the sound of isolated shots did not help me settle down to routine.

Much later they told me the accident had occurred once they'd shot one pig, and not seen any other after circling the brambles various times. Then, quite unexpectedly, another sprang out from the undergrowth directly in front of Bob's horse making it shy and rear abruptly, throwing Bob to the ground. The boar didn't delay one fraction of a second to attack. Rushing at the unprepared, unarmed man on the ground, it dug its tusks into his leg. The damage would have been far greater had Donald not been rapid to swing round sharply and plug the beast with a couple of bullets before it made its second attack. Still not defeated entirely, the *jabali* rushed off again, limping badly, into the undergrowth. Donald and Sydney pursued it for a while, shooting at random, but it was lost from view immediately.

Instantly Bob was rescued but his leg was badly wounded. There was a lot of blood.

'D'you think you can make it as far as the house?' Sydney asked him as he regained the saddle. 'We can get the cart to bring you home in otherwise.'

'I'll be all right,' he affirmed, 'but it's devilishly painful.'

———————

Bob remained almost six weeks at Las Palmas, his visit was extended by his leg wound which kept him laid up for many days.

Due to Bob's accident we were at once thrown into a certain amount of extra work and elementary nursing. During the two weeks when he was not allowed to put his foot to the ground, he was confined to his bedroom upstairs, and although he was in no way demanding, there was endless carrying of meals up and down.

Ada proved herself absolutely marvelous with her help. She was always willing to climb the stairs to the top floor to reach him his food. Every morning she'd be up before us, taking in his breakfast tray before we even appeared downstairs. She was as quick as lightening and seemed to enjoy these tasks. I preferred to visit him later in the morning when food was not involved and a certain amount of entertaining necessary.

Very early on he'd read our entire library of books, which were not many, and it was then we started on cards, ending with Bridge, an extension and improvement on the simple Whist we played. The only inconvenience with this card game was it needed four willing and unoccupied people to play. Bob and I were a sure fixture; members of the household who played boiled down to Donald and Sydney, as Willy was on the ground-floor and was unable to go upstairs any more, otherwise we had to depend on visitors and neighbours. Ada emphatically refused to play any card game, but one day Donald suggested she remain and learn.

'Waste of time!' she declared, 'it's much more fun to be out with the animals than cooped up over a table of cards. No thanks! Not for me! And she was gone.

'The speed with which she moves is incredible,' laughed Bob as he began dealing the cards. He and I were always partners and I looked forward to our evening games; it was a pleasant culmination to a long summer day and I think we all felt the same.

It was different and easier when Bob was well enough to come downstairs and could walk with a stick. This gave him more maneuverability and he could attend meals and intervene in family activities. Soon he became the umpire for tennis matches and the organizer of the tournaments. Even handicapped by his wound, he was still extremely good company. We also discovered he had a fine tenor voice and enjoyed singing. We invited the Harrisons over more frequently for Margaret was the best piano player in the district since Billy had gone.

Our parties round the piano became well-known and the sound of music and singing was constantly heard through the summer open windows. Of course Celia could play the piano nicely, but she was too shy to lead a group in song, and if I insisted too much, she'd retire to her room to escape the ordeal.

It was quite a surprise then, on returning from a ride one morning, to find the piano being played and Bob singing. Stealthily I crept into the house and peered into the drawing-room. Celia was playing the simple chords of 'Tea for Two' while Bob sat on the piano stool beside her and sang.

It was a beautiful duet and Celia's face a picture of pleasure as she also followed in song, completely oblivious of being watched by me. As the song came to an end I applauded vigorously and they both turned in surprise.

'Come here, little mother,' called Bob, 'we want you to hear what a perfect couple we make.' He stretched out a hand to me in welcome and drew me onto the piano stool too.

'Do we fit?' I asked. It was cramped and perfectly uncomfortable but I placed my arm round Celia's shoulder and Bob put his around me, each supporting the other, and thus we sang 'Tea for Two' again.

The body contact with this man was exciting, he was so masculine and virile. Admirable the way he'd got Celia to play and sing the duet with him.

CHAPTER 28

The pageantry of autumn began to unfold; the Virginia creeper was just beginning to redden and our wonderful summer spent with Bob Courtland was into the past. We could not complain; it was a good time to look back on. I stored up many treasures in my memory chest: smiles and tender looks which had passed between this splendid man and myself.

Eventually, once Christmas had come and gone and the New Year on its way, he went back to Buenos Aires for his leg was much better.

To us at the estancia it was inconceivable that yet another cry of 'Civil War!' arose at the beginning of March. This time it seemed more serious and lasted for six months impoverishing the country and casting many Uruguayan families into mourning. It was a depressing time for us all.

Again the winter proved a severe handicap to Sydney's health. During June he caught another bad cold which systematically turned to bronchitis. He was bedridden for days and even after a lengthy convalescence he was advised to be cautious of the cold weather, Dr. Owens forbade him to go out into the fields until the warmer weather came round.

Donald was overloaded with work; we saw no relief from this harassing situation and it wore him down.

'It's time we took on some help,' Sydney observed one evening when Donald had returned particularly exhausted.

'The thought has been lurking in the back of my mind also,' said Donald. 'The only reason for not taking action is because I don't know where to begin looking for somebody appropriate — somebody reliable.'

'We'll have to advertise in the newspapers at home, I suppose, as we did for the governesses.'

'It's a sound idea, of course, but it takes a long time to get a favourable reply. Six months can easily go by before we get a response, and that's too long.'

'Something's got to be done,' continued Sydney, 'I can't stick this climate any longer and Donald can't manage alone.'

The gruesome shadow of Sydney's possible departure hung over us all winter. The ultimate climax and his decision came when, after another threatened asthma attack, he announced his plan to leave for Ireland at the end of September.

'Just as soon as I get to Dublin,' he promised, 'I'll advertise for a manager for Las Palmas, don't you worry.'

'Why are you going away and leaving us, Uncle Sydney?' asked Paul forlornly.

'I'm not going for ever, Paul. I've not been well, as you know, and I need a change and rest. I'll soon be back once I'm better.' Silently I wondered how much truth there was in these words of Sydney's, or whether this was the end of his participation in our pioneering.

Sydney's imminent departure from Las Palmas was dispiriting us all, of that there was no doubt. I could not imagine life on the farm without him. His ruddy face at table, his immense breakfast appetite which could only be equaled by his brother's, his quiet reliability and outspoken honesty, the twinkle in his eyes when a pretty girl appeared, all added up to the man Sydney. He was Donald's right hand.

I tried to make him desist from going. I spoke for hours about the opportunities of recovering here with the assistance of doctors in Montevideo or Buenos Aires. I said he ought to try all possibilities in the River Plate before deciding to leave.

'I accept the fact there are certain possibilities of recovery here, but I've suddenly got a bee in my bonnet about going home for a break; my health is the excuse,' he replied. 'I've been out here well-nigh twenty-four years with no return... like all of us.' He smiled and pressed my hand affectionately, knowing Donald and I had also been here the same time. 'I must take a complete change. It'll do the trick.'

'What makes you so sure?'

'I don't know,' he confessed, 'but I want to see Bonny Ireland again. Play Cricket on a real Irish green. See the mist; feel the drizzle, breathe deeply on a 'soft' day, you know, the things we don't get here.' He laughed before adding: 'Hear the yokels singing folk songs in the Pub!'

I found I had no further arguments after this. I only whispered: 'We're going to miss you dreadfully, you know.'

'I'll be sending you a new manager. A younger man and I bet he'll keep you entertained,' he chuckled and I wondered what he meant.

Some weeks went by.

Many attempts at making peace in the country had fallen through, when unexpectedly a tragic incident ended it all.

The government ordered the usual annual festivities in the city of Montevideo to celebrate the Fiesta Patria on August 25th, commemorating the 72nd year of Independence, despite the fighting going on in the interior.

President Borda attended the traditional Te Deum in the Cathedral of Montevideo, and was walking with his retinue to Government House when, on reaching Sarandi and Camaras, he fell, murdered by a bullet in his heart.

The untimely death of the President so shocked the people that, during the interim government of Lindolfo Cuestas, a Peace Treaty was signed and peace and quiet came to the land.

With the good news of the Peace Treaty, we all rejoiced at the prospects of quiet times ahead and at one point thought Sydney might change his mind about leaving but we were mistaken. He left in October.

———————

Donald was gazing despondently into the hazy distance one evening shortly after Sydney's departure and my heart bled for him. He seemed to have lost all his natural optimism and faith. Normally obstacles did not depress him, they were to him all part of the game. But I knew things were different now without Sydney; we were all changed; we felt strange.

The shearing was approaching and more hands were needed to be taken on. Sydney used to fix these details at Don Ignacio's *Pulperia*, (general store) with Donald taking no resolutions. Now however, it was all in his hands and he was undecided whether to get the men through Don Ignacio or whether to take on the team which had appeared on the premises today, offering their services at a lower price.

He sat there miserably irresolute for half an hour while he revolved this new difficulty in his mind. I held out my hand to him, trying to give him some stability and strength, but he didn't seem fully aware of my presence. He sighed: 'I miss old Syd and he's not been gone a month.'

'The trouble is you're overworked and tired,' I said, 'it'll be better once the new manager comes. Pity it takes so long...'

'What about asking in Buenos Aires?'

This brilliant idea came from Ada surprisingly, as she sat curled up in a chair with a book. This idea of hunting for somebody from the Anglo Argentine community was immediately discussed and approved by all. Why had we not thought of it weeks ago? Then, with thoughts of Buenos Aires, we remembered Bob Courtland and the fact he'd not settled into anything permanent and gave us hope the position of Manager at Las Palmas might interest him.

We invited him over to talk personally to him, and of course he came immediately.

While the first strident screeching of the *chicharras* (cicada) in the trees was heard at the beginning of the summer of 1897/1898, Bob remained with us as a guest who was considering the manager ship.

Even as I must mention Donald's joy at having Bob with us, it also should be noted how all members of our family thrived with his presence.

Ada was already twenty-one and was supposed to be growing up and becoming a young lady, yet she still seemed childish in many ways. The words of the Bishop came to mind when he'd said of her: 'She's so alive in her youthfulness'.

Even Celia had matured more than Ada. Celia was now fifteen and rapidly becoming a dignified little lady despite her shyness. I often felt I was with an older person when speaking to her and not so when trying to get some common sense out of Ada. In the meantime, Celia had fallen love. One of the young Dawson lads had caught her fancy and they were committed in an engagement of their own.

Ada was contemptuous of her younger sister: 'They're so stupid and soppy, they make me sick! Holding hands and gazing into each other's eyes — such fools!' She was often heard to criticize in this manner. Whether her contempt was born of a wee bit of envy, we did not know, but she ridiculed them often. Celia and Charles seemed blissfully oblivious of this criticism in their rapture of being in love and together.

Bob was a boon for the twins; as most lads of ten, they were open to anything taught and Bob was there to teach. He was teaching them to shoot and this gave the boys a new feeling of power and maturity they'd not felt before. Paul handled his rifle best for he was more stable than his spitfire brother Simon.

I gave thanks for Bob's dedication. He was exactly what we needed to fill some of the gaps existing in the family these days.

'He's a marvel!' declared Donald one afternoon when we were riding and Bob was ahead with the workmen and the sheep. 'We'll be more than fortunate if he decides to take the post of manager.'

Bob Courtland did accept the position as from February 1898; in fact, he never went back to Buenos Aires before taking over his duties. He very ingeniously slid from the role of a welcome guest into an efficient manager.

From the moment Bob accepted the position, a delightful change came over Donald. From the elderly, preoccupied man who'd been walking about as if all the cares of the world were on his shoulders — slightly bent with burdens and thin drawn lines forming around his mouth — he was suddenly transformed into somebody almost youthful again. A Donald whose eyes shone with enthusiasm and walked with a light step and a swing to his body.

Almost the first thing Bob did as manager was to get rid of all Mr. Brown's cattle off our fields, and we terminated the business deal with our neighbour.

'Much as I respect your herdswoman business, it's unproductive to have all that cattle feeding off our pastures. We'll get rid of them and fill the fields with our own animals,' he said. The need which had originally brought about the relationship with Mr. Brown no longer existed, and although I still made a good profit, the estancia did not thrive, so they had to go. Surprisingly I felt no remorse. On the contrary, there was a great sense of relief at not being bound to the horrid little man up the road any longer.

The Las Palmas lands were for once put to their correct use and advantage. Bob had capacious inner sight and a fine intuition as well as a good business head. Everything which had been neglected or used incorrectly, was at once put right. Bob and Donald did wonders in a rapid hand-over of heavy duties and responsibilities.

In the midst of this noticeable uplift of things, Willy's health which was plainly deteriorating caused a great deal of preoccupation. Dr. Owens came as frequently as required, but even the doctor's years were beginning to tell on him and he did not move about the countryside as much as he used to

Willy needed a lot of attention.

'Ada dear, will you go and stoke the fire in Willy's room and take him his supper tray?' I asked her one evening. She was in her usual place on the sofa reading while we were playing a few hands of Bridge, taking advantage of Mr. Dawson's overnight visit to make the fourth.

'All right; I'll get to the end of the chapter first,' she said absent-mindedly.

'Four Spades.' Bob called a game in my suit, so I'd play the hand while he went down on the table as dummy. He put his cards down and rose to his feet. 'Don't worry, Child,' he said to Ada, 'I'll see to Willy while I'm dummy.'

She looked up and smiled gratefully at him. He was out of the room before anybody could stop him.

'Is Willy all right?' Donald asked on his return.

'Yes,' replied Bob. 'He was asleep in his chair when I went in and then said he felt very tired tonight. He says he wants to go to bed as soon as he's eaten, please.'

'Right-ho!' said Donald whose job it was to get Willy to bed each night and up in the mornings.

In the meantime, our game was over and I went to see about dinner. Admissions of tiredness such as this were becoming more and more frequent with Willy; he preferred to be left alone in his room in the evenings and not be brought into the drawing-room.

With all this warning then, it ought not to have been such a shock to us when in the month of August Willy was found dead one morning when Donald went in to get him up.

Donald was accustomed to tap lightly on Willy's door each morning before entering.

'Come in.' Willy was always awake by the time Donald came in and he often felt a pang of guilt at having kept Willy waiting for his breakfast.

'Morning Don. So good of you to give me a hand. Sorry to be such a nuisance.' Every day Willy greeted him with the same words of apology.

'No problem, old man — it's a pleasure.' Donald had to reassure him daily. 'Give me that arm and I'll help you up — there we are!' The toil of 'fixing Willy' for the day began: toilet, dressing, settling him in his chair and finally bringing in his breakfast tray.

But today there'd been no answer to his knock, no cheery 'come in!' and once the curtains were drawn aside Donald was surprised to find Willy still lying on his side as if fast asleep. He touched him lightly and when there was no response, he'd realized the truth. Willy had passed on in his sleep. A blessed way of passing on, but a terrible shock for Donald who'd found him.

I'll never know how the Bishop heard of our bereavement, but within a day we had word he was coming to see us and would read the Burial Service if we so desired. Nothing on earth would give us more comfort at this particular moment and anticipated his visit with gladness.

We'd only seen the Bishop once in Fray Bentos since his gracious visit to Las Palmas so many years ago. We'd attended a service at which he was officiating and we'd lunched with him afterwards. The warmth of his saintly personality had enchanted us again. It was no wonder we welcomed this visit when our sorrow was deep; we wanted nobody else to officiate at Willy's funeral, particularly when we knew how fond he was of Willy.

The Bishop arrived in the afternoon and we had the funeral the following morning. Near to where our infant daughter lay, Willy came to his final rest.

'Dust to dust, ashes to ashes...'

The Bishop said a few brief words on the true Christian life that our cousin had led. Words and phrases which I could hardly hear through my grief. I could feel Donald's hand shaking under my elbow as we stood forlornly at the graveside and heard the Bishop's gentle voice: 'his unlimited kindness... his love of little children... his boundless patience and Christian charity... his dignified resignation to ill health...' every word the truth about Willy.

With Willy's departure some of Donald's previous depression returned in spite of having Bob with us.

'The old place is no longer what it used to be, is it?' he asked me time and time again. 'The younger folk are gradually taking over and the older generation must step aside. It's sad. I find I await Sydney's letters anxiously and still miss his cheery company.' He sighed, 'and now with Willy's passing I find I have nobody left to compare notes with, or play the old game of 'do-you-remember?' After a short consideration and regret, he added: 'I know you are my greatest blessing, Evie darling, but I'm needing a man to talk to at times.'

I understood partially, yet not completely, for I felt differently. I was content with Las Palmas as it was, even though there were moments when I missed both Sydney and Willy for their individual fine qualities, but the new generation was filling my life satisfactorily; the world was changing and one had to look at the world differently for the world was looking at us differently.

Now I had to admit Bob's presence on the farm was making a big difference. It added interest to my animal breeding which had lagged very noticeably since Alberto had left, and I was looking forward to the time when our estancia got down to agriculture. Bob was constantly pushing this for he had the conviction that most of the country's wealth was going to be in agriculture and, like Donny, in vines.

Donny wrote from France regularly. He'd completed his courses in Bordeaux and taken a position on a vineyard, but his letters always implied he'd soon return to Las Palmas with his knowledge to be put into practice.

It made me sorry then, to find Donald in his retirement, giving up his interest because of the loss of his two life-long companions.

'I miss 'em,' he said, and with a small shrug to his very painful shoulders, he walked away into the open fields alone. But the past has to be forgotten, I thought, one can't live it over again. Bob helped me forget. He entertained and accompanied us; he was the heart of everything; we relied on him completely and his decisions were never over-ruled; his word became law.

I loved this easy way of life where all responsibility was on another's shoulders and all the pleasures mine, and I knew I had Bob to thank for this.

One Sunday Ada and Bob returned slightly late for lunch from their ride. They'd been fox-hunting all morning and judging by their flushed faces they must have ridden back at a high speed. It was not usual to be late for meals.

'Sorry about the time,' Bob apologized, 'but we have a surprise for you.' His arm was resting casually on Ada's shoulder and she was smiling radiantly, her eyes alight with happiness. I thought how young she looked with her wind-blown copper hair in an unruly mess and her cheeks aglow.

What was the surprise this time, I wondered? Last time they'd brought back a 'surprise' for me it had been a new horse. The time before it had been a young teru-teru bird with a broken wing which I'd eventually cured and raised and then domesticated and she now lived with her mate in our gardens. The terus had been trained to belong to our household and served to announce visitors or strangers approaching the house, quite as good as any watchdog.

I smiled at the prospect of another surprise, and Bob was looking directly at me, 'Yes?' I asked.

'Ada and I have just become engaged to be married,' he said, 'and we hope it meets with your approval.' Suddenly embarrassed, he turned to Donald for his consent.

It was such a shock to me. 'Good gracious!' I cried shrilly, springing to my feet. 'Ada's much too young for that sort of a thing. She's a mere child!' I laughed and my mirth sounded unreal. I felt strange.... Ada and Bob? Ada and Bob engaged?.... Whatever was this.... Bob was Donald's and my friend, the manager of our estancia, nothing to do with the children, and yet... I began to feel dizzy.

Donald came to the rescue; he put a firm arm around me and extended his hand to Bob and shook it heartily: 'Of course we're delighted with the surprise news! Congratulations!' He bent and kissed Ada's happy cheek and patted Bob's shoulder in approval.

The awkward moment had slipped by and then we were all hugging and kissing the new couple and Donald rushed out and opened a bottle of wine to celebrate the occasion. This helped, a glass of wine always cheered me, exactly what I needed at the moment.

Somebody said: 'Ada's already twenty-one, the same age you were when you got married, Mum, so we can't consider her too young.' Although I pretended to be pleased, I felt an extraordinary sensation of, in some way, having been cheated.

Bob was my man, at least mythically so. He advised me, he was my confident, my Bridge partner. We rode together, went to the village and shopped together, he knew what provisions to bring for the workmen; he helped with my children; he taught the boys to shoot and fish; played duets with Celia; rode with Ada, I'd thought in all innocence, but now a thousand suspicions came to mind about their outings together. Not long ago they'd come back from the river after sunset, laughing and jesting about who'd caught the biggest fish. We'd not been anxious for Ada was with Bob and no harm could come...

What a change this engagement had brought about.

Everything was different now. I could no longer lean on Bob; he was Ada's fiancée and soon to be my son-in-law. I laughed bitterly. What a fool I'd been thinking his preference was for me; his tender 'little mother' as he called me would sound false. A changed meaning the words would hold 'little mother-in-law' — ugh!

Donald, on the other hand, was delighted with the engagement. 'The best person on earth for our Ada!' he declared happily. 'She always wanted to remain at Las Palmas and by marrying the manager, it secures her position. How wonderfully it's all working out for her!'

'I feel he's a bit too old, don't you?' I ventured. 'Bob's already thirty and she's such a child.'

'It's of little importance. It's better for the man to be older than his wife. I worry more about Celia's choice for I feel that Charles Dawson at twenty-one is young to be settling down in marriage.'

CHAPTER 29

The big wedding took place at Holy Trinity Church of Montevideo.

It would be impossible to explain the confusion flustering me during the weeks of preparation for Ada's wedding.

'We've decided we'll have our wedding at Holy Trinity Church in Montevideo,' she informed me one day.

'Oh!' I exclaimed, quite taken aback, 'why not here?'

'Here?' she echoed. 'It's much too small.'

'What do you mean, too small?'

'Mother, you must remember this is the union of two families, not just our little group of friends who couldn't even fill a hay *galpon!*' (barn)

I gasped. It was hard enough to keep up with Ada in her present turmoil of excitement, but her reference at this particular moment to the hay *galpon* which had burned down on such a memorable night, was more than I could take.

'Why do you say hay *galpon* of all places?' I cried in dismay.

'Oh dear,' she laughed, 'I said a hay *galpon* metaphorically as I might have said a pig-sty or anywhere.' She was laughing at me as usual I was sure.

'All right Ada, Las Palmas is too small for your wedding, I'll accept that, but why do you choose Holy Trinity, may I ask?'

'Well, it's Bob's idea mainly. He says Montevideo is mid-stream for both of us, not at home for me nor him, and it's an idea I agree with.' So the argument was closed and the wedding was planned to take place at Holy Trinity.

'Have you fixed a date yet?' I asked nervously, hoping she wouldn't tease me again. Ada grinned: 'As soon as possible; Bob wants it on the twenty fifth.'

Suddenly I wanted to help. I wanted to be a real mother to Ada perhaps for the first time in her life. 'Ada, count on me for anything you need in preparation.' I wanted her to know I did approve of their marriage deep down inside me, although I'd not shown it until now. Her gaze softened.

'Thanks, Mum, you're really a good old stick, aren't you?'

'Drat you Ada!' I cried, vexed. 'I'm NOT old!'

She laughed in her throaty way and it returned us to our habitual position of uncertain mother and willful daughter.

After the wedding the young couple had a short honeymoon touring Uruguay, seeing some of the country which was new to them. At first they went to Punta del Este the beautiful seaside resort and spent a week there, later another week in the city of Montevideo. On their way home they visited Colonia Suiza an inland paradise of palm trees and fertile dairy farms and subsequently home.

The newlyweds returned to Las Palmas full of joy and excitement for living. I'd never seen Ada look so well and happy, she was virtually blooming. The new couple automatically stepped into the position of head of the household while Donald stepped directly into his retirement. Immediately he suggested Bob begin looking for a foreman to help, because he personally would not be working.

It was a different and strange environment for us and especially for me, so I became more companionable to Donald. We went fishing together when the weather permitted and we enjoyed the freedom of those outings. The twins came with us often, each armed with his rifle and fishing cane.

Sundays were special days now more than ever and even though we'd always kept the Sabbath and read prayers, Bob now introduced Sundays as a day of complete rest. Only a skeleton staff was allowed in the kitchen and nobody else was requested to work. All the workmen had the day off, many of them rode into the village to spend their weekly wages on wine, women and song.

The first Sunday Bob and Ada returned from their honeymoon they spent the day in a curious mixture of love-making and economic discussion. They got a pencil and paper after lunch and jotted down some essentials to buy on their next trip to Mercedes. While sitting out on the porch I overheard Bob saying to her: 'The power of money is relative. It depends on how one spends it. Badly administered money can be of little or no value.' Ada had laughed in his face and Bob had caught her roughly in his arms and kissed her. 'You have a lot to learn, Child, and you'd better make a start soon.'

The mail brought a long happy letter from Sydney, very descriptive of all the joys of living in the Old Country again.

'It's wonderful to hear Syd's not disappointed with his decision of returning home. I think it ought to be ours too.' Donald put his arm around my drooping shoulders. 'We've done our part in civilizing this land. We'll be leaving it well attended by competent family, carrying on our good work. Nothing will be lost if we leave now.' I said nothing, and then he went on: 'Next year the twins will go to school in Ireland. None of our boys have returned yet though Donny claims he will but Billy with all his music and art has little to attract him here. Ada's now married and settled, she never wanted to leave Las Palmas anyway. This only leaves Celia unsettled.'

'Why are you wanting to leave at this particularly beautiful time of year? It'll be cold and snowy over there.'

'There's nothing to keep us here any longer. Haven't you noticed we're surplus now?' Silently he stroked his chin meditating on the cycle of events which had brought us to this. 'Bob and Ada by rights ought to be using the main bedroom but while we're here they don't want us to move out. So here we remain, in excess.'

'I've thought we might build ourselves a cottage somewhere on the grounds in which to retire. Wouldn't that be lovely?' I cried feigning enthusiasm.

'All that mess and headache of building again. No. I can't face it. We must go; it's our time to leave, don't you see?'

We discussed this subject aggressively.

'No, Donald, we can't go back to Ireland permanently. We can go for a visit if you like, but not for ever. No, no, no, we can't walk away from all we've built and worked for all these years.'

'Why can't you understand the time has come for us to retire?' Donald sighed as if the subject tired him. 'We're now the old generation and must give way to the young. We must let go, Evie dear.'

'Retirement has arrived. All right, I'll accept that, but why can't we retired here? What links exist over there that'll give us the happiness you imagine?'

'Old Syd seems happy enough. We wouldn't have to face any more petty revolutions. We wouldn't have to live in an uncertain society, never knowing whether armed forces are suddenly going to arrive and take what they fancy. We'd not have to face the stealing and plundering. I'm tired of it all and I want some peace in my old age.'

'Will you be at peace knowing half our family has remained to face those problems alone?'

'Not alone!' he cried, 'the girls have strong backing here. Ada and Bob together. Bob's doing wonders with what we've begun. There are improvements everywhere — there's no holding this young man, he's a success already and Ada's the right person to be at his side. They love each other and she has this place born into her very bones... she's part of the land...'

We argued and argued. We were both right; we both had our convictions firmly grounded. Donald wanted to go back to his roots, content with the knowledge of having completed what he'd originally come for, sure he was doing the right thing. I clung to what we'd built, worked and struggled for and couldn't conceive leaving it forever more, but how to convince him?

I wanted him to see my point of view, and he tried to make me see his.

'I won't go without you, Evie darling,' he said, 'do try and be reasonable and understand how I feel about it. You MUST! I can find out about berths on steamers soon and perhaps we can be home for Christmas. We can have a lovely white Christmas.'

'I had more than twenty white Christmases when I was young!' I cried. 'My Christmas will be hot and dry this year! It'll be here, not in Ireland anymore.' I sat silent and indignant. 'Don't do anything about berths on steamers before we have this fully decided upon. If you want to get a passage, get one for yourself only.'

'NO!' he cried, 'I repeat, I'll not go without you!' At length I was able to persuade him to postpone the journey for different reasons. First, our beautiful greyhound bitch was expecting her litter in one months' time and I insisted on being here for the birth.

'I have two of the puppies promised to another family; then we've to see how many of them remain at Las Palmas and if there are any more to be given away. This is my responsibility being a thing I began when we bought the greyhounds for breeding and I wish to see it ended.'

In view of this Donald agreed to wait but deep in my heart I knew — bitterly — I was merely delaying the inevitable evil moment.

I had to find something truly authentic to keep Donald at Las Palmas where our feet had taken root. Here was our destiny. We'd given too much of ourselves, our youth and vitality all now planted in Uruguay. Surely he'd miss the open fields, the sheer beauty of being surrounded by nature by day and night. He'd miss the challenges we faced every year, the gigantic cycles of drought and flood.

When Christmas was approaching and the New Year not far behind, I arranged special celebrations for both these important events: Christmas as the last one of the 19th Century and the New Year as the first of another century. We had guests and parties nonstop. I invited some people we hardly knew existed in our area, hoping to capture Donald in a new and attractive friendship which might make him consider remaining.

This had its partial success and Donald did enjoy his summer and forgot his age, his rheumatism and his retirement. He hardly had a moment to reflect as he rushed from tennis tournaments, Bridge competitions, *asados* (cookout), fishing, sing-songs and dances; we were thus obliged to forget the existence of work. It was Bob and Ada's concern now and we were simply living for the sake of enjoyment and pleasure, quite unlike our real selves.

Another incident keeping us at Las Palmas for another period was Celia and Charles Dawson's wedding. On hearing about our possible return to Ireland, they decided to marry although it meant living with the Dawson's for the first few years. Theirs was a small, quiet wedding at Las Palmas.

Gradually, very gradually, as summer faded and autumn began to take over, Donald's spirits descended and remarks such as 'when we go back home...' or 'it'll soon be spring over there...' entered into his conversations again. I saw we could not keep up the summer trend of entertainments all the calendar round. Something was going to snap. And it did.

Donald and Bob had gone to Mercedes, and on their return we all sat down together for tea.

'Pass the butter, please,' said Bob, 'I'm famished.' Paul obliged and Bob began spreading it generously on his bread.

'How did your trip go today?' I asked.

'Mmmm, very well,' replied Donald, 'very well indeed. Bob's business went off on rails and I went to the shipping company.'

At this moment Simon burst into the room and flopped into his place at table. 'I've a joke to tell!' he shouted. 'Oh, shut up Simon.' 'No, please I must tell it before I forget it. Why does a cat lift its tail when you run your hand along its back?' There was a deep silence during which Simon looked pretentious. 'Anybody know?' he asked eagerly.

'No.'

'It's to let you know the cat ends there!' Simon let out a bellow of laughter hardly getting the last few words out before exploding with glee at his own joke.

'That's a very good joke, Simon,' I said, 'but now will you be quiet and let us hear what the gentlemen have to say about their day.'

'There's a steamer about the middle of March,' Donald continued, 'on which there are berths available.'

The arrow struck home and I immediately felt sick. My eyes sped around the family table. Donald, in spite of having shot the dart, was tucking into his food with relish. He didn't look up from his plate, nor did either of the twins. I saw a fleeting look of alarm turn to one of resignation on Ada's face, and she quickly looked away. I caught Bob's eye and our glances fixed and held for a moment. Was it pity I read in his eyes? He smiled kindly at me and handed me a slice of nut bread which I accepted absently, too dumbstruck to eat it.

I left the table soon and walked over to the stables, a place of refuge for me since the hay *galpon* (barn) burned down. In here I found a few preparations for the night underway. Most of our riding horses were already in and my beautiful Fiona was eating her oats from a nose-bag.

'Oh, my beauty,' I whispered in despair, 'what's to become of me?' I sat on a low stump near to her as she munched her ration, snorting contentedly: there was no heartbreak for her. With my head between my hands I tried to collect my thoughts. From some source I had to learn to accept my destiny, but who was going to teach me?

I felt hot, bitter tears roll down my cheeks, I couldn't stop them, they eased the tension inside me.

I heard a step and then felt a hand on my shoulder.

It was Bob. He'd followed me over, guessing my condition. When he saw my tears he said softly: 'Don't cry, little mother.'

'It's that I...'

'I know how you must be feeling. It's a very hard pill to swallow but you must be brave. You can't let Donald down, can you? He depends so much on you. And he loves you so!'

'But why...' The tears rolled down again and I sniffed. Of course I had no hanky. I felt like a foolish schoolgirl, weeping and sniffing in front of this man, my son-in-law, so I hung my head to hide my embarrassment. Everything was going wrong. He searched deep into his *bombacha* (baggy pants) pocket and handed me his hanky, not perfectly clean, only smelling a bit of animals and of him. I blew my nose and handed it back.

'Thanks.' I almost smiled at the picture I must have been portraying. The nose blow had eased things and I could talk.

Bob was understanding; we went over the whole situation time and again, back and forth various times, without any positive conclusion for ultimately Bob felt I had a commitment to Donald.

I'd hate leaving my home, my farm, my mare, my greyhounds, my old chum Trixie, yet I had to go.

I'd weep for my daughters whom I felt I was abandoning, but I had to find courage and go.

I'd yearn for the feeling of the strong black earth under my feet, but I'd eventually forget.

I'd long for the smell of a distant skunk, sweet and sickly, reminding me of the days gone by and Emma and her pet.

I'd miss the odour of smouldering eucalyptus leaves heavy on the air of a summer evening, but I'd have to adapt.

I'd halt and listen for the cooing of a dove on a summer morn, or the screech of a nearby *chicharra* (cicara), but I'd hear neither.

Was it not too much to ask of me? Bob reassured and explained, he gave me all the reasons for going back with Donald. He stayed with me, and we talked until late afternoon, when the other horses were brought in for the night. Fiona was no longer eating and there were soft whinnies in the stalls, settling down for the night.

We left the stables together.

'I'll be looking in at the men's quarters to see about their rations for tomorrow,' he said. 'You all right now? No more tears, little mother.'

It was almost dark now so I had to ride at a gallop all the way. There's a very short twilight in this country, once the sun sets it's soon dark. I was riding Fiona, of course, and it was only a few moments since Bob and I had been talking in the stables.

In my despair I was going to the person whom I'd most trusted in all the years in Uruguay: Señora Pintos. She was very special to me and if there was help to be had, she was the one to extend it. I could not face another meal at Las Palmas with this predicament hovering over me, nor did I wish to see any member of the family, least of all Donald.

I rode like the devil towards the Pintos' *Puesto* (outlying farmhand housing) and at last I came within view of the humble house set among the trees, enveloped in the first dusk.

Now I was free of Las Palmas and the cordial atmosphere of the *Puesto* reached out at me. Lights shone in the windows through the drooping leaves and I could barely distinguish the figures moving at the back. Dogs barked as I rode up. The greyhound pup leaped in delight. Mario came out to see who this lone rider was.

'Hola Señora!' (Hello Madam) he cried out, surprised when he recognized me. Before dismounting I asked: 'Is your mother at home?'

'Si Señora,' he replied, coming forward to take my mare.

The Señora Pintos was also openly surprised to see me at her humble dwelling at this time of the evening, alone. She immediately sensed something was amiss. She was cooking the evening meal when I arrived and only Mario was at home. Pintos had gone to the *Pulperia* (general store) and was not yet back.

Señora Pintos was one of the few people I knew who did not seem to have been touched by the years. She was exactly the same as when we first met. Her dark skin was smooth and finely stretched over her high cheekbones and her black eyes were bright and lucid like a young person's still. Tonight she was wearing a large blue apron around her ample middle, fitting for her simple kitchen duties.

It didn't take long to confess my predicament to her, she was a good listener, and I poured out my heart. 'I can't go back! I don't want to see anybody!' I wailed. 'Can I stay here?'

The Señora Pintos was suddenly placed in a commitment altogether new to her. I was the wife of the boss apart from being a lifelong friend.

If she sided with my willful request, she'd become an accomplice. This she might have been willing to risk by herself but she was not alone in this. Pintos' job was at stake.

The anxiety and alarm my sudden disappearance from Las Palmas must be causing would doubtless lead to a search party setting out. This was very likely already organized and the Pintos' *Puesto* was one of the first places to be visited. They would be dreadfully involved; didn't I understand? she asked.

I understood but didn't have the ability to side-track the difficulty. My spirits sank... what would Pintos think when he came home shortly? The Señora Pintos had the intuition to see I could hardly reason any more.

'Do you wish to remain here for the night?' she asked.

'Yes, if it can be arranged. I need time to think.' She'd made up her mind about something, I could tell, and I trusted her judgement completely.

'Pintos must not know of your presence here. He's not a good liar if he should be questioned, so it's better if he knows nothing about you.' She got to her feet and said: 'Come.'

There was a small shed attached to the house which she rapidly prepared for me to spend the night in.

'I don't need any extra comforts, please, just a bare bed to sleep on, that's all.' She brought me blankets and as she turned to go: 'I'll bring you something to eat.'

By the time she returned with a hot meal, I'd remembered Mario. 'What about Mario?' I asked her, worried.

'You've no need to worry about Mario. I'll explain to him,' she smiled, 'but there's the problem of your horse. Pintos will recognize her unless we hide her... I don't know where.'

In the end Fiona was brought into the meagre shed with me. The Señora Pintos and I talked some more about my situation and then she said: 'I'll leave you now but remember to reflect on your position as wife.'

As the door closed behind her, a still dark silence only remained, but before long the inevitable happened: the sound of horses and carriage wheels was heard. A contingent hunting for me from Las Palmas had arrived. I distinctly heard Bob's voice raised in query and then Ada's. Señora Pintos was talking in soft terms as they went to the front of the house and no sound reached me in my shut-in shed.

Gradually all factors began to fall away, and the only person left in my mind was Donald. While the night dragged by, one sleepless hour after another, I began to miss him, just as I always did whenever we'd been separated at night. The place felt lonely and slightly chilly despite the blankets, and I couldn't close an eye.

I kept hearing their words coming back to me through the darkness: 'You can't let old Donald down now, can you?' Some terrible thoughts of Donald going off alone to Ireland and myself remaining at Las Palmas, lost and bewildered. Donald's stoop of defeat as he walked away; the recriminating look he'd throw me when we said goodbye.

And then: 'He depends so much on you.' Did Donald depend on me? I asked the darkness. Often there'd been: 'Please help me, Evie dear, it's too much for me alone.' After Sydney's departure: 'Thank God you're still with me. I can't face it alone — don't ever leave me!' And the final blow of Willy's death, his hand shaking under my elbow by the graveside.... And there were mealtimes: 'Where's your mother? We can't sit down without her.' It made me wonder what was happening at supper tonight. I saw Donald's lost expression as he stood by his place at the head of the table and my empty chair.... Perhaps Bob was right, he depended on me. He depended on me to go back to the old country with him and start afresh, he'd never do it alone: 'I won't leave without you, dear.'

And finally, 'He loves you so.' Of his love I was more than sure. I'd never received reproaches from him, he accepted me as I was and loved me despite my faults. He had no resentment (he knew not what the word meant) about Alberto and me and the destruction of our priceless hay *galpon* (barn). His forgiveness had been complete for his love was always unwavering and firm.

The Señora Pintos had said a few moments ago: 'He's given you so much.'

There before me rolled a vision of my life and everything I valued had been given me by Donald, starting with the South American adventure, hard though it had been at times, it was the centre and core of my entire life. He'd given me six wonderful children and a good life-style, but above all he'd given me his complete love and devotion. His gentleness and beauty of soul were, in the deep shadows of the small shed, like those of an angel, although I knew him as human through and through, having longings and desires like all of us, yet knowing how to control and best use them. His love of all humanity was above reproach and he'd always be a true Christian to the end of his days. His religion was an enormous part of him and was his warm consolation.

What had I given him? Apparently nothing except a sheaf of headaches and a little companionship. I suddenly saw myself as a very ungrateful person and wondered at this behaviour of dashing away selfishly from the home without even a word to anyone, sowing fear and anxiety in the family. I could change nothing now. The family had been here and they'd moved on with the weight of uncertainty pressing them down as the night hours went by. I felt vile.

Suddenly I was squatting on the floor. I'd never get up again! Before me in the dark, dank little shed, three windows appeared representing The Past, The Present and The Future.

In The Past window there was light and warmth as my life had always been, full of love and affection and the spoiled feeling of being the only woman, the sole important female for so many years. Only when Ada had matured, the first sign of another important woman arose, making me have to share the affection of all my menfolk. She was fully grown but still I'd not accepted her womanhood until Bob had claimed her as his bride, and the truth became established before my eyes. I'd suffered for a short time but Donald had come to my rescue, helping me accept what was self-evident: our Ada grown and in love. Donald shared my life always, with sunlight all the time. What a lovely window to peer into but it was in The Past and now I had to see The Present.

The Present was all darkness. Flashes of indecision, anxiety, mistrust, blame....The Present was a small smelly shed, far away from my home and people. I'd chosen it, but there was nothing pleasant here.

The third window was The Future and it had an enormous Question Mark filling it but as I looked it began to clear. The Question Mark appeared to be receding and in its place there appeared an image of me living at Las Palmas without. Donald. He had retired to Ireland leaving so much adjustment for me. The removal from my own bedroom with its heavenly view of the open fields, wooded lanes, spectacular sunsets, green vales where cattle grazed peacefully and my entry into another smaller room, with merely half my possessions. Ada's voice: 'You can't take all this junk into the other bedroom! It won't fit, be sensible.' Myself tossing all night while trying to get used to a different bed; cold at night without him, and the surrender of my place to Ada for she was head of the household. I hated being one of the group on the side of the table. Ada in my place asking: 'What will the old lady eat today?' and she served me what she felt was good for me. I would tell her: 'I want more gravy with my meat.' And her reply: 'Oh Mum, don't be greedy!' and me recoiling into my shell with the label 'GREEDY OLD LADY' hanging round my neck. Later I was telling them I'd enjoy a game of Bridge tonight, but Bob was tired and Ada was laughing at me: 'Nobody plays that game anymore, Mum, it's old-fashioned.'

The pain of bidding goodbye to my twins next year became perfectly visible in The Future window. Their schooling must begin. 'Don't cry, Mum,' Simon was saying, 'we'll be quite all right because we'll be with Dad most of the time.' My tears increased. 'We'll come back to visit in the holidays,' Paul promised.

More unpleasant adjustments drifted onto the scene of the future: 'Bob and I are going over to Garcia Otero's place to choose new riding horses.' Donald and I had always gone together to buy the horses, why couldn't I go now? Why was there no further room for my opinions nor me?

I shuddered in the chilly shed. It was the shiver of a lonely soul.

There'd been many times in the Past I could take comfort from, particularly the deep involvement with my husband, much as I'd kept a self-imposed detachment from the children, the attachment to husband and farm were total. Nothing else was important, it came up clear tonight. I loved my children but was not dependent on them, with Donald it was different. I had to change The Future window.

Astonishingly the huge Question Mark was again in the middle of the window. Here was my chance!

I made a gigantic effort to push the Question Mark into the background and see a different future.

Irish fields and meadows spread before me in beautiful peace and grandeur. A warm familiar hand was holding mine as we walked in the late afternoon sun. Donald said: 'It's so wonderful being here with you; it'd all mean nothing without you, my darling.' The unmistakable magic of his voice had its heavenly effect on me. I smiled contentedly.

A pretty cottage with my favourite hollyhocks growing by the front wall. Our cottage. Simon and Paul arriving back from day school, hungry, spreading thick honey on the scones I'd just taken from the oven. 'Oho-o-o! Mum's scones — the best ever!' Paul was tucking in. Donald and I laughing happily over our growing lads.

A soft mist spread over the valley and my soul was at rest. I knew I was in the right place.

'I'll build a little fire to have the cottage nice and warm before Sydney arrives.' My heart lurched. Sydney coming to visit us, I couldn't wait to see him again. As Donald came in with an armful of logs, he turned to me and said: 'You look so lovely and young in that soft mauve colour and your hair...' he lifted a gentle hand to touch one of my tresses.

I bent forward and kissed him.

At long last I could resort my relationship with God, and prayed: 'Dear God, show me the way.' I saw I could look to God to supply all my needs for a good, joyful future life in Ireland. My place was clearly beside Donald. It was part of God's great unfathomable plan.

Right now I needed the warmth of Donald's presence to reassure me that I was not so dreadful as I appeared. Donald's love shone so strongly, it made everybody see me in a better light.

Where was he now? I had to go to him at once...

I made a rush for the door of the shed and threw it open wide, intending to leave and return to Las Palmas, but the deep darkness of the exterior world hit me like a slap in the face. There was nothing visible except the immense sea of blackness pressing me back into the shed. There was no moon and few stars scattered in the sky for it was partially covered in cloud. Everything was silent, dark.

I stumbled back and the door swung shut. Fiona snorted. I collapsed onto the blankets and must've slept a little, for when I awoke, away in the east there was a slight grey hue and the Pintos roosters were crowing an early welcome to the day.

I felt better since my decision was made, and I wanted to get to Donald quickly. I led Fiona quietly from the shed and saddled her up. Only some of the dogs were aware of my movements but I'd have to waken the Señora Pintos and tell her of my decision and tell her goodbye. She was so sage, she must know already, but I had to thank her.

I lead my mare along the gravel drive to the front of the house. Mario came out of the kitchen with the milk pails. He was off to do the morning milking.

'Is your mother up?'

'Si Señora.' And I saw her in the kitchen putting on her ample apron. I went inside.

'I've reconsidered,' I told her. 'I'm returning to my husband.' She smiled knowingly. 'I'm glad,' she said, 'we were not wrong.'

I didn't stay for I wanted to get to Las Palmas before Donald got up. I wanted to fling myself onto the bed beside him, see his surprise, and tell him I loved him.

I made my mare gallop swiftly, the track was good between the *Puesto* and the homestead and I was making excellent time. Down the slope to the first *cañada* (small stream) and as I took the next rise rapidly, I saw a horseman approaching at a speed. So early.... I wondered who.... It only took me a few fleeting seconds to recognize Donald. We neither of us slackened our speed and on reaching each other we dismounted and ran into each other's arms.

'Darling, darling!' I sobbed, 'I'm sorry...'

'Don't!' he gasped, 'nothing matters. You've come back to me. I love you so!' We stood locked in each other's arms for a long while not wishing to break the magic, and we kissed and laughed and sobbed until at last he said: 'Let's go home.'

On the way I asked him if he'd had a very bad night, but he assured me he had slept.

'Weren't you worried about me?' I asked a little disappointed.

'No, we'd been over to Pintos place last evening looking for you and the Señora Pintos told us in confidence you were safely in her care, but you should be left for the night to reflect.' He smiled. 'We went home satisfied that you were safe. Now I was on my way to bring you home.'

———————

A load of hay came down the track, the great feet of the horses treading softly in the dust. The scent of jasmine filtered in through the open window.

Donald, hindered by his aching shoulders, was struggling into his disreputable old jacket which he proposed travelling to Fray Bentos in because it was one of his most comfortable garments. 'I don't care what I look like, it's comfortable!' he exclaimed when I'd reprimanded him for wanting to wear it.

We were packed up, waiting for Bob to bring round the carriage which would take us to the steamer.

I crept from room to room seeking some measure of consolation. It seemed as if the very doors and windows stared at me with reproach.

The tumbled bed which I'd never sleep in again, had been stripped bare and it looked strange and accusing also.

The house was silent, spectral and austere.

The Future was here.

I heard again the words of the prophet Micah saying:

> 'I go forth from this place knowing that this is what God asks of me, only this: act justly, love tenderly, and walk humbly with God.' (Micah 6.8)

THE END.

About the Author

by Philip Campbell

Heather Beatrice Cobham was born in 1927 in Uruguay, to her parents Irene Baker and Ralph Lowndes Cobham, both born in Argentina. She is the second child of a family of four siblings, Elizabeth, Charles and Aileen.

She lived her childhood mostly in Montevideo, and some years in Buenos Aires, in the Hurlingham neighbourhood.

At the age of 21, she married Leslie Grahame Campbell, born in Uruguay of British parents, and had five children, Virginia, Philip, Robert, Janet and John. During the early years they lived in their house on Luis de la Torre street in Montevideo just around the corner of the British School, and half a block from the "Ombu" landmark. In 1964 they moved to their house in the neighbourhood of Carrasco, following the move of the School there also.

In 1968, Heather started a pre-school at her home in Carrasco, for children of 3 and 4 years old, where they were taught the basics of the English language and culture, which helped many of them with their admission to the British School later on. Her daughters Virginia and Janet worked at the pre-school for some years, as well as her granddaughters Malena and Ingrid, at different intervals. The pre-school remained in operation for 30 years, and closed after Heather's 70th birthday.

During these years, Heather also gave English conversation classes at her home in Carrasco, to local businessmen wanting to improve their language skills, which would help them in their international business ventures.

"In Open Fields" was written in the early 1980's, but was never published until now. It was first edited by Jazz Azkoul, husband of Clarissa Whitaker, youngest daughter of Elizabeth Cobham, Heather's elder sister. It is a mixture of fact and fiction, based on the story of the emigration of the Fitzherbert family from Ireland to Uruguay, in the second half of the 19th century, and all their trials in establishing and running a large farm in a faraway and foreign country. It also incorporates some interesting historical information about Uruguay in those days, when political and civil strife were quite common, and how it affected their lives on the farm. It also depicts some clear contrasts, apart from the language difference, between British and local Uruguayan cultures.

In later years this farm, named "Estancia Media Agua", came to be owned by the Cobham family, through the marriage of Edward C. Cobham with Alda Fitzherbert. One of their sons, Arthur Cobham, Heather's cousin, owned and managed the farm for most of his life. He married Wendy La Brooy, and they had four children, Susan, Christine, Alec and Phyllis. The farm now is owned by the Cobham-La Brooy family, and managed by Alec and Phyllis.

Heather will be 90 years of age in 2017. She now lives at The Green Residence in Carrasco, Montevideo, a small cozy home for elderly people, founded in 2014 by her daughters Virginia and Janet. This initiative was in response to the need in the British community in Uruguay, for a place for their elderly to live in comfort, maintain traditions, while being close to their friends. It was made possible initially by donations from different individuals and families of the British community. Wendy La Brooy Cobham also lives in the Residence since its opening.

The publication of this book is a joint effort of all Heather's children, as a celebration of her 90th birthday, as our loving Mother, and in honour of the outstanding heritage of the Fitzherbert-Cobham families.

Printed in Great Britain
by Amazon

27050266R00169